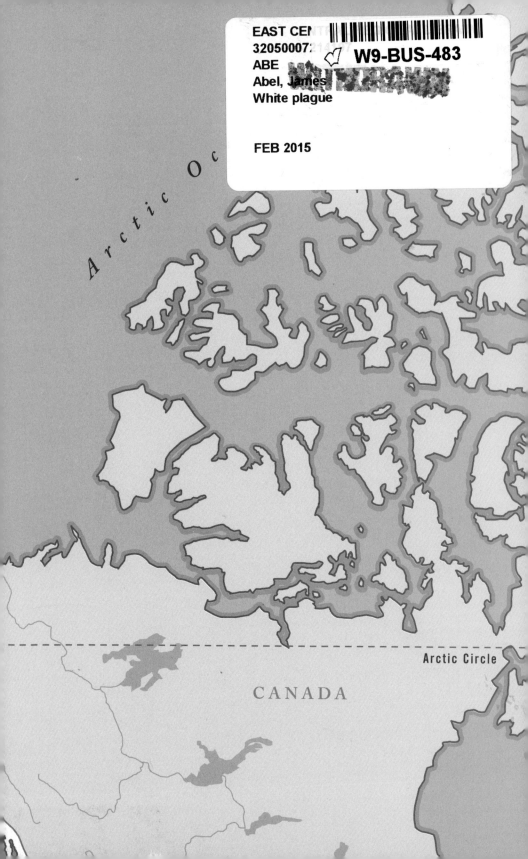

Arctic O

Arctic

Arctic Circle

CANADA

WHITE PLAGUE

WHITE PLAGUE

JAMES ABEL

BERKLEY BOOKS, NEW YORK

THE BERKLEY PUBLISHING GROUP
Published by the Penguin Group
Penguin Group (USA) LLC
375 Hudson Street, New York, New York 10014

USA • Canada • UK • Ireland • Australia • New Zealand • India • South Africa • China

penguin.com

A Penguin Random House Company

This book is an original publication of The Berkley Publishing Group.

Library of Congress Cataloging-in-Publication Data

Abel, James.
White plague / James Abel.—First edition.
pages cm—(A Joe Rush novel)
ISBN 978-0-425-27632-7 (hardback)
I. Title.
PS3568.E517W45   2015
813'.54—dc23
2014027519

FIRST EDITION: January 2015

PRINTED IN THE UNITED STATES OF AMERICA

10   9   8   7   6   5   4   3   2   1

Cover design by Richard Hasselberger.
Cover photos: *Submarine* © U.S. Navy Photo/Alamy, *Dive into the cave* © littlesam/Shutterstock,
and *Abstract radar illustration* © IndianSummer/Shutterstock.
Endpaper map by Virginia Norey.
Interior art: *Under the Artic ice* © Hayri Er/Getty Image and
Ice floe floating on water © Purestock/Getty Image.
Interior text design by Kristin del Rosario.

ACKNOWLEDGMENTS

I owe many people thanks for their generous help during the research, writing, and editing of this novel.

At the U.S. Coast Guard, thanks to Admiral Thomas Ostebo, to Captain John Reeves of the icebreaker *Healy*, to Marcus Lippmann, and to the crew of that icebreaker. Thanks for a great trip.

Thanks to retired General Dana Atkins of the U.S. Air Force. At the Navy, to Robert Freeman, once again, and to Lieutenant Commander Jason Weed, and to David Fisher, retired, all of whom put up with lots of questions. At the U.S. Marine Corps, thanks to Captain Tyler Balzer.

Several magazine editors gave me assignments in the Arctic over a three-year period. I'd like to thank Daryl Chen and Janice Kaplan at *Parade*, Carey Winfrey of *Smithsonian*, Dawn Raffel at *Reader's Digest*, and Chris Keyes at *Outside* magazine.

In Barrow, Alaska, thanks to Edward Itta and Richard Glenn, and also to David Harding, formerly of Barrow.

In Anchorage, huge thanks to Mead Treadwell.

To Bruce Seligman, inventor of the Arktos amphibious craft, many thanks for taking the time to answer my many questions.

Thanks to Patricia Burke and Charles Salzberg, good friends who gave terrific advice during the writing of the book. So did James Grady and Phil Gerard.

The list of people I ran imaginary scenarios by includes Jerome Reiss, Samantha Reiss, Marsha Price, Gabrielle Rosenthal, Ken and Ann Smith, Ginny O'Leary and Kirk Swiss, and Dr. Tio Chen. Michael Pillinger at NYU was hugely helpful on the subject of viruses. Thanks.

ACKNOWLEDGMENTS

Many thanks to Tasha Mandel, and to Seicha Turnbull.

To my publisher, Leslie Gelbman, and my editor, Tom Colgan, thanks for believing in the book.

I'm lucky to have agents like Esther Newberg, Josie Freeman, Daisy Meyrick, and Zoe Sandler.

I'm luckier still to have Wendy Roth at home.

There is no resemblance between any real person and the fictional characters in *White Plague*. The real icebreaker *Healy* is not the fictional icebreaker *Wilmington* in the novel, and the crew of the real ship has no resemblance to the crew of the fictional one, except that they both have my respect and admiration, as do the men and women of the U.S. Coast Guard for the superb job they do.

Any factual mistakes in this novel are mine.

WHITE PLAGUE

ONE

The pleas for help stopped coming just after five in the morning, Washington time. The Pentagon staffers cleared for handling sensitive messages sat in horror for a moment and then tried other ways to reach the victims. Nothing worked so they called the director, who phoned me. I was awake anyway, as I often am at 1 A.M., Alaskan time, running a fifteen-miler in the coastal city of Anchorage, where I live.

I have trouble sleeping. I don't like the dreams that come when I do.

The director said, "Joe, the submarine USS *Montana* is in the Arctic Ocean, five hundred miles north of Alaska, on the surface, on fire."

"What started it, sir?"

"Unclear. Everything happened fast, in the last few hours. Something toxic hit 'em. Chemicals or gas probably. They're sick apparently. Their air circulation system went out and then the fire started. Or maybe the fire started first. They can't dive. They can't move. The *Montana* carries a crew of a hundred and fifty-four men and women. Last report, one hundred and seven were still alive. Nine are critical. The medical officer burned to death."

"Radiation leak?"

"It's not radiation."

"Intentional?"

"Possible, Joe."

"What's the surface temperature?"

"Plus two. At least the sun barely goes down in late August. Darkness drops it another twenty degrees."

I blew out air. "Where are the survivors, sir?"

"Anyone not fighting the fire evacuated. They're on the ice, in insulated tents and covered life rafts, with portable generators. They've got fuel for two more days."

I swore. "Rescue helicopters?"

"Nothing has the range or space. Plus our closest subs are eight, nine days out. And, Joe?" I heard thick frustration in the director's voice, and grief. "The satellites are blind. Three days of bad weather and more on the way. Some kind of polar superstorm. We can't send planes, even those tough little Twin Otters. And nothing can land anyway on that ice. It's a goddamn rubble field where that sub came up. Might as well be boulders."

I thought fast, breathing with exertion, standing in running shorts and Reeboks on Treadwell Street in front of the old Russian church, with its hemlock and Sitka spruce trees scenting the air, along with the clean tang of the Chugach Mountain Range foothills, and with dead marble eyes of dew wet statues—saints and ocean explorers, Vitus Bering, watching the solitary runner with an encrypted cell phone in his hand. The yellow cedars were heavy with green. A traffic light blinked red in the plate glass window of Rosa's Brooklyn Bagels. "Maybe the

Russians can assist, sir. Don't they have twenty icebreakers? They must have something closer."

There was a long sigh. The director said, "Can't."

In the silence I heard secrecy and disgust for politics and necessity and all the reasons why our biohazard response unit had been formed in the first place. The director was a rotating public servant—corporate to government for twenty years—and lived in a world of high-level trade-offs. He was far more comfortable in the backstabbing world of high-level Washington than I. I said, the drumbeat of urgency growing, "Why, sir?" and the bigger picture began coming out.

"She's a Virginia-class sub, newest thing we've got. Most advanced weapons and guidance systems. We can't have President Topov's boys getting a look at them, sharing them with their friends in Damascus and Tehran."

"So it was a spy mission."

"They have spies," the director said wryly. "We have intel. Joe, get up there." His voice grew angry. "The United States Navy . . . greatest in the world . . . and we only have one working icebreaker at the moment and it's used for science, not even under Navy control. The Coast Guard has it. At least it's only four hours out of Barrow," he said, naming the northernmost city in Alaska. "It's been up there doing sea bottom surveys. We'll jettison the scientists, board you and Marines."

"I want Eddie with me," I said, naming my best friend.

"He's on the way."

"And an expert on Virginia-class subs."

"Yes, yes, with Major Nakamura, coming up from Seattle," the director said. Major Nakamura was Eddie.

He added, as if needing to underline urgency, "The new Russian government makes old Vladimir Putin look peaceful as Gandhi. They've made control of the Arctic a keystone of military policy. The Arctic is melting, Joe. A whole ocean opening that wasn't passable before. Oil. Gas. Shipping. It'll make the Atlantic sub game look like third grade. They're stronger than us up there. I've been trying for years to get more money from Congress for Arctic ops."

"You mean *intel*." My joke fell flat.

"Save the ones you can. Secure or destroy that sub. Joe, whatever happened up there, whatever started it, you've got the qualifications to handle it. You make the hard choices. I'll back you up."

I felt my pulse go up and more sweat break out on my forehead. *One hundred and fifty-four people.* A sharp ache gripped my gut. My mouth was dry and a cold shadow seemed to pass over the city, even though it was a hot night for Anchorage, temperatures around seventy degrees.

The director said, more softly, "I know you gave notice, Joe. I know you only have two weeks left."

I'd been looking forward to quitting, moving back East. "Oh, I'll be back before then," I said, which might or might not turn out to be the truth, I knew.

"Thank you." I heard real gratitude in his voice. "You'll fly from Elmendorf to Fairbanks," he said, naming the city an hour away by air where my ex-wife lived with another officer. "You'll pick up Marines and head to Barrow in a Globemaster. You should arrive the same time as the icebreaker, so no time lost. Get me a list of what you need, soon as possible."

Christ, help me.

But Christ, I thought wryly, had not listened last time I needed him. He had not helped at all, so I'd done things that had put the last nail in the coffin of a long-failed marriage, kept me awake most nights now, and made me a pariah among men and women I'd worked with, U.S. Marines.

The worst part was, I knew I'd do it again if I had the choice.

The director seemed to guess what I was thinking. "Joe, you were a hero last time. I wish the truth could come out someday."

I wasn't going to give him absolution. So I said nothing.

"Good luck, Colonel," he said, and hung up.

I started toward home. The twenty-minute sprint would be spent planning. No use waiting, calling a cab. In my head I began drawing up a list of what I'd need—antibiotics and antivirals, body bags, burn medicines. I'd take the thumb drive library, a portable case containing just about everything we know about bioweapons. The questions came hard and fast.

They're sick? Sick from what?

I thought, feeling my legs pumping, my heart roaring, that I'd never really understood secrets until I'd joined the director's unit. Only then did I see that owning one made *you* a secret. I was a living secret, and I knew with dread, as the darkened foothill houses went by—here a cedar ranch-style home belonging to an Air Force Raptor pilot I knew who was often sent up to the U.S. border to monitor Russian bear bombers buzzing U.S. soil; here a condo in which lived an *Anchorage Daily News* editor who wrote editorials urging the beefing up of Arctic military budgets; and there, a dark spot a half mile off, an Air Force research lab where I'd done occasional work for the last few months, looking at virus behavior in cold climates—that one day the things that my unit dealt with would kill them, and their families, all of us, in warm beds as we slept, on a lovely night like this.

■ ■ ■

My name is Joe Rush, and you won't find a description of my real job in my dossier at the Marine Corps. It's been sheep-dipped, altered so that what remains contains—like Washington itself—enough truth to fool a casual observer, and the rest a fabrication designed to protect the

Corps, me, and the nation from learning things that people like the director have decided you ought not to know.

Thirty-nine years old, the dossier says. That part's true, at least. Six foot two. The photo shows hair as black and thick as my great-grandfather the Welsh coal miner's, eyes as blue as those of the Norwegian peasant woman, my great-grandmother, who met "great-gramper" on the deck of the coal-powered steamer that brought them into New York harbor 130 years ago. The Massachusetts town they settled in is in the file, too, because I grew up there: the textile mill village of Smith Falls, population 250, a hamlet nestled in the green mountain foothills, ten miles south of the Vermont line on a cracked two-lane rural road.

There, three generations of Rushes worked on the assembly line of Brady Textiles, making Army uniforms in World War One, Air Force uniforms in World War Two, and Naval uniforms during Vietnam, but by the Iraq War, Brady had moved operations to Honduras, where they paid workers less, and the men and some women in my family had become the electricians, plumbers, and roofers maintaining the second homes of people from Boston or New York who summered in our region, and went home to their condos and Long Island suburbs when the air grew chilly each fall, and I boarded a rusted yellow bus and rode to a country school where, if we wanted to keep our football team equipped, our moms baked pies that we kids sold door to door to the college professors in wealthier Williamstown.

State troopers and soldiers were our success models. *"Be all you can be,"* said the Army commercials I thrilled to on TV when I was nine. *"The few, the proud,"* said the ads for the Marines. I grew up dreaming of the ocean and travel, feeling trapped by familiarity and smothered by love. I wanted far away. I'd never traveled more than forty miles from home. The smells of summer grass and February snows were odors of my prison. The kiss of a girl and even the camaraderie of friends were, to me, tricks to bar escape to the wider world.

So I left that girl, said good-bye to those friends, and the "education" part of my file correctly indicates that I attended UMass on a ROTC scholarship. The early Marine history is right also: Parris Island, Quantico, amphibious duty in Indonesia, and the Philippines, everything right up to the second tour in Iraq.

But the second tour is not mentioned in that file.

Under "awards," you'll see the Silver Star and the Legion of Merit, and a Navy and Marine Corps medal awarded for actions taken in combat during the global war on terror. True. All true. But you won't find out what the "actions taken" were.

Under "skills," you'll learn that I can hit a moving target with a rifle at three hundred yards, and can afterward, thanks to my MD degree, remove the bullet, stitch the wound, prescribe proper medications, and run any field hospital or field lab in the world, to hopefully identify chemicals or germs released in combat against our troops.

I am also qualified to lead an assault on an enemy bioweapons bunker, secure it, decontaminate it, treat injured staffers, and then arrest them, so they can be interrogated, tried, and hung by U.S. military tribunal, under obscurer laws of the Republic. If my skill set seems contradictory, you're starting to get an idea of why you need access to several files to get a complete picture, why I now live alone and run long distances at night, instead of going to sleep.

After my wife left, I went through the drunk phase and bar fight phase. I went through the period where you sleep with lots of women, and tell yourself you enjoy it, and the phase where you stop enjoying it, and if you ever saw my "eyes only" psychiatric file, you'd read that I cut myself off from friends, except for Eddie, who knew the whole truth.

If you have big enough secrets, you can't have friends.

For the past year—after getting out of the hospital—I've been on partial duty, teaching a few biohazard classes at Elmendorf, several miles from my home, hitting the pistol range three times a week, occasionally traveling to remote Eskimo villages along the Bering Strait with Air Force doctors to study new strains of rabies.

My memo to the Secretary of Defense—which brought me to the director's attention five years ago—suggested that the military should prepare for the possibility that the next big outbreak of human disease might come from a cold climate, not a hot one, not a jungle, as is usually assumed . . . but from a microorganism released by melting ice, after being encased in it for hundreds or thousands of years. Or a mutant variety emerging as the region warmed.

Now, going home—I raced along Stevens Boulevard, beneath a lone hooting owl, and to the sound of a distant loon, and past evergreens draped with moss that shimmered beneath streetlights. A certain degree of cynicism is healthy in a longtime servant of the Republic. I'd achieved the level commensurate with a man who'd been seconded to an obscure biohazard unit comprised of two-officer teams of doctors with intense combat experience.

I was ranking officer on my team.

I admired the director but was also wary of someone who always believed he knew the best course for the rest of the world.

The director liked to quote Benjamin Franklin. But I think he was talking about himself.

"Patriotism is relentless."

Franklin was not a soldier, but he signed the Declaration of Independence. Had America lost its revolution, he would have been hung. He understood choice, and that is my measure of a man, the ability to make decisions.

I arrived at my small cedar-sided home in twenty minutes. A black Ford pulled into my driveway sixty seconds after that.

By 2:30 A.M., I was in an Air Force Falcon clawing through a late-summer thunderstorm as it flew toward Fairbanks, and I read a series of encrypted "eyes only" reports on the submarine *Montana*, my heart pounding.

I kept thinking about 107 surviving men and women on the ice, far north of me. It seemed like a big number. It would be small compared to the danger I headed toward in the end.

TWO

From the air, Barrow looked more like the last place on Earth than the place where our world could end, which, I'd learn soon, was the case. The big Globemaster transport made a wide turn over the frigid ocean and angled back toward the airport's lone runway, its four mighty engines spewing air. The roar was tremendous. We were at the top of North America. The town of 4,500—mostly Iñupiat Eskimos—hugged the junction of the Chukchi and the Beaufort Seas, waters frozen for centuries until recently, now passable to ships in summers. The water looked black as anthracite. I didn't see any ice out there. The big stuff, the pack, I knew, would come farther north.

Alaska is so big that if you superimposed it over the continental United States, one end would cover North Carolina and the other would touch California. We'd roared over the Brooks Range, the peaks seeming to reach up and try to knock the plane from the sky. Dall sheep stared back from snowy crests. Then the mountains had dropped away and the land had become brown tundra, rolling grass-covered hummocks and thousands of elliptical freshwater lakes. Shaped like sunglass lenses, they threw back golden glare through rainbows of vapor: mist tendrils, fog, drizzle. The sense—gazing out—was of flying through gigantic lungs.

I'd slept for an hour, files on my lap, and had the dream about a girl from Smith Falls, more memory than imagination: a time-lapse vision of a slim twenty-year-old with long chestnut hair, fawn-colored eyes, and an Irish freckled face, a stunner, a beauty, naked, her legs folded, sitting on an old yard-sale carpet in my old college dorm; a beam of morning sun slanting in to highlight the curve of hip, smooth inner thigh, triangular three-freckle pattern on a small foot, above clenched toes. A girl doing something mundane, speaking to her mother on a telephone, on the first night we'd slept together. *Yes, Mom, I'm fine. No, Mom, we didn't drink wine.* A girl who, at that moment, had seemed the most breathtakingly beautiful image I'd ever seen. I'd married that girl, but the early vision we'd shared of each other had not lasted.

Still, it had not occurred to me then that years later, after many stunning views— elephants grazing at dusk in Angola, glaciers two hundred feet high calving in Antarctica, the moon on jungle canopy in Nicaragua—the simple image of a girl in a dorm room would stand out.

Some people think nightmares are the worst dreams from which to awaken. But it's beauty that gets you. Not ugliness; glory that ambushes you with the bittersweet touch of remorse, slipping through the unconscious to a thirty-nine-year-old bachelor who traded family for duty; the barest whiff of regret that comes when you open your eyes in the morning, before the tasks of daily living wipe it away, that glimpse of solitude that, I'd realized, in rare moments, comes with membership in the unit, although no one tells you that when you join.

I'd chosen to confess to my wife what I'd done, and watched her close up to me forever.

The last image, before I shot awake, was a coiled, black, old-fashioned rubber telephone cord pressed against a white breast, leaving a pink mark. Can you beat it? Just a plain phone line, and I'd woken with a hole in my gut, the copilot's hand on my shoulder, and with the sour knowledge that the man who shared Nina's bed now was behind me in the plane.

■ ■ ■

"Sir, we've raised the ship."

I tried to wipe the dream from my mind as I made my way to the cockpit. I saw, at sea, a red shape on the horizon. Up until now we'd been unable to reach the icebreaker, and I'd cursed the poor state of U.S. military technology in the Arctic. The mightiest military power on Earth is more than ten years behind the other polar nations, having spent all our monies on wars in the Mideast.

The copilot gestured me to the jump seat and I pulled a headset from the cockpit wall. The coming conversation would be delicate. All Captain Maurice DeBlieu—his file said—knew so far was that his normal scientific mission had been canceled, he'd been ordered to send all research staff ashore, he was about to undertake an unknown mission, and that the Secretary of Homeland Security herself (Homeland Security, not the Pentagon, runs the Coast Guard) had hopefully told him to give a Marine lieutenant colonel named Joseph Rush platinum-quality treatment on his ship.

The voice that came over the line was clear, professional, vaguely

Southern, Virginia or northern North Carolina, I guessed. The file on my laptop held a photo of a black man with a thin, neat mustache, thick black framed glasses, and dark brown eyes that looked directly into the lens, as if challenging the photographer to finish up so Captain Maurice DeBlieu could get back to work. He had nine years in the Arctic, six as top man on the ship.

"DeBlieu," he said.

He hadn't been appointed guardian of the nation's lone functioning icebreaker by being a laggard. The Coast Guard was used to hosting guests in the Arctic, but not having guests tell them what to do. This next part could be awkward, especially as I'd requested that he *not* be informed yet as to the exact nature of the mission.

So when I asked him to meet me ashore, instead of on his ship, he requested that I hand the headphones to the pilot, and a moment later, the pilot politely but firmly requested identification. When he read the laminated card to DeBlieu, the captain still insisted that during personnel changeovers he preferred to monitor things from his ship, and not go ashore.

"Safety reasons," he said. "If something happens to us out there, there's no one to help. We're it. So I like to watch everything up close."

"I understand, sir. Security situation."

He paused, curiosity in his voice. "Look, Colonel. I'm sure my people and yours can deal with loading issues. My understanding is that wherever we're going, we have to hurry. So why not talk on the ship while boarding proceeds."

This was precisely what I needed to avoid, and I said, "I'll explain onshore. Also, I'm afraid I have to ask you to cut off all communication from the ship now. No e-mails, no cell phones. Cut all satellite access."

No response.

I said, "Captain, if you'll take the first chopper over, I'll meet you in the terminal and explain fully."

"Explain? I've got thirty pissed-off scientists here, and one furious Assistant Deputy Secretary, State Department, demanding explanations for kicking them off the ship. No one told us why. These scientists get a seven-week research cruise each summer. If they miss the window, once the big ice comes back, they lose the year."

"They're not my concern," I said.

I hung up, knowing that resentment was building two miles away. I'd not been told that a State Department official was aboard, and hoped the director had dealt with that. The last thing I needed was a high-end squabble.

At least the captain didn't call back. He would fly ashore.

■ ■ ■

The runway came up quickly, abutted by high grass, tundra. I saw a two-story Easter egg–blue corrugated metal terminal and a warehouse-style hangar beside it, inside of which I glimpsed, through open sliding doors, a couple of small jets and two copters. Men in yellow foul weather gear wheeled an old Bell 412—*North Slope Borough Rescue Squad*—out, into light rain. It would—along with a parked Coastie copter, ferry Marines and supplies out to the ship, and displaced scientists back.

Good. Three copters means faster loading.

My two dozen Marines—sitting in bolted-down airline-style seats, or affixed to net webbing on the sides of the fuselage—were dressed like science research and support staff, our cover story for locals. Anyone watching us, especially tourists with cameras, would see "civilians" who lay whale acoustic buoys or fix machinery; they wore thick jeans, Northern Outfitter boots, hooded parkas, and wool caps, enough of a disguise to fool casual observers in an airport, as we didn't want some Eskimo kid or tourist or scientist tweeting or sending Facebook messages about Marines boarding ships in Barrow. The clothing was perfect, but considering the jarhead haircuts and the way the guys stuck together, and the efficient way they took orders, they wouldn't fool a professional observer for fifty seconds.

Arctic tech crews are usually big, jovial, loose-moving bearded boys and high-spirited women from Minnesota and Wyoming, or ropy types, motorcycle racers and boat bums from Cape Cod. My guys were clean shaven, serious, quiet.

Also back there were crates we'd taken on in Fairbanks, from the Arctic combat school, an impressively named, but undermanned, basement warren at the air base, for which the generals were perpetually trying to get more funds.

The crates were stenciled: WHALE ACOUSTICS BUOYS; BOWHEAD STUDY, WOODS HOLE OCEANOGRAPHIC INSTITUTE AND LAMONT-DOHERTY EARTH OBSERVATORY.

In reality the boxes contained M4 carbines, M16s equipped with 40 mm M203 grenade launchers, Kevlar vests, eight kinds of antibiotics and burn medicines—including Cipro, zanamivir, ribavirin, and xapaxin—chemical decontaminants, snow goggles, portable propane generators, incendiary explosives, snow camouflage uniforms, microscopes, oxygen canisters, surgical masks, terrestrial satellite-jamming equipment, oil drums of bleach, encrypted sat phones, snowshoes and cross-country skis, three-finger mittens and boot liners, all the gear the modern Arctic warrior needs to do his job on a rescue mission while knowing there may be combat involved.

Another coffin-shaped crate, labeled TOOLS, carried Bibles, small wooden crosses, four small Jewish stars, and 154 folded-up plastic zip-up body shrouds.

Farther in back of the fuselage were two tied down big Arktos amphibious carriers, superb hybrid vehicles built in Canada, tank-like cabs with thick glass windows and steel tank treads, that could bull over ice but float on water. Propulsion in the water came from high-thrust, low-speed jets.

Each Arktos could hold fifty people, more on top. They were ungainly, a pumpkin color, built for visibility, not stealth, good for rescue, but not a fight. We could carry extra sleds and skis for Marines on top. The crafts would be driven on their own power to the *Wilmington*, and loaded by crane.

I tried not to think about the men and women trapped on the ice, five hundred miles north of Barrow . . . winds rising, snow blowing, medicine and food running out, their medical officer burned to death, possibly no one alive by the time we got there at all.

The director had told me an hour ago, "No change, except that the storm is getting worse. Gusts at fifty-three now."

We halted and a trio of forklifts growled toward the plane. With a mechanical groan, the back of the Globemaster shoveled open to form a ramp. Cold wind and rain blew in. The Marines unlashed themselves from side netting, and got to work unloading. Two squads, twelve men each. One major, two gunnery sergeants, and the rest enlisted men, none of whom I'd ever met. They moved efficiently, but there was also something in the faces of those men, the young ones and veterans alike, something hard and unpleasant when they glanced my way. A guess as to the source would be Major Donald Pettit, who lived with my ex-wife, and commanded the rapid response squads that had been put under my control.

I'd first learned of Pettit's existence on the day that Nina moved in with him. She'd phoned me to make sure I heard the news from her, not from anyone else. She'd assured me that she'd met the guy eight months after our separation, and had not dated him until three months after that. I believed her. Nina doesn't lie. But that didn't mean I didn't feel like taking a swipe at Pettit's jaw when I met the big man on the tarmac in Fairbanks. I suppose he felt something of the same, and his guys sensed the extra testosterone saturating the air.

Marine males locking horns.

Pettit seemed to avoid looking my way.

I suppose we'd have to deal with this eventually, but at the moment, with things to do, the clarification session would come later. I saw a copter landing. It would carry the captain. And I needed to talk to that man now.

Get yourself under control.

Look, I respect the Coast Guard. I've always admired the altruism involved in joining up, the choice to serve the country by providing humanitarian aid, helping victims of hurricanes, fires, ship sinkings. But combat-wise, even on a normal cutter you find, at most, a handful of crew allowed to carry weapons, there to arrest drug runners or smugglers. The *Wilmington* was built for science. It was a floating lab. Its crew consisted of a few veteran chiefs and otherwise mostly kids, eighteen- and twenty-year-olds whose expectations of emergencies ran to fires or sinkings, not battle, terrorism, or disease.

The good part was, they had extensive training in first aid and rescue. I'd need both. But if fighting broke out, they couldn't help me. I'd asked the captain ashore because, until precautions were in place, I couldn't discuss that on the ship.

■ ■ ■

"I shut down communications as you requested," Captain DeBlieu said with a slight standoffishness marking his professional courtesy, "but I'll need a reason why if you want me to keep that order in place."

We occupied cushioned swivel chairs in the Borough Rescue Squad office, taking the measure of each other, alone, as the pilots had given us privacy. The room was divided into comfortable cubicles with landline phones, computers, Atlanta Braves coffee mugs, and logbooks on desks. We could have been in any town in Idaho or Arizona.

I glimpsed boarding proceeding out a window—ship scientists to shore, crates to the *Wilmington*. Beyond the airport were some of the town's one- and two-story wooden homes, perched on concrete pilings to keep them from melting into permafrost when they heated. I saw gravel roads. Traffic. A three-story office building. Eskimo kids on bicycles, wearing Windbreakers, even at thirty-six degrees. Satellite farms sat out on the tundra, huge dishes and golf-ball-shaped geodesic domes to protect sensitive equipment. Barrow's radar, the old DEW line warning system, had been set up during the Cold War to warn of incoming Russian attacks. Local equipment still served as America's Arctic front line. But it had been designed for threats from the past.

"Colonel Rush, my crew has been at sea for three months straight without a break. They're tired. They miss home. They want to talk to their families. I'd like a good reason why I'm telling them they can't."

He was a short man, with excellent posture, an ex-academy shortstop with top grades, I'd read, Ohio born, both parents engineers. Over the years I've learned that small men in positions of influence tend to be more efficient, contrary to the usual view. They've had to prove themselves, especially the top athletes, all their lives.

When I told him about the submarine burning, his horror was genuine. When I explained that we could not tell the crew or call out for assistance, his eyes narrowed, and I watched him process the logic. He didn't need a map to understand why we had to move fast and secure the sub.

"But why shut off my crew's communication?"

"I don't want anyone else knowing our route. I don't want anyone getting a fix on a phone and monitoring us."

I also told him with some delicacy that the reason I'd asked him ashore was that I intended for the Marines to sweep his cabin, the wardroom, and also my quarters—former chief scientist's room—for listening devices before we could have serious talks on the ship.

He bridled. "That's a bit paranoid, Colonel. We're a science ship. In all my years on the *Wilmington*, the State Department never asked for this."

"Then they should have. The Marines will also activate jammers, in case someone on board," I said, meaning a spy, "has access to a foreign satellite, or a corporate one. Once the ship is secure, you'll announce we're on an emergency drill, simulated rescue of a tourist ship taken by terrorists. Further north, we'll tell them the truth."

He saw holes in the story. "We've done other rescue drills, and Marines weren't part of them."

"Neither were terrorists. You need Marines."

"We need satellite information for navigation."

"My understanding," I said, having spoken to the director about this, "is that your officers are quite competent with charts, in case sat access goes down."

His silence acknowledged this. "It's happened in bad weather."

"Your crew will do what they're told," I said. "Also, if we need sat access, we can open it up every once in a while, stagger it, in ten-minute increments, but only we know when. Now! My understanding is that we can reach the sub in two days. Is that correct? What's your top speed?"

"Seventeen knots, at first," he said, "but once we get into ice, we slow down. In heavy ice we back and ram. We can push through four-foot masses at a couple miles an hour. That pack may not be ten feet thick like it used to be, but it's still heavy in places. Hit it the wrong way, it can crack us open. Plus we've got that storm up there."

"Two days," I said.

"Two to five, depending on conditions. I determine speed," he said. "Unless you want another hundred and fifty people in need of a rescue."

I blew out air. He made sense and even four days would get us there before the nearest U.S. sub could reach the victims. But would anyone still be alive? Would anyone else get there first?

DeBlieu's mind was on other matters and he asked, with some tightness, "Colonel, do you have any evidence to support this idea of yours that I may have a spy on board?"

"Evidence, no. But it's a logical possibility."

The brown eyes veered between irritation, doubt, and amusement over my cautious behavior. He'd come up through the ranks as an engineer, his file said. He had no combat experience. "Why logical?"

"Because trillions of dollars are at stake up here; because the Russians have declared the Arctic to be the probable site of the next big war, over mineral rights or trade routes. The Chinese want the minerals and routes, too. We spy on them. They spy on us."

"The Cold War is over," he said.

"The cold peace never is. It's perfectly logical for them to try to keep track of the research, screw it up or try to slow you down. *They've* made the Arctic a priority, even if we haven't."

I preferred to make this man an ally, not an enemy, so I explained further, in a softer voice.

"Saudi Arabia was wasteland two hundred years ago, and the countries who got control of that oil and those Mideast trade routes ruled the world. You ever read Rudyard Kipling, Captain? It's the great game, jockeying for power in remote places. Hell, if not the Russians or Chinese, just an oil company that wants access to your surveys. *We need to keep this mission secret.*"

To his credit, he thought about it. Slowly, he said, his voice losing some stiffness, "We haven't had any problems."

"How would you know? Furthermore," I said, "the civilians you carry receive only low-level vetting. And, Captain? Even if there's *no* spy aboard, any blogger, tweeter, an innocent e-mail home saying *We're on a rescue mission* could blow it. If a spouse back in Pittsburgh phones the local TV station, or she's got a brother at the *Washington Post*, maybe a niece on that sub, the instant the public hears, *Arctic submarine on fire*... I guarantee you, our satellites would suddenly track every Russian icebreaker within a thousand miles make a run at intersection. And some of their icebreakers have artillery. You have a few M16s."

"You think we'd really fight?" he asked, not believing it possible in the new century.

"If our sub is in international water, abandoned? It's drifting. It could drift into Russian waters. Next time our boys and girls are submerged off China, Syria, you want their lives in jeopardy?" My voice hardened. "You want a test?"

He nodded, unhappy. "So it's a race," he said.

"A race."

He was eyeing me differently now. "Just what kind of doctor are you anyway?"

The kind who treats worst-case scenarios.

I said, "Oh, hypothermia. Frostbite."

He sighed. It would be all right with him, at least at first. "Right," he said. "And you won't tell me what really happened on that submarine?"

Finally I could tell the truth, not that this relieved me. "I wish I knew what happened."

Ten minutes later I learned that one of the Arktos propulsion units was broken, and could not quickly be repaired. There was no way to get the second rescue craft to the *Wilmington*. We'd have to leave with just one.

Two hours later we were under way, heading toward the North Pole at full speed, to start, at least, seventeen knots.

THREE

"If you spot a polar bear," I told the man who shared my ex-wife's bed back in Fairbanks, in a dry, academic voice, "record it in the log."

Major Pettit almost responded, "Yes, Colonel," but he changed it, at the last second, to "Sure, Doctor."

I unscrewed a ventilation shaft door, peering in, scanning for hidden microphones, running a meter box. I kept talking because the meter was supposed to jump if a transmitter was sending. "Bears use ice as platforms for feeding. When the ice melts, the polar bear population drops."

My quarters consisted of a two-room suite on the level four deck, which also housed cabins for the captain, ship's officers, scientists, and held a radio room and helicopter control station. There were electronics shops and a pantry. We were one level down from the ship's pilothouse.

My cabin was large, light streaming through a porthole. The sea was calm and there was no sense of movement, although I felt a low vibration from the diesel engines below. The sun outside was a hazy orb, as if viewed through gauze, a glow which would circle low in the sky, horizon to horizon, but in late August, almost never go away. If I needed to sleep, I'd close the porthole cover.

Inside, two more Marines were silently up on steel chairs with screwdrivers in hand, reattaching grills to ventilation shafts that hung between the two single beds on opposite sides of the room, both crisply made. A lance corporal was going through the two upright steel lockers with a meter detector. A private was in the bathroom. My quarters smelled of pine-scented cleaning fluid.

The ceiling was a mass of insulated pipes and bunched multicolored wires.

I said, "I hope the food here is good."

Major Pettit slid out from under my desk and shook his head. He'd found nothing. I pointed at the screws fixing porthole cover to hull.

A conference room abutting my cabin—which we examined next—held a bolted-down steel conference table and eight metal chairs. There was a topographical map of the sea bottom off Alaska, with areas shaded blue for "U.S. Zone" and yellow for Russian. On the map the Arctic Ocean resembled a jagged lake and its surrounding nations: U.S., Russia, Canada, Norway, Greenland, Iceland, and Sweden.

Major Pettit shook his head. No mikes.

"I saw the menu. Steak tonight," he said.

In recent years, I knew, voice-activated mikes—Phillips screw tops, minis, or stick-ons—have been recovered in, among other places, the golf bag of the general who runs Elmendorf Air Force Base in Anchorage, the Lexus leased by Shell Oil's head of Alaskan offshore exploration in the Arctic, the sunglasses of a fighter pilot sent out regularly to monitor Russian bear bomber activity off our border, and the laptop computer belonging to a University of Alaska professor advising the U.S. Navy on which ships to build to handle a region with less ice.

It is not known who planted these devices, but the director believes they originated with Russian or Chinese military or commercial—shipping or mining—interests.

I liked the silent concentration with which the Marines moved and used hand signals. I admired the focus on details and the way they operated as a team. I was less pleased with the continued coldness emanating from them. Marines are trained to keep emotions in check, and as it takes one to know one, I was picking up almost minuscule muscle tightness, extra distance in voices, the barest rigidity.

Why? And will it hamper our mission?

"All clear, Colonel," Pettit said.

"Thank you, Major. Stay a moment."

The men left. Pettit was a bulky, broad-shouldered blond in his mid-thirties, with deep laugh or frown lines around his mouth, suggesting an inner life of strong emotions. He had thin brows, a boxy face, a strong jaw, and eyes of robin's egg blue, which somehow lacked the warmth normally associated with that color. He was my height, about six two. He'd done duty in Afghanistan, in winter, where he'd won a Navy Cross and Silver Star after being shot in the thigh and saving two wounded men, carrying them, under fire, to safety. He'd also excelled at joint maneuvers with Norwegian Arctic troops, in Europe.

I fought off a vision of this man in bed with my ex-wife. *Stop it!*

Now, told to relax, Pettit moved his feet apart slightly, but his back remained straight, wary. Good Marines can broadcast disdain with nothing more than a minuscule adjustment of the spine.

I'd not yet fully briefed him on the mission, as I'd spent my time on the plane reading the files of *Wilmington* officers, and about the submarine. Now I gave him the bare-bones picture, but unlike Captain De-Blieu, who, upon learning about the sub, was horrified, Pettit gazed directly into my face, as if questioning why of all people I'd been sent to deal with it.

"Major, I'm detecting some issue here, perhaps something you'd care to discuss, affecting the mission."

He regarded me coolly. "No, Colonel. There's no issue!"

"Major, my powers of detection are vast, powerful, all seeing, and mysterious, and I believe you meant to say something else. So here's the deal. What if I told you that for the next two minutes, two only, you could say anything and it will stay between us. Marine to Marine."

The eyes shifted, came back. He made his decision. "Then, Colonel, I would tell you that I heard a story about you and I would appreciate knowing if it is true."

The pulse started up in my forehead. I'd thought this was going to be about Nina. I felt hot. "What is that story?"

Those robin's egg blue eyes went darker now, intelligent, measuring, yet to his credit, I detected hope, so he was fair. "It is that you personally panicked in combat, sir, and blew up a truck carrying nine Marines. That you killed your own men. The incident was hushed up and you transferred out."

"Where did you hear that story?"

"I'd prefer not to share that, Colonel."

Another plus for him. My head throbbed. I said, "And?"

"If the story is true, I believe it my duty to tell you that I think you are the worst sort of human being, a disgrace as a Marine officer, and that you should have been cashiered and put on trial. Also, if it is true, I don't understand why you are in command here."

"Will these feelings hamper your ability to follow orders, or slow your responses even a fraction of a second if I tell you to do something on this mission?"

He shook his head. "My men and I are good Marines!"

He didn't need to add the rest, *unlike you.*

"Then I will inform you that the story you heard is not true."

The eyes relaxed a little.

I said, staring directly into those pupils, "There were eight Marines on that truck, not nine. And I choose not to explain anything else to you."

He seemed to be hit by a small force in the back, so that his posture, seemingly perfect before, stretched even higher as his gaze shifted away. I could have lied to him, but I was finished with that. You dominate people with truth as well as falsehoods. Or was it that, like a shrink once told me, I needed to keep punishing myself?

I asked, in a hard voice, "Anything more, Major?"

"Yes."

I waited. He said, almost reluctantly, "It didn't come from Nina. She's never said anything bad about you."

"Thank you. You will complete sweeps of the captain's cabin, exec's, and wardroom. You will make sure the boys get chow, and sleep. You will then map all routes from forward areas to the helo hangar, where we will set up a field hospital. We won't be carrying a chopper on this trip."

He exhibited no hint of the animus he had displayed a moment earlier. He saluted and left.

I sat on the bed, slumped, my insides grinding. For a moment I flashed back to the only time I'd ever defied the director. It was in his office in D.C., two months after the killings. He'd sat me down and explained with some pain in his voice that a rumor had gotten out about the incident. He did not want me to be surprised if I heard it on a base, a gathering, or worst case, if I received a call from a reporter. He assured me that he intended to track down the source and prosecute the Marine who had leaked the story.

"After all, Joe, all witnesses were sworn to secrecy. I'll lock that damned leaker away for so long that—"

"No," I'd blurted out.

"Joe?"

"I'd appreciate it if you left it alone, sir."

"Joe, this isn't just about you. Those people were warned, told what would happen to them if anyone spoke—"

I'd stood up, heart slamming in my chest, my breathing hot, seeing, in my mind, a sand-coated tarp-topped truck racing toward me. I'd said, through pounding in my ears, "Sir, I won't have anyone punished because of what I did. I don't care what else is at stake. If you do this, I'll be the one to go to the papers. *Drop the inquiry, now.*"

He'd seemed angry, and then, in turn, thoughtful, and sad.

"All right, Joe. For you. I'll leave the punishment out of it. But we need to stop that story."

Eight dead Marines, I thought now. Fuck the story. Who cared about a story? I cared about the truth.

I killed eight good U.S. Marines.

■ ■ ■

Thirty seconds later came a knock on the conference room door and I said, "Come!" I composed myself. I'd given DeBlieu a list of people I needed to see immediately, whose participation would be vital to the mission. They were waiting in the wardroom, and would be escorted here one by one by a Marine, who would keep anyone else away.

I always prefer personal meetings—even brief ones—to give me a sense of people I must work with. Later would come group strategy sessions. Now I wanted a close-up look.

"I'm Marietta Cristobel," the woman in the doorway said.

The nation's foremost Arctic sea ice expert—"ice forecaster"—was plump and fortyish, with curly black hair streaked with gray, brushed to her shoulders. The eyes were black, skin a tea color, clothing loose but warm looking: corduroy painter's pants over Eastern Mountain lace-up boots, red and black checkered flannel shirt, fleece zip-up vest with an outer pocket showing the tip of a thin cigar.

This woman's ability to pick open routes through hundreds of miles of sea ice could determine the success or failure of the rescue. We sat beneath the map of the Arctic Ocean, blue at the fringes, white showing the permanent ice cap, a jagged presence at the top of Earth.

Marietta's name was on every report I'd read on the plane—Naval, Coast Guard, scientific task force—dealing with future military ops in the Arctic. She worked for NOAA. Mother of two. Home in Miami. Her parents had fled Cuba under Castro, when she was four. Husband a professor of biology at Florida International. I asked, "How did a Cuban get interested in ice?"

"We like it in rum and Cokes," she said, and smiled. It was probably a standard answer to a question the Stanford graduate got all the time.

"How bad will the ice be ahead?"

She leaned back, easygoing but thoughtful. "Colonel, used to be, twelve years ago, we'd be in ice now in August/September, but within a couple hours we'll start seeing *bergy bits*, little pieces of white. Later, *growlers*, bigger ones. Then slush and *pancake ice*, a glaze over the surface, then light first-year ice. The big pack won't come for a day."

"The captain says that can damage the ship."

"Even an icebreaker can be holed if it hits too hard, or at the wrong angle. Or we can be trapped in heavy ice. This ship carries a six-month supply of food if that happens."

"I'd prefer to avoid that," I said.

"Me, too. My daughter's sixteenth birthday is in a month." She grinned. "I plan to be there."

I liked her. "Tell me how you forecast ice conditions."

Marietta slid an electronic tablet across the table. She worked with the National Ice Center in Suitland, Maryland. "Normally, with satellite pictures. But you've shut down communication," she said. "I lost contact forty minutes ago. I can't see anymore."

I envisioned my Marines—first thing they'd done—placing a portable terrestrial jammer on the high point on the ship, the aloft conn, a closed-in nest above the bridge. The jammer was effective at a range of two miles, at least on all known frequencies.

On Marietta's tablet, I read: NO RECEPTION.

"If you want forecasts, I need access," she said.

"I'll give you ten minutes once in a while, then we close it up again. What's the minimum amount of time you need to pick up information?"

She sat back, considering. "Well, with the storm, we may get nothing even when it's on, but give me ten minutes every two hours, and hope that's when cloud cover lets us see." She shook her head. "You couldn't have picked a worse time for a drill."

"Ten minutes then, at staggered intervals."

"Thanks. But even if it works, we'll learn the extent of the ice, but not thickness, and *thickness*," she said, "is what's dangerous. I have a drone on board which we can fly in wind below twenty miles per hour. It'll show open routes. But winds lower than that?" She laughed. "Don't hold your breath. It's worsening up there.

"Also, about this rescue drill," she added. "I'm curious, how did you pick the spot where we're going?"

"We're heading for a buoy dropped by plane," I lied.

"You know that it will drift with the ice, and won't be where you dropped it, right?"

"The buoy has a radio beacon on it. At a certain point, we should pick up the signal," I said. This was true; there was an emergency transmitter on the *Montana*. Normally it was good at long distances, but in a storm, who could tell?

I added, "Dr. Cristobel, please keep the sat channel access arrangement a secret between you and me."

She nodded. She'd been at enough Naval war games to know variations. "No problem. By the way, if you *really* want an ice expert, talk to Clinton Toovik."

"Who is Clinton Toovik?"

"Our Iñupiat Eskimo observer. The North Slope puts a marine mammal watcher aboard every cruise. Clinton's a whale hunter. He reports back to the community on animal conditions, and truth is, he's more the ice expert than me. He can tell from watching clouds what kind of ice is ahead. Mist, whale movements, wind, currents, even light reflection, to him they're clues."

"Where is Clinton?"

"He hardly ever sleeps," she said. "He's usually up on the bridge, watching and writing in a little book. The Iñupiats have a hundred words for ice. The National Weather Service only four. To Clinton, it's alive, like some kind of animal," she said as a loud argument began in the corridor outside, and a man shouted, "I don't care what your orders are. I demand to see him instantly!"

Marietta recognized the voice and rolled her eyes. She said, "Those Iñupiat words don't just describe conditions. They describe safety. One word means ice you can walk on, another is ice you better walk on fast, a third is ice that looks safe but isn't. It will turn on you, trick you."

The man in the corridor yelled, "Do you know who I am?"

"That's our friend from the State Department," Marietta said, standing, giving me a look of sympathy. "Oz the great and powerful. Assistant Deputy Secretary Andrew Sachs."

She let herself out. I called out for the Marine to send the shouter in, and a thin, red-faced man stormed through the open door.

Andrew Sachs was supposed to have gone home with the scientists. I'd vetted him, crossed his name off the passenger list. Clearly, he'd had other ideas, found a way to stay here, hidden, and had now come out.

■ ■ ■

"I don't take orders from you. Do you have the *slightest* idea of how much trouble you're in?" Sachs demanded, refusing a seat.

"You were supposed to go ashore on the copter," I said.

He was tall and thin, balding off both sides of the front slope of his forehead, dressed in thicker versions of the Arctic clothing Marietta had worn, heavy fleece vest, cords, lace-up Merrell boots, but in his case everything was new, while hers were comfortably worn. He wore a blue Coast Guard *Wilmington* cap, the kind that the captain presents to VIPs. His watch was thin and gold, the waving hands fragile white, the angular face purple with rage. The surprisingly deep voice combined the nasal consonants of old New England breeding: Groton to Yale— with the in-your-face attitude of a Bruce Willis character. The cheek-bones were sharp; granite specks floated in the iron-colored eyes like mines. A small swath of boyish chestnut hair flipped over the otherwise balding high forehead. I judged him an unhealthy forty.

"*You*," he said, "don't tell *me* what to do. I insist on phoning Washington! Your men are jamming transmissions!"

My ex-wife once took me to the National Gallery in Washington to see a Botero painting exhibit. The artist had captured South American leading families as collections of pudgy childlike figures; innocent looking and dressed as dolls, bunched in groups, archbishops and admirals, presidents and little fat children. Botero used circles to depict privilege, greed, and inbred ignorance. Picasso chose parallelograms to show Spanish peasants in their sharp complexity. But an American artist, showing Andrew Sachs, would prefer long thin triangles, like a dowager's dangling earring, a ropy geometry spanning generations of his DNA.

"What the fuck are you up to?" he hissed.

Clearly, breeding lapsed when it came to language. He did not wait for an answer. His finger was a rapid pendulum, his bobbing nose a divining rod assigning blame.

"A *drill*?" he snapped. "You canceled important research for a drill? I didn't hear anything about that. Nobody at State knows about it. I checked on the way in."

"It will only take a few days, sir," I said, wondering how much force I could use with an Assistant Deputy Secretary of State.

"You will cancel it now. You will call your superiors and tell them that the exercise is off. Do you know why?"

"Why?"

"Because you have interrupted a crucial scientific mission that has immense strategic importance to the United States. The researchers who you cavalierly kicked off the ship were conducting bottom surveys, to be used by the State Department to apply *this year* for vast tracts of undersea territory under the Law of the Sea Treaty. Trillions of dollars are at stake. Stop the research, you set us back a year!"

"I'm going to have to ask you for your satellite phone while you're on board," I said. "We'll arrange for you to take a copter back. Sorry.

Orders," I said, curious. Was the man's rage too profound, I wondered, to represent mere professional ire?

His eyes mocked me. "Orders? What are you, a Nazi? Very well. I was specifically ordered, *ordered* by the Secretary, to stay on board throughout this . . . whatever you're doing . . . get you off as soon as possible, and continue our work."

"The chopper should be arriving soon," I said. "You might want to make sure you're packed."

He sat back and his face changed as he saw that intimidation was not going to work with me. He was probably used to getting what he wanted whenever he said "the Secretary." He'd probably grown up getting his way. But then the face grew shrewder, and I saw that I wasn't going to get what I wanted either.

"The copter," he said. "You're going to drag me onto the copter, just kick me off the ship, is that it?"

I said nothing. I waited.

"Because if you do, I can't wait to get back and tell my people, *and* my friends at the *Washington Post*, that the Marines have taken over our only working icebreaker, and brought body bags on board—yeah, I saw them when a crate busted during unloading. I was hiding—and we're rushing north for some secret reason. Scientific equipment? A drill? Don't make me laugh! What's in the other boxes? What are you up to? Why are Marines dressed like civilians?"

"Part of the drill is to maintain secrecy."

He smirked. "Well, I guess you won't maintain it," he said. "Especially if you send me ashore."

The ship's intercom came on with a crackle, and a voice announced that a helicopter was about to land. That would be my best friend arriving, I thought, with the submarine expert the director had sent. The question was, would the copter carry back to shore this angry load of human dynamite?

Assistant Deputy Secretary of State Sachs sat back with a prim look that made me want to arrest him, lock him in his cabin. But he was right. He was not under my orders. He had, in fact, been lead voice on the ship until a few hours ago. I was filled with curses inside. I wondered for a moment if the director knew he was on board, and had dumped him in my lap.

"You're in big trouble," he said, bent toward me over the desk. "I'll tell the Secretary personally about you."

"Thank you for your input," I told him, and shrugged, making my decision. "I suppose it won't hurt to have you along during the drill."

Better to keep him close. At least he won't be able to use his satellite phone with the jammers on. I'll decide later if I'll take away his unit when we turn 'em off.

He'd gotten part of what he wanted. His lips formed a smile but the rage remained in his eyes. He left and the door whispered closed, quiet as a man tiptoeing barefoot down a hall at 3 A.M., keeping secrets from others in the house.

Why is he so angry? I thought.

■ ■ ■

I needed to meet the submarine expert but first wanted to talk to the *Wilmington*'s medical officer, who would assist with victims, if anyone from the *Montana* was even still alive.

Next into the room was Lieutenant Janice Cullen, looking neat in her blue Coast Guard uniform, her auburn hair cut regulation short, neck length, her name in white script at the breast pocket. She wore black CG lace-up boots. Coast Guard Academy, her file had read.

Originally from Brownsville, Texas; divorced, childless, ex-college gymnast; formerly posted to the Pacific Ocean, on drug interdiction cruises. There was one mention of an "anxiety episode" suffered when her cutter was caught off Panama in a hurricane. After that she'd transferred off.

She emanated fitness, but I also saw muscle tightness—tension—around her mouth. The face was round and cheeks cherubic, rosy, eyes light undersea blue. She wore small jade earrings, dots of color in the white lobes. A girlish package on the surface, if you didn't look twice.

"You've done rescue drills before," I said. "How many victims can you handle?"

Her voice was low, slightly hoarse, and I had a feeling she was one of those smokers out on deck during breaks. "Well, with more tourist ships coming through the Northwest Passage, we did a drill last year, mock sinking, a hundred and sixty victims. We set up the copter hangar with cots. A hundred and sixty is how many were on board when that cruise ship went down in Antarctica a couple years back," she said.

"How did your drill work out?"

"Fine. This crew has excellent training in first aid, evacuating victims by Zodiac, sled, triage, keep 'em warm, get 'em on board. We're who you want in an emergency. In that exercise, though, we had smooth water. Victims were airlifted to the hospital in Barrow. We've got enough food in the two freezers aboard to feed plenty of extra people. The crew ran scenarios with burns, smoke, frostbite, hypothermia."

That sounded good, but she was chewing her lip. I also noticed chewed-down fingernails. She added, "But the drill postulated an accident closer to land, and, uh," she said, turning slightly pale, "better weather."

"You don't like storms?"

"Hey? Seventy-foot waves? What's not to like?"

I didn't laugh. She said, realizing that her fear showed, "I was in some bad ones in the Pacific, but this one will be worse, the captain said."

I agreed. "Things will get a lot worse."

I had no idea how much worse.

FOUR

His name was Thorvald Weir, and he was a very good sea captain, but the chase was almost over and he was losing, and he knew, with a sinking feeling, that by midnight he'd probably be dead; leaving a widow in Seattle, two babies without a thirty-year-old father, a family burial plot with no body in it, just a headstone marking the mystery of his disappearance, and any evidence; floating wood bits, oil slicks, bits of blown-up movie cameras and tripods, shot to pieces by the Bolshevik gunship closing from behind.

I never should have taken the money from the War Department, *he thought, fighting the twenty-foot chop, pointing his "fishing trawler," Anna, north, watching for rocks or floating timber that could smash the bow. The black volcanic beaches of Russia slid by on the left, sixteen miles off, and the ragged cliffs of Alaska were twenty-eight miles to the right, and the cold zone was dead ahead, the frigid Arctic seas of ice and storms. The sun was out at 11:45 P.M., a low-hanging orb spotlighting the* Anna, *allowing the Red bastards to push closer, with their deadly deck gun. The* Anna *did eleven knots; the ship behind had to be moving at thirteen.*

A few more minutes and they would be within range.

Thor crossed himself, coughed from a bad summer cold the crew shared, knew that in another few minutes, if no miracle occurred, all men aboard would be turned into food for the birds, orcas, Pacific cod.

It was August 1918 and the world had turned upside down: war in Europe, kings overthrown, nations ended, millions of soldiers dead, their corpses hanging on barbed wire in France, men succumbing to mustard gas and bullets, sepsis, poison gas, flu, newfangled weapons like lumbering tanks, and airplanes that actually dropped bombs from the clouds, and on top of all that, American troops were in Russia, Thor knew, battling the godless Reds. President Woodrow Wilson had sent doughboys out of Michigan, big strapping boys off the Ford auto lines and family farms, sent 'em away from the killing trenches of Europe, and seven thousand Michiganders fought with the White Russian army against Lenin's hordes in the forests of the west, as another three thousand God-fearing Americans guarded the rail lines along the Pacific Coast against the fanatics who had overthrown the Czar, pulled Russia out of the Great War, made peace with the German Kaiser, and sought to turn the rest of the world into a cemetery for decent folk.

I had to say yes, Thor muttered to himself.

He was a patriot and a veteran of the Spanish War, where he'd fought with the great Teddy Roosevelt, charged up old San Juan Hill with the Rough Riders, greatest day of his life. So when the men in suits, the men from Washington, had told him that a seemingly innocuous "quickie trip in and out of Russia" would help the national effort, how could he say no?

He'd lied to his wife about the destination . . . Edison's making a silent movie about Eskimos, he said . . . and the five-man film crew from Fort Riley, Kansas, had stomped aboard and shot plenty of film, all right, in coves and in caves and on islands, until twelve hours ago, when, as they idled on the Russian side in a seemingly isolated bay, a forty-degree, foggy day, about ten thousand walrus on a black beach ahead, pink and fat and stinking of salt and excrement, suddenly the peaceful part was over. The prow of a Bolshie gunship had jutted from a cloudbank—an armor-plated 237-footer—and the first shell had missed them, splashed into the cove and echoed in the fir forest that thickened the curved black shore, and even as Thor hit the throttle and spun the wheel, he'd seen the enemy, angry men wearing a ragtag collection of uniforms . . . sailors in red caps, civilian troops in red scarves, factory workers and even a gigantic barking dog beneath a huge handmade flapping hammer and sickle flag half obscured by coal dust clouds, men yelling foreign words as the two ships plowed through the walruses, churning them up, turning the sea red.

Thor had not understood the words, but he understood the tone.

Stop or we will kill you.

Stop and we'll kill you anyway.

I should have never allowed the film crew aboard. *They never explained what they were doing with their secret maps, cameras, sure, but also rifles, wooden boxes, nets.*

Going ashore. Disappearing into the forests.

Shoulda . . . woulda . . .

Now he was in a race. A miracle. That's what they needed. A bay or estuary to escape into. An accident aboard the gunship; a spark in the ammunition room. A prop smashing into a gigantic log. An angel swooping down to confuse the Bolsheviks. A collision between the pursuers and an undersea boulder tearing a hole in their hull.

Thor handed the wheel to his first mate and went on deck for a better view. The Army men stood in a group on the fantail, camera and tripod idle, watching the big ship draw closer. They had Springfield rifles in their hands, and one man held a .44 sidearm, as if those pathetic weapons would be of use against artillery shells.

Still they were brave, and the ship behind them—far north of any Rus-

sian town of note—was bigger every time he checked, single stacked, spewing smoke, an old Imperial Russian Navy boat seized by the revolutionaries, its 130 mm deck gun capable of firing five shots a minute.

A boom *sounded behind him. A high-pitched whistling announced the shell coming, a speck growing impossibly bigger. It was going to hit but instead sent up a tower of water off the fantail, close enough to splash the men on the ship.*

Then Thor's heart started racing because he'd spotted a chance. Maybe the miracle was happening, maybe Saint Christopher had heard him. The cloudbank a half mile ahead was low and thick and hugged the sea, gray as death, a roiling curtain.

He headed for it, asked Saint Christopher to hide them. He promised that he'd be a better father, a minder-of-his-own-business, if the great Christopher would mislead those godless bastards behind.

A geyser erupted ahead.

The cloudbank growing closer.

The next explosion came fifteen yards away, rocking them so much that the screws lifted out of the water, screaming and spinning before they bit back into the sea.

One man on the fantail fired uselessly at the big ship.

The air getting shockingly, instantly colder.

The mist reaching out with tentacle-like arms, coated them with a smell like wet earth. They slid into its clammy folds. The temperature plunged even further.

The ship behind them was actually gone now, at least for a minute, as they seemed to cross some kind of boundary between the upper Pacific seas and what lay in the great High North.

The Bolshies gone. The air almost liquid.

Had the miracle happened?

The little Anna *stabilized, and Thorvald zigzagged north and prayed the fog would hide them, and it did, at least for a while, and finally after ninety minutes the mist thinned and they emerged from the cloudbank.*

Five men stood in the pilothouse, two crew, three cameramen, one coughing because he had not brought a heavy coat, thinking it was summer, and he was shivering, all of them peering ahead like Columbus's sailors gasping at the New World, wondering what sight would meet their eyes with the fog gone.

And now they saw it, and stiffened.

"Dear God," whispered the first mate.

Holy fucking . . . said one of the men from Fort Riley.

Thorvald staring, his mouth gaping, his belly churning, his face white with a different, and almost indescribable, terror. It could not be. It was absolutely impossible. He'd heard of these things, but had not truly understood. And now it seemed they had not escaped the fundamental problem, not by a long shot, no, he thought, knowing he'd never get home now. Never see his wife and children. Not at all.

FIVE

The helicopter—a Dolphin—swung wildly in a crosswind. Watching from the aft deck, ninety feet below, I felt my intestines clench and feared, looking up, that it would crash, killing my best friend. A twenty-five-mile-an-hour gust slammed the needle-nosed craft, knocking it sideways like a gigantic hand as I held my breath. The pilot—I could see him through glass—fought to steady the bird.

Beneath my feet the *Wilmington* pushed north toward our rendezvous, through whitecaps. The orange copter shuddered, veered away and safely up as if it were a conscious being, reconsidering the wisdom of being here, then suddenly and swiftly it set down in the center of the white circle on deck, and began powering down.

The *Wilmington*'s flight crew ran forward and lashed down the Dolphin, placing chocks against the wheels. The door slid open and two figures climbed out, wearing Mustang suits, zip-up orange float apparatus that would have kept them alive, kept them from freezing to death, for about three minutes in the icy Arctic water had the copter plunged into the sea.

From the V-shaped build of the taller figure, I saw it was Eddie, and as he leaned back into the copter and spoke with the pilot, the second passenger exited and pulled a small attaché case from inside. The person—it had to be my sub expert—was small as a boy, a moon-suited figure the size of a thirteen-year-old forced into big brother's Day-Glo-colored hand-me-downs. Then the helmet came off and long silver hair spilled out, falling past the shoulders.

The woman's hair seemed to catch light, hold and improve it. It wasn't gray, wasn't dry and aged, no, it was too filled with vibrancy, as if a teenager had dyed her hair silver for a party. The small elfin white face scanned the deck and then with clear purpose she strode toward me, as if she knew who I was, as if they'd shown her a photo.

"You're Colonel Rush." It sounded more like an accusation than a fact.

She had a low, direct voice, and judging from the movements beneath the bulky suit, I guessed she had the build of a teenager. Her face, close-up, put her somewhere in her early thirties; Icelandic clear, perfect skin, burned pink from wind, eyes the color of ice in a crevasse, voice a surprising Ozark lilt as she extended a slim, ungloved hand, and gave a shake that seemed firmer than the small, slender fingers would have implied.

"Dr. Karen Vleska. Electric Boat," she said, naming her company.

She'd just flown four thousand miles after being roused from bed at 2 A.M., tossed about like a bug in wind, ordered onto an alien ship in the Arctic, and although the urgency of the job came through, she seemed no more surprised or ill at ease than if she'd walked into a diner on Broadway and West Ninetieth Street in New York. She seemed a pro.

"Glad you're here," I told our sub expert.

We had to shout over the gusting wind. The eyes looking up—probing me—were keen and direct, and even though there was anger there, I experienced a shiver of the sort I'd not experienced in a long time, a sensation which I'd thought I would not feel again.

The landing pad smelled of diesel fuel. Communications antennas rose up forward of where I stood. Fire-fighting equipment was stored around me, reachable fast. Safety nets had been extended off the pad on all sides, to catch any hapless traveler or crew member who fell off. And I could see the top of the ship's big A-frame winch below and behind the pad. The rear deck usually functioned as a research platform for scientists—doing dredging for samples, or buoy work, measuring currents, listening to whales—so down there were also rolls of thick cables necessary for hauling coring pipes or sample nets from the bottom of Arctic seas.

Man and woman meet amid the technical equipment of an ice-breaker. A musky whiff of perfume came to me over the odors of sea and fuel.

"Crew error," she said.

"Excuse me?"

"Just wait. That's what it'll turn out to be, not toxic release from any material *we* put on that sub," she said. "If they're sick, it's not because of us, let's get that straight. We run tests, Colonel, *hundreds* of tests, on every piece of fabric, rubber, composite, electronics, anything you can think of. We burn them and freeze them. We mix the chemicals. If a fire started, if they're sick from it, it'll turn out to be crew error. That's what causes most accidents."

"You seem pretty sure," I said, taken aback, and off balance because of my fierce reaction to her.

"The *Miami* caught fire in '88," she said, naming a U.S. sub accident in Kittery, Maine. "An angry yard worker did it, set the blaze on a bunk.

He was working too hard, he said. He wanted a break. Four hundred million dollars in damage *and at first they blamed equipment.* The Russian *Kursk,* '03, a hundred and eighteen dead, caused by a misfiring during practice with a torpedo, probably started from propellant believed to be new liquid fuel. We don't use that stuff. Want more examples?"

I realized I was still holding her hand. I let go.

"Dr. Vleska," I asked with some irritation, "are you the company lawyer? Because I thought they sent me an engineer, to figure things out, not to fight."

She looked about to snap back, then stopped, seemed to reconsider the surroundings, and her frown turned into something more self-aware and clearly embarrassed.

I couldn't help thinking, *She's lovely.*

I said, "Why don't we save the blame and concentrate on trying to get those people safe."

She took a deep breath. Her whole body seemed to ease up. "Of course," she said wryly. "Look, they woke me up. Said get on a plane. They wouldn't tell me why at first. Everything's a secret, even when they need you. Then some of your guys said some pretty angry things, before we even got the story. Accusations. I guess that made me hot."

"Apology accepted," I said.

She smiled. "I didn't say it was an apology. I said I didn't want to take it out on you." She laughed. "Oh, God. I hate planes. Truth is, I'm scared of them. I don't mind going down four miles in a mini-sub, enclosed space, dark, cold, I love it, but put me up in the air in a Boeing 737 and I need Valium. It got to me. I could use sleep."

I liked the shoulders, the loose easy movements and the smell, and the feminine way her hands wove exclamation marks. She said, "Sub accidents are so horrible. Then everyone points fingers. Now I just did it. I promise to start over and be more coherent after I close my eyes for a bit."

I told her, "No need to start over. We're good."

She turned away and swayed through the steel roll-up door into the copter hangar, where a crewman met and escorted her away to her cabin. The wind flipped her long hair. *Jesus*, I thought.

I pushed it away. Now my partner and best friend, Major Eddie Nakamura, stood before me, a welcome sight: jet-black hair from his Japanese dad, with one white streak, greenish eyes from his Irish mom, a surfer's weathered skin, lightness in his movements from three types of hand-to-hand combat training, grinning the idiotic way only a best friend would after watching my exchange with Dr. Vleska.

"Your type, Number One," said Eddie.

"Eddie, you're Samurai, not Jewish mother."

"She's even better looking with the flight suit off. Lives in Alameda, but long-distance relationships are a good way to start."

"This isn't the time."

He grinned. His easygoing outer nature is deceptive. He's actually one of the most dangerous people I've ever met. "It's always the time, Uno. And to you, it's never the time. I've been telling you for two years, as your physician I advise you to get a life. Watch movies. Get laid. Eat something besides PowerBars. She's divorced. Clever midair interrogation revealed a boyfriend—a company lawyer—but as I am a trained truth-finder, I have ascertained that he is but a piece of lint to be brushed away by your firm hand."

Eddie sang the title of the old Cole Porter tune, softly, over the hissing wind, "*Tonight I love you morrre.*"

"Eddie, can it. Did you find out anything else about the sickness? Symptoms?"

We clomped forward, into the gigantic copter hangar, amid our crates, a basketball court, stairs to labs, and then onto the spray-slick outer deck on our way to the suite, which Eddie would share to make more room for survivors, hopefully. His luggage would come later.

Eddie said, "Before I answer, Colonel Uno, get any sleep lately?"

"Plenty."

"No, huh? Eat anything in, say, the last eighteen hours?"

He always knew when I was lying. "I had a Mars bar on the flight."

"Well, then I'm sure you're firing on all cylinders! It's important that the boss keep himself tip-top, so he can make good decisions that affect us all!"

We ducked through a hatch and bar-locked the door behind us. The passageways were white, utterly clean. I was in a blue Coast Guard parka, CG stocking hat, and Thermolite gloves. Eddie—shed of his mustang suit—wore an olive-drab parka with fur hood, and thick-soled rubber boots.

"Eddie," I repeated warningly. "Symptoms?"

He sighed. "No new transmissions, but we went back and pieced together a little more that the director didn't know when you spoke. There was an early reference to bleeding."

"What kind and how much?"

"Nose, ears, mouth. Several crew members had it."

"Did they work together? Eat together? Any idea what started it?"

Eddie blew out air. "Sorry."

"Anything else?"

"Fever. Chest pain. Purple spots on the skin."

I stopped outside a room labeled SCIENCE LOUNGE. Inside I saw a comfortable space filled with cushioned chairs, computer terminals, and lockable cabinets with books inside. It had to be a library.

I said, frowning, "Petechial hemorrhages?" These occur when there are capillary breaks near the outer skin, creating discolored patches. AIDS victims get them. Mold victims can, too. Toxic poisons, even some common cleaning fluids, if ingested, can trigger eruptions.

I said, thinking out loud, "The sub was out at sea for weeks. I can't see someone intentionally introducing something on board that late in a cruise. They'd be trapped with everyone else. It has to be an accident."

"Never say 'has to,'" Eddie said. "Could be viral, hell, some insecticides cause those symptoms. I wish I knew more, like if they sprayed that sub for pests recently. Rats. Roaches. The Navy insisted they only spray in dry dock, and no one boards for twenty-four hours after that. But who knows? You're underwater. An infestation breaks out. Someone decides to spray . . ." he said, testing a theory out loud.

We were thinking as a team, but one lacking information. "Food poisoning?" I said.

"Won't give you the skin marks."

"Carbon monoxide."

"Won't cause marks or bleeding. But marks have been known to happen with *chaetomium*," he said, naming a black mold found in the Tropics, in dirt, in plants, and in one recent case, a disgustingly ill-cleaned Nashville college fraternity bathroom.

I shook my head. "You don't get bleeding with that."

"The *Montana* was in Indonesia before heading for the Arctic. Who knows what fucking bug came aboard inside a sailor, or skittered on from a dock."

"Eddie, if something got on in Indonesia, it would have erupted earlier."

Eddie looked frustrated. "Unless we're dealing with something new. Or intentional. Look, those guys in the sub didn't even mention sickness until the fourth or fifth SOS. They were concerned about the fire. And nobody in D.C. asked about it. Nobody linked the two. Everyone assumed the sickness was a plain old cold at first, you know subs, everyone shares colds, but then the hemorrhaging started, and by then it was too late to ask about it because the transmissions stopped."

We fell silent. It was all frustrating speculation until we reached the sub.

I told Eddie, "We might need to seal the ventilation system on this ship if it turns out to be a pathogen."

"Get some sleep," he said.

"The director said the fire could have released something toxic, in a new material. I'd say we need to talk to Dr. Vleska."

"She does seem defensive, but I must say, cutely so. By the way, as it's my duty to report important issues to you, I must inform you that she is a sea kayaker who likes jazz and Mexican food. You won't be bored by her. She has strong opinions."

"I have one. It's that you should shut up."

I knew Eddie was right about sleep, knew that staying up too long could cause me to make a mistake. I couldn't do that. I just couldn't. And if there was something toxic in that sub, if I had to lead Marines inside . . .

No, not again. I don't want to do this again.

We headed toward our cabin.

Then suddenly alarms went off all over the ship.

SIX

The emergency announcement blared again as we hurried toward the bridge. Three figures in white fire retardant suits burst from a hatch and lumbered past us, heading aft. Clear polycarbonite shields protected their faces. One person wielded a fire ax and the others carried canisters of fire retardant on their backs.

A calm male voice announced over the intercom, "Smoke in the aviation office."

The bridge would be the control center in an emergency. But we were new here and the corridors a maze. We rushed past cabins with name tags outside identifying berthing for officers. Infirmary. Electrical workshop. We pushed through a door accessing a steel stairwell that rose, switching back at each deck, and took us hopefully toward the bridge. I heard boots pounding on steel below. A woman shouted, "Move it, Robb! You dead or what?"

As we reached the next level up, the intercom came to life again. "Man overboard, port side!"

Eddie and I halted, looked at each other, stunned at this new emergency. Then we understood and Eddie's face broke into a smile. We burst out laughing at the same time.

"A drill," I said, my heartbeat slowing.

Sure enough, as we stood there, tension draining away, the voice added a third disaster.

"Smoke in the bow thruster room!"

Eddie grinned. "Bad luck ship, all these problems only two hours from shore."

"I needed a laugh," I said.

The truth sank in. The drills addressed real possibilities. They underscored our ship's position as lone U.S. nautical presence within a thousand miles. Were a disaster to befall us, any scenario for which the crew was drilling, there would be no second icebreaker to send after us. We would be as vulnerable as the crew of the submarine we were on our way to try to save.

"Eddie, let's get someone to show us around."

■ ■ ■

Eddie and I followed Captain DeBlieu through a maze of steel stairways and decks. He'd left his usual bridge staff in charge of guiding the ship in so-far ice-free waters. He wanted to stay close to us to find out more about what we planned to do. As we headed for the engine room, I mentally reviewed my situation.

Two Marine squads who don't trust me. One State Department Assistant Deputy Secretary who should not be here. One ice expert who grew up in a communist country. And a crew that has not been vetted for high-security situations. All it takes is one person who's pissed off because they lost a promotion, or a friend died, or they need money for a car, vacation, trip to Vegas . . .

Or they've decided, in the twisted compartments of their brain, that Al-Qaeda is right.

The ship was a marvel of complexity, a floating city of steel; but clearly it had been designed for research. Rescue missions, yes. Warfare, no.

"The *Wilmington* was built as a compromise," DeBlieu told Eddie and me as we made our way aft from the mess, where Eddie had insisted I fortify myself with some caloric intake. The bacon-on-wheat sandwich, generously proportioned, smelled mouthwatering, and the caffeine rush from the mug of heavily sugared Maxwell House sharpened my thinking.

"Our rounder prow," DeBlieu said, "optimizes ramming. We sacrificed maneuverability. There's no miracle formula to getting through ice, gentlemen. You slug through or back up and ram it. You try again. If the ice gets too thick, you stop."

Eddie said, "Sounds like the Marines, except for the stopping part."

DeBlieu explained, "Congress only allocated enough money to keep one icebreaker running at the moment. The other two are under repair. NOAA—the National Oceanic and Atmospheric Administration—assigns our missions, except during the annual summer cruise when State takes over. By the way, I hear you met Secretary Sachs."

"We had a friendly chat," I said.

DeBlieu allowed himself a smile, clearly familiar with Sachs's friendliness.

I need to plan. Within hours, these peaceful-looking decks might be transformed into a field hospital, a launch point for combat, platform for Arctic war.

From outside, the ship had looked impressive, but in a boxy, cruise ship way; its prow more rounded than sharp, as it would have been the case with a Naval ship built for speed, fighting, and evasion.

The superstructure was an enormous white box, top-heavy, crowned by the bridge, the icebreaker a maze of twelve levels. Inside four upper levels, humans slept, ate, or relaxed, and layouts were similar; with two long passageways running along port and starboard sides, lined with bunk rooms, individual ones for senior officers, group cabins for other crew below, then supply rooms, lounges for crew and scientists, and various mechanical shops.

Passageways held regular caches of fire-fighting equipment, and to go fore to aft, we had to continually pass through watertight steel hatches, unlatching steel levers and locking them behind us once we passed.

"Main control on the bridge. Propulsion's diesel electric. Horse-power's 30,000 max. We can carry 1.2 million gallons of fuel. Length, 420 feet. Aft area is mostly for science. We've got labs there as good as those at Harvard, freezers for sediment samples, whale samples."

Well, that's one good point, I thought. *If we've got to analyze a disease or toxin, we'll have labs.*

"I thought it's not legal to kill whales," Eddie said, out of curiosity.

DeBlieu nodded. "We only take samples if we find a dead animal and need to figure how it died. Believe me, if we ever hurt a whale, Clinton Toovik would have our heads. The Iñupiats took oil companies to court and stopped them from drilling offshore until they agreed to stay away during hunting weeks. The whole culture up here depends on whales. The locals have millions of dollars from taxing oil on their land, and they use it well in Washington."

"Having Clinton looking over your shoulder must be a pain in the ass," Eddie said.

"No. Marine mammals are protected, and even if Clinton weren't here, we'd have observers on the bridge—private company provides them. Usually college kids. If we're on a collision course with whales, they can order us to divert."

Eddie was always irritated at civilian meddling. "You're telling me a college kid can order you around?"

DeBlieu shrugged. "Part of our job is to protect the environment."

"But the only thing up here besides animals is you."

"No, every year there are more ships: seismic ones, oil company ships, tourists exiting the Northwest Passage . . . we don't even know they're coming until they show up."

Eddie flared, hands on his hips, "So if we get into a firefight, we need some kid's permission before we shoot, in case we hit a walrus?"

DeBlieu laughed.

"Somehow I know you'll do the right thing," he said.

I liked this captain, the way he didn't engage when it was pointless, the way he stood up for things when he was right. I interrupted him as we dropped through a hatch, donned noise-suppressing headphones, and eyed the ship's two immense shafts turning, operating screws out back.

"I'm posting a guard here. Also in the engine room," I said.

By now the captain clearly regarded my security concerns as excessive, and his answer came immediately.

"They don't touch anything. I don't need an overzealous Marine doing damage. Unless they see someone actually starting a fire, they'll leave my crew alone."

"Fair enough."

My tiredness was creeping back, and my coffee mug was empty. Boots appeared in the hatch above, and Major Pettit climbed down to report that his men had found no listening devices in any of the spaces they had checked.

"All clean."

DeBlieu smiled. "What a surprise."

■ ■ ■

The bridge stretched port to starboard and was a large, comfortably lit space, its windows providing views in all directions. A twenty-foot-long waist-high console dominated the area, manned by the three-person bridge crew, constantly monitoring a plethora of screens: wind speed, temperature, latitude and longitude, and frozen, the last satellite image received of sea ice ahead, a white mass, but I was too far away to see how many miles separated us.

Clad in fire retardant Kevlar suits, an emergency drill crew of four stood around in back, doing nothing. Their job was to extinguish fires here, and since there weren't any, they waited for the drill to end.

Another half dozen men and women clustered around a large chart table, peering at a map. One officer was plotting a route.

The crew, most in their late teens or twenties, wore standard-issue dark blue uniforms, black lace-up boots, some in hooded sweatshirts with WILMINGTON in white letters, some in peaked caps, or blue stocking hats, or woven red hats with gold lettering.

"Red for 'polar bears'—Arctic veterans," DeBlieu said.

My eyes went to the vista outside the slanted windows. It was astounding and I caught my breath.

I looked down on an expanse of black ocean and a few bits of bobbing ice—small from seventy feet up—amid whitecaps, like scouts probing for weakness in the hull.

Despite the urgency, I was awed. So this was the southern Arctic Ocean, which had smashed ships to pieces for centuries, and those ice dots were *growlers*, remnants of the once mighty ice sheet. They seemed to tumble in slow motion, white on top, bottoms the turquoise of a

Caribbean bay, or the green of a dollar bill. I saw a spout of water erupt from the surface about a hundred yards to starboard, then two more, beside it, all three heading away from the ship.

"That's a pod of belugas," the captain said.

The more murderous ice that could smash bulkheads awaited us north, in a place where survivors of a submarine fire hopefully still struggled to stay alive.

"It's gorgeous."

"Colonel Rush, these shots of the storm were taken three hours ago," DeBlieu said.

The printouts he handed me showed a mass of corkscrewing gray-black inside the Arctic seas, covering an area as big—when I checked proportions—as Nebraska. It was well formed, with a tight, clear center.

But the view here was pristine, air so clear that I could see three weather systems simultaneously. Directly above, the sky remained pale blue, washed out with cold, that gauzy sun visible. To starboard lay a low, gray mass, the sky of an altogether different planet. To port, a direction which the ship unfortunately seemed to be turning, awaited a ragged, bruised color, a thick, dirty violet that seemed to pulsate with malevolence, smearing the horizon, an advertisement to turn away.

"Clinton says we've got a few more hours before we get into the bad stuff," said DeBlieu.

He indicated a tall, broad-shouldered, barrel-torsoed man standing with his back to us, beside an empty captain's chair by the port-side window. He scanned the sea with large binoculars. He wore no jacket or hat, just faded jeans and an old brown T-shirt reading, BIG MIKE'S ISLAND SAUCES . . . HAWAII.

Clinton Toovik calmly lowered the binoculars and wrote something in a small leather-backed notebook, in ink. Then he pulled a plastic pillbox from a pocket, snapped it open, removed something small and pinkish with thumb and forefinger, and popped it into his mouth.

"Pickled muktuk," he said when DeBlieu introduced us. He held out the open container. "Bowhead skin and blubber."

"It looks sweet," Eddie said.

"The black part is skin, the pink fat." Clinton was about twenty-seven, I judged, with a soft voice, short black hair, and intelligent almond eyes set into a large head.

I tried the muktuk, and found it fishy, not to my taste. "Mmmm," Eddie said.

Clinton peered ahead, binocs at his thigh. "I been watching that polar bear," he said, "on the ice floe."

"What floe?" I asked. I saw no ice.

"There." I saw, squinting, a series of vague discolored specks on the sea. Or did I see them?

"What bear?"

"Right there."

I borrowed his binoculars. Now the vague specks looked like ice.

"Look for yellow," Clinton coached. "It's fat under the fur."

Finally I saw a pinprick dot which might have been a pus color. The dot moved right to left. Or was there a dot?

"Big male," said Clinton. "The female passed with a cub fifteen minutes ago. Males kill cubs. If the cub dies, the female goes into heat earlier. So Mom's on the run."

Eddie sighed. "Horny guys the world over," he said.

The bridge smelled of coffee. The helmsman steered the big ship with a small wheel. Some joker had placed a tiny plastic toy, of an old-style inch-wide ship's wheel, the size of a Cracker Jack prize, atop a joystick. I noticed a wooden handrail running the length of the ceiling, behind the console, and above rubber flooring.

"You'll want to hold on to that when the weather hits," said DeBlieu. "But one advantage of ice is, when we reach the storm, waves'll be smaller."

The bridge was a spaceship traversing another world. The U.S. flag snapped ahead. The planet's curve was evident on the horizon. I borrowed Clinton's binoculars, and in the distance, a white city skyline leaped into view; a row of high-rise buildings, white as snow, thrust upward; they had to be ice. "There's land here?" I asked, surprised. "What the hell is that? An island?"

Clinton grinned and DeBlieu said, "It's your first mirage. Wait until the upside-down ships appear. You're looking at pancake ice, light stuff, not even a foot thick, but from a distance, with the earth's curve, well, everything's different from a distance here. You'll see when we get there in about twenty minutes."

The sense grew stronger that we were entering a world where rules were different. Clinton's smile sank to a frown as he eyed the purple-gray skies. He went outside onto the outer deck, in the wind, then came back five minutes later, none the worse for wearing only a T-shirt. He did not look happy.

"When I was a boy, our elders warned about that," he said, nodding at the sky ahead.

He looked into my eyes. His own were calm, and I saw deep knowledge there.

"We're on a rescue drill, right?" he asked.

"Yep."

"An exercise. Make-believe."

"You got it," said Eddie with confidence.

Clinton nodded. "Then I suggest we turn around."

My mouth felt dry. I looked at the white city that wasn't really there.

"Oh, we can't do that," I said. "Timetables. It's all about timetables. It takes months to draw up these games."

He didn't seem surprised. He just let out air. "Any chance I can have a few minutes to call my wife? I've got my own sat phone. The borough's paying. So you don't have to worry about cost. Can you open it up?"

I felt a chill. Eddie, over Clinton's shoulder, had his brows up. *Can't do it.*

I knew that Clinton wanted to say things to the woman he loved that wives need to hear from husbands, and husbands need to say to wives. I especially knew this because I had not said them when I should have. I wondered if Clinton had children. But I also wondered, even as I hated myself for thinking it, whether the call Clinton wanted to make really was to his wife.

I slapped him on the shoulder. "It'll be a great story to tell her when you get home."

I sounded like a fool, probably like every trader or whaler who'd ever told the Iñupiats a falsehood during their long history. Joe Rush, professional liar.

But I couldn't open up the sat lines, not yet, not until we were closer, so close that even if the Russians or Chinese discovered what we were up to, we'd get there first. I needed to keep a fucking piece of inanimate machinery out of the hands of strangers. That was more important than this one man talking to his family.

I sounded like every sorry bureaucrat who'd ever frustrated logic, hope, desire, or human need.

"Sorry, Clinton. If we let you call out, we have to let other people do it, too."

He took it in stride. He just nodded as if his request would have been too easy. I think he knew we were not really on a drill. I'd tell the crew soon enough, but just now, something fatalistic moved into the Eskimo's deep brown eyes.

With a duckish gait, Clinton turned to leave the bridge, shoulders slightly slumped, his cadence as measured as his quiet voice.

"Where are you going?" DeBlieu called after him.

"My cabin," Clinton said. "To pray."

I'd given up on God in an Iraqi bunker one day, years ago, when I saw things that changed me and Eddie. But at the moment, I'd settle for sleep, I realized; restful unconsciousness—just for a while—as my personal savior. For what is God if not the voice in your head that tells you to worry, and when trouble is coming, helps you prepare?

SEVEN

My Humvee rumbled forward, filled with Marines. I looked out and saw desert sky roiling with black smoke from burning Kuwaiti oil fields, to the south. The world was on fire, the air orange, the color of hell, at midday. Ours was supposed to be an easy assignment, but I felt, looking in my binoculars, a premonition, a claw on my spine, a catch in my throat.

"Something's wrong with that village ahead," I told Eddie over the radio.

We were thirty miles into Iraq. Our column—four Humvees and an armored personnel carrier, containing my rifle platoon—had been detached from the main attack for special duty, protecting the flank, patrolling outlying villages, dots on the terrain map on my lap. Eddie on the ride-along. "Make sure they're free of fedayeen, ambushers," the major had said, sending us out.

Joseph Rush and Eddie Nakamura, two years into the Marine Corps, both wearing silver bars denoting us as first lieutenants.

"Nothing moving," said Eddie's barely contained voice in my earpiece, from the second Humvee. "What's the problem?"

"This road."

"What's wrong with it? It's just tar, man."

"It's new. Brand-new highway in the middle of nowhere. Why build a four-lane highway out here?"

My face felt like sandpaper. The landscape was hard desert, prickly hills and rocks blasted by sun in daytime, split open by freezing cold at night, as if the earth here was unable to decide how to torture you, and had become as schizophrenic as the tyrant we'd come to fight. Southern Iraq resembled 29 Palms, the Marines' high-desert training area back in California—filled with sandstorms, winter storms, blasting heat one day, freezing wind the next.

Eddie snorted at my worry. "Why a new road? Saddam's cousin Achmed is a road contractor. So he needed a job."

"Then he would have built a lousy road. This is top quality, built for a reason."

Fragmented radio reports told us that the main action was south or far north, where coalition forces blasted Saddam Hussein's Republican Guards from their bunkers. Burning Russian tanks and Iraqi corpses littered the main highway. Our smart bombs had hit the power plants and communications centers. The regime was collapsing.

Overhead, three F-16 Falcon jets shot past.

We'd taken some sniper fire from behind rocks, nothing major. An hour ago the pings of AK-47 rounds had bounced off my Humvee, and my gunner had killed four teenagers who could not have been older than seventeen, and who we'd left in the dust.

Now Eddie laughed, high on combat and victory. He was happy-go-lucky, the lone child of two San Francisco accountants who'd been horrified when he chose a military career, and his jocular surface hid a dangerous fighter who could come out if provoked by unequal odds. Back in college, where he'd been my ROTC roommate, I'd seen him wade into a street fight once, to help a small kid. I couldn't figure the fury. Then he told a story. At age nine he'd been in a plane hijacked by PLO terrorists. He'd been on vacation with his parents, sitting next to a sixty-year-old Jewish lady playing magnetic chess when gunmen took over the plane.

The lead man had walked up to the boy and woman, spotted the Jewish star hanging from the woman's neck, and shot her in the face.

The man had told the shaking boy, "Why sit with kike pigs? Come sit in a cleaner place."

Eddie said now, "You're looking for reasons, Number One? This country is a madhouse. Bridges built over desert, not water. Mansions filled with gold statues of movie stars. Mercedes upholstery of real tiger skin."

Looking out, ahead I saw pathetic poverty-stricken architecture dating back to Babylon's King Nebuchadnezzar.

Inside the boxy Humvee, I smelled men after days without baths, dirty feet, cordite, peanut butter.

I said doggedly, eyeing the collection of mud and wattle huts coming up at the end of the black highway, "No, there's something more . . ."

The air was filthy orange through dust goggles, and thick with sand particles that stung exposed flesh like flies. The surface of the planet was the bottom panels of the Sistine Chapel, where tortured figures—onetime men—emerge howling into eternity.

After three days my thirty-seven guys coughed sand and spit crud out every few minutes, and blobs of heat-caked yellow phlegm marked our passage.

"Come on, man, in and out, like the other villages," Eddie said.

This one rolled closer. I saw walls ahead, a dirt village square, a collection of huts each the size of an L.A. maid's room, shimmering in heat that seemed to throw back the sound of our mechanized advance. The hair on my neck began to stand up.

"Be ready for ambush," I told my guys.

"Hey, Numero," Eddie said, "little bet. I say it's nothing. You say fedayeen."

We'd started the competition in college. Our race for better grades spread to everything else. Who could drink more beers on Saturday night? Who would win the motorcycle competition, the weapons competition, raise more money for the leukemia walkathon? Name it. It became a contest.

He won the best rifle shot, the push-up competition by a hair, and hand-to-hand combat, after four ties. I won the hot dog eating, beat him by one and a half seconds on the obstacle course, and I led the Red Team in war games, creeping over a forested western Massachusetts ridge in a surprise assault during a thunderstorm that captured the "general" of the Blue Team. That ranked me number one in the graduating class, hence the nickname.

We'd lost contact after graduation. Eddie went to Pendleton, I to Lejeune. And now we were rolling those final hundred yards toward Al Rassad, and the rooftops grew clear to the naked eye. I scanned the tops of walls for the glint of metal, a ducking head.

Nothing.

We stopped fifty yards short. I looked for the usual buzzards circling. The sky was an empty furnace; a lone smeary cloud seemed glued in place, almost two-dimensional.

The heat seemed to expand inside my head.

Now Eddie saw something. "Hey, man, no garbage."

"No busted cars. And look at these tracks in the dirt. They're from big trucks. Heavy treads."

"Clean as a Hollywood set, One. No Coca-Cola bottles lying around, no chickens . . ."

"No dogs," I breathed. *"No damn dogs!"*

That was the crowning touch—no yowling dogs, those big mustard-colored Iraqi canines that seem more like hyenas than domesticated pets. Dogs that make your average Manhattan pit bull look as pitiful as a Chihuahua. The dogs always stay behind in evacuations. They belong to no one. They seem to have sprung to life from rage itself, the yellow desert become flesh and hair.

We'd halted just inside a newly constructed ghost town. No creaking wooden doors left open to wind or looters, no shutters banging, no whiff of human shit marking the community ditch, not even any chicken droppings.

Just the hiss of sand scouring walls.

"Eddie, from the air, this place would look like a typical village. It's a set!"

My guys went in, house to house, and in the very first one found that people had lived here, all right, but they hadn't been peasants. Army cots, empty weapons racks, electrical appliances and generators, and the dirty rags of villagers hung on hooks . . .

"Troops disguised as villagers, but for what?"

Then, inside the third hut, we found what they'd protected, the entrance to a bunker, a steel doorway built into rock. Twin surveillance cameras aimed down on us.

"Engineers!" I shot the cameras out.

They blew the door with C4 and sent it flying. Eddie's squad raked the entranceway with fire, and when there was no response, I told my guys, "Watch for booby traps. Go slow."

We entered a tunnel, angling down into the earth. It was wide as three Humvees, with an arched roof fifteen feet high. The walls were blasted-away limestone. Bare bulbs overhead remained dark—but everything glowed green from the night goggles. Ahead, the tunnel turned right.

We wore bulky, tough-fibered two-piece camouflaged chemical suits. We carried M16A2 rifles, firing 5.56 mm rounds. I heard our equipment jangling. My heart seemed loud inside my chest, and my breathing was audible.

Lower, ten feet down, fifty. We shot out more cameras, dead eyes, maybe someone watching, maybe not, and after about three hundred feet we found ourselves spilled into the complex. Lights were on and bright.

At first, it could have been a hotel subbasement, with pipes and wiring, the part of the building the guests never see. Cool air down here. I saw an official warning sign in red, in Arabic, a cartoon drawing of an Arab man with a Saddam mustache—it must have been the law here for all guys to wear them—the guy in a yellow hard hat, air filter over his mouth, finger in the air as if to say, "Danger!" Beside the man was a skull and crossbones, but none of us could read the words. I cursed. Our translator had been sent away, to help in the main attack.

Maybe one of my guys hit a tripwire. Maybe the place had been wired and a timer set. All I knew was that suddenly the ground began trembling. Then shaking. "Down!" I yelled as a chain of explosions went off below. Blue smoke poured from the vents.

"Masks!" I yelled.

We donned the bug-eyed masks. Now the smoke was all around us, coming from beneath doors, filling the hallway. But nothing bad was happening—no itching, no catch in breathing, no burning, at least not yet.

I decided to stay.

There's something important down here Saddam does not want us to find.

Then I saw something moving ahead, something living staggered toward us through smoke. It was small and two-legged, a child. A goddamn kid. A silhouette in agony, hands waving in the smoke, maybe to surrender. Head whipping back and forth.

I yelled, "Hold your fire!" The figure fell and stood and then continued forward with a crazy side-to-side gait. Up. Down. It was hurt or ill. A voice in my earpiece gasped, "What the fuck is *that*, Lieutenant?"

I breathed, staring, "A monkey."

The thing began screaming, *"Kraa . . . kraa."*

It had a snout like a dog or a baboon and pink hands like a person. It had a pink face and white fur on its chest. It jerked in crazy circles, not seeing us. Blood was pouring from its mouth and nose, and when it turned sideways, I saw red ooze dripping from its ears.

Concussion from the explosion?

The animal took two steps forward, rubbed its eyes, cocked its head, my guys froze, and then it seemed to see us. I could not imagine, in my wildest imagination, what it must be thinking.

The monkey screamed one long eruption of rage.

It lurched forward but fell down and began convulsing.

By the time I reached it, it was dead. It had hemorrhaged out from every possible orifice. Black, clotted, evil stuff spread out, pooled on the concrete floor.

Shit, shit, what were they making in here?

Eddie's voice in the earpiece was saying, "We're coming in, One, behind you."

I saw a sign half in Arabic, half in English. AL HAZEN IBN AL HAITHAM INSTITUTE RESEARCH SATELLITE FACILITY.

"Eddie, it's a lab down here. Stay out."

■ ■ ■

I kept going.

The smoke thinned and the screams started.

It was hell, a tunnel to hell. Now the echoes came through vents all around us. "*Kraaaaaaa!*" It sounded like hundreds more animals were down here somewhere, grunting, screeching, and there were tearing noises and retching, and I did not think there would be humans down here anymore, but I still could not be sure what waited behind the next bend.

The toxic gear better work, I thought, and we stayed a couple inches farther away from the walls. We passed a half dozen paintings of the dictator, the madman king of this madman house; Saddam on a white horse, wearing white flowing Bedouin robes. Saddam cross-legged by a desert campfire, reading a Koran, the wise military sage.

I was proud of my guys. Eighteen and nineteen years old and they held discipline. The point men going in first, the other two behind.

The first room turned out to be an office. There was a steel desk, wood-paneled walls, and in the flashlight beam, I made out medical certificates in biochemistry. A panel read: DR. MASSOUD AZIZ. He was, in the photo, on a beach with a plump, fortyish woman and two smiling teenage sons. There were lots of reports in blue binders, a TV set in the wall, a pair of backless slippers on an oriental rug, as if the owner had laid them carefully down, expecting to return. I opened a photo album with my rifle. I was looking at photos of dead people, their faces bloated, bleeding, their eyes red from blood.

The next room was a locker room. Medical whites hung on hooks. There was a break room with refrigerated glass cases filled with orange juice cans, and dishes of what looked to be hummus or baba ghanoush, olives, tomato slices. I saw small bloody tracks . . . animal feet . . . on the linoleum, a loose pile of bloody stools on a table, an overturned sugar bowl. Those tiny hands would have been in there. There were sugar strands on the table.

The cacophony was growing. A symphony of agony came through the vents, echoed between walls. I heard sobbing, hiccups, metal rattling. I heard hacking and sneezing. I was in Bosch's hell, and somewhere ahead, behind a door, behind smoke hovering by the floor, were the creatures.

The smoke didn't kill them. Or is it killing them now?

I recoiled as my light beam hit the dead face of another monkey in the hallway; bled out, belly blasted open, ears a mass of clotted blood.

Did the doctors open the cages before they left? Did they leave because the cages opened accidentally, or because we were getting closer? Are these animals contagious, and if they are, will our suits protect us?

Each time we opened a door, we stepped back and waited for a charging animal. A pharmacy closet had been looted of drugs. The doctors' quarters were equipped with DVDs and TV sets, refrigerators, porno and religious magazines.

The operating room had two tables, a small one for a child, or monkey, I guess, the other one for a larger primate or human adult. Built into both were bloodied iron manacles for hands and feet. There were vials on shelves and an electron microscope. I saw drawers labeled in Arabic. I smelled urine, shit, fear.

I opened the next door. The screaming exploded.

At least a hundred monkeys were inside, in cramped cages, on tables spread along four long aisles. I walked the aisles, horrified, disgusted, terrified, hoping the hot air in my suit remained clean. I saw animals with bloated stomachs and blood leaking from their ears, noses, mouths. I saw monkeys dead in cages, popped open at the intestines, flies buzzing by their heads. The live ones panicked, grabbing bars, possibly driven insane by what was going on around them, or by their treatment.

Monkeys watched me with eyes too sick to care. Monkeys lay in their own shit. Monkeys reached through bars like condemned prisoners, beseeching another species for help, with those pink human-like hands.

One male, the biggest, went berserk, throwing himself at me, trying to smash through his cage, when I looked into his eyes. *Crabeater monkeys*, I'd learn later. An Asian variety hunted in the swamps of the Philippines and shipped to labs all over the world.

I gagged but held it in. One of my guys was puking in a hallway. His mask was off. I sent him up top, fast. I was snapping photos for our major. Panic was trying to get out of my chest, into my thinking. *What more do I need to do?*

I felt something land on my shoulder and I whirled and it was Eddie. I felt better for a moment until I saw, behind him, like a ghost, through curling smoke, a man charging him, no, not a man because it was coming too fast.

My M16 was going up. Eddie saw it, threw himself left. The creature was in the air, canines bared, and it would have landed on his neck but my shots drove it sideways and into the wall and it slid down, whimpering and thrashing, torn and bloody, and a moment later it was still.

Eddie stared down in horror. "Shit. If it bit me . . ."

"Get out," I ordered everyone, having had enough.

We retreated, all of us, before invisible microbes.

Then I ordered the place blown up, used flamethrowers on the wreckage, and watched it burn.

■ ■ ■

That night we lay by our vehicles below the stars, when they weren't obscured by smoke from burning oil fields. The temperature had dropped but we couldn't make our own fire, and risk alerting stray fedayeen that we were here. Tomorrow we'd rejoin the main column. Tonight everyone who had been below was wondering the same thing, and fear floated among my men like airborne germs.

Private Lionel Pettibone, nineteen, asked me, "Did you see the monkey with the stomach busted open, Lieutenant?"

"I'm sure you won't catch it," I lied.

"But I took my mask off! I breathed the air! It smelled funny! Was it chemical or germs?"

"I don't know, Lionel. The docs will check you out."

"Oh man, why did I take that fucking mask off?"

I wanted to know this new enemy. I wanted to answer his questions. When I'd joined the Marines, I'd envisioned foes as two-legged, but now saw that they might be invisible, yet do more damage, if unleashed, than an atomic bomb.

I lay awake, thinking about my wife, my beautiful young wife back in North Carolina. I thought about my parents and friends. I saw the crowded cities, Chicago's Loop and Manhattan's Fifth Avenue, except in my head, the crowds were screaming like the monkeys, bleeding and convulsing.

"Lieutenant, I'm getting a sore throat!"

"You had a sore throat yesterday, Platt. Remember?"

There was no way to know that the knowledge I sought would, in the end, drive me from all the people who, at that moment, I wanted to protect. My wife. My lovely wife. Average people. Poker pals. Kids I'd grown up with.

Eddie lay a few feet away, in a sleeping bag.

"We'll know in a few days if we'll get sick," I told Pettibone, who was unable to sleep.

In ROTC, and at Quantico, I'd learned facts about toxic warfare: symptoms, delivery systems and antidotes and gestation periods. But it had not been real, not like what I'd seen today.

The sickness was monkey hemorrhagic fever, I'd learn months later, when interrogators discovered the truth. *It doesn't kill humans, but the Iraqi docs were trying to figure out how to make it jump species, mixing it with common colds.*

"I want," I told Eddie suddenly, "to work on toxics."

"Great minds think alike, Number One."

"You, too?"

"Hey, it's another chance to beat you out."

We'd seen a weapon that was so horrible that most people don't want to know about it, a weapon grown in glass tubes, sought in jungles, farmed by men in white coats. We'd seen up close a possible future that was terrifying. Oh, we'd imagined *something* before, but it was distant, like a movie. You simply leave the theater when it's done.

We'd seen a weapon that generals desire but no one wants to talk about, a weapon that never marches in proud public military parades.

Eddie grinned. "You saved my life."

"Are you kidding, Eddie? One taste of your blood, that monkey would have keeled over, man."

We became best friends that day, not just old roommates.

After all, before that we'd had common experiences and friends, and we'd lived in the same location, but now we had a common enemy.

What can draw people together more than that?

■ ■ ■

I shot awake. Eddie was shaking me. I lay in my bunk on the *Wilmington*, remembering where I was, remembering the monkeys becoming human in my dream. Eddie's face looked concerned through the red nightlights. The porthole was closed. The clock read 9 A.M. I'd been out for six hours.

All the humor was gone from Eddie's face, the lines by his mouth standing out, tense, drawn, bad news.

"We heard from the director, Number One, got through to him when the jammers were shut off for ten minutes."

"Say it."

"They know. *They found out.* Washington's picked up something moving toward the sub."

EIGHT

"The Chinese," the director said.

Like an armed torpedo zeroing in on us, the red blip on screen turned slowly in our direction, and aimed just north of our yellow boat shape, to intersect. I watched it begin sliding over grid lines superimposed over the Arctic Ocean.

"The *Snow Dragon* is their first icebreaker. The second should be in operation this year," the director said over the intercom box on the captain's conference table.

The pressure in my chest mounted as I eyed another blip, this one green, pulsating in the sea.

"It is also possible that the Chinese have a Jin-class nuclear-powered submarine somewhere in the Arctic, but we're not sure. They're not usually up there with subs, but last we heard, it was headed in that direction, weeks ago."

The somber-eyed group of ten around the conference table included Eddie and me, Dr. Karen Vleska, Assistant Deputy Secretary of State

Andrew Sachs, Marietta Cristobel, and Clinton Toovik, our ice experts. On the crew side, with DeBlieu, sat his executive officer, a competent-looking fortyish man named Gordon Longstreet, and his communications officer, Brooklynite Lieutenant Peter Del Grazo, who managed to seem cheery despite the danger. Major Donald Pettit sat on my left. It was time for the key players to know the big picture.

The screen changed to the actual *Snow Dragon*, its hull red, its superstructure white. Arctic ships tend to be painted colors that stand out. The icebreaker was smashing through three-foot-thick ice, pushing chunks the size of boulders left and right, seeming to bull off the screen and drive straight at us.

The director briefed us dryly. "The Chinese are not an Arctic nation but they have huge interest in new shipping or attack routes around the top of the continent, and in access to seabottom oil. They're investing in a deepwater harbor in Iceland. The *Snow Dragon* may be carrying troops for ice maneuvers, although usually it's just scientists. Their top speed roughly equals yours."

"So it's a toss-up who gets there first?" Eddie asked.

The director sighed. "It could come down to minutes. Get as close as you can. If the ice blocks you, send a party on foot, or in those vehicles, depending on terrain."

My mouth was dry. Major Pettit had switched off our jammers for the conference, after an announcement went out prohibiting unauthorized calls or e-mails from the ship.

In the brief window we had now, Marietta had checked in with Maryland for updated ice information. Sachs had called Washington. He had a look of anger on his face. It probably related to why, with an international incident possible, the director was on screen, not someone from State.

The director just glanced left, so someone else is in the room with him. Someone higher up, I bet.

The director, on H Street, went in and out of focus, as if the storm ahead infused itself onto the screen. Snow-like interference drifted across his face, which degenerated into lines resembling wind-pushed current; as the High North played with us, just as it had teased sailors for centuries. *You're not so different from hundreds of others. They were as confident as you.*

I asked, "Sir, do we know how the Chinese found out?" I hoped to eliminate the *Wilmington* as a source.

The blocky head—ex-college fullback—shook side to side. "We got word that they know, that's all. You. Electric Boat. Washington."

Button up your ship, he was saying.

I asked, "Has Beijing asked to help?"

His smile was half visible through the interference, and sour. "Oh, we're both pretending that nothing is going on, so in a worst-case scenario, it stays private."

That's why State isn't the lead. Is someone from the White House with the director, then? Homeland Security?

Andrew Sachs spoke up shrilly. "Worst case? *Combat?*"

The director sounded exhausted, leaned left, and seemed to consult someone, then was back. "Our Navy and theirs are facing off more regularly in the South China Sea. And you, Secretary Sachs, know better than anyone that a Chinese sub collided with one of our destroyers during Pacific maneuvers last month. We had no idea they were there until then. But they said we did it on purpose. They lost twenty-eight crew. So . . . under these circumstances, things can go wrong. Big storm blowing. Tempers hot. Our sky eyes blind. Then guns go off. The apologies come later, and diplomats make nice, and the scapegoats who were positioned all along to take a fall go down, *but they have the Montana.*"

Sachs seemed shocked. "That's absurd! Take some responsibility! If you tell your people to stand back, they'll stand back."

The director said coldly, "It's our people, our sub. We're not the ones who will stand back."

"Even if you start a war?"

"Don't be dramatic." The director sighed. Sachs was trying his patience. But the director was a political animal and clearly knew he was talking to the Secretary of State himself through Sachs. "Like I said, excessive zeal by officers, human error, soldiers shooting blind in a storm, et cetera et cetera. It stops short of war."

Sachs stared. "You're setting this up for a fight."

"I don't consider forethought a setup."

I asked, eyeing the Chinese icebreaker, "Those projections you're showing us, sir, are they actual ship locations or computer guesses?"

"Last known position, coupled with current, wind, floe direction." The director brightened. "Conditions are pushing our sub in your direction. But reaching her first may depend on ice. So! Marietta! Where are we on that?"

Ice, I thought morosely. It looks hard; it has the geometry of rock. You can walk on it and climb it, but it is always moving. Sometimes you see the movement. Sometimes you don't. Imagine a city block constantly drifting. You walk outside and the supermarket is a hundred yards north of where it was yesterday. Then it drifts back fifty yards. Then the block splits in two, and the traffic light goes one way, and you, across the street, move the other. The landscape has viscosity. Solid is a lie, one more mirage.

Now, Marietta typed on her keypad and the picture on screen split:

director on the left, sat shot on the right, a jagged white peacock shape; a grid superimposed over it, like a wire fence. The grid, she said, divided three thousand square miles into pixels. I saw a few patches of black spilling across lines. I saw a blotchy gray area containing darker speckles. It was like looking through a microscope at virus growing in a specimen of mold.

America's foremost ice expert fingered an unlit cigar, worrying it like prayer beads. She still wore the baggy clothes she'd been in when we met. "This is our last projection, nineteen hours old. We've had problems with reception because the sats keep dropping into standby mode due to solar flares. They shut down during periods of intense activity to avoid damage. So! Aqua, our most advanced eye, uses microwave scanning. Each pixel represents a six-by-six-kilometer area; good overall, but when we get close, problems start. You see, if Aqua picks up sixty-five percent ice cover in one box, the computer turns the whole pixel white. Less than sixty-five percent, black. So if we're heading for an area with only sixty percent cover, but it's big, ship-killing stuff, the computer thinks it's ice free. In the end, we need human eyes or the drone to know exactly what lies ahead."

I said, "Then how do we pick the best route?"

Her mouth was a tight line of frustration. "Using luck. And Clinton."

The director asked, "What are those gray masses?"

"Gaps in information due to the solar disturbances."

Eddie sniffed. "This is the best we can do?"

"If we had more money, we could do better," she said bitterly. "Also, Aqua sends photos every five hours. So even when everything is working perfectly, it's possible that we're making decisions based on hours-old information, since the ice keeps moving all the time."

Captain DeBlieu raised a finger, like an engineer worrying a technical question. "Can you change the speed of transmissions, get them at, say, thirty-minute intervals instead of five hours?"

"No, that ability would have cost more. NASA was ordered to streamline costs during Iraq and the fiscal crisis. They ate up all kinds of capabilities. Don't get me started."

The director's lips were a hard line, and I knew that he was cursing inwardly. I'd had this discussion with him plenty of times over beers. *We've been warning Congress for years that we need better equipment, Joe, and they never give it. Washington's gridlocked. Sooner or later something like this had to happen.*

"Thank you, Dr. Cristobel," said the director.

She smiled unhappily. "For what?"

■ ■ ■

Thinning light seeped in through the cabin's portholes. DeBlieu's walls were hung with photos—mug shots of the Arctic that would have been lovely in an art gallery, but were daunting just now. One old shot showed a snow-swept ice sheet, jagged icebergs, in sepia, nature's pillars, trapping a twin-masted steamer between them, circa 1931, like massive pincers.

The framed shot beside it showed an ice storm, thousands of pellets driven sideways to create a translucent curtain half obscuring a trio of roped-together scientists tap-tapping their way like blind men, with walking probes, over a floe. Astounding beauty, but it reduced humans to insignificance. The scientists in the photo had about as much presence as a lone flake of snow.

The director said, "Dr. Vleska, your turn."

She sat directly across from me, projecting an image of a Virginia-class nuclear sub on screen. The long black tube resembled an immense eel, and featured a jutting egg-shaped mast about a fifth of the way aft.

I thought that Karen's lips looked nice.

She said, "The Chinese know what's on our sub in theory, because it's public, but not how it works. So you might as well know, too."

Her voice was soft and she'd changed into a red and black checkered flannel shirt over a black wool turtleneck that showed an inch of soft throat. She seemed petite and fresh from sleep. Her hair was worn long, its silvery mass draped over small shoulders, probably brushing her seat cushion. Her hands were small, but rough, strong, an outdoors-woman's. I saw a pale band of whiter skin on the fourth finger of the left hand. A wedding or engagement ring had been removed recently and left a mark.

Click. The torpedo was shaped like a large, finned, green baseball bat, tapered from narrow tail to front. "The new prototype Mark 80," she said, "capable, while closing on a target, of calculating hull mass and detonating at optimum standoff distance, guaranteeing the best chance of destruction. Best torpedo on Earth."

Click. Two subs passed each other, underwater. "Our acoustic coun-termeasures are way ahead of Beijing's."

Her eyes met mine. I had not noticed the gray flecks in the blue before. "The *Montana* is whisper quiet from electromagnetic signature reduction. The enemy may detect her presence, but has no way to de-termine which exact unit she is, no way to track specific boats."

Eddie piped up, "Any way to do that for people, so I can keep the director from knowing where I am?"

Marietta and DeBlieu laughed. Sachs rolled his eyes. Karen Vleska smiled. "I know what you mean," she said.

"The Virginia class has been modified for combat in littoral waters, shallow ones like those in the Mideast or the areas around Taiwan. She can slip inside the enemy's air defense and unleash salvos of up to six-teen tomahawk missiles. She's less detectable on the surface with the periscope gone. She uses a mast-mounted photonics array instead. She's got hull-mounted mine detection. The acquisition by an enemy of this craft would jeopardize thousands of U.S. military personnel around the world, and our ability to wage war. When we get there, I go in first to check things, and you all wait outside."

I started. I'd not envisioned taking her in, or taking her at all if we had to go on foot. "Dr. Vleska," I reasoned, "you have to understand . . . conditions won't be optimum. I suggest the Marines and I go first, and once we secure the boat—"

"No! There are things I need to do before anyone else can enter."

The director remained silent. Why didn't he stop her? I started to say, "You don't understand . . ." but noticed Lieutenant Del Grazo, across from me, grinning.

"Do you mind explaining what's so funny?" I snapped.

His and Vleska's eyes met. They seemed to share something amus-ing. I felt an irrational stab of jealousy, even while I waited to hear what the hell was going on.

Del Grazo said, grin broadening, "Karen *Vleska*, Colonel. *Vleska*. Remember? She's *that* Karen Vleska."

Marietta Cristobel let out a sharp breath. "That's *you*?" she said, staring at the submarine expert.

I was baffled. But now Eddie got it, too, sat back and turned to me, joined in the grin festival, at my expense. "Colonel, she's probably got more polar experience than all of us together. She was on that expedi-tion to the North Pole two years ago, the skiers . . . *Fifty Nights* . . . the documentary. Won the Oscar. All-woman expedition. Remember?"

Now I did. I remembered the ads for it. Shots of four women in a blizzard, on cross-country skis, hauling sleds. I'd not read her file on the way up, figuring she was already security-cleared since she'd helped design the sub. Now I envisioned a different sort of body beneath those thick clothes, tight and muscular, like the hands.

Karen Vleska ignored the looks. She said reasonably, "Look, we've got a security leak, and I will not take the chance—however remote—that the person responsible is among us. So I go down first. I cover up anything sensitive. Then you gentlemen are welcome to drop in and have a big cocktail party, do whatever you want."

"There's something toxic in that sub," I argued. "There will be bodies in there."

"I go in first."

"How about we discuss this later?" I suggested.

"If by that you mean after I go in, Colonel, fine."

There was a coughing sound from the intercom. The director was fading like Marley's Ghost, but he was still there, a pale outline, a consciousness from afar. But his voice came out strong and clear. "You'll go in together."

That convinced me. *He's not running things.*

He was disappearing as if his essence were being sucked away to be deposited in whatever Situation Room, Pentagon room, State Department, or task force room he'd be reporting to next, to face the usual round of Washington high-level second-guessers. *You should have sent more Marines! We should have asked our allies for help!*

The director was gone.

■ ■ ■

"I'm going, too," Andrew Sachs said.

All eyes went to the Assistant Deputy Secretary, who had drawn himself up in his chair, fortified by a satellite phone call with the Secretary of State.

"*She's* going. The *Marines* are going." He sounded like a ten-year-old to me. "The Secretary has instructed me to go, too."

Sachs sat taller, the overhead light gleaming off the bald spot on his narrow head. His thin lips were tucked together. He was the stern New England schoolmaster or preacher. The iron gray eyes dared anyone to disagree.

Sachs was one of those men who lecture rather than talk. "The last thing we want is an international incident. There's going to be a U.S. claim to territory up here and we'll need all the support we can get. Negotiation may be required. *You* are not trained to do it. The issues are greater than the fate, however important, of one submarine. To be honest," he said, using a phrase that in my experience identifies consummate liars, "confrontation must be avoided at all costs."

Karen bristled. "Meaning, give them my submarine?"

"Meaning no trigger-happy posse, Wild West style."

Eddie said, aghast, "What about the sick crew?"

Sachs's lecture finger was up, wagging. He answered to one God and it was the Secretary of State, and he had spoken from his C Street Mount Olympus. "The fate of one hundred and fifty people versus three hundred and twenty million. You are *not* to fight."

"That's not what the director said."

"The Secretary assured me, that's what the President said, and your director, last time I checked, doesn't run Washington. If we get there first, fine, do what you want, recover the sub, sink it. But if we . . . *I'm coming along!*"

It was a surprise voice beside me that spoke up. Clinton Toovik, the Iñupiat marine mammal observer, said softly, very calmly, "May I ask a question?"

Sachs glared at the interruption. "What question?"

Slowly, he said, "Well, what if we don't get there ahead of the Chinese because, well, because of you, sir?"

"Me? What? Me? Ridiculous!"

"Mr. Secretary," Clinton asked, unperturbed, "have you ever been in an ice storm?"

"If *she* can do it, I can."

"I'm sure that is true. I'm just saying. We might need to climb ice ridges thirty feet high. And wade through seawater ponds . . . That wind peels skin from your face. My uncle Dalton, he likes his vodka, and he came in too late once and had *no skin left* on the right side and had to be airlifted to Anchorage."

"Your uncle Dalton? What does he have to do with this?"

But I noticed that Sachs, envisioning a different sort of future, had turned slightly paler, as he said, "I'll wear heavy clothes, like everyone else."

"Uh-huh. Also, anyone could fall in. The ice looks safe. You might even see a bear walk on it. Then you walk on it. Down you go. It's all about weight distribution. But don't worry. We'll be roped together. We'll move extra slow for you. And then, when we report back, we'll explain how we *had* to go slow—lose time—because we didn't want anything to happen to you."

Sachs was blinking more rapidly. Looking at Clinton, the big body, Hawaii barbeque T-shirt, the open, amiable expression, I knew I'd just seen one of the best conference ambushes I'd ever witnessed. I wanted to applaud.

Clinton said, "It's not your fault if you're the one who has never been on ice. I know the Secretary of State will understand if you cause us to lose out."

Sachs insisted weakly, "I won't slow us down."

I said, joining in, "Secretary Sachs is right, Clinton. If anyone falls behind, we'll just leave them."

Clinton nodded thoughtfully. "That is for the best."

Sachs looked sick.

I felt a tap on my leg, from Clinton. He pushed a folded piece of paper into my hand. I looked down. He had good handwriting.

Sachs = asshole.

Clinton brightened. "Well, if you do come, you can help carry packs, fifty-pounders, well, feels more like eighty in a storm. We'll suit you up . . . Can you snowshoe? Or maybe we'll need crampons to get up and down the ivus and—"

Sachs broke in. "Ivus? What's ivus?"

"Mountains of ice that just come, suddenly, out of nowhere. My aunt Martha, once she was out on the beach, and . . ."

Sachs poured himself water from a carafe.

Sachs said, pompously and thoughtfully, "You make some points, Clinton. Thank you for providing this perspective, yes, interesting. A need for speed. Speed is crucial. Hmm."

He's going to drop out, I thought.

"We don't have to decide right at this minute," Sachs said, trying to save face.

The screen remained dark but suddenly the director's voice was in the room again, amid static.

"Secretary Sachs is to come along if contact is imminent," he said, as if he'd heard the last exchange. I knew then that Sachs had been right about one thing. If he was coming, backroom Washington was now fully in the mix.

As if the director understood my thinking, had given me a moment to catch up, he added, in a tone I understood, and which was also clearly intended for whoever sat with him, "Colonel Rush, you remain in charge, of course."

Meaning: *I'm sorry he has to come with you. Ignore Sachs if you have to fight.*

Easy for him to say. Sachs would be with me, not him.

■ ■ ■

"Last thing. Security," I said. "I want all phones checked on the ship, see if anyone even tried to call out. I want all deck cameras checked to see if anyone was outside at any time, trying to call out."

DeBlieu okayed it, but said, "Colonel, the better sat phones can access out from the cabins. You don't need to go outside to use them."

"Do it anyway," I said, angered at the lapses. "Also, from now on when we open sat channels, the crew goes on the buddy system. Two-man teams. *And* you'll announce that anyone trying to call out for any reason will be violating national security laws, and arrested."

DeBlieu stared down at the table, and when he looked up, I saw a quiver of anger on his lips. But I'd misread the reason. He had no problem with security precautions. It was my attitude that pissed him off.

"I don't know where you got the idea that my crew is not professional, Colonel. They're every bit as patriotic as your goddamn Marines anywhere on Earth. You tell my people the sub's in trouble? Well, they're working at one hundred percent now, but they'll up it even more. You tell 'em this is high security and they'll button their mouths faster than my ex-wife used to when I'd call her during the divorce. I *welcome* the chance to show you what we do. We're the eyes of the United States in the Arctic. We're up here in the snow while you're lying in the goddamn sun in summer. So tell us what you need. But you will not disrespect my crew. Understand?"

I liked him tremendously, the little engineer with the quivering mustache and dark, goofy military glasses and very real rage. And I saw pride in their captain in the eyes of the chief exec and the communications officer.

"Captain, I apologize. I'm asking for your help."

"For my *crew's* help."

"Yes, your crew's help. Thank you."

DeBlieu told the exec, in a dry voice I'd not heard from him previously, "Make sure to interview the Marines who came aboard, too. Colonel Rush and Major Nakamura also."

"Everyone," I agreed.

"That's better," DeBlieu said. "That's just a damn sight better. I get sick and tired of you guys sometimes."

Chief Exec Gordon Longstreet calmly absorbed the information. Clinton Toovik looked resigned, as if he'd expected bad news all along. Marietta Cristobel seemed weighed down with despair, her inability to help more. The worst-looking face belonged to the ship's medical officer, whose fingernails drummed on her yellow pad, and whose trembling made me decide to drop a pen, and look under the table. Her right knee was bouncing. She was terrified.

Suddenly the ship jolted.

There was a sound resembling steel chains dragging along a trash Dumpster. Then a crunch like a crumbling Volkswagen, and then a soft grinding noise like a 7-Eleven Slurpee machine.

Clinton looked up, almost as if he could see through the hull, to the source of the sound. Now it became claws trying to break through steel, scraping.

"We've reached the ice," he said.

I do not know if fate has consciousness, but thirty seconds later, as if some higher power feared a momentary lessening of resolve, as if the

Arctic felt it had to bait us to keep us going, the cabin phone buzzed. DeBlieu picked up quickly. The bridge crew was under instructions not to call unless it was important.

Answering, he listened for a full half minute, said "Thank you," and put the phone down, lips taut.

"We picked up the *Montana* radio beam locator," he said, standing. "They're two hundred and seventy miles ahead."

NINE

The storm blasted out of the north and we were blind. Satellite reception was gone now, even with the jammers off. Nature accomplished what the captain had commanded previously, blocking all communication, cutting off the ship. Visibility was reduced to radar. The bridge crew peered like Romans reading entrails at a screen that pulsated with reddish Doppler readings of wind and precipitation. Gusts at 55 mph and rising. A flag that stood straight out beyond the snow-smeared window, and seemed ready to rip from its mooring and disappear into the void. Combine wind and temperature and the chill had dropped to minus eight.

From the bridge she looked small and alone on the forward deck, amid the wet lash of flying snow. She pushed into the wind and reached the prow and stood there, looking out at the ice into which the *Wilmington* now plowed at a reduced speed, seventeen knots had become fifteen, thirteen, then eleven. I went to my cabin and zipped up my parka. I pulled a stocking hat over my head and went down the corridor, where I pushed down the steel lever unlocking the hatch.

When I stepped outside, the wind that had been muted inside the ship exploded. The steel railing was coated with ice spray and more rocketed into my face with each fierce gust. The wet lash of pounding snow drove me sideways as I left the slight protection of the overhang, marched forward toward the living figurine who stood gazing out as if the day were clear, the wind a pleasant breeze, and she a happy tourist eyeing the northern ocean ahead.

I joined her and said nothing, opting for silence over interrupting thoughts. She seemed unaware of my presence for a few moments, but she knew I was there. When she spoke, it was to shout over wind, but her face remained turned to the storm.

"It's beautiful. The blizzard boutique."

"Excuse me?"

The face shifted fractionally in my direction. Her presence was a physical force that shifted molecules of air. "This storm, so powerful. Yet we can just walk inside and take a hot shower and snuggle into bed. When I went to the pole, we didn't bathe for six weeks. Each night we'd get into the sleeping bags, and our breath would condense, turn to ice. After a while we slept in it. The bags got heavier each day." She smiled. "My least happy memory of the trip."

"But still a happy one."

I could not see her shrug inside the bulky parka, but I sensed her do it. Her sigh was a line of white vapor whipped away by wind. The ship had assumed an up-and-down rhythm timed to oncoming swells. "Colonel, I always feel like the best thing about anything is also the worst. People, for instance. My girlfriends and I, when we were twenty, used to play a game about men. We called it, *I married him because . . . I divorced him because . . .*"

"What was the game?"

"Ah, I married him because he was the life of the party. I divorced him because he never shut up. I married him because he was stylish. I left because he couldn't stop buying clothes. See? If you're not prepared to live with both sides of anything, don't get involved."

She seemed comfortable in her own skin, seemed to know why she did things. It occurred to me that what I'd taken for bluntness earlier, rudeness, was merely an impatience with saying things in roundabout ways.

"Why submarines?" I asked.

She looked at me sharply, as if wondering whether I'd really asked, *Why submarines for a mere woman?* But I hadn't meant it that way, she seemed to know it, and the look subsided as quickly as it had come.

"Because submarines go places where people can't."

The ship struck something harder and we bounced off but continued moving. Her face was elfin inside the furred hood. The gloves made her hands huge on the handrail, and melting ice ran in rivulets down wind creases in her cheeks. Her skin was an outdoorswoman's, abraded by nature. It would age faster than other women's skin. Her eyes would remain younger. Her posture was an inverted bow, so that she thrust forward into the violence, as if welcoming it, and her answer came as if we'd been chatting like tourists getting to know each other on a pleasant Arctic cruise.

"Submarines," she said, "reach a different world."

"And going on the polar expedition? The same?"

"If two things are the same, why do them?" she said.

She kept looking forward, not ignoring me, simply not wanting to miss the view. The ship wallowed in a small open area—a gap in ice, then slugged through a mass of gust-sheared, flat-topped waves, and plowed into a new floe. But the ice was getting thicker and was clinging to us now.

I looked down. Clumped ice covered every inch of my parka, a coating of gray rubbly slush.

"If you never do anything twice," I said, "you must get bored with people."

She peered out through ice-rimmed lashes. I'd been overt, asking that personal question. I was surprised I'd said it, even thought it. I'd not launched into this sort of stumbling, adolescent probing session since I'd met my wife. *Some tough Marine you are*, I thought.

"Colonel, my father was a history professor. My mother was an engineering professor. All they did was talk. Their friends, also academics. We'd sit at the dinner tables, or in backyards, at parties, and they'd talk and drink and talk and eat. They talked about fascinating places and never went there. They talked about policies and never voted. They made the world outside seem exciting and made me want to do the things they feared, and see places they avoided. For a long time I thought they were scared, and I mocked them. But I just didn't understand them. One time, I was eighteen, having an argument with my mother, I yelled, *You never do anything! You just talk!* And she smiled, patted me on the head, and said, But, darling, we like to talk. You're different. Do things. It's who you are."

It was a funny sort of talk to be having in a blizzard. It was the sort of talk you have with a girl at a small restaurant table, with a candle burning between you, with an open bottle of chardonnay. She seemed just at home with herself in a sixty-mile wind as in a restaurant.

"Sounds like you had good parents," I said.

"I didn't answer you just to make a chat, Colonel. I answered because now I get to ask you one," she said.

"Oh?"

"The Marines call you 'Killer Joe.' Why?"

I never knew it possible to feel so much heat in a blizzard. They say that Scotch whiskey will warm a man, but it's nothing compared to the blast I felt at that moment from my face to my toes. She explained that she'd overheard the Marines talking in the mess, at a table behind her. I'd heard the nickname at Quantico: *Killer Joe.*

Her eyes turned full on me now, and through the flakes hissing between us, I saw the keen glow of scientific curiosity. For a moment I'd forgotten who I was, and why I no longer deserved things that I'd once thought a basic human right. I'd been wrong to talk with her about anything except the submarine *Montana*. I deserved this.

The coldness in my voice startled even me. "Why didn't you just ask the Marines what they meant?"

"I don't like gossip. If you have a question, either ask the person directly or shut up," she said.

"Marine nicknames are hard to figure out," I said.

"Meaning you don't know why they call you that name? Or that you're glad the answer isn't obvious?"

What was I seeing in her face? Amusement at my discomfort? Challenge to the mission leader? Rampant, directionless curiosity that never stopped?

"Meaning that we all have to live with who we are."

The answer seemed to surprise her. She studied me. "Fair enough, and who *you* are," she said, "is the man in charge when we get off the ship, out *there*," she said, indicating the storm with a wave, "even though you're not the one with the most polar experience. So you're not the only one who has to live with you, Killer Joe."

She looked like a slush statue, eyebrows white, hood rimmed with white, shoulders coated, breath white.

I retorted, "That seems like a valid reason to ask the Marines. Why come to me?"

"So that's your answer?" She didn't seem angered. It was like anything I said provided information. She peered into the microscope. I was the specimen on the slide.

"Yes, that's it," I said.

I left Karen Vleska at the prow of the ship, and later, an hour afterward, saw from the bridge that she was still there, a lone human figurehead, her face forward into the elements, the fierce snow blowing around her, as if all else in the world was gone.

■ ■ ■

Time crawled by. The radio beacon flickered on and off . . .

Ninety-two miles separated us from the *Montana* . . .

Seventy-four miles . . .

Satellite communication remained blocked, so there was no way to know if the Chinese icebreaker was ahead of us.

DeBlieu announced to the crew the truth about the crippled *Montana*. There was no point keeping the rescue quiet anymore. He told them—as they stopped work, as they stared at intercom boxes—that we were in a race to save fellow sailors, but he gave the impression that the race was only against time. He did not mention any Chinese icebreakers or submarines. He did not mention potential Russian movement in the region.

Thirty-two miles . . .

The wind was now audible, even when inside the ship, in those rare moments when we didn't hear ice. It had thickened and both engines ran at full power—probably damaging them, DeBlieu said—and we were like a steel bronco smashing, pushing, nudging, and backing and ramming our way north. In the stairwells we needed to hold railings, moving between decks. During sleep periods the ice clawed and screamed at us on the other side of the hull. I lay in my bunk. I could not sleep. I stared at the mass of wires and vents bouncing and quivering with each impact of steel against ice.

"Colonel, good news. The floe is moving them *toward* us at a good three miles an hour. We picked 'em up for a minute. Then they were gone again."

Twenty-two miles . . . Crewmen with ice mallets and baseball bats smashed at ice coating the railings.

As DeBlieu had predicted, once the mission was known, his crew doubled the intensity with which they worked. They brought new care to each job, more attention to detail, whether it was serving steaks in the mess, or checking on the Arktos. It was in their posture and faces and the way the crew, in ones and twos—kids to me—came up in the corridors or mess and volunteered to be part of the rescue trip, if we needed help.

"I grew up in North Dakota, sir, and can move fast on cross-country skis . . ."

"I have a sister in subs, sir. I know she'd want me to go with you."

I was humbled by their drive, and realized that—as DeBlieu had assured me—his men and women constituted a greater asset than I'd given them credit for. I'd been the too-proud Marine.

Still, it was a race, against time, against death, against the worldly powers opposing us. The ice thickened outside. We had to stop, back and ram, then race through a lead, then hit another floe, then back and ram again. We made teeth-jarring progress. The first iceberg went past, jagged and tall and like a mini-mountain easing by fifty feet to starboard. I saw ice pillars. I saw a floating ice half moon. The bergs came and went like frozen monuments just beyond any clear field of vision.

Meanwhile the wardroom—a large, lit, comfortable lounge down the passageway from the captain's cabin—became our headquarters. It had a long conference table, thick carpet, comfortable chairs, and was stocked with coffee machines and snacks.

A Marine guard stood outside while Karen Vleska, Eddie, and I went down a list of materials used in Virginia-class subs: rubber compounds, wiring, computer chips, plastics, and parts of strategic metals, anything new, anything that might—if subjected to extreme heat— produce toxic gas. Eddie tried to match the results with charts of toxic chemicals, trying to identify the possible source of the illness aboard the *Montana*.

Neither Karen nor I made any mention of our previous conversation on the deck.

Eleven miles . . . but we'd slowed to four knots.

Had the Chinese icebreaker gotten there yet?

The beacon failed and lit and failed and came on, and DeBlieu said we'd sailed to the east, or maybe the current had moved the submarine west . . . so we had to change direction.

Eddie and I pored over encrypted files that had blasted through from the director during the brief period when the sat line had been open. Eddie was in his bunk, me in mine.

"Listen to this, Number One," Eddie said:

The U.S. has become more militaristic since they abandoned a draft Army for a volunteer force. Their Congress, having fewer veterans in it, is more inclined to fight. Democrats wish to prove that they are tough. Republicans see enemies everywhere. The result is a crippled giant seeking to bolster popular support at home—and gain advantages abroad—through military adventurism.

"What are you reading?" I asked.

"It's a paper that was published by Admiral Xu Lingwei Ha in 2014, identifying the U.S. as the most likely enemy China will face in a future naval war, and urging speedy preparations for a, quote, 'wide-ranging confrontation that will occur in numerous locations across the Pacific and High North latitudes.'"

Eddie kept reading, "The U.S. sees China as its principal adversary in the Pacific, and the Arctic is a source of wealth and power in the next century. The Russians see the Arctic as their private lake. As tensions heat up and the region becomes more critical to world economies and security, it is likely that both countries will turn to military aggression to defend their spurious claims. Chinese Arctic policy—since we do not border the ocean—must be to obtain every possible advantage now in this opening region before the inevitable clashes occur."

"Peaceful guy," I said.

"Yeah, blame every possible problem on old Uncle Sam. Got a toothache? Americans did it. Your Beijing-made car stops suddenly on the Lhasa highway? Evil satellite technology from Silicon Valley, most assuredly! And by the way, as I am an expert at smoothly switching subjects, Number One, I saw you outside with Dr. Karen before."

"Consulting," I said.

Eddie grinned. "Hey, if you're lying about talking to her, I sense the earth moving beneath your feet."

"That's ice, and it's always moving."

"Did I tell you that she's a surfer?"

What I heard in my mind was her asking, *Why do they call you "Killer Joe"?*

"A surfer? *A surfer, Eddie?* That's particularly relevant at the moment. Let's get something to eat. In another few hours we'll need the energy."

Nine hours to go, the instruments said.

■ ■ ■

I've always been amazed at the normalcy that constitutes impending violence. The banana cream cake you fork in as you wait to pick up an M4 and go out into a blizzard looks exactly like the slice you ate at 3 A.M., in a bathrobe, in your home kitchen. The coffee that steams before you emits the same rich aroma that a mug of Folgers did when you read the Sunday sports section in Cleveland, parked on a couch one Sunday, as your wife and kids scowled at you, preparing to go to church.

The cooks broke out the good stuff in expectation of impending danger. The chow line snaked back from the galley, into the main passageway, and the crew heaped their trays with thick steaks and mashed potatoes, and there were four kinds of soft drinks and the fruit bins bulged with Washington State apples, Oregon pears, red bright cherries.

We ate and watched big-screen Armed Forces Network shows: *CSI*, Yankees baseball, *Jurassic Park 2*, antisuicide and don't-drive-drunk commercials. A soldier, weaving out of a bar at 3 A.M., started his car and—

Boom.

The mess deck canted sideways, slowly, and all conversation stopped. "*No promotion, for me, honey, all because I had a couple of drinks,*" the red-faced corporal on screen was saying. Food hung on forks, midway between plates and mouths. The big hangings on the wall; photos of hard-hatted seismologists working the pipes and winches on the fantail; photos of crew playing touch football on the ice, shirtless; a photo of the launching of the *Wilmington,* in far-off Louisiana . . . all seemed to be slightly off-kilter.

A creaking and groaning reverberated through the hull. The XO was already heading briskly from the mess. Eyes swung upward. I smelled steamed string beans and potatoes, tuna salad and chocolate sundaes. A wedge of banana cake that had teetered on a table crashed to the deck.

Eddie said what everyone was thinking, "What did we hit?"

DeBlieu stood up, still holding his favorite dessert, bacon coated with milk chocolate and sprinkles, on a stick.

"All we do is hit things," he said. As he spoke, I realized that the heavy shudders that had been jolting us every few moments had ceased.

"The good news is, if we were holed, alarms would be ringing." DeBlieu said, although he hardly looked happy.

"Then what's the bad news?"

"Can't you feel it? We've stopped," he said as he headed for the bridge, and I rose to follow. "We're stuck."

TEN

The Arktos hung in space, swaying like some prehistoric animal in a cradle, a 16,000-pound terrified creature hanging above Earth. The amphibious vehicle was being lowered—one of its two units at a time—by the starboard side crane. Assembled, it would look like two tanks connected by a mechanical arm. The cables looked frail as thread. The ship canted sideways in a seventy-five-mile-an-hour gust. Unloading proceeded on the lee side, providing at least some wind protection. I watched the orange craft dangle at the halfway point between deck and ice.

"Slowly, slow-ly," Captain DeBlieu ordered, his hand on the shoulder of a lieutenant named Matheson, at the crane controls. We'd squeezed into a glass-sided compartment. The storm's residue was shoved away every two seconds by fast-moving two-foot-long wiper blades. The contrast between the warmth inside, and cyclonic violence inches away, made the scene unreal, a sense magnified when, momentarily, I got a glimpse of the world beyond.

"Touchdown! Too bad the other Arktos never got aboard. You'll be pulling a lot of sleds with this thing, bringing everyone back, Colonel."

I gasped with astonishment. It was genesis reversed, as if we'd reached some gyroscopic center of planetary energy. Because how can you be stuck in place if everything around you is moving? What natural law demanded that the *Wilmington* keel over, slanting five degrees, while all we saw around us swept past? I saw ice boulders, football-sized fields, pillars. It was vast, beautiful, and terrifying. It was birth and death on a planetary scale. I'd been briefed about this but seeing it was different. A century ago the view would have been solid ice, so thick that a hundred-mile-an-hour wind couldn't move it; ice that had been present when Rome was sacked, when Vikings found America.

But recently the heated-up ocean had welled up, and like ice cubes left out in a martini, the ice had begun to ooze. Thousand-year melt speed had accelerated to five. Warmed below by current, and above by sun, the ice cap had weakened and everything out there swirled in different directions—ice fields the size of Belgium crashing into each other, ice Alps, ice mountains, ice plateaus coalescing into a white hell, vortex of storm-topped earth.

"We're pinned, Colonel," said Executive Officer Gordon Longstreet, pushing into the cab from outside. "We've got a block of ice the size of a Chevy wedged against a rudder. I don't know how it got inside the ice horn," he said, referring to the massive steel boxes encasing the rudders. "But it's lodged. That wind is pushing us sideways, with ice piling up on starboard."

"Back and ram it," DeBlieu said. "Back and ram."

I asked, "How long before we break free?"

The captain's face was a study in tension; the cords on his jaw stood out. "Could be thirty minutes. Could be three days, or," he said, voice dropping, "weeks."

I found Major Pettit in the copter hangar, where the Marines were checking weapons. "Suit up to leave."

A voice in my earpiece said, " We're lashing on skis and sleds. Passengers ready, sir."

As we headed for the deck, Peter Del Grazo's voice started up excitedly in my radio. "I picked up the *Montana*! Talked to someone! They're alive, at least eighty of them. Then I lost transmission again."

"How far away are they?"

"Seven miles, sir."

"Are the Chinese there yet?"

"We're the first to arrive so far."

The *so far* told the rest of the story. Seven miles, I thought bitterly. Only seven miles separated us from the survivors, maybe less if wind kept pushing them toward us, although the same gusts would be in our faces.

I could run seven miles in under an hour. I could walk it at home in two hours.

Del Grazo was coming with us, I decided, as most qualified to run communication. The Marines clomping into the outer deck wore Day-Glo vests to see each other in the storm, over snow camouflage shells, over their extreme cold weather gear: windproof heavy-duty parka and snow pants and three-fingered mittens—enabling them to shoot—with inner woolen linings. Their eyes looked robotic inside slits in their balaclavas. Their M4s were slung over their backs. Two men carried M16s equipped with M203 40 mm detachable grenade launchers.

Karen and Clinton met us on the ramp—or brow—lowered from the 01 deck to the ice. Marietta Cristobel—ice expert—would stay on board. She'd told me. "I know ice from a lab. I couldn't help you find a ten-story-high rum factory out there. Use the extra space for the sick. You'll need it with the second Arktos stuck back in Barrow."

That Arktos can carry fifty-two people, sitting upright, like crew on those old Civil War–era confederate submarines.

Andrew Sachs appeared on deck, dressed like everyone else, but somehow he looked different, as if the gear was so alien to his body that it imprisoned him inside. He moved stiffly. I was glad we'd go in a vehicle, and not depend on him on the ice. There was no question he'd slow progress down if we had to walk.

Clinton Toovik was a solid presence at the top of the brow. He pressed his head against mine to be heard against the wind, and even then he had to shout.

"In the Arktos, better keep the temperature low so we don't sweat. You don't want to sweat if we have to go out."

"Right."

"Also, I want a rifle," Clinton said.

"The weapons are for the Marines," I explained.

His breath smelled of minty mouthwash. "There are bears. And there might be Chinese, you said. Always travel armed here. I was in the Army. I know how to use an M4."

"Clinton, the Marines will protect us."

He snorted. "I was an Army Ranger. And I'm a hunter."

I soothed him, curbing my impatience to get going. "Yes, of course, but these guys have *combat* training in the Arctic."

Clinton's laugh was carried off by wind, so he seemed, in the shrieking maelstrom, to be miming good humor. He said, "Where? In Norway? Norway's a hundred degrees warmer some days. Seventy below in Barrow. Thirty above in Norway. Norway gets the Gulf

Stream. Those waters warm it. You want me to come with you? I want a rifle, Colonel."

I said, growing testy, "They're not for civilians. Now let's get going, okay?"

"Civilians? Then I guess the *civilians* will stay on board, Colonel."

I sighed. "Get him an M4," I told Major Pettit.

Andrew Sachs was there suddenly, chiming in, and also demanding a rifle. He surprised me. He could move quietly.

He was saying something about belonging to a shooting club.

"Sorry, Mr. Secretary. But feel free to threaten not to come, too," I said, hoping he'd accept.

■ ■ ■

We ducked one by one into the Arktos. The Marines took seats along the walls, backs straight, balaclavas off, jackets unzipped as the heating system began oozing fifty-five-degree air into the cab. I sat beside the lance corporal driver, following news from the ship. At least ground radio worked this close to the *Wilmington*, but the worried voices I heard from the bridge did not build confidence.

"Both engines stop! They're burning out!"

The icebreaker, trapped, couldn't even back and ram anymore. Ice held a rudder fast.

Karen Vleska squeezed into a seat beside me. I smelled, over the diesel odor, her coconut-scented shampoo. Our headlights switched on. Time was topsy-turvy. At 11:30 P.M. it should be dark, but the sun was up. If the sun was up, it should be light but the storm darkened visibility. I recalled lithographs showing ships trapped in ice a hundred years ago, the ice actually reaching high enough to breach railings, creep across decks, spread into living quarters, crush whole vessels.

Eddie, a bulky presence behind me, demanded of the driver, "Why aren't we moving?"

"Um, which way, sir? The GPS isn't working."

Shit. "Can we get a fix on the sub's radio beam?"

"It disappeared again."

I turned to Del Grazo. "Then use the goddamn compass."

The normally jovial Brooklyn-accented voice sounded distressed.

"Sir, this far north compass needles get screwed up. Magnetic north and regular north are different. Rely on a compass, we're likely to get thrown off."

"Well, for Christ's sake," I snapped, momentarily at a loss. "You mean we'll just sit here?"

Karen Vleska spoke up from beside me, calm and rational and peering beyond the slashing wipers into the melee outside. "Clinton? You or me?"

"Me," he replied. "I'm better at it. Open the door," he told the driver. "I'll go out and lead."

"How?"

"Sastrugi," said Clinton, as if it was an explanation.

Eddie said, "Anyone speak plain English here?"

Clinton was zipping up his parka. "It is English," he said. "Keep me in the headlights, Jarhead. Sastrugi are lines in the snow, from wind. The wind's from the northwest, so sastrugi will face southeast. We use the snow lines as pointers. Works every time."

"Sorry," said Eddie.

"Buy a dictionary," Clinton said.

"Why not just stay inside and point from here?" I said.

Clinton gestured at the window, the rime on the panes, the snow and darkness. The storm threw the powerful headlight beams back in our faces. We couldn't make out wind lines on the ground.

"Oh."

Moments later we were following the big man, who *shoosh*ed ahead on skis. His back was a Day-Glo orange mass between wiper blade passes, his M4 a whitish slanting line like a Sam Browne belt across his back. He was moving at least, and the speedometer said we chugged north at a blizzard-respectable but frustrating four miles an hour.

For half a mile.

Then the figure held up a mittened hand to stop us. The radio— hooked to his mouth mike—emitted screechy static. I heard Clinton battering on the door.

Eddie the joker called out, "Who is it?"

"Open it," I said.

Clinton's head stuck in, along with swirling snow. "Weak ice ahead. I'll climb up on top now. When you hear me pound, start moving again."

I looked into a gray mass that seemed no different than the land-scape we'd moved through for the last half hour. We waited while Clinton climbed up and then we lurched forward, and suddenly experienced a deep rumbling below. We were tilting forward, sliding faster. I felt buoyancy take over and knew that we'd crashed through ice, plunged into a lead. Water swirled outside the window, at neck level.

The pilot switched to jet propulsion power and we wallowed through a field of floating boulders. Ice clunked against Kevlar as we threaded a minefield of sharp-edged blocks. The tread spun, trying to get a grip on solid pieces, but pushing them below. Our bottom half was under-water. We struck something and the Arktos tilted upward and climbed from the sea to resume crunching forward, left edge up, now the right, on a field of ice rubble.

Clinton banged on the hatch, we stopped, he got off and began leading us by foot again, sometimes leaning down to check the direction of sastrugi, pointing when he wanted a course change, or merely slogging off to the left or right.

Andrew Sachs had been quiet the whole time, and when he spoke, his voice seemed higher. His normally white face seemed paler. "Maybe the ship has broken free," he said. "Maybe we can go back."

Del Grazo shook his head, "It hasn't broken free, sir."

I failed at first to hear the engine noise changing, the mechanical sputter starting, as I was giving orders.

"Major Pettit, when we get there, I'll want surviving crew back on the *Wilmington* fast as possible."

"Yes, sir."

"We don't know what made them sick, so wear masks."

"You men hear that?" Pettit announced to nods.

Now I grew aware of a metallic coughing coming from inside the vehicle. If we were in a car, I would have said the muffler was broken, or a tailpipe. We continued our progress, but now the grinding grew louder, coming from below.

"If the *Wilmington* can break free, we'll try to tow the *Montana* out."

The Arktos was shaking now, from something internal, not the ice outside.

"But we also need to be prepared to scuttle her if the reactor is leaking or if the Chinese—"

We'd stopped, yet nothing blocked our progress. Ahead, Clinton continued forward, unaware that we were not following, but now I saw him coming back.

The driver frowned at his controls, reached like the suburban driver of a stalled Volkswagen to turn a key, press an accelerator, try to restart the engine, peer at a red warning light where no light had been on before.

Electricity still on, wipers streaking, air blowing . . .

With the engine off, the storm noise intensified. We'd halted between two jagged pillars of ice, lumped shapes, an ice Stonehenge. The wind here shook us side to side.

"Colonel, the tank reads full."

"Check it manually," I said. "I'll go, too." After all, we carried extra fuel. Perhaps some stupid error—or faulty meter—had misled us into thinking we had a full tank when we needed to put more in.

Or did someone tamper with the Arktos?

Eddie and I exchanged frowns as I zipped up my parka, uncoiled myself from the seat, hunched past the expressionless Marines, and ducked out into the storm.

First the Chinese turn toward the sub, then the Arktos stops.

Wind blasted into my face. There was a burning sensation in my throat, and I felt it closing. I could not breathe directly into the wind. The storm made me see everything as if in a white tunnel, the sides a kaleidoscope of movement. The driver and I made our way to the rear. Ice had frozen shut the panel protecting the gas cap, so we had to retrieve a Ka-Bar from the cab, and chip ice to open her up. The driver pulled out the fuel cap dipstick—a modified Arktos feature. Newer Arktos crafts featured fuel-tank entry from inside the vehicle. We rode in an earlier model.

"Almost full, sir." Then he peered closer. "Shit, sir, what's this blue coating? It's not fuel."

I peered at the stick, then, with a sickening feeling, looked more closely at the cap door itself. I saw pry marks along the chassis where the cap opened, damage streaks resembling the scrapes you see on an automobile door, when a thief has tried to jimmy the lock.

Someone tampered with the fuel.

Or was it, I asked myself, hoping against logic, that the striations had been caused by steel cables during loading, by an impact going in or out.

Get a better look at the dipstick.

I climbed back into the relative warmth of the cab. My eyes hit Eddie's. I nodded slightly. His mouth was set in a solid, angry line.

I unrolled my mittens from around the dipstick, and held it up.

"What's this blue stuff? Anybody know?"

Del Grazo's breathing quickened and his eyes narrowed and he reached for it, held the stick to his nose and sniffed and grunted unhappily.

"It's . . . it's fire retardant, Colonel."

I cursed. He said, "It's what we carry in the canisters. My job used to be to check them, when I first joined up. We were in the Pacific. I'll never forget the goddamn smell. But how did fire retardant get into the . . . wait . . . *during a drill!*"

I had a vision, a memory of the emergency drills that had marked normal life on the *Wilmington*. A bell goes off. Minutes later the ship fills with groups of white-suited emergency crews. Men and women with their faces covered. People carrying axes and tools that could have opened a fuel cap. People scurrying around while the Marine guard who was supposed to be in the hangar allegedly watched.

"You'd only need thirty seconds to pry open the tank, stick the hose in, spray, screw up the fuel line," I said.

Eddie added, "While twenty other people in suits just like yours distract the guard, simply doing their jobs."

I said, "Major Pettit?"

"I had a guy there all the time."

"One guard?" I accused, which was unfair, because one should be enough. But I wasn't going to apologize, especially not to the man sleeping with my ex-wife.

"Yes, sir. One."

Del Grazo's mouth was a tight line of fury. "We'll ask the captain to question everyone who worked in the hangar."

Eddie shook his head. "Anyone could put on a suit and look like he belonged to that crew."

"Or *she* belonged," added Dr. Vleska.

Major Pettit looked around at the faces around us: Karen's stiff, Sachs's tense, the driver's fearful, me trying to stay bland, as if I maintained hearty confidence. Eddie just voiced what we were all probably thinking.

"Is the person who did it on the ship? Or with us now?"

"Get ready to walk," I said.

■ ■ ■

Lieutenant Del Grazo radioed back, asking Captain DeBlieu to order a review of all security tapes made over the past few days of the helicopter hangar.

"Maybe we'll see something."

Eddie said morosely, "Yeah, twenty people dressed exactly the same, with no faces, and who is to say it even happened then? Maybe it happened in Fairbanks. Or Barrow."

"Everybody out," I said.

With the hatch open, snow blew in. Outside, we helped the Marines unload sleds, piled on the medical supplies, explosives, and propane—heat—for any survivors.

"Stay close. Pay close attention to the person in front of you. Obey Clinton or Dr. Vleska, whoever is leading at that point. Lieutenant Del Grazo, can you stay in contact with the ship while we're outside?"

"Do my best."

We started into the maelstrom. The Arktos—our magic carpet—

disappeared. Clinton knelt and peered down and adjusted course and slid north, cutting diagonally across wind lines in the snow.

I looked behind me at the straggling, jagged line: the Marines, Karen, Eddie, Andrew.

Who's the spy? I thought.

What will you do next?

ELEVEN

Plant your pole, push and glide; that's the way you're taught to do it. But it was impossible in this shrieking violence, especially when we hauled Kevlar sleds on which were piled up to—depending on the hauler—two hundred pounds of supplies.

Three steps and glide became two, then one, then we were stepping forward as if through heavy water. The rubbly plain became a field piled with close-packed ice boulders. The sky tilted sideways as, linked to the sled like a horse, I pulled it into a gap, and there it stuck. Pettit materialized beside me, reached wordlessly to help me.

"Together, Colonel. One . . . two . . . *pull!*"

The group was roped together like a slave caravan. The ice went spongy suddenly, and I saw Clinton's shoulders drop, felt a sickening lurch as the surface gave way. I was falling, expecting to feel seawater, but I'd merely dropped into a small ice ravine. Shaken, still standing, I stepped out, slid back, pushed forward, and froze as I heard a vast rumble beneath me. Then came a long cracking sound above the screech of wind, as if solid rock were tearing apart down there. As if sped-up plate tectonics ripped at granite seams. It was the sort of sound that sent coal miners scrambling for exits.

The echo stopped. I never thought I'd be happy just to hear a screaming wind.

Clinton slogged away into the dark, a half-visible figure in my yellow headlamp beam.

We carried salt pills against cramps, burn salves, and medicines. We carried military rations that self-heated if you tore open the pouch. There were tents, if we had to stop. There were vaccinations and aerosols. There were hydration packets. There were waterproof blankets. There were splints, hazmat suits, goggles, chemical sample kits.

How much time passed? An hour? Two? The cold wind elongated each second. I felt the sled working against my upper arms and thighs. The wind lessened; was it stopping finally? No, no, it was only teasing, and it sped up again.

Suddenly Major Pettit pushed past me up to Clinton and the forms came together in the semidarkness, and from Pettit's angry hand gestures, I gathered he was shouting. His gloved hand jabbing left. Clinton's parka hood shaking back and forth, *no!* When I skied up to them, they were arguing over Pettit's ice-rimmed compass, which he wielded—shaking it—like a prosecutor producing exhibit A.

"You're going the wrong way!"

Clinton calmly knelt, traced a gloved finger along the almost invisible line of a wavelike snow, sastrugi.

Pettit shook his head. "That's east, not north."

The earth was a monumental tuning fork. The hideous tearing noises started up again. I felt the ice shuddering and rumbling, a metal animal. Clinton's face was before me, eyes oval, features hidden by the black balaclava, lips white, nose white. Clinton assured me, "It's just moving down there, but not breaking up. Still, we'll circle around that flat area ahead."

"But that will slow us."

"If we don't, we'll fall in."

Our ski trails filled with blowing granules. Karen moved easily, head down, bulling forward. Eddie slipped but kept up. Pettit traveled up and down the line, making sure his men kept going, like every line of sailors which had disappeared into the polar void for the last five hundred years.

Peter Del Grazo materialized beside me, having conferred with Pettit. "It's *Clinton*, Colonel. He's taking us the wrong way!"

His eyes were fierce in his balaclava, and his voice, that Brooklyn accent, had lost all trace of the good humor marking it previously. "He goes where he wants on the ship. He doesn't report to anyone. He could just ski off."

Ice rime hung from his balaclava, his breath was white brume, his anorak matted crystal.

"Get back in place," I said.

How far can the fucking submarine be?

■ ■ ■

We stopped for a ten-minute rest on the protected lee side of a huge ice column, a lone formation like a sandstone form in Utah, a tower that shielded us slightly from direct wind. Someone produced cocoa. My fingertips were losing feeling. We sat shoulder to shoulder for warmth and inside my mitten liners I imagined skin turning solid, blood crystalizing, fingers as blood sausages, legs as statues unable to move.

Andrew Sachs had done surprisingly well, I thought. He'd not complained. He'd shut up. I'd been surprised at his acuity on skis, at his hidden resources, his ability to pull a sled. He sat off to the side, alone. One of the Marines suffered from the freezing together of his lips. His frosting breath puffed out from both sides of his mouth, and his fitful breathing resembled that of a horse.

The man wordlessly endured the ripping apart of his lips. Karen Vleska advised him to keep his mouth open as he walked, and to turn away from the wind, to keep the running blood from freezing his lips together again.

Del Grazo pulled the radio from his sled, tried for a fix on the submarine, looked up, and nodded happily.

"Hey, he was right, Colonel! It's still ahead."

■ ■ ■

Clinton switched off with Karen, who took the lead for a while, and then they switched back. He probed ahead with his long ice gaff.

"Weak ice."

Gingerly moving, he played out rope. His form grew dimmer and I thought, *This is what Pettit predicted. He'll uncouple. He'll ski away. He's leaving us.*

The form was coming back.

"There's a way through, but just a small one. If we go fast, we can ski right over the water."

"*Ski into water?*" Eddie gasped.

"It's only water on top. There's ice just under it. If you go fast, you'll be fine."

"That water is what . . . like thirty degrees?"

"In and out," said Clinton. "Otherwise, it gets deeper east and west of here."

"But thirty degrees—"

Clinton said calmly, "Just keep moving. The boots are waterproof. If you get wet, the wool socks will keep in heat. What's the matter, tough Marine? You chicken?"

"I'll go first," I said, to shut them up.

He was right. It was easy. The water came up to my ankles. But the ice held, and we passed. The socks held the extreme cold off my feet.

■ ■ ■

We built up speed, made good time, the wind at our backs for a while, which made no sense, but then, nothing did here. Then the wind dropped and the light turned gray and ahead rose a range of looming shadows. Ice mountains. My heart sank. *Ivu*, Clinton called it, the up-thrust edges of two floes that had collided.

"We have to climb *that*?" Eddie said beside me. They had to be at least forty feet high. Forty feet of ice. A four-story building. How do you climb up forty feet of ice, with sleds?

Wind hissed down from the saddle shape above, whooshed into our faces, and drove ice pellets into our exposed skin.

Clinton said, "It's not that hard."

"Maybe not for you," Eddie said.

"Either way, Jarhead, you do it."

"You have a problem with Marines, Clinton?"

"You have a problem with Army, elitist?"

The sleds seemed to weigh double poundage going up over the ice. We all hauled and pulled, helping each other, inching them up, and trying to keep them from crashing down, and finally, exhausted, we got over the top.

One Marine had sprained an ankle. We were beat. We'd been out for seven hours, but had probably suffered an equivalent energy drain of two days of normal athletic activity. The storm had dulled senses and battered bodies and I knew that it might make us careless.

So I called another rest, a longer one, and two sleepless hours later, we pushed off again and made decent time overcoming a much smaller pressure ridge, pros at this now, pushing through an ice field—and two hours after that, from the top of yet another ridge, and through still falling snow, I looked down, a quarter mile ahead, and glimpsed the long dark form of a nuclear submarine along the edge of a lead in the ice.

We made it.

It was like seeing a sub beside the bank of a river, except instead of land on either side, there was solid snow-covered ice, which just looked like land.

I recognized the configuration of the sub.

It was the *Montana.*

Nearby, on the ice, sat a motley collection of oblong-shaped covered black life rafts, with tented roofs, and a couple of orange Arctic tents. The survivors would be inside. The small generators running the heaters inside the shelters sat on the ice, rumbling and sending up thin plumes of grayish smoke. I saw no people.

My spirits lifted, but as we started down the rubbly incline, the ice began shaking. There was a sound like a railroad train, and the deep vibrations began again, from below. To me it sounded the same as before, but Clinton stopped abruptly, cocked his head, and held a hand up to halt us. He began scanning the ice plain spread out at the foot of the pressure ridge. And we waited with him.

Suddenly I heard a deep ripping noise, a shredding sound reverberating inside the wind, low, alive. It echoed far in the distance, thunder exploding many miles away, except sound was all wrong up here, I knew. So maybe it wasn't far. Maybe it was close. And then I saw, with horror, only four hundred yards from the collection of tents and rafts, a jagged shadow appear on the surface. It ran quickly toward us for a quarter mile, from the open water right up to the rubbly hills where we stood, watching.

"It's breaking up," said Karen. "My God!"

The crack had missed the tents, but it was widening. It stopped suddenly, as if an earthquake had ended.

It's going to start up again. This ice is unstable.

We climbed down, hauling sleds, in a different sort of race now. At bottom, we raced toward the tents, as men, *Montana* crew, several upright, in parkas . . . or on all fours, began emerging into the snow.

They moved like apes, half hunched over, swaying, cavemen, Neanderthals, evolutionary throwbacks. One man fell down. Men waving. Burned, sick men. Now a woman, coughing, half bent.

These were probably the healthier ones.

The ice underfoot was a shattered mirror.

Sick or not, I've got to get that crew out, fast.

TWELVE

Captain Zhou Dongfeng, commander of People's Republic of China nuclear attack submarine type 094, its newest Jin-class underwater craft, lowered his periscope, and ordered the vessel backward, quietly, away from the American Marines skiing toward the crippled USS Montana. *He was a medium-sized, thickly black-haired, superbly postured thirty-three-year-old, and he was furious that they'd beaten him here, but he also knew they had no idea he was present. This meant he still might be able to complete his mission.*

I have never failed and I will not now, *he thought, recalling the admiral's call to him, a day ago, as he cruised north of Alaska, west of the cyclone. The admiral was a well-known leader in the Chinese Navy, whom Captain Zhou admired, and studied, but had never met.*

"The American submarine is carrying the prototype Mark 80 torpedo, most advanced underwater weapon in the world. It is also possible that they carry some bioweapon that released. We have heard there is a strange deadly illness aboard. This sickness greatly troubles me."

Captain Zhou Dongfeng had beaten long odds since he was ten years old, son of a poor farmer in China's arid northwest. He'd hated pig farming and had excelled at school, and then at Naval entrance exams, driving himself to succeed, working, sleepless, while all around him, privileged sons of government or military officials rose through the ranks with assisted ease.

Now his ceaseless work had paid off. He had been entrusted with one of the People's Republic's newest submarines, dispatched to the High North, a region that Beijing believed would be crucial to the twenty-first century. When the call came, he had been patrolling new ice-free areas, which Beijing believed would soon become shortcuts for Chinese commercial vessels. He was carrying forty crack Marines. Captain Zhou knew that the United States had stationed long-range missiles in Alaska, aimed at China. If war ever came in the future, and more than a few officers he knew believed this a possibility, knowledge of northern routes and undersea terrain could make a difference. Jin-class subs carried nuclear missiles.

"As you know, our relationship with America is bad at the moment," the admiral had said. "Two weeks ago one of their ships hit a Chinese submarine in the South China Sea, during their war games. The Americans claim this was an accident, that our vessel ran so silently they did not know it was there. Twenty-eight Chinese died. The sub was lost."

The admiral's fury was palpable. "Beijing has chosen to accept the U.S. explanation."

It was clear that the admiral believed, as Captain Zhou did, that the Americans had no business conducting war exercises so close to China, and that the alleged "accident" had been either a deliberate challenge, or the natural result of American aggressive posturing. Neither was acceptable, and the loss of the sub and so many lives had been a humiliation and disaster.

The admiral had said, "You will arrive at the abandoned submarine before the Americans. You will offer the survivors medicines and food, both of which will be airdropped to you before you enter the storm area. You will, while assisting the crew, do all you can to learn about the Montana's systems.

You will say you are on a humanitarian mission. You will take control of the vessel. You will wait for the arrival of the Snow Dragon, *so the American submarine can be towed, if possible. You will acquire a prototype Mark 80 torpedo, along with any blueprints, plans, and technology available. I want samples. I want hard drives. I want blood taken from their ill, if possible. I want them to know that tender toes will be stepped upon.*

"Also, regrettably, any one of your crew who enters that sub is to wear protective clothing, and undergo full decontamination when rejoining you. Chemical shower. Quarantine. They will transfer to the Snow Dragon *later. You, and they, will be doing a great service for China."*

The admiral had no patience with excuses, and Zhou had seen the man destroy the careers of officers who did not live up to his expectations. A certain captain—a rising star—might be marked for better things. Then, failing the admiral, he would be transferred, demoted, or would languish in the bureaucracy for years.

Just a vision of the admiral's bald head, thin eyebrows, set mouth, and stern face—from China's Naval News—*made the captain's mouth dry. He imagined a tiny room with no windows, a pile of paperwork on a desk, a one-room apartment for his family, a dusty wind blowing and the smell of pigs . . . a lone man and hung head—the fate of a failure.*

Moments ago, through the periscope, he'd treasured the view of the crippled $2.4 billion bonanza that, the admiral had said, "will help us thwart U.S. adventurism!"

"The bioweapon, sir. Do we know anything more about it?" The notion of toxic gasses and human-made germs made the captain's skin crawl.

"It is unclear whether the illness is that at this point. There may be a natural explanation."

"Sir, what if the U.S. rescue team arrives first?"

The question, of course, was logical, but in the silence that followed, Cap-

tain Zhou broke out in a sweat. The admiral's voice seemed cooler when he responded.

"All cats love fish, but fear to wet their paws."

Meaning, fearful people are of no use to me.

The admiral added, "I am certain, with your speed, this could not happen. In addition, we have an asset aboard their icebreaker slowing them down."

Captain Zhou knew that under international law, any ship in danger of sinking, or of damaging the environment, was permitted to be boarded, rescued. But military ships were tricky; the law said they belonged to their host nation. He had asked the admiral, the issue of a fight on the table, "For clarification, sir. If any of their crew is on the sub, you still want me to board her?"

The admiral provided the excuse. "Should ice crush the submarine, the environmental disaster would be profound, especially if their reactor is damaged. You must prevent this catastrophe."

"The Americans may, sir, have other ideas."

"Undoubtedly. But their satellites are blind. And thanks to our asset, the American rescuers cannot communicate with Washington. He's jamming them. They think the storm is blocking communication."

What the admiral meant, the captain thought, is that no one else will know what happens on the ice. Just as in the collision in the South China Sea, there will be two versions.

The admiral added delicately, "If they start a fight, no one can blame you for defending yourself. Remember, defeat cannot be bitter if one chooses not to swallow it."

There it was. Give them medicines, look helpful, but get the American sub, no matter what you have to do.

Captain Zhou Dongfeng had no illusions about the other part of the admiral's message. If you fail, if anything goes wrong, you will take responsibility, not me.

The admiral went on, "The Americans are tricky and lie constantly; they are dangerous and dying as an empire. Even their great diplomat Henry Kissinger recently predicted that war may erupt in the future. Our own great naval thinker, Li Zhenfu of Dalian Maritime University, has said that whoever controls the new Arctic routes will control the new passage of world economics and international strategies. Captain, you may save millions of lives through thoughtful action. I have no doubt that you will bring honor to China, and to yourself."

The captain recalled a lesson he had learned in officer training school, about Russian submarine captains who refused to fire nuclear missiles at America during the 1960s, when the Americans blockaded Cuba. Those captains prevented nuclear war, and were broken for it back home, and became scapegoats and pariahs.

The admiral broke into his thoughts, providing the identity of the spy with the Americans, the code word used for identification, and an encrypted photo of the asset.

"You will bring home this person if assistance is required."

Captain Zhou Dongfeng had been filled with admiration for Chinese ingenuity when he learned the identity of the spy.

But now he needed to move fast. He looked around the control room, at the tense faces of his crew. He called up on the monitor photos taken from the submarine and beckoned forward the major who led forty shipboard commandos, troops whose training mirrored that of the U.S. Delta Force. They were tough men who'd received cold weather training in the subzero temperatures of Manchuria. They'd been sent north to practice landings and maneuvers on the polar ice pack in international waters.

It was pure luck that they'd been within range when Beijing discovered the location of the crippled U.S. sub.

The major was a wide-shouldered, trim, and dark-haired perfectionist named *Li Youyoung*, who quickly took in the photos as Captain Zhou issued orders.

"We are backing out of view of the Americans. You will land and circle around them on skis, using the ice ridge as cover. Once you set up your field of fire, we will surface. Do not shoot unless ordered to, or fired upon."

"Yes, sir."

"They have a State Department person with them, urging cooperation." The major snorted.

Captain Zhou Dongfeng added, "I will begin a dialogue with them, keeping the channel open to you. If at any point you hear me say, 'I am trying to be reasonable,' *show yourselves so that they understand they are surrounded. I want them to see that their position is untenable; you behind, us in front.*"

The major told Captain Zhou Dongfeng, "I had a cousin aboard the Victory," *giving the nickname of the Chinese submarine sunk by the Americans in the alleged accident last week.*

"My condolences, Major."

The major's men, Zhou Dongfeng knew, carried bullpup assault rifles equipped with under-barrel grenade launchers, and two QJY88 tripod-mounted machine guns.

The captain said sternly, "We prefer to avoid a fight. You are not to start one. But if you hear me say, 'I'm sorry. I have done everything possible,' you will preemptively, immediately fire."

"Yes, Captain."

"This is a photo of a friend of China who is with them, but works for us. If at any point this person seeks asylum, provide it."

The captain jabbed the shots on screen, grainy from falling snow—but the layout of the American position was clear.

In the photos, the Montana *lay crippled in a lead, a gap between ice floes.*

It seemed to be tied by hawsers to stanchions hammered into the ice. The lead was so wide that the sub almost seemed docked along a meandering oxbow river. The "shores" of the river stretched, at the moment, at least almost half a mile apart, enabling Zhou's 094 to maneuver. But, of course, the ice was constantly moving, and leads could widen or close at any time.

At the moment, the sub was backing off to remain out of view when they surfaced.

But the insulated tents and life rafts housing the American survivors of the Montana *disaster were in plain view on screen, clustered thirty feet from open water, about a hundred feet from their crippled sub.*

Captain Zhou Dongfeng told Major Li Youyoung that the U.S. Marines had probably entered the sub by now, but he knew their numbers and so knew that they had left no guards in the rear. Nobody was looking for a Chinese submarine surfacing a third of a mile away, around a bend, in a blizzard. No one was guarding the backs of the Americans.

The major inclined his head in understanding.

Captain Dongfeng liked this major. "Prepare your men!"

The major saluted, turned on his heel, and hurried off.

At the periscope again, the captain saw that he'd successfully moved his craft out of view of the Americans.

It was therefore safe to surface now.

His mouth tasted of copper, and bile.

"Prepare to unload troops!"

THIRTEEN

It was a coffin made of steel, a coffin made of ice. I followed Dr. Vleska through the $2.4 billion wreck. Our headlamps cut the dark as we maneuvered through blackened passageways, stirring up a film of particles underfoot, even the unburned areas coated with soot. Our bulky toxic suits were made for cold weather and worn over Coast Guard parkas.

Somewhere in here a poison had come to life.

Outside, in the tents and life rafts, Eddie Nakamura and half the Marine contingent were preparing the ninety-six survivors for evacuation. Eleven more of the submarine crew had died of illness or burns since my departure from Anchorage. Speed was essential. But so was care.

The ice continually groaned out there, threatening to break up.

Our guides were a *Montana* chief of the boat, Sam Apparecio, and a SEAL commando, Lieutenant Mark Speck; both of whom had fallen ill, but survived. Apparecio had trained to work in a hazmat suit, but not Speck. We kept bumping into things, the suits restricting movement. We had to move sideways through the narrowest passageways, twenty-one inches wide.

Both guys survived. Why?

We breathed air from canisters and I felt like a mine inspector after a cave-in. The *Montana* echoed in places from wind swirling in up top, and we left hatches open as we passed through, to allow water flow in case I had to scuttle the sub.

It seemed inhuman to expect the two sailors—after what they'd been through—to function. Apparecio was a kind-faced Minnesotan of about thirty-two years old. He had a blackened hand, from the fire, bandaged, and he coughed dryly like a coal miner. Smoke damage, I thought, not a wet hack like the crew in the tents. Speck was a pockmarked, hook-nosed, big but surprisingly light-footed man, with an arm in a sling. He'd broken a wrist during the evacuation.

But they responded magnificently to my questions with a forced cheerfulness that made me want to weep with pride, as we tried to bottom-line the status of what had been—only days earlier—the pride of America.

"Can the *Montana* dive?"

"No way, sir. No controls."

"The reactor?"

"No telling if it was damaged. The skipper was quite clear on that. Can't turn it on."

"What about electrical power?"

"Well, sir! Electricity might be different! Let's just pry this here console loose. *Might* be possible, sir. *Could* happen," mused Apparecio, peering out at the guts of the console, through his faceplate, like a car mechanic examining a Honda's undercarriage. "Bit o' this, sir, bit o' that. *Might* be able to get auxiliary power. Shall I try?"

"Why not?"

"We probably still won't be able to move, sir."

I said, "But if you have electricity, you can fire torpedoes."

Three pairs of curious eyes flickered at me in the headlamps.

"Just in case," I said.

The faceplate nodded. "Well, we usually keep fish in tubes one and two. Let me check, see what I can do."

We left him behind, a man in a cave. As we continued aft, Dr. Vleska paused to examine Medusa-like clusters of burned wiring, and smashed computer screens. Plastics had melted, and without heat, ice stalactites hung above us, and we avoided sharp edges—protecting our suits—as I scraped samples; pink residue from a vent, burnt skin off a corpse in a passageway, mouth scraping from a man—dead of smoke inhalation—sprawled in a head.

Some compartments had been devastated by fire. Others were just smoky.

The passageway between engine room and crew quarters swirled with particles, fire-blackened curtains that had shielded bunks. The portable chem-alarm, wielded by Speck, remained silent. If it detected toxic chemicals, its tinny beeper was supposed to go off.

But chemical alarms don't work as well in temperatures below freezing. They are not made for this climate.

Somewhere in here sickness had erupted and killed sailors, and was still killing them outside, inside their makeshift shelters.

Before descending into the sub, I'd seen those rafts and tents and knew the scenes inside would always haunt me: the mix of horribly burned men and women and hideously sick ones, wrapped in salvaged blankets, or sleeping bags, or lying on salvaged mattresses; suffering 103-degree fevers, wracking coughs, blotched chests and faces . . . the cramped spaces dripping with condensation if heaters worked, weighed down with crystallized breath on domed canopies if the heaters had run dry; temperature outside now at two below zero, twenty below in wind.

Originally the sub crew had been triaged into four covered rafts for the badly sick and the worst burn cases; three for lesser sick and milder burns; tents for the healthy.

But over the last two days, the sickness had spread; triage lines had collapsed. Now all the shelters hosted a mix; the sickest people, clearly dying, coughing up frothy blood, which froze on their cheeks, ran down their throats. I'd tended crewmen and women with their skin peeling, with hands that smelled of rot, faces needing grafts, the odor of burned flesh and hair everywhere.

Everyone on the evacuation detail wore gauze masks, but precautions that worked in temperate climates failed in subzero wind. Breath solidified and ice coated fabric, and then you couldn't breathe anymore.

Two Marines had discarded their masks, and Major Pettit had let them. If they couldn't breathe, they couldn't work.

Eddie and I had administered morphine to those in extremis. We'd tried to clear air passages by scooping out the masses of phlegm, blood, and mucus with gloved fingers.

I'll check their blood back on the Wilmington, *in the labs off the helicopter hangar. There are microscopes there, sample freezers, instruments, a lot I can use. I'll call the CDC in Atlanta. The director will assemble the wise men—a committee—to deal with this on screen. We'll try an assortment of antibacterial and antiviral medicines to see if anything works.*

But just now our worst-case victims were lying in vomit-soaked salvaged bedding, shaking like malaria victims, groaning from stabbing pain in their joints—elbows and knees—crew wrapped in blankets that stank of diarrhea, as blue patches, the size of dimes, blossomed on frozen cheeks. The same man might have black areas from fire on his face, white ones from frost on his hands.

I'd asked the men, *"Where are your officers?"*

"Dead, sir."

"Do you know where the infection started?"

"No."

"Did your medical officer figure out what the sickness is?"

Hands gripped my forearm, fell away, clawing. *"I don't know. I have kids at home. Help me."*

"Major Nakamura! More xapaxin here, fast."

We had no idea if any medicines would work, and if so, which ones. We acted confident around the victims, telling them things would get better, especially once they got to the *Wilmington*, once they were air-lifted ashore to warm hospitals . . . but when we were outside, Eddie had slumped and said, "Christ, this is about the worst thing I ever saw."

"Get them on the ship soon as possible. Quarantine the hangar. Block all contact between *Wilmington* crew and rescuers. Everyone who came here stays in the hangar."

"Numero, no one will do more for these guys than you. They're lucky to have you."

"I don't want lucky. I want them cured."

Then I called Major Pettit aside and explained that his men would need to stay in the hangar once they got back to the ship, stay clear of the ill, and wear masks. Anyone who'd been exposed to the *Montana* crew might become sick, too, I said, and needed to be quarantined.

The hangar isn't as secure as—say—even a level-three biohazard lab, but if we keep it closed off and the hangar doors open, and ventilation system off, hopefully any contagion can be contained for the time it takes to get to shore, or for airborne help to arrive.

Pettit told me coldly, almost accusingly, "Marines don't leave any-one behind, Colonel."

He's thinking that I'm afraid. Well, fuck you, Pettit.

I wanted to be going with them. But the source of the illness was in the sub, and I needed to identify it and either scuttle the *Montana* or guard it until the *Wilmington* broke free of ice, and arrived to take us under tow.

Eddie will start out without me. Clinton can guide them back to the ship.

I wasn't even sure what I was looking for. A mold? Mold could have taken root in their lungs, and started growing. A gas could have dissipated, liquefied, frozen.

If it was mold or gas, why did the sickness spread after they left the sub? Because the toxin was already inside them; and it took a couple days for it to work?

No, it's more likely that a germ did it.

I shuddered.

A germ.

A random germ? Or a planted one?

I told Karen and Speck as we moved, "An airborne germ would have spread through ventilation. Hell, one crew member gets a cold and soon half the crew has it. Each sick person amplifies the spread."

Or was the source, I wondered, the Arctic virus or bacteria we'd been waiting for? A virus like the one that Russian scientists pulled from a Siberian lake a few years back, fully formed, a tiny life that woke up in a heated lab?

I was so preoccupied that it took some time before I realized that something else was bothering me.

Why is it that as soon as we arrived here, I got a funny feeling in my scalp, an itching, the sort of warm tickle I used to feel in Afghanistan when it turned out we were under observation?

Maybe it's just normal itching. After all, my scalp is itching now, inside the sub, probably from sweat from the balaclava.

No, that's not it, I thought.

I feel watched.

■ ■ ■

"Chief," I asked Apparecio, "tell me more about your mission."

"Sir, we set up a weather station and then we were testing weapons capability in cold conditions."

"Anything biological?" I prayed the answer would be no.

"Just the new torpedoes, sir. But then we got an emergency message to drop everything."

"Emergency?" I said, surprised.

"We were told to meet an explorer who needs assistance. An American . . . some guy walking and paddling to the North Pole."

Karen spun around and stared at him.

"He'd sent out a message. He'd stumbled onto something. What was his name? Nate . . . Nate something . . ."

"DiLorenzo?" said Karen.

"Yeah, that's it."

"I know him," she said, sounding concerned. "He's on a one-man expedition this year, to dramatize ice melt. Foldable kayak and sled. Nate was in trouble, you say?"

"It wasn't that, ma'am. He'd found something. Anyway, we got there, surfaced. Sunny, beautiful day, ma'am. I went out with the rescue crew. Your friend. He was fine, but . . ."

"But what, Chief?"

"Well, it was what he showed us, Colonel. It was the damndest thing. I'm out there and I can't believe what I'm seeing because it's like my six-year-old daughter's dollhouse, you know? A cutaway section, like the hull of a boat had been torn away, but one cabin had been *saved*, intact, sir, embedded and *sticking out of a half-melted iceberg.* The rest of that boat, maybe it was crushed, on the bottom. What was left, *two frozen men at a table."*

Karen and I looked at each other, holding our breaths.

Apparecio said, "They'd probably been there for years. They'd died at that table. What's the word, sir, when you're in second grade and you make a scene in a shoebox, a picture, you know, to show your class?"

"Diorama," I said, my heartbeat rising. *Why didn't the director tell me about this? Or did he know?*

"Yeah. That's it. Like an exhibit in a museum, behind glass. There was old film equipment there, a tripod with an old camera. There was a pot of coffee with the stuff frozen inside. Weirdest goddamn thing."

"You took the bodies aboard," I said, feeling the worst sensation— heat—spread inside my skull.

"Yeah, those frozen guys were U.S. Army, right? The film container said ARMY, and we took it, too. Battered old canister, sir. Really old. Blankets. Knives. We wouldn't leave them. The doc was supposed to keep the bodies in the freezer, but he wanted a look. So I heard from Chief Duerr that he took a body out, to examine."

My headache worsened. "And it thawed out."

"Only thing I know is, two days later the doc was sick, and then the skipper, and so *fast.* He was fine in the morning. He was dead that night. Then it spread. Colonel, the XO told Washington about this before he died, and . . ."

I stopped dead in the passageway, looking back at the open, round, kind face of the chief—the five-day beard. The shock spread through me.

"He *told* this to Washington?"

"I was there, sir, he plain out said it."

"That you'd taken aboard frozen bodies."

"Yeah. By then lots of guys were coughing. *It spread so fast.* It got hard to do normal work. Lieutenant Robbins died. And then Chief Duerr was *really* sick but working three jobs, because everyone else was out, and Duerr—he was exhausted, sir—he made a mistake and the fire started. It was an accident."

"What was the name of the person the XO spoke to?"

"I don't know, sir."

Karen was staring at me angrily. "Nobody told me about this," she said. "Or any accident."

"Nobody told me either."

She studied me in the beam, deciding something.

"Then someone lied to us both," Karen said.

The fury started as a small beat in my chest and spread down into my belly. The director! Had he known? Had he sent us five hundred miles from land, into a blizzard, into this, and *not told me everything?*

Or was someone in Washington holding back from him?

I said, "We need to figure out what infected these people."

She said calmly, "Before it spreads."

"We need to find that old film. Maybe there's something on it that . . . Chief, do you know what happened to it?"

"Maybe it burned up. Maybe it melted. Maybe it's in here somewhere. I don't know."

■ ■ ■

We couldn't find it. Or any overt clue.

I cursed inwardly as we looked for records: a captain's log, a book, a diary, a file; a thumb drive that would explain what the *Montana* had taken aboard . . . but finding things amid the wreckage seemed impossible. The captain's cabin, wardroom, the infirmary, useless. The control room. You'd need a month in here to do this right.

We pulled open blackened steel desk drawers, opened lockers, bashed a lock off a soot-smeared desk, covered with a snowfall of burned insulation. Nothing.

Our Marine Motorola emitted static. Possibly someone outside was trying to reach us, possibly they were just talking to each other. Inside our cold cave, I couldn't make out words, so we kept going. If it was important enough, a message for me, a Marine would come down.

What is on that film? Can it even help us?

Digital monitors had exploded. Plastic keyboards were frozen blobs that clicked emptily if you touched them.

That film is probably burned up or useless anyway.

In the sub's mess were soot-coated stainless steel cabinets and cookware. A red and white cardboard box of Sysco Kosher Salt lay by the sink.

"There's nothing here the Chinese could use," I said.

Karen made a *tsking* sound. "Oh, they could learn plenty from those prototype torpedoes in the bow."

I envisioned the twelve Marines outside, stationed beside the *Montana*, watching to make sure that the ice did not start to move, start to break up, float off with the submarine attached, or with the sick on top.

I recalled a lecture from one of our old biowarfare instructors at Quantico.

"Back in the 1980s," I said, "the Soviet Union designed chemical weapons for cold climates. Their gasses could kill in forty below zero. Their mustards worked below their freeze points. Their hydrogen cyanide," I said as we walked, probed, took samples, "solidified at fifteen below into particles you could send through ventilation systems."

I said, "In extreme cold, chemical contaminants are harder to locate. Gas goes solid, breaks into bits that can cling to clothing. Chemicals can be carried on a hazmat suit into a warm room, where they vaporize, go airborne, sicken people who think they're safe . . . Lieutenant Speck, hold that detector lower. Some chemical agents settle by the floor."

"Yes, sir."

Karen said, "You wanted to know why I decided to go into submarine work? Man, why did you go into *this*?"

"I love the Tropics."

She turned and hit me in the arm, grinning.

Her first nonprofessional act toward me.

The radio emitted more static. What were they saying out there? Where was the damn movie canister?

I glanced through Karen's face shield, got a flash of cheekbones, and eyes looking back, felt a dry beat on the roof of my mouth.

She's beautiful, even at a time like this.

■ ■ ■

"I'm not leaving them on the ice," I said.

Our search was interrupted, from outside, as I grew aware of a new sound against the hull, not the irregular scrape of ice, but a rhythmic pounding of a person out there using something heavy against steel. Three hits and stop. Three and stop. Whoever had been trying to reach us via radio had given up, and was using a more urgent method.

As I turned to go, Karen's glove reached out and brushed the arm of my hazmat suit, too lightly for me to feel it. "You really think that film is important?"

"I don't know."

"Let me try the captain's cabin again, and the exec's. I've got to think they'd keep anything important there. Maybe there's a place we missed. I mean, we're moving around here so fast."

"Good."

I had a vision of the ice field outside splitting, those deep cracks spreading, and the sub floating off, powerless, the sick and burned sub crew drifting farther away. I rushed through the passageways, the banging more urgent on the hull. I felt an ice stalactite snag at my shoulder, at my hazmat suit. I reached the ladder and climbed as quickly as the bulky garment allowed, to emerge outside, onto the bridge.

What I saw out there froze me in place.

It was big, and black, closing slowly, five hundred yards away.

Through the snow and gloom, I recognized the tapered shape from images the director had forwarded, and the red flag made identification unmistakable.

It was a Chinese submarine.

FOURTEEN

From the bridge, I saw the Chinese sub halt about three hundred yards away, inside the lead, its bow facing our midsection, far enough away, if the commander was confident he could withstand a blast at that distance, to enable him to fire. If he used a spread, he'd hit the *Montana* and also kill the evacuees from the sub, at the edge of the ice. *Or he can just go after the survivors and seize the sub.*

Their sail flew a white flag, requesting parlay, along with the red flag of the People's Republic of China.

As Dr. Vleska and Lieutenant Speck came up from below, I watched Chinese crewmen lower a Zodiac boat into the sea. Two figures in bulky parkas and fur hats climbed onto it, one at the bow, the other steering, avoiding bergy ice bits that swirled in the crosscurrents, their sharp edges capable of ripping a hole in the small craft.

I placed my Marine Motorola to my lips, hoping that I could reach Chief Apparecio in the engine room. "Chief?"

No response.

"Chief?"

I heard static. Then, "Here, Colonel."

"We really could use that electricity."

"Working . . . on . . . Maybe in . . . *buzzzzzzz* . . . ten . . . *buzzzz*."

The Zodiac was a hundred yards off and closing. The wind had died, the falling snow had gentled. But the currents below seemed even more violent, ice swirled in different directions, floes collided, moving north and south. Natural law seemed held in abeyance. Even math and logic degenerated into anarchy this far north.

"If you get electricity, how long till you can arm the torpedoes, Chief?" I asked as Karen's head jerked in my direction.

This time he came in clear. "A couple . . . minutes, sir."

"Hurry. We may need it."

There was a pause. The chief said with some irony, "Colonel, last time I looked, our bow pointed straight at ice. An explosion at forty yards, the concussive power, could crack us open. And even if I get power, I'm not sure we can fire or program the fish. Controls might be damaged in the torpedo room."

"One thing at a time, eh? Electricity first."

The Chinese captain had positioned his sub perfectly. I envisioned his open torpedo tubes beneath the waterline, enormous snouts. Inside lay finned missiles. He wouldn't even have to guide them, as we lay straight ahead. The ones destined to destroy our sick and wounded would be wire-controlled, so as to curve left upon launch.

I tried to reach Major Pettit as, on the ice, Andrew Sachs skied toward me, waving his arms and moving faster and abler, I noted, than he had while getting here. A fast learner? Clinton Toovik had exited a tent, and was also coming. So was Peter Del Grazo. All the homing pigeons converging to help.

Or is one of them coming for a different reason?

Pettit's crackly voice came back, via his neck mike. "I see it, Colonel."

"Turn the evacuation over to the chiefs. Don't fire. Get more men over here! Can you find any cover?"

"Negative, sir. We'd need axes to break up the ice."

"No hummocks, ridges, something to get behind?"

"Flat as a pancake if you want us close. Plus, no way to move the sick out yet. They're not loaded."

Bobbing thirty feet away, the Chinese Zodiac's fur-hatted passenger turned out to be an officer who spoke English, his language skills one more Arctic ability that our party lacked. The man smiled and waved and knew not to try to get up on deck, but he tossed up to Lieutenant Speck a ziplock package containing a handheld Chinese radio. He seemed like every Good Samaritan ever to arrive at the scene of an accident. His captain wished to help, he said. But the goodwill on his face was marred by the threatening bulk of the sub behind him.

The officer said, "We understand that you are in trouble. My captain wishes to speak with you, sir. I will translate." He explained the operation of the radio. It was similar to our Motorolas, handheld or neck-mounted, encrypted and probably equipped with automatic frequency jumping to discourage monitoring or jamming. Good at short range, in good weather, lousy at long range, in any weather. They could cut off reception on the set remotely, when they wanted. And like our models, if you wanted to share conversation, all you had to do was instruct everyone else with similar sets to tune to the same mode.

I had a feeling more than one person would be monitoring what came next. Maybe someone all the way in China.

Is it possible he can reach home, but we're blocked?

The green light on the unit glowed on, meaning that the figure on the bridge of the other sub, waving, was ready to talk. I wasn't. I turned it off. I pretended to speak into the unit. I shook it, as if it was not working right. I kept the red light on, pressing a gloved finger firmly over the mike, in case the thing was transmitting anyway. With my other hand, out of sight, I activated my Motorola, raised my voice, and pretending to address the Chinese set, spoke loudly to Pettit over the other line.

The Chinese Zodiac below had pulled back, too far away to hear. I turned my head, in case they had a lip reader.

I told Pettit, "Move the sick behind the pressure ridge, out of the line of fire."

"I'll tell the chiefs, but they're still loading."

"No shooting. No sudden moves. Easygoing, right?"

"Yeah, Colonel. Easy."

Assistant Deputy Secretary of State Andrew Sachs reached the mass of tumbled boulders abutting the hull, discarded his skis, and began a clumsy ascent toward the bridge, slipping back, scrambling up. He was a wild card. But the presence of an important U.S. official, even when communication was out, might give us some leverage. I let him come.

Sachs shouted up to me, "Let me talk to them. I speak Chinese."

You do?

No way would I give Sachs a radio. But maybe he could translate snatches of Chinese if any came over the thing.

Clinton came up behind Sachs and began a slower, but steadier, ascent. I could use him when it came to predicting ice behavior.

Del Grazo knew electronics so maybe he could help Chief Apparecio below. I waved him up also.

I couldn't delay the parlay any longer. Heart thumping, I pressed the right-hand button on the Chinese unit. A twinkle of green came on.

■ ■ ■

"I am Captain Zhou Dongfeng," the translator said cordially on our three-way loop. "I am sorry that we meet under such terrible circumstances. We picked up your distress signal and can share food and medical supplies. I have an excellent physician on board to assist."

The accent was more British than American, and the command of English excellent. Andrew Sachs reached the deck and headed for the tower. I gestured Del Grazo to go below. Captain Zhou repeated, "My medical officer is at your disposal."

Yeah, to grill our guys while he works. No thanks.

I told Zhou Dongfeng, trying to sound gracious, "Thank you for coming, Captain, and for risking your ship in this terrible storm. I'm happy to say, though, that we've gotten the situation under control. We'll be moving our injured to our icebreaker. It is close. As for the medicines, we'd sure appreciate those."

Sachs, coming up to me, reached for the set, miming, *Let me talk to him.* I shook my head.

Zhou's voice was all sympathy. "Ah, sorry to tell you, but perhaps you are unaware that the *Wilmington* is stuck and cannot move. Actually, it has drifted further away from you, since you started off."

Christ, how does he know that? Or is he lying?

Zhou added, "Colonel, my doctor is well trained in treating burn victims."

Now he's telling me he knows my rank, too.

Sachs reached for the radio again. I shook my head and told him to make sure I got a real translation of Zhou's words, and to also translate any errant bit of Chinese—in the background—that came through. Perhaps Zhou might talk to someone else on the other tower, with the unit on. You never know.

Sachs stepped toward me, unused to being ordered. "Colonel, I expressly—"

My expression stopped him dead. He actually backed away a step. He held up both gloved palms, as if to say, *Okay, have it your way. But I don't like it.*

Three hundred yards, I thought. A torpedo, launched at three hundred yards, would require less than fifteen seconds to reach a target. We'd never hear the whoosh of discharge. We'd never hear the hum of the motor coming on. Without sonar, we'd never hear the torpedo tube doors opening, that is, if they were still closed. Perhaps we'd see a small wake through the falling snow.

That captain would be risking blowback from an explosion that close to him. It was chess with human beings as pieces. I suggested to Captain Zhou that he send the medicines ashore, where we'd take them over, and Sachs nodded, as if telling me he approved. *Asshole,* I thought.

Zhou Dongfeng countered with, "Very good. Also, I've been instructed to put our fine lab facilities on the incoming *Snow Dragon* at your disposal. My physician can take samples of blood, and perhaps this will help you identify the illness."

Sachs nodded, as if to urge me, *Why not?*

Did I imagine a long sigh coming over that radio when I declined? Or was it static? Zhou's voice grew firmer, losing the overtly helpful note. "Very well! I will send the drugs, and the other offer stands, Colonel. Meanwhile, if you will kindly exit the sub, I will send over a damage assessment crew and hook you up to tow you from harm's way. You are in danger of being crushed by ice. And your reactor has been weakened by the fire, most certainly."

Yeah, and the second your guys are here, they'll begin taking things apart, snapping photos, grabbing parts, making diagrams, no way, Captain.

"Colonel, neither of us wants to see a leaking reactor go down," Zhou added reasonably, both of us probably knowing—I would bet—that the reactor was not leaking.

I hoped that Chief Apparecio, his headlamp glowing in the dark below, was making progress turning on the auxiliary power. I couldn't remember how far the auxiliary power area was from the torpedo room. But I saw no lights coming on below, felt no vibration, just the dead stillness of a sub at total rest. I had to delay and figure out how to keep Zhou off.

If I tell the chief to scuttle her, he'll open the sea cocks if he can, and she'll go down fast. If the Chinese hear that happening, hear the rush of water, will they fire? Will they try to board and stop it? Why would they fire? It would serve no purpose. It wouldn't get them the sub.

I had another, more chilling thought.

But what will I do if Zhou threatens to fire at the survivors on the ice?

"Chief? Can you hear me?"

"Almost there, Colonel. Power should have come on by now. But this . . . this stuck panel here . . ."

"How much time to scuttle her?"

"Don't know, sir. The ballast controls are jammed. If I can get to the sea cocks and open 'em, ten minutes to do that, maybe another fifteen to sink. But moving around, sir, some places are blocked, and the heat fused some controls."

That captain knows we can't talk to Washington. What he's doing is blatant and brilliant and no one will see what happens here. All I can do is play for time and hope something changes and that he won't use force.

It was, I thought, a perfect ambush.

Onshore, some of the Marines who had tended the sick had turned over loading to healthier crew from the *Montana*. Moving with exaggerated slowness, they drifted toward me on the ice.

I told Zhou, "We expect to fix these problems shortly. I'll decline the tow. The *Montana* is not abandoned. As you see, we are aboard."

I heard a snatch of rapid, agitated Chinese and then the unit went off.

Sachs said, "Someone was arguing with him. Telling him to go ahead . . . to do something . . . but I couldn't hear . . ."

The green light came on again, and this time there was strain in the British-accented voice, which was clearly losing patience. "Colonel, the *Montana* is in immediate peril of being crushed. You've lost power, steering, and diving. You've got a nuclear reactor on board—possibly leaking. I must insist on assessing damage. I expect the arrival of our icebreaker *Snow Dragon* imminently. I'm sure that our governments will work out any details. That part is for diplomats. Meanwhile, we must prevent an environmental catastrophe, I know you will agree."

I saw more activity on the other deck now. A hatch open. Figures climbing out. My stall time was over.

I said, "That won't be possible."

"Colonel, if you act aggressively, I will be forced to defend myself and I fear that many sick and injured men may be harmed. I am trying to be reasonable."

This was followed a moment later by a gasp on my headpiece, and Pettit's startled, "Shit, Colonel! They're on the pressure ridge! They circled behind us!"

Zhou Dongfeng gave me a few moments to appreciate the situation. A line of Chinese troops had showed themselves a hundred yards from the survivors, at the ridge, and then sank back in place. Our entire party was now caught in a potential cross fire; the *Montana*—and the little collection of life rafts, tents, and sleds—sat dead in the sights of their torpedoes. The Marines were in plain view of Zhou's soldiers on the ridge. Almost everyone in my care would be decimated in seconds if the Chinese opened fire.

Chief, get that electricity working!

I said, "I hardly find your actions friendly."

"Please, Colonel. Pure precaution. After all, your twenty-five Marines," he said, naming the exact number of troops here, "could misunderstand our purpose."

"I think I understand that purpose quite well."

Captain Zhou said, "I'll send some helpers over. You will, of course, allow them aboard."

■ ■ ■

The ice was groaning out there, straining, and the tearing noises came again, echoing in the wind. It sounded like laughter. Someone was pulling at my sleeve. It was Clinton. He pointed at the Chinese radio. He wanted me to turn it off. He seemed to have something important to say. So far he'd come through each time he'd suggested solutions, so I shoved the Chinese unit into my parka, in case the thing still relayed talk, even when its light was red. As in, they'd given me a trick unit.

■ ■ ■

Clinton whispered, "Ten minutes!"

"Meaning?"

"Hold them off for ten minutes. It will change then."

"How?"

Clinton swore, in Iñupiat. He gripped my sleeve and looked out over the landscape. He hissed at me, as the Chinese boarders climbed into three Zodiacs, "You all keep forgetting that ice is not land! It's moving. All the time! It's not land so it won't stay where it is!"

I looked out and took in the scene: the oxbow-shaped "river," which was actually a lead between floes, the "shore," which was actually two fields of ice, neither one land, and the Chinese sub facing us.

He was right. In my mind, those boundaries had seemed as fixed as if we were facing off in the Hudson River.

But it was not a river.

"The ice will help us," Clinton said.

I still did not understand.

"Look at the damn currents, Colonel."

"They're going in all directions."

"That's the point." Now he looked angry. "I was in the goddamn Army, Colonel. I'm a veteran. Those assholes are not getting this submarine," he said. "When the ice speaks . . . *do what you have to do!*"

■ ■ ■

Captain Zhou was back. "I must insist, Captain, that your Marines stop moving, and stay in one place."

I pretended the radio was broken again.

He said, "If you can hear me, Colonel, I will count to ten, then my men will assume hostile intent and be forced to fire defensively if the Marines keep moving. One . . . two . . ."

I told the Marines to stop moving. They halted, spread out, about forty feet from the sub, in easy range of the Chinese on the ridge, and close enough to the ice edge to be killed by a torpedo.

I asked Karen over our Motorola, "If the chief gets power, can you help in any way in arming torpedoes, in launching them?"

"I'm familiar with the system."

"And?"

"We'll do our best. But if you launch this close—"

"Just do it," I said.

■ ■ ■

Zhou said, "By the way, Colonel, we have excellent hearing over here, and should any machinery switch on in your vessel—hydraulics, doors—I will be forced to assume hostile intent."

He was no fool. There was only one possible way to stop or slow him for Clinton's ten minutes, and I went for it.

I told Zhou part of the truth. "Captain, we have a highly contagious and unidentified disease on board. We will be able to solve the problem, I'm sure, in a short while, but for the moment, as you can see, we're in hazmat gear. It is not safe below, for you or for us."

Did he laugh, or was it just static I heard?

His men were now in their Zodiacs. They pushed off from his sub. There were wooden crates in there with them. For all I knew, they were bringing their own hazmats.

I tried again. "Captain, did you hear? We have a pathogen of unknown nature here. We're trying to determine its origin."

"Yes, I heard you. That is an interesting story, Colonel," he said, a new and harder note in his voice. "So, as I understand it, you admit that your vessel was carrying a bioweapon, which somehow got loose, infected your own crew."

I was stunned. This was the last possible response I'd envisioned.

"That is absolutely not what I am saying. There's no bioweapon!"

He had taken the truth the wrong way. But then another, horrifying thought hit me.

He's been right about everything else. Is it possible?

No, no, it's not possible, if it started with bodies brought aboard from a long time ago.

I said, "I'm telling you that we're close to determining the source of infection. Do you hear me? Captain?"

He was silent. The wind came up suddenly. The storm, which had been easing, grew instantly, violently worse. The snow fell harder. I could barely see him now, much less guess his intent.

Even the static grew louder.

I shouted into the set, and braced for gunfire or torpedoes. It was the worst possible moment for communication to fail.

FIFTEEN

"A bioweapon," he repeated, twenty seconds later.

At least the set worked, but I cursed the distance. I wished I could see his face. I wondered if he was in contact with Beijing. I wondered if he was alone in making decisions, as I was.

I said, stalling, as the snowfall thickened and ice pellets resumed their machine-gun rattle against steel, and the exposed areas on my face, "If it will help to convince you, please do send your physician. Take the blood samples. We would very much appreciate your medicines and any assistance in identifying the pathogen here."

I hope Clinton was right about the ten minutes.

The Marines remained in place, vague statues through snow, vulnerable to the Chinese guns, a very long forty feet from the sub. Even if they reached us, they'd have to clamber up those slippery ice blocks to reach the deck, backs exposed. If shooting started, they were doomed.

Captain Zhou said, "Good, I'll send over Dr. Liu, with the medicines."

I raised binoculars and saw shadow figures on the opposite bridge, one gesturing angrily, the other in a posture of subservience. He was playing for time, too. He had his own ideas of what to do. Andrew Sachs stood staring into my face with an intensity that I did not like, and I wished I understood what he was thinking.

I know you are angry, but why?

I also thought, *Zhou is using different satellites for communication than I am. Does his system work? Is he in contact with Beijing? He's not going to give up on the* Montana.

The green light went on and Zhou, back now, was straining at being cordial. "Come now, Colonel. What's the expression in America? The laying of the playing cards on a table? There was an accident. A release of an experimental toxin. Perhaps a defensive weapon only. Yes?"

What is he doing? Recording my answer? Recording this so the Chinese can release an American admission of guilt?

How can I convince him that I'm telling the truth?

Zhou suggested, "It got out of control, and made your crew sick."

"That's not what I'm saying."

"An accident. A warhead. Yes, a bad accident."

Between the static, the pellets pounding the hull, the stamping of Sachs to keep warm, and the wind, I was only vaguely aware of the new sound, a low vibration, like a far-off train, approaching through a tunnel.

"After all," Zhou continued, "your sub was conducting cold weather weapons trials in the North, was it not?"

Who tells them these things?

I said, "I won't comment on her mission, but please let me assure you—"

"Yes, I would like your assurance."

"The United States does not use biological weapons. They are illegal and immoral and we have signed every treaty banning them."

"I am familiar with immoral acts, Colonel. Like ramming a Chinese submarine last week in the South China Sea, causing the deaths of twenty-eight of our sailors."

He is recording this!

"That was a terrible accident," I said.

"Ah, *that* was the accident."

It struck me, with perverse humor, that Zhou had his torpedoes pointed at us, was attempting to steal the *Montana*, that he had sent soldiers to encircle us, and yet *he* was acting like the aggrieved party.

"The two things are not connected," I insisted.

Suddenly the hull beneath me lurched.

I looked down. We were not under power. So what had hit us? For a second, I feared it was a dud torpedo. Then I realized it had been ice.

Clinton jabbed me and nodded at the shore. There, the ice boulders had shifted slightly. The top ones had tumbled away and the pile now seemed a foot farther away from the hull than it had been a moment before.

Clinton nodded. *Five minutes*, he mouthed, holding up five gloved fingers. He'd removed his mitten for a moment to do it.

It occurred to me that the ice sounds might mask any noise coming from the *Montana*, if our power switched on.

I told Lieutenant Speck, "Get down there. Tell them what is happening, to get a torpedo ready and power on."

As he descended inside, he kept off his bulky head gear. He'd be breathing possibly contaminated air, risking his life to move faster. His resolve—and a vision of those men in the tents on the ice—fortified me.

I will save every one of you that I can.

The *Montana* lurched again, this time to a sound like fingernails on a blackboard. The vibration seemed to pass through the hull, to set the steel trembling beneath my mittens.

Clinton nudged me.

"See? Behind their submarine? *See?*"

I raised the binoculars and peered into the mass of flying ice pellets. I saw the ghost sub, and the vague line of ice pack behind it. The "shore" had been an inverted bow shape before. Now it was a jagged line, closer to the rear of the Chinese sub. Suddenly I understood exactly what Clinton had been telling me. My hope rose. If the ice pushed Zhou's sub, it could swing the bow away from us, and their midships toward us, and, if *we* kept moving also, then . . .

She'll be sitting in front of our tubes. The threat will be reversed.

I would have had no idea that the ice was about to move if not for Clinton. Zhou may be as ignorant as me. Neither of us knows ice.

I heard a *cr-ack* below, as if some large mass had snapped in half, and almost simultaneously, a soft hum sounded; a vague glow shone, and looking down, I saw yellow light inside. We had electrical power!

Had Zhou's people heard it come on?

There was no comment from the Chinese sub.

Well, the director said to scuttle her if I have to.

■ ■ ■

Their Zodiac boats, their boarding crew, were ready.

I felt the choice facing me as a series of emotions, played out in fractions of seconds. If broken into solid thoughts, they would have sounded like this.

My God, what do I do? Decide!

Which is more important, saving or scuttling the Montana, *or saving the people on the ice?*

The people.

And which is the best way to do that? To give Zhou what he wants? To try to scuttle the sub? To hope that the ice swings us around?

If I order a scuttle, if Zhou sees her listing, they'll try to board us before we go down, try to stop it. That will likely start a fight. My Marines won't have a chance.

If I give him what he wants, hand over the sub, there will be no reason for him to kill us.

No, that's not right. He's angry about the collision with the Chinese sub last week. He's already committed an act of war; and he's doing it because he knows no one can see what is going on. If he leaves witnesses, he risks escalation.

I have no idea what he's been commanded to do.

Is Zhou so cold-blooded that he'd order the murder of the entire party onshore?

Maybe he's been ordered to do that.

He already tricked us once, parlaying while he sent his troops to circle us.

Do I want to risk finding out if he'll honor his promise, if I hand over the Montana?

Hell, let him take the sub, order in his men, and let the damn sickness take them all and send him to the bottom, screaming with pain.

I made my decision, what to do.

■ ■ ■

I felt another jolt, and this time the ice to which we were chained broke off, and the bow of the *Montana* began to swing into the lead.

At the same time I saw a jagged crevice open and snake four hundred yards east, missing the Marines, and tents. The pack—on my side of the lead—was breaking up fast.

I did not know if Zhou was aware of this. His Zodiacs were now a hundred yards off and closing. I put my mouth to the Marine radio, and felt the "on" switch give beneath my three-finger mitten.

"Major Pettit, slowly, move position, flanking."

"Yes, sir."

"Chief Apparecio?"

"Torpedoes in tubes one and three, sir."

"What do you need to do in order to fire them?"

In the worsening storm, the Chinese submarine dimmed to a bulky outline. The figures on their deck disappeared. The Zodiacs were dark gliding dots. My Marines would now be invisible to the Chinese gunners on the pressure ridge, a hundred yards from the survivors.

I heard a groaning sound from "shore" and a reverberating echo—a tremendous burst of thunder—followed by loud crackling. I could not make out what was happening on the ice pack behind Zhou. But the outline of the Chinese sub was suddenly swinging around in a manner too fast to be caused by his engines, and in a direction contrary to where he wanted to be. His bow went in sixty seconds from facing us to facing left. The ice was pushing him, fast.

Zhou was probably giving frantic commands. *Back up. Reverse engines. Get us out of here. Fight the push.*

On my Motorola, Apparecio's voice came through, loud and clear for once. "Ready, sir. There's a good chance they'll hear the outer doors if I open 'em up, although with all this noise, who knows? After that, two seconds to hit a switch."

"Open the outer doors. But don't fire."

"Yes, sir."

Here goes, I thought.

I pushed the button on the Chinese radio. I watched the little emerald light twinkle on. If the other sub managed to overcome the pushing ice, I'd lose my advantage. It would only last a few minutes at best.

"Captain Zhou? You are now sitting directly in front of our open torpedo tubes. We are ready to fire. You will immediately order your men on the ice to throw down their arms. You can then bring them back aboard. I have a translator with me and want to hear your order go out. I want to hear your men respond. I want that right now!"

Silence.

"Captain, you threatened me and now you have thirty seconds before I fire. Twenty-nine . . . eight . . ."

Sachs had stopped translating and was screaming, "No, don't!" His eyes were wide with panic inside his balaclava.

Zhou had been ready to fire and I was, too.

A burst of Chinese came from their radio. Zhou was giving orders, I guessed from the tone. Andrew Sachs stopped shouting. He seemed to deflate.

"He's telling them to leave their weapons. He's telling them not to fight, and, and *they're acknowledging!*"

My knees were weak. But it was not over yet. I kept Zhou's channel open while I gave Pettit instructions, trying to keep my voice steady, which was not the way I felt at all. "Major Pettit, pick up your weapons and escort the Chinese out of there, to their Zodiacs. Treat them politely. Treat them like guests. They are bringing us medicines. Their people are going back to their sub."

"Yes, sir." For the first time, I heard admiration in his voice.

"Captain Zhou, I hope you heard that. It will do neither of us any good if we fight. You are not going to get the *Montana*, and there is no bioweapon aboard. Turn around. Go home safely."

No answer. But he was there; I felt his fury and humiliation coming over the line, more palpable than words, as if the set itself were breathing, issuing malevolence into the air.

I added, "Captain? Just so you know, I meant what I said about the sick. If you still wish to provide medicine, I welcome it, with thanks. Those medicines could save lives. I do not think we will provide you with blood samples, though. Probably it is better to limit contact, at this point, between our crews."

No answer. It was funny how the striations in the radio set, the plastic lines, resembled a mouth, set hard, set straight.

"I would appreciate your word of honor, Captain. No fighting. Sir? I need to hear you say it."

"I . . . give . . . it."

I thought, hope rising, *This is going to work.*

Out there the soldiers would be moving toward each other, in the storm that never stopped, like two dangerous electrical currents that needed to be kept apart or they'd spark. Two groups of distrustful men.

Yes, it was going to work, I thought. It was. But, of course, just when you think that, things go wrong. The ice cracked somewhere, a single, high-pitched snap that sounded, quite unfortunately, to me, like the firing of a bullet.

And once the first "shot" was fired, the real shooting erupted, all around.

SIXTEEN

The Arctic murders by illusion. Refracted light forms a rescue ship you rush to meet, only to plunge into frigid water. Floes seem solid but you better not step on one. A ridge of ice snaps off, quick and loud as a bullet.

"Ground fire! Ground fire! Ten o'clock!" a voice on the Marine band radio yelled.

In the storm, it sounded like a whole army was fighting. The cacophony included the thump of Marine M203 grenade launchers, the three-round bursts of M4s, the crack of Chinese bullpups, and always, like low rumbling laughter beneath it, the straining field of ice.

The radio net was alive with voices of men groping and calling out through the storm, shooting blind, trying to pinpoint the origin of enemy gunfire.

"Bowhead one-two, bowhead one-two. This is bowhead three. Do you hear me? Over."

"Shots coming from Sierra echo, that's a bull."

"Go! Go! On the left, take him out!"

"I got hoofprints in the snow, bowhead one-two."

I shouted, "Cease fire! Cease fire! It was the ice breaking off!"

The echoes rose, fell. There was no way to know where anyone was located.

"For Christ's sake, cease fire, Marines!"

I had a sickening flash of the injured and sick from the submarine, torn apart by fire. The tents, Eddie, the grouped sleds, caught in a cross fire or mowed down by the Chinese. The sick, strapped down, were too weak to free themselves and crawl away to seek even bare cover.

"Get down!"

I did not know if the combatants knew the location of each other. The likelihood of being hit by a stray bullet was as great as being struck by an aimed one. I shouted over the Motorola for Chief Apparecio and Karen Vleska *not to fire a torpedo!*

Did they even hear me?

Major Pettit and his squad leaders directed men to spread out, crawl toward the pressure ridge, or the sleds. They'd be humpbacked forms, wriggling toward the last place they'd seen the Chinese, who would naturally be somewhere else by now.

On the Chinese set I heard another stream of shouts.

Andrew Sachs bore up well, considering his civilian status. He remained rational, and seemed horrified. "Now someone's yelling about a bear! A polar bear! Is that what started it? A starving bear and . . ." He was laughing now, but not sanely. "A damn bear! This place!"

"Tell me everything they say."

"Now someone is warning them that we've got one of their radios. Saying we're monitoring what they say."

The Chinese radio went silent.

There came the *cr-ack* of rounds overhead, and then a zipping noise, which meant that whoever was firing had adjusted angle so that the bullets came level with my head. I pulled Sachs down. A barrage slammed into the bridge. My M4 was up but I didn't fire back. It was possible that a Marine was shooting out there. I shoved the Chinese radio at Sachs and bellowed for him to tell them—yell into the set no matter what—that we hadn't started it, to stop firing, to say I was trying to get our guys to stop, too.

"This is Colonel Rush! Cease fire, Marines!"

Sachs said that the Chinese had probably switched bands. But he kept turning dials and babbling into the set. Maybe he'd been the one to tell them to switch bands in the first place. I had no idea what he was really saying.

"Doc! Doc! Freed is down!"

"Enemy incoming! Rapid fire!"

Then I heard Major Pettit. "If you keep firing, Crowley, that hand-set of yours will get shoved up where the sun never shines. The colonel said to shut it down!"

Nobody *likes* being shot at. If you hear the other side stopping, you tend to do it, too.

The shooting—at least the U.S. side—seemed to be slackening, or was it my imagination?

The bullpups fell silent.

All the firing stopped.

There was only wind now, like laughter, and the groaning of men, and someone screaming.

I tried to reach Eddie. "Major Nakamura?"

"All good here, Colonel." I felt some relief that he was okay. "Nobody hurt, but they goddamn shot up the snow, holy shit, son of a bitch! They killed the goddamn snow two hundred times. That snow is deader than Julius Caesar."

I switched handsets. "Captain Zhou? Can you hear me?"

Stiffly, after moving bandwidths, on the third try, I heard an answer, flat and cold. He'd probably turned his radios on again. "I hear you."

"It was the ice started it. Or possibly a bear. We did not fire first."

Silence. Did he believe me? He had to know I could have torpedoed his vessel, and hadn't. He must have been waiting for the impact and explosion on his end. He must have heard his own guys yelling about the bear.

I tried again. "Captain Zhou."

The interpreter's voice said grudgingly, "The captain says he knows about the bear, Colonel."

I ordered Chief Apparecio, so that Zhou could hear, "Scuttle her. Open the sea cocks or torpedo tubes. Set explosives. Do whatever you can do as fast as possible and get out."

"Yes, Colonel."

I told Zhou, "Let's continue what we started. Tend the wounded. Take your men aboard. If you still wish to give us medicines, thank you. Then let's go home."

■ ■ ■

Pettit reported the Chinese soldiers filing back to their Zodiacs, carrying two wounded. Pettit commandeered one of their Zodiacs. The Chinese would get their weapons back when they reached the sub. I knew that combat could still break out again at any provocation.

Sachs asked me, as we climbed down to the ice, as the roar of water flooding into the sub reached us, as the sub began listing and ice crept closer to the bridge, "Do you really think he'll go away?"

"No. I think he'll submerge and wait for orders. But I'm not about to blow up a Chinese submarine and start World War Three."

I told Zhou, feigning bitterness, giving him some bragging rights at home, some face, giving him a recording of the American commander, "If it weren't for you, we could have kept her afloat, Zhou. Could have saved her."

Let his bosses think that Zhou caused us to lose a $2.4 billion submarine. Well, technically speaking, he did.

But I still have to figure out what is making the Montana *crew sick! That sickness may be more dangerous than losing the submarine.*

Maybe my gesture did it. Maybe Zhou would have done it anyway. But he sent over two Zodiacs loaded with crates of medicines, a few of them the same ones we carried, the same ones any prudent doctor would start out with against the symptoms I'd seen in those tents and life rafts. It was funny, I thought, eyeing the Chinese and English logos on the crates, the names of the companies that supplied both countries, funny because our weapons to kill each other were different. But our medicines to save lives were the same.

Everyone seemed shaken, but glad to be alive.

■ ■ ■

She went down slowly at first, tipping forward at the bow, where the torpedo tubes were flooding. Then the long cylinder shape started sliding forward. I watched the eel-like form glide into the frothing lead, sending up spray . . . and then there was only a fin in the air . . . and then that, too, was gone, only foam indicating that the craft had ever been there.

Two dead Marines lay in the snow. Two others, wounded and bandaged and shot up with morphine, could not pull sleds. Now we had Marine patients. Thirty sailors from the *Montana* lay coupled on sleds, in various stages of illness, some slack from drugs, some glaze-eyed with exhaustion or fever, the worst hacking up yellow bile, putrid bits of contagion that left a trail on the snow.

As for the dead, I hated giving the next order. Leave them. There were not enough sleds to move them, and we needed every spare second to get the needy to safety, if we wanted them to live. Later—after the storm passed—another mission could be dispatched to collect the bodies or incinerate them, depending on what—in the end—had made them ill.

The Marines wanted to take their dead, but I told Pettit, in no uncertain terms, that if we did that, we'd have a riot on our hands from the *Montana* survivors, who would demand the same treatment for their friends.

No one was happy. But Pettit understood. The healthier *Montana* crew would help pull sleds. Clinton would lead us back toward the *Wilmington*, or at least the direction in which our radio locators said she'd be.

The Chinese sub was gone, at least on the surface. Eddie skied beside me in silence for a while.

"You think Zhou's directly underneath us, or to the right or left?" he said, eyeing the ice rubble field.

"What I want to know is, who's talking to him?"

We looked over the moving figures, the jagged line probing its way back toward the warmth of the *Wilmington*, if Clinton could help find her again.

"Sachs?" Eddie threw out a name.

"He speaks Chinese. He wanted us to hand over the sub. But he did a good job during the fighting."

"Our lovely Karen Vleska?"

"Hell, she knows so much anyway, she could just tell them half the things they want to know. She didn't need to come all the way here to do that."

"Is that logic talking, or love?"

"Eddie!"

"Okay, okay. Clinton, then? He's always there when we need something, always around."

"What are you saying? That the most helpful guy is guilty because he helps?"

"Well, if the truth was obvious, we'd know it by now."

Glumly, I concurred. "A lot of the Iñupiats do have relatives in Russia."

"And what exactly does Russia have to do with China?"

"I'm just saying," I snapped. "You know. They're both rivals."

"I keep going back to Sachs. Or Del Grazo. Mr. Communications. We never think about him. He knows how to fix equipment, so he knows how to screw it up. He looks over everyone's shoulder, and no one looks over his," Eddie said. "He could be the one, plain and simple."

"I thought of that. Plus, Del Grazo kept pointing his finger at Clinton."

"Like you did back there?"

"Del Grazo was in every meeting."

I looked back at Del Grazo, who was skiing beside a sled and talking to one of the wounded Marines, Del Grazo bending to adjust the man's blanket. He was a constant positive presence. Only in our upside-down world would support constitute a clue.

"Pettit was in the meetings, too," Eddie mused. "Hey, that would be great if your ex-wife's paramour turned out to be a spy. She always did have bad judgment in men. I mean, look who she married."

"Not funny. I don't think it's Pettit. I think the Chinese had someone in place on the ship before we got there, someone monitoring the original mission. That's more logical than them lucking out and managing to place someone inside an emergency rescue so fast."

"More logical, but not necessarily right."

I sighed. We scanned our sled convoy. Ahead looked like behind. The ice rumbled below, as unstable as a tropical volcanic island. I heard a tearing noise, like fabric ripping, and felt the surface heave suddenly. There came a single tremendous lurch and a crevasse ripped open, running past us, widening, faster than we were, a maw a mere terrifying eight yards to our right.

The ice settled down again.

"Shit," Eddie said, awed and horrified and remembering, as I was, how we'd left the *Montana* site just as the lead closed and the two floes crashed together behind us, a convulsion that pulverized in seconds ice edges that had been solid moments before. The earth was unstable. The groaning never stopped. It occurred to me far to the south, in the marble halls of Washington, men in comfortable chairs called this process "global warming." There it was academic dinner argument. Here I watched a planet disintegrate before my eyes.

"Eddie, we need to get these people inside, and warm," I said, realizing how right the Eskimos were when they gave ice a hundred names, treated it like an animal. "And I wish we could have found that film, the goddamn film."

Eddie nodded toward the sleds thoughtfully. "The latency period for spread . . . if we're going to start getting it, too, I wonder, once we're on board, how long before—"

I cut him off, snapped, "I just almost started a war to save these people. I'm not losing any more, not abandoning them to die, or fall in when the ice cracks open again."

"Hey, I'm with you, man. I'm just saying."

"Well, don't just be saying. Figure out what made them sick. Be useful, for Christ's sake. For all we know, the antibiotics will knock it, or weaken it. Two days from now they'll all be better. Scare over. Welcome home, Marines."

Eddie hesitated. "That movie, what year do you think it was made, Numero? It was old, the chief said. Nineteen sixty? Nineteen eighty?"

"We'll never know."

"Ah, maybe it was old porno. Maybe it was bullshit. Hey, remember those monkeys, One?"

"I never forget them."

"I dream about them sometimes, and in the worst dreams the monkeys get human faces. People I love. Then ones I don't know. One gets sick. Then another. Buses. Trains . . ."

We skied in silence for a while. There was some small comfort in mindlessness, but then I reminded myself that to do anything mindlessly out here could be fatal. Simple relaxation was not an option.

Eddie said in a low voice, "Thirteen forty-seven."

"You're filled with happy thoughts today," I said.

I halted and our eyes met through the slits of our balaclavas. He'd finally mouthed the nightmare that loomed over this whole mission since I'd found out that the sickness had preceded the fire aboard the *Montana*, that—with the sailors coughing on the sleds—would have occurred to any doctor in our unit.

"Marseille," I said, naming the French Mediterranean port that was famed for its role that year. "*Yersinia pestis*," I said, naming the infamous passenger that had come ashore there in 1347.

I knew that Eddie and I both were seeing the first map that we'd been shown when we'd joined the unit. It was a map of the past—the year that the black plague sailed out of Astrakhan, in central Russia, tacking its way south to Sarai, on the Sea of Azov, and then past the great Turkish port of Constantinople, until the tiny, cramped ship docked at Marseille.

"To burn through Europe," I said.

"Yeah," said Eddie miserably as we stood to the side and watched the progression of sleds pass, pulled by healthier Marines and Navy guys. Del Grazo helped. So did Sachs. Karen Vleska skied up front with Clinton.

The nightmare of nightmares had started *on a ship*. One ship that disgorged, along with coughing sailors, a few rats. Black ones, not the brown kind you see in the New York transit system. *Rattus rattus*. Rats that carried fleas. Fleas that carried bacteria. Bacteria that entered human bloodstreams when the fleas bit a dockside vendor or two, maybe a beggar with his hand out, maybe a fat, fur-clad merchant in his rich home overlooking the port.

Day one, a scattering of men and women, just a handful, scratching idly at their ankles and wrists, where fleas bite. Same day, a few locals grow feverish and have headaches. By day three, even for the strong people, here come the chills, first like a cold coming on, then chills become shakes and shakes become convulsions, and those little bite marks bloom into buboes, and soon after that, *other* family members who touched the sick, or breathed air they exhaled, maybe fed them a bit of soup, maybe told them a bedtime story, maybe changed a bandage, *they* began to get fevers, too.

"We may not know what our guys have," I told Eddie, eyeing a moaning man being hauled past by a Marine. "But the good news is, it is definitely not the plague."

"Ninety-five percent," Eddie said.

Which was the percentage of people who contracted pneumonic plague who perished from it across Europe. *A kill rate of 95 percent.* Add in people who got just regular old plague, black plague, not the pneumonic kind, and you ended up with between thirty and seventy million dead. Clinically speaking, hiding horror with math, the way scientists prefer to do it, that was an overall 30 to 75 percent death rate, all starting with a couple of skinny, hungry *rattus rattuses* jumping off one ship in Marseille.

One ship.

And in *those* days far fewer people lived on Earth. And there were no airplanes, cars, and trains to spread things.

"I'm not letting some scare story keep our guys from getting all the care they need," I said. "Whatever it is, it isn't going to be another 1347."

"Absolutely." Eddie nodded.

But, I thought, we were heading for a ship, and that ship would hopefully take us back to Barrow, and Barrow had an airport, and cars, and trucks, and planes that took people—tourists, locals, scientists—all over the world so . . . well . . . you get the picture Eddie was painting.

Stop being paranoid.

I told Eddie wearily, "Take off the rose-colored glasses, Eddie. Stop being so positive about things."

"Why didn't the director tell us they knew about the sickness, One? Or the bodies they took aboard?"

"We'll ask him when we can. Maybe he didn't know."

"You have some decisions to make before we reach the ship."

I stopped and my voice hardened. "No I don't. I made them."

He leaned closer, but I didn't give him the opportunity to say any more.

I snapped, "You want us to leave them on the ice? Walk away? Is that what you're saying? How about us then? You and me? The Marines? Everyone here? We were all there. Because if it's what you're saying, have the guts to outright say it instead of making stupid jokes."

He looked hurt. "That isn't what I was saying."

"No? Then you tell me, Doctor, what *were* you saying? Leave them on unstable ice near the ship? Throw them in the water? Inject them with too much morphine? Just what the fuck were you saying? Half these people won't last till tomorrow, we do that."

He lowered his eyes.

"Not a word about this," I ordered. "We don't even know what it is, and we'll beat it. They didn't have antibiotics in 1347, they didn't have one percent of what we do—and their medical world was about as efficient as America's health care plan. We're going to save these people. That's all I want to hear, so otherwise shut up."

He said nothing, but I knew what he was thinking.

"Eddie, this has nothing to do with what happened in Afghanistan. I'm not making up for that now."

"Sure, One. I know that."

"I would do the same thing either way. In Afghanistan, we knew what we were dealing with. Here we don't. That's the difference."

"I know. I do. Absolutely."

"You're not the one making the decisions."

"And I'm glad of that."

"Then make it easier instead of being an asshole."

He dropped back. He skied alone. Later I saw him tending to the sick, and he did not flinch or pull back or spare them any attention. He was a good doctor. He knew he was in harm's way. We didn't speak for the next few hours. I felt bad that I'd snapped at him. He'd only been sharing things, not trying to make me change my mind. He had every right to be terrified. He had every right to share his thoughts with his best friend.

Thirteen forty-seven, I thought, pushing forward and gliding, pushing and gliding, hearing the hacking men over the swoosh of runners on snow. The storm was lessening again, although by now, having been through several false endings, I fully expected the wind to rise up again at any moment.

Del Grazo knelt, back to wind, and picked up the radio locator signal from the *Wilmington*, and it turned out that we'd gone off point, but only by a few degrees. Clinton had been taking a generally accurate path.

"Two miles to go, Colonel. We're just about there."

I looked into his eyes. I saw black irises, cooperation, hope.

"Thanks, Del Grazo."

"Hey, no problem, sir."

A New York phrase, not Chinese. Well, I thought, if he's a spy for China, he's not going to run around saying things like, *As Confucius said and my spymaster stressed, he who learns but does not think is lost!*

"Two-hour rest behind those ice ridges, out of the wind, then we push through the rest of the way!"

Del Grazo said, "I'll try the sat phones again."

■ ■ ■

"Knock, knock?"

Dr. Vleska's head poked around the ice boulder that I leaned against, lee side of a pressure ridge, giving us cover from the wind. We'd broken out hot chocolate. It would be too involved to get the sick into tents, too laborious to unload and load them again, so we'd broken out the portable propane heaters and fired 'em up and circled sleds around them, or clustered in groups, like bums of the Arctic around trash can fires.

The privilege of command. I had my own private heater.

Her eyes looked big inside the slit of the black balaclava, ice blue and touched with white, a dime-sized patch of frostbite forming above the left brow.

"I have only three boxes of Girl Scout cookies left," she said. "Well, that's what I used to tell people at every house, when I was a kid, till all the boxes were sold. Effective sales technique. If I said one box, they just ordered one. But if I said three, they ordered them all. I tried four once, but that was too much. Interesting question. Why does three work and four fail? Harvard will jump at the cookie study, ten-million-dollar grant."

"Got mint chocolate?"

She nodded approvingly. "Popular item, especially in the Arctic. It's that cool sensation in your throat."

"I'll take three boxes."

"Can I sit down?"

"You already have."

"Who's the spy?"

Once again, the on-again, off-again storm was lessening. The thermometer was up to a balmy four degrees. I'd taken my turn at hauling a sled and now felt sweat drying, bad idea in the Arctic. I sipped hot chocolate and stared at her, my question obvious. *How do you know?*

"Give me a break," she answered, sitting, baggy snow pants akimbo, like a girl attending a yoga class. Her back was straight. She probably did go to yoga. She said, "That Chinese captain knew you were a colonel. He knew how many Marines we had. *Who* told him, do you think?"

When I just smiled, she held out her wrists.

"Oh, it's me? You going to handcuff me?"

Is she flirting? Or just probing? When in doubt, always answer a question with a question. I said, "Who do *you* think it is?"

"You."

I started to laugh. I couldn't help it. It was the relief that I needed. Just a great big circle, being out on the ice, I thought. Let's just all kill each other. Let's sit around like an old British drawing-room play and figure out who's the one.

"Well," she said, "no one checks on you, do they? *You* have the best access to communication. *You* get information first. *You* had that one-on-one talk with Captain whatever his name was. *You* magically stop the shooting. And," she said, leaning close, "*you sank my sub.*"

"As in, the whole crazy thing was coordinated?"

"Plans *can* work once in a while."

"How do you explain the bear showing up?"

"If you were a spy, you'd say that very thing!"

"What can I say? You nailed me."

This time when we looked into each other's eyes, I felt something different. We held the gaze for longer than politeness or accusation allowed. Whoever said, *Eyes are the windows of the soul,* didn't know what he was talking about. Eyes are curtains to prevent you from seeing. They're rabbits that climb out of a magician's hat. Eyes are the last thing you see smiling before a bullet slams into your midsection. I'll take pulse rate over eyes as clues any day of the week, and my rate was up.

She slid closer. There was a wet wool odor over the granular snow smell, and the oily propane, and the whiff of bad electronics. The hint of sweat-tinged perfume had to be the part manufactured in my head.

"I'm going to close my eyes a bit," I said, meaning she should go away.

She rose and her sigh came out as a thin cloud that expanded and dissipated. Her breath, if solidified, would resemble an icicle pointed at my throat.

"Well, if you're not the spy," she said, "then what you did back there was pretty remarkable."

I raised my brows.

"You didn't fire the torpedo. You stopped the fight. You prevented a massacre. You put everything on the line."

We watched each other.

"Surprised?" she said. "That I care more about the people than the submarine?"

"Your bosses hear that, they'll dock your pay. Two billion. That'll take a few years to work off," I said.

The way her hands hung for a moment conveyed a vulnerable awkwardness. She said, "Sometimes I have trouble saying the nicer things. I'm better at the other."

"My ex-wife was like that. Is it all women? Or just ones I know?"

"I don't understand why the Marines call you Killer. It doesn't seem right. It seems cruel. You're not a killer, are you? You can do it, but you'd rather not. So what is that about? They seem to have the wrong idea about you."

"Excellent interview technique," I said. "You ever leave Electric Boat, I can find a good berth for you at the unit, as an interrogator."

"Well, if you're not the spy, I guess I can give you this," she said, smiled, reached into her parka, and when I saw what she pulled out, the force of it pulled me to my feet. I could barely believe what I was seeing.

"The XO brought it out of the *Montana* when they abandoned ship. It was on one of their sleds. I found it while poking around, looking for rations. The man who had it—he was unconscious when we got there— woke up. He said the exec told him to get it to the rescuers, if any came."

The canister was old, all right, about a foot in diameter, olive colored, the universal hue of military issue. It was battered and dented and stamped on the metal container were the words PROPERTY OF U.S. ARMY.

"Pretty old," she said. "What do you think?"

"I have no idea."

"Nineteen fifty?"

"Your guess is as good as mine."

After she left, I sat staring at the canister, heart beating rapidly, but whether from her visit, or the object in my hand, I was unsure. I slid off a mitten. Instantly the air closed around my fingers like a cold vise, and I knew that even to touch frigid metal could stick skin to it, and bring on severe frostbite.

I put the mitten back on and considered using one of the ski poles to pry the can open, but in a storm, with wind blowing, I knew that old film—if it was even stable—could easily crumble or be destroyed by such savage elements. I shook the canister. Something rattled around inside, all right. Was it cellulose nitrate? Was it even a clue?

Don't get so excited. You'll do something stupid. You'll ruin it before even seeing it.

Karen Vleska seemed to be watching from twenty feet off, where she knelt beside a sled and an injured man. I wished I could see inside the canister, wished I had x-ray vision, like Superman did in movies I loved as a kid. PROPERTY OF U.S. ARMY. It was the color of uniforms, vehicles, canteen covers. It was an announcement confirming that the film inside related to death.

Reluctantly, I put the canister in my pack. It would have to wait for opening on the *Wilmington*.

Twenty minutes later we saddled up again, and moved out.

■ ■ ■

I saw an upside-down ship in the distance, hanging in the sky. It looked solid as the sun emerging through gray, at 4 A.M., to reveal the gigantic inverted icebreaker, a steel piñata. I gaped. Hundreds of thousands of pounds of solid metal floated upside down; decks, antenna, escape boats, winches. Everything else was inverted here. So why not logic itself?

As we got closer, the upside-down antenna seemed to lower and then I saw a second *Wilmington*, right side up, beneath it, on the sea. Two ships of equal size, identical images, yin and yang, foot by foot.

Closer still, the mirage started to merge with the real ship, and then the sun broke out, and suddenly an enormous prism filled the sky, like a pipe organ in a cathedral, a shining rainbow that made the two ships less distinct. Then the two ships blurred, and then abruptly, the one in the air vanished. The welcome form of the red hull was dead ahead, at about a half mile, and it was coming toward us, breaking ice.

Eddie came up beside me.

"Murphy's Law," he said. "As soon as you reach the stuck ship, it's able to move again."

With binoculars we could see men and women lining the prow, waving. They seemed to be celebrating that we were alive, and their joy made my plan for them crueler, more dangerous, but I pushed that notion away.

I was thinking that Eddie had been right earlier. In less than twenty minutes, when we rejoined the *Wilmington*, I would take the biggest risk of my life. Because it involved more than just my life, but the lives of others.

Am I doing this because of what happened two years ago?

I was going to put the sick aboard the *Wilmington*, and gamble that we could figure out what ailed them and at the same time prevent the thing inside them from spreading.

I would gamble that we were smarter than a germ, and that the thing inside them was smaller than our ability to stop it.

The ship got closer, and the image I saw merged into some other version, a past one.

I saw a memory all too clearly, and it was one that I wished had been the mirage.

SEVENTEEN

Majors Joe Rush and Edward Nakamura looked down from the open door of the Chinook helicopter taking them and twenty Marines south from Kandahar Air Base toward one more alleged hidden biological laboratory, this time near the Afghan border with Pakistan and Iran, in the southwest.

The base commander had been taken aback by two officers from Washington appearing out of nowhere, irritated at the "special orders" requiring cooperation, and reluctant to release the copter. He'd argued that the aircraft was needed for a raid on the Taliban, to the north.

"We'll need Marines, too," Rush had replied.

Joe and Eddie had been chasing rumors, a whisper in a village bazaar, a prostitute's boast, a tip from a beggar, a monitored e-mail, a voice fragment on an NSA phone snag. This time the "information" had come from a bloody man strapped in a basement chair, screaming for the Afghan security officers beating him to stop: "They're mixing chemicals!"

Eddie said, as the copter hit an air pocket, "Another wild-goose chase, want to bet?"

After all, the "hidden lab" in Teyvareh had turned out to be nothing more than a filthy pharmacy the size of a closet, its cracked glass shelves filled with ten-year-old aspirin, and dried seaweed that the "druggist" called Viagra. The "cave of equipment" near Daulet Yar had been deserted, burned charcoal as evidence that the Taliban had once used it. They'd found a pile of gnawed goat bones, and a latrine area crawling with rock rats, but nothing else.

There was no doubt in Rush's mind that Al-Qaeda sought biological weapons the world over—sending buyers to Russia, for stockpiled chlorine bombs; to Syria, wanting nerve gas; to Sudan, where hidden labs toyed with that country's strain of the Ebola virus.

Phone calls had been picked up by satellites, snatched e-mails pored over in Virginia.

Back in D.C., Joe and Eddie had sat with the director, peering at Manila passport control shots of men claiming to be "importers" when in fact they sought germs or chemicals for use against U.S. troops, or targets like London. Madrid. New York.

"I didn't know they even had lakes in Afghanistan," Eddie said now, looking down.

"They dried up," Joe said.

"Look, there it is, a goddamn ship laying in a desert," Eddie said, as the copter angled down, as the pilots strained forward, nervous, watching for white puffs below, streaking smoke tails marking the flight of shoulder-fired missiles rising from the mud flats, skimpy cornfields, watermelon patches, and refugee camp, the entire vista pathetic remnants of what had once been one of the most magnificent lakes in Central Asia.

The man strapped down in Kabul had told the Afghan officers, while Eddie tried not to throw up, "The doctor from Pakistan made the ship into a laboratory. They put explosives on the bottom of oil drums, chemicals on top."

"I read about this region," said Eddie, fixing the strap on his helmet.

"Used to be otters here, leopards, and freshwater farming. Look at this mess. It's worse than Secaucus. A thousand-square-mile dump."

They passed over a mass of tents, through a gray cloud formed by four thousand cooking fires. The acrid smell of human waste and swamp washed through the open gunner's door. Nine miles later they set down on a slightly raised area, on cracked hard earth, surrounded by softer clay, from which tall reeds sprouted like the last stubby hairs on the skull of an eighty-year-old with cancer. The Marines jumped out and, to Joe's orders, rapid stepped through a foot-wide path in the reeds, their brittle straw-colored tops higher than the moving helmets, toward the now-invisible wreck lying like a dead whale three hundred yards away.

The only sounds were mud sucking at their boots, and flies. Joe glanced down to see, discarded, an empty canvas sack stenciled UNAID. Something living wriggled inside it. A rat or snake. He saw a mud-spattered Little Debbie snack cake, still in the wrapper, Debbie beaming, probably surprised that she'd landed ten thousand miles from home. He saw a wad of crumpled International Herald Tribune that some smuggler probably used as toilet paper. The whole place was a cornucopia graveyard for manufactured crap from the first world, where Hostess Twinkies and Dallas Cowboys T-shirts go to die.

The prisoner in Kabul had been a clerk in a hotel, a small, soft man, picked up by Afghan security guys after he left one of their agency-run brothels. Under torture he'd started crying. Eddie had gone outside, after watching what the officers did to him, and had been sick.

But with his functioning left hand, the prisoner had drawn a map smeared with blood, and later, a passing satellite had confirmed the location of the wreck, but spotted no human movement, then glided away, in the void, where military eyes peer at rooftop laundry, seeking hidden antennas in souks far below.

"*They make the gasses there,*" *the man had gasped.*

Eddie said, "Iran to the west, Pakistan to the south. Welcome to smuggler heaven. Even if the ship houses a lab, five to one it's for heroin."

The vista opened up abruptly and the ship lay ahead, on its side, as if it had fallen from the sky. Was it rigged to explode? The men sank into mud the color of iron oxide. Flies rode each air molecule. The heat made the ship shimmer, and it seemed larger, the closer they got. Once it had been a fish factory. Its nets had pulled glistening masses of catch from the lake. Now the lake was a thin layer of dirty water hosting bottom feeders and speedboats, but no longer heavy craft.

Once this discarded rust bucket had provided food and respect for locals. Those days, and benefits, were gone.

Eddie said, "Boot and sandal prints. At least twenty guys. Truck tracks, too, light here, then heavy. Was it delivering or removing cargo from the wreck?"

"Major Rush, we found a ladder in the reeds!"

The Marines formed a cordon to protect Joe as he went up first, M4 ready. At the top he heard movement, but it was just a fat rat waddling down the slanting deck—owner, captain, crew.

They all reached the deck without incident.

Eddie let out an amazed breath, minutes later, when they opened the door of the former mess room.

"Fuck me, One. That clerk told the truth."

A lab.

■ ■ ■

The Marines roused two guards, teenage boys with AK-47s, asleep in a cabin where they'd been screwing. The stubs of two fat marijuana stogies lay on the deck beside them. The ship reeked of mold, hemp, sex, and piss.

"Where are the other men?" the Marine translator—a Yemeni immigrant from Orange County, California—demanded.

No answer.

The translator aimed a .45 at the head of one of the teenagers. Joe lowered it when the bluff didn't work.

The Marines reported the rest of the ship empty, then took up defensive positions on deck, in case whoever worked there came back.

"Major, they must have seen the copter," the lieutenant in charge of the squad said. "I suggest we hurry."

"Where'd they go?" said Eddie.

"Maybe they got invited across the lake for a Big Mac at the local Iranian Ministry of Intelligence Office. Maybe there's a clue in our little lab."

■ ■ ■

"Someone's done a pretty good job in the build-it-at-home league," Eddie said admiringly, and uneasily, some minutes later.

Joe eyed the "lab" by flashlight, danger ticking in his throat. The portholes had been welded over, so no outside light came in, no air could flow in or out. The fume hood and small vats were state of the art. Four large electric fans filled a jury-rigged anteroom, a sort of airlock welded between the cabin, and outer door to the passageway. The fans faced inward, to keep air from escaping. It was a primitive version of up-to-date biolabs. Air was never supposed to be able to escape those labs, in case something deadly got loose. Fort Detrick level fours had vacuum antechambers, air-sucking fans, and triple-sealed hinges. But the jury-rigged lab here used household fans from some desert bazaar. Add in rubber tubes, vacuum bottles, water hoses, bleach and water decontaminant, steel milk cans and pumps, and you got Dr. Frankenstein's lab-in-a-ship.

"Don't try this at home, kids," said Eddie. "Or you could wipe out your family."

"Whoever worked here had guts," Joe said.

"Maybe they don't care. All those virgins waiting for them in heaven. I never understood what's so great about virgins anyway. They thrash around and knee you in the groin," Eddie said.

"All women knee you in the groin."

There came, over the decrepit smells, whiffs of old alcohol and Lysol. Hanging in rusted steel lockers were chem suits, goggles, face masks, and on shelves, cardboard boxes filled with rubber gloves. There were three vintage Maytag refrigerators, but with no electricity on at the moment; whatever was inside would be moldy at best.

"Open it."

Eddie, biomask on, reached for the tarnished handle. Inside were racks of empty test tubes, empty vacuum jars. Both other fridges were empty.

Joe frowned. "That clerk said they had oil drums, made 'em into bombs."

There was a long wooden worktable, upon which a thick green ledger sat, except, when Joe opened it, it did not show rows of figures, but diagrams of oil drum bombs.

"Where are those oil drums now? What's in 'em?"

"Maybe those prisoners will tell us, although they don't exactly look like scientists. More like the dropouts hanging near the Taco Bell by my house, sniffing glue."

But then came—after months of frustration—one of those dumb luck moments that happen. Admiral Yamamoto's plane gets shot down after Americans break the Japanese war code. A Union soldier in the Civil War finds a discarded cigar box containing General Lee's secret orders, and the North wins the battle of Antietam. Two U.S. majors in Afghanistan find a ledger in an old desk. Flipping pages, they see lists of chemicals in English.

Methylphosphonyl difluoride.

Isopropyl alcohol.

Isopropylamine.

Eddie looked at Joe. "Oh no."

To bioexperts, those three chemicals were a signature.

Joe saw, in his head, aerial photos of the Kurdish city of Halabja, with bodies, about five thousand of them, dead in streets, squares, alleys, stadiums. Bloody Friday, the locals still called it. Nineteen eighty-eight, 150 miles north of Baghdad, when Saddam Hussein's gas shells rained down on the civilian population. Ten thousand injured. And thousands more to die in the coming days from vomiting and diarrhea, shortness of breath, convulsions, paralysis, from a gas that had been developed originally as a German pesticide.

"Sarin," said Joe.

It was three hundred times more toxic than cyanide. In even a mild form, released by terrorists in the Tokyo subway, it killed fourteen commuters in 1995. It was possibly the deadliest chemical weapon in existence, and Joe, staring at the ledger, belly hollow, said, "What else is in that book?"

The next page was about expenses, not sarin. Rice cost. Cheese cost, the Yemeni-born Marine translator said.

"One book for everything. Keep turning."

"Whoa, call the porno squad," said Eddie. "But tear out that top shot. Interesting position! Next!"

Next page showed a diagram of a big circle with jagged lines around it, maybe mountains, and arrows pointing from left to right, and little x's in the circle, and little y's inside the jagged lines. Men? Tents? Trucks? Planes?

"Who the hell is that?" Joe said at the next page.

This time they were eyeing four photos of a swarthy, handsome, dark-haired and uniformed U.S. Army corporal, and Arabic writing underneath. In two shots, the corporal stood before a small, neat, clapboard home, with Mideastern-looking parents, and a younger boy who looked like him, brother probably. The proud soldier back home.

In the next shot he was in Afghanistan, judging from the dun-colored desert and the rows of trucks in the rear.

Joe asked the translator, "What does the writing say?"

"It's his name. Rana Amir Khan."

"Why is he in this book?" said Eddie.

"I'm calling the director," said Joe.

Joe went out on deck, and powered up the sat phone. Sometimes the gizmos worked like magic. Sometimes, in seconds, your voice bounced off a sat and came down in Washington, and when you talked to the director's secretary, her precancerous smoker's voice came through as well as if she stood a foot away, shouting into a megaphone.

"The director is in a meeting, Major."

"Get him out, now."

■ ■ ■

Rana Amir Khan turned out to be, records said, the oldest son of Pakistani immigrants living in Mankato, Minnesota, Joe knew by the time he was back in Kandahar. Rana had graduated with straight B's from high school, then joined the Army Reserve, and was almost immediately sent overseas. When his tour was up, he was sent there again.

Under "religion" in his application, he'd checked "Moslem."

"Plenty of fine U.S. soldiers are Moslems," Eddie said.

"Their pictures are not in the ledger," Joe replied.

They left the ship/lab in flames and brought back the prisoners. By the time they reached Kandahar, the director was back on the line, having read the riot act to his contacts at the National Security Agency. Emergency search warrants had been acquired. Army investigators headed toward Corporal Rana's parents' home, and were trying to locate Rana through the computer systems. It should have been simple.

"There seems to be a snag," the director said.

That night the prisoners confirmed that whatever had been manufactured *on the ship had been trucked off. Neither man knew the destination. They'd not talked originally to the Yemeni translator, they said, not because they were uncooperative, but because they couldn't understand his accent and they were terrified of being shot.*

"We loaded oil drums," they told interrogators. "Then the Pakistani doctor went home. We were told to keep people away until someone came for us. That was two weeks ago."

At midnight the director forwarded to Joe a disturbing series of e-mails from Corporal Rana Amir Khan to a sister, the early ones, from the beginning of his deployment, happy and chatty, although complaining about being sent overseas, instead of attending college, the reason he'd joined the Reserves. Then, over time, the cheery quality degenerated. It started when other men in his platoon nicknamed Rana "Raghead."

"I laugh with them, but it infuriates me," the corporal wrote. "I'm as good an American as they are. I do not think they are really joking."

Months later, with the teasing worse, Rana Khan learned that his best friend was being discharged twenty-four hours before he would have been eligible for college tuition aid.

"The Army did this on purpose," Rana wrote. "They don't mind getting us killed. But they mind paying our tuition if we don't get killed. I think those bean counters prefer us to die, to save a few bucks."

He grew more bitter. Days turned to months. Rana felt trapped. He stopped referring to other soldiers as friends. He turned to religion for solace, quoting the Koran, but stopped going to the Army imam, as his hatred grew overt. By 2012, when the news broke that several Marines had burned Korans, and that a staff sergeant named Robert Bale had massacred seventeen innocent civilians, half of them children, in a small village near Rana's base, the e-mails were unrecognizable as belonging to the same man who'd typed messages two years before.

"Afghanistan is hell and we are the demons," his last e-mail said two months ago. "I won't be writing for a while. I'm on a special mission. Don't worry. Much love."

Joe asked the director if Rana was on a special mission.

"Not for us," the director said. "Find him, fast."

■ ■ ■

"SNAFU, motto of the U.S. Army," Eddie snapped twenty-seven hours later. "Situation normal, all fucked up."

It had taken that long to pin down Rana's location, thanks to errors up and down the line, started when some half-illiterate or bored clerk had punched in a two-digit mistake in Rana's computer file, *"6"* instead of *"4"* on the social security number, *"l"* instead of *"r"* on the name.

"We have no Corporal Lana Khan stationed in all of Afghanistan," a captain in personnel assured Joe.

The mistakes followed their search like an electronic leprechaun. There was no soldier named *"Rane"* stationed at the air base at Nimruz, they were told.

"Not Rane. Rana."

"Ah! Well, there's a Sergeant 'Hanna' Khan at a supply depot near Kabul. And a Lieutenant Mohammed Rana from Orange County just shipped back to the States after a tour in Iraq."

"He's a corporal, for Christ's sake."

"Ohhhh! Yes! Why didn't you say so! A Corporal Rana Khan is stationed seventeen miles from a base near an old lake in—"

"My God, he was sitting half an hour from where we started out," Eddie said, eyeing a clock on the wall, as if it were the timing device on a bomb.

They flew back to Kunar Province, to the base, shared by Army and Marines, where the Army colonel in charge told them that yes, Rana was assigned there, but no, he was not actually on base at that moment. *"He's on his way back with a joint Army/Marine humanitarian mission to a refugee camp near the lake."*

Joe and Eddie standing in an air-conditioned prefab Quonset hut, asking what humanitarian mission is that?

"Hearts and minds, gentlemen. Win their hearts and minds and the province follows, that's what I say."

"What mission, Colonel?"

"Well, we had some extra turkey after Thanksgiving, and cranberry sauce, and we figured, donate it, with the usual fuel. Corporal Khan is a driver bringing in the food, hauling back the used oil drums."

Joe leaned forward, his heart quickening at the words "oil drums." In his mind, he heard the prisoner back in Kandahar saying, "We loaded oil drums on trucks."

The colonel was a small, hard-looking man, crew cut, with pale blue eyes and sunken cheeks. His accent was Boston. His family, pictured on his desk, seemed to be sitting in stands at a high school football game. His pride in the humanitarian mission was evident. He explained, "They use generators at their hospital. If we don't send fuel, they run out mid-month. The Army gives us more diesel than we can use." He was interrupted by his phone.

"Ah! The convoy is a few miles off, coming back now."

They ran for the base entrance and reached it in time to see the dust thrown up by the approaching convoy . . . Humvees in front and back, as armed escorts; nine tarp-topped cargo trucks in between.

"Tell them to stop where they are, pull over," Joe told the guard. He still hoped that the drums would be empty, and Rana would be just one more pissed-off but professional soldier. But he didn't think that would be the case.

The lead Humvee was a mile off. Three minutes away at the crawly twenty miles an hour they moved.

"I said stop them!"

"Sir, there have been ambushes . . . It's a bad idea to stop in the open. Sir, I need to check with the captain."

"There isn't time!"

There was a delay in reaching the captain.

Plus, Joe, a visiting Marine major, had no authority to order an Army guard what to do.

The "front gate" was actually just an opening in the Hesco barriers and concentric rolls of concertina wire surrounding the base; the sandbag guard post housed two, and there was a .50-caliber M2 machine gun there. Entering vehicles had to thread a zigzag maze of concrete-filled oil drum bomb barriers. After passing through a second checkpoint, and searched, they could proceed into the thousand-acre base, which housed two thousand troops, tents, prefabs, warehouses, and gym.

A stiff wind blew at the base from the direction in which the convoy was approaching.

The guard told Joe, still holding for the captain, "You'd think the wind would let up, but it don't."

Joe, looking around, fixed on the M2. It was to be used against truck or car bombers, if one was coming, and you knew it, which was, he knew, rarely the case.

Joe walked into the post, to get close to the M2 on its tripod. Neither guard tried to stop him.

The trucks were now a half mile from the base.

The guard reached the captain finally and, after receiving orders, was on his radio telling the trucks to pull over. Almost instantly, all Humvees and all the trucks except one did exactly that.

The truck that had not pulled over passed by the pulled-over vehicles, and kept heading for the front gate.

In his binoculars, Joe had a view of the driver for an instant, through the windshield. It was Rana Khan. There was a passenger, but the passenger was slumped in his seat. The other passengers would be in back, with the oil drums.

"Shoot," he said.

The gate guards seemed confused.

A voice on the unit radio, Khan, said, over static, "I've got a wounded man here."

"Fire," Joe repeated. At least neither guard was trying to stop him.

The voice said, "Code one! Code one! He needs medical attention."

"Sir, there are Marines on that truck, too," a guard explained, as if this would make Joe countermand the order.

Joe grabbed the man's radio. "Pull over or we will fire!"

Suddenly Khan began chanting, "There is no God except Allah the generous and patient. There is no God except Allah the Almighty and all-wise . . ."

The truck, a hundred yards away, accelerated.

"Oh, Allah, pardon my sins . . ."

Joe shouted for the guards to run. The wind was coming sideways. He knew that even a drop of sarin on the skin could start the reaction.

He held the twin grips on the M2 and fired, heard the heavy BANGBANGBANG of the weapon and felt the recoil in his shoulders and arms. The guards were scattering. The oncoming windshield shattered but the truck was armored. Joe swung the muzzle and tracked the truck and kept firing.

Khan sang, "Allah be merciful and . . ."

The truck exploded.

One second it was hurtling toward them, the next a thousand hot pieces of steel blew out and up and scattered in a mushroom pattern over the desert floor. There came a rain of machine parts on the spot where the guards had stood. The truck had been two hundred feet from the gate. There must have been explosives in there. The wind was like artillery. Someone screamed at the men running toward the wreckage, to help, but Joe screamed at them to get away.

He'd been so preoccupied with the shooting that he'd not seen the goat-herd, fifty yards from the explosion—side of the road, man and flock, and the man was suddenly engulfed by a cloud, his hand going to his throat, a man on his knees, animals falling sideways, a man convulsing like an epileptic, while the skinny goat legs waved and went still. The truth sinking in to the Army guys.

"Holy shit, sir. What . . . what's the cloud . . . what's . . ."

And Joe, on his knees, knowing he'd just killed eight innocent Marines, not just Rana Khan, answered, "Sarin."

That part was hushed up. The guards were sworn to secrecy, threatened with prison if they talked. No one wanted the other troops or the American public to know how close the attack had come to success, or that a U.S. soldier had facilitated it. No one, the director explained, wanted Congress to restart the debate about pulling out. The Pakistani professor who made the sarin had been "dealt with." Corporal Khan's parents got a letter saying their son died "in an accident." So let's put it to rest.

And later, when Joe couldn't sleep, when he relived the scene nightly, when his emotions caught up and passed his logical mind, and when he was losing his wife, he decided fuck orders, and he told her. He'd given the director three years of his life at that point. He wasn't going to give the director his wife, too.

But it was too late, she said. "I know you're a hero, Joe. I know you saved lives. But you're not who I married. That man would not have been able to make that choice so quickly."

"Is that so bad?"

"No. You saved a thousand lives. But that's not the issue," she said, know-ing, without rancor, after ten years with him, where the holes in his veneer

lay, to get inside. "I'm not leaving because you saved people. I'm leaving because when I look at you, I see dead ones. It's my fault. Not yours. I'm not strong enough for you."

He'd sat numbly, too guilty to protest, their home, their voices, the city of Anchorage outside just a hollow stage pounding with his heartbeat, and with loss.

"Joe, my father told me something. He said we all find a life to justify what's inside us. I can't help thinking, I wish I didn't, but are you sure you didn't enjoy the power at some level? I can love a flawed man. I need one. But not a flawed God. If you can't be perfect, don't play God."

■ ■ ■

Joe broke from his reverie. Men on the sleds were coughing, growing sicker. They were being carried up the brow, to the ship.

He thought, in agony, *I'll kill them if I have to, if I really have to. Because letting them die is the same thing. But maybe there will be something good on that film.*

Do we pick a life just to justify urges inside us?

When did our weapons start depriving us of choice?

EIGHTEEN

"Don't open the canister," the director ordered.

The *Wilmington* pushed back toward Barrow, the storm over, crystal air—aftermath of the cyclone—making the view stunning and unworldly from the aft deck. I was on another planet. I saw four suns: the main one a hazy orb, floating on mist like a New England lake's, above the white vista. But there were three more suns, too, smaller stars or "sun dogs," Captain DeBlieu had called them; a diagonal row of accolade satellites whose coronas formed prisms of ruby, emerald, turquoise, cobalt.

The temperature was a sharp twenty degrees, and fine diamond dust, ice bits, fell as if out of nowhere, like glitter at a party. The ship nudged small floes from its path, the ice suddenly as cooperative as a meek dog. The thick pack that we'd struggled through on the way north had been pushed west by wind and current. We moved faster. We'd eaten a good meal, brought aft from the mess while we worked. We slid through ice passages and between floating sculptures: a hilly ice island, a truncated ice cathedral, a series of ice church pipe organs thrust into the sky, as if to blast out Bach, the whole seascape rolling out beneath one perfect cumulous cloud. I stood alone, unsure whether I'd heard the director properly, hoping I had not.

"Sir, we need to identify this thing, and fast."

His pause when I'd first mentioned the film had been a buzz on the sat line. He'd gone away for several minutes. Then he'd come back.

"Joe, I know how important the film might be. And how delicate it is. That's why you need to leave it alone so experts can handle it. People who know how to keep it intact. People at the national archives military section, in Culpepper." His voice dropped into a soothing range. "We don't want it crumbing in your hands, man. Look, when you're in range, we'll send a copter, get the film back East. Meanwhile, do your best."

"My best, sir? For that, I'd like a shot at the film."

I stood, phone in hand, eyeing rescue work around me; gauze-masked Coast Guard crew moving men and women on stretchers through the unrolled sliding door into the copter hangar, open to the Arctic air like the enormous maw of a hospital emergency room. Inside, six rows of cots bolted to the deck—three short ones for the sick, three longer ones for the quarantined, off to a side—had transformed the former makeshift basketball court, floating warehouse, dance class area, and Saturday night movie theater into a hospital. Janice Cullen, ship's medical officer, had assigned each patient, crew member, or Marine to a cot, taken names if possible, or got them from other patients; the whole orderly system working just as smoothly now as it did in the drills the crew endlessly practiced; but I knew what lay beneath it; and it was not what initially seemed like control. It was anarchy and terror.

Saline and antibiotic bags hung from metal racks above cots. Janice

Cullen and Eddie went patient to patient, taking vital signs, asking about symptoms, looking down throats, into noses, and ears, and measuring blood pressure. The pneumonia-like signs looked bacterial. Many chests were filled with fluid. We were prescribing Cipro and Bactrim antibiotics.

"But the bacterial stuff is secondary, I think," Eddie had told me. "I think a virus started it, weakened them, and then double pneumonias hit. We're giving the aerosol antivirals, ribavirin, zanamivir, and xapaxin, which, thanks to our buddy Zhou, we have extra. At least something good came from that. I'll get a look at blood samples in the labs. They've got microscopes back there for their mammal work. Whoever would have figured they'd need the labs for this."

The worst should have been over—the sick and burned under care, more doctors on their way to Barrow to meet us, copters readying to pick patients up when we got within range, and American attack subs converging in our direction, in case Captain Zhou Dongfeng remained somewhere nearby.

The director switched to his no-nonsense voice, the voice of the old Washington insider, the high-powered New York boardroom voice, the friend of important people voice, the I-know-things-that-you-can-trust voice. "Please acknowledge instructions, Joe."

"I hear you, sir."

"You did a great job and we're all proud of you. You kept the *Montana* out of unfriendly hands."

Something was off. When we'd reached the part about the canister, all the hearty concern had dissipated. He was my personal Machiavelli and he explained with paternal authority—support that was also denial, "We'll get that film checked out, chop-chop."

"I urge you to reconsider, sir."

"Foresight now may save lives later."

"Sir, I'm not sure that I've fully relayed the seriousness of the situation. Perhaps if I—"

"Joe," he cut me off, "you were chosen for this job because you make the tough choices. You tried to save the sub, and scuttled it when you couldn't. You outmaneuvered an unfriendly when he seemed to have you trapped. You give a thousand percent. I understand your desire to do everything you can but you are also tired and strained and that means mistakes."

"But, sir," I ventured, "I suggest that I start the process, go slow, unroll just a little at a time and—"

The director snapped. "Colonel! Let this one go! We'll have an answer in five, six days. Understood?"

"I do."

"You don't sound enthusiastic, Joe. Try again."

"Five, six days, we could lose more people."

The voice grew modulated as he'd won the point. "Joe, I'd be frustrated, too, were I you. But we'll get this dealt with as soon as possible. I've put you in for a medal. Now! What are you doing to try to locate the spy you believe is aboard? That is our immediate concern. Stopping the leak."

"I've asked the captain to review security tapes made during ship drills, sir, in the hangar. Possibly we'll get a glimpse of whoever tampered with the Arktos. The XO's doing a locker-to-locker search; cabins, storage areas, labs. The communications officer will go through all laptops on board, see if he can find piggyback programs inside, foreign software."

"And who's checking on him?"

"His number two. Also, sir, when you and I are finished here, we'll shut down the sat lines again. When we get within copter range— DeBlieu says that will be in another hundred and seventy miles if weather holds and ice stays clear—I advise sending in security folks to ask questions. Hold everyone aboard while we do. And, of course, we'll have to open it up for consultations with the CDC."

"There won't be any consultation just now," he said.

I felt my breath catch. "Excuse me?"

"Joe, until we know who you've got on board, passing information along, we simply have to block all calls out. We're shutting *you* down. Communication quarantine. We'll open her up and call if we need you. DeBlieu keeps the radio off on your end. But you've got that thumb drive library of yours, that kit of memory sticks, probably hundreds of books' worth. Plenty of medical information in there. You've been building that collection for years.

"In the meantime . . ." He hesitated and I had a vision of his secretary standing in his doorway mouthing, *Your eleven o'clock appointment is here.*

He said, "In the meantime, Joe, I have full confidence in all your decisions."

Yeah, except when I want to open the canister.

He added more softly, "Even the upcoming tough ones."

What does he mean by that?

"You know, Joe, you more than anyone understand that our country is at a huge disadvantage in the Arctic. We, the Pentagon, we've been trying to get four consecutive White Houses to pay attention to this region, but we've only got the *Wilmington* up there breaking ice. If we lose her, we lose the ability to move. We lose *access* to a whole ocean opening up. The country can't afford that."

Is he saying what I think he is? I felt a tickling, an itch on the roof of my mouth, a numb feeling spreading down my esophagus.

"Joe, if that sickness amplifies, if you decide that keeping the ill ones on the ship is risky to others, I'm just saying, you know, to remember the vast stakes."

I gasped. "You want me to *put them off*?"

"No, no, of course not. I'm not telling you that. I'm not on site. You are. I'm just saying, Joe, that you're always good at balancing tough considerations."

My God! He's telling me that it is okay if I leave those guys on the ice, if I decide they'll contaminate the ship! That's why they're cutting me off from the CDC. They don't want a committee involved in the decision. They don't want anyone extra knowing. Jesus God!

The director said, "Well, I'm sure it won't come to that. Good luck. I'll call *you* every few hours for updates. We'll open the line when I do."

"Sir, perhaps, if you'll excuse a request, perhaps if I spoke directly to whoever—"

"I have full confidence that you'll do the right thing."

He was gone. His praise tasted like ashes. Eddie came up to me, took one long look into my face, and said, "What's wrong, Uno?" The canister lay in my left hand, gripped as if it might jump overboard if I relaxed. My jaw hurt. My neck cords were tight. I held the container up between us. I shook my head.

Eddie jerked as if struck physically. "He said *no*?"

A wave of tiredness washed over me, then a wave of fury woke me up.

"He said leave it to the experts. He made sense on the surface, but I got the feeling," I said, reliving the talk, "that he knew about the canister before I mentioned it."

Eddie, waiting while I thought out loud, went back over the conversation.

"He was surprised, yeah, *surprised for sure*, but I can't figure it exactly. He wasn't surprised in the right way."

"And what would be the right way?"

I smiled grimly. "That's the question, isn't it? Need to know, friend.

And you know what? I can think of eight good need-to-know reasons to open the canister."

Eddie's breath came out as a long white line.

"Eight dead Marines," I said. "In Afghanistan."

"This is a different situation."

"That's the point. In Afghanistan there was no choice. Here there is. And I can think of one hundred more reasons right there," I said, nodding toward the parade of stretchers moving toward cots. "And," I added, gazing up at the ship's superstructure, envisioning, inside, men and women in the passageways and bridge, "there are even more reasons up top."

"You sure, One?"

I laughed. "Sure? Who is ever sure of anything? But I'm opening this. They can't do anything to me—I'm retiring—so you stay here. If the film starts to disintegrate, I'll close it up. If I find something, you'll be the first to know."

"No, I'll be the first to know because I'm coming with you."

"Then officially, you're coming to talk me out of it, right?"

Eddie grinned. "Don't do it. Do not do it! I'm urging, pleading, begging you to follow the director's orders."

He wiped his nose on his sleeve.

With sharp concern, I said, "You getting sick?"

"Nah. It's the ventilation system. But," he said, a frown on his face, "frankly, I don't like the look of Clinton."

Captain Maurice DeBlieu broke off from the rescue work and followed us through the hangar, up steel steps, to the warren of labs on the 01 level. This was the first time in my military career that I had disobeyed a direct order.

Director, what do you know that you have not told me?

Our boot steps rang on steel as we reached the hallway housing the labs; some used for analyzing bottom sediment, others for weather analysis or sonar imaging work, and then the bio lab, similar to those I've worked in, in Washington, or in tents in Afghanistan. I knew this room. I was comfortable here, if it was possible, under these circumstances, to be comfortable at all.

Up until now this lab had been used by researchers—DeBlieu told me when I first toured the ship—to quantify ocean acidification, examine starved polar bears, or walrus air sacs, which kept males afloat when ice was gone . . . Or to look at codfish, which were migrating into newly warm waters, DeBlieu had said, or grasshoppers that had fallen from the sky, all new life-forms appearing as the High North warmed.

But none of these samples might be as important as the one I awaited seeing.

I had my pick of familiar instruments: tweezers and magnifiers, chemicals and monitors to show images, and there was even a shower decontamination room in case—on a normal day—a chemical accident occurred.

I lay the canister on a table that had probably been used for slicing open fish bellies. I wore a mask, apron, and rubber gloves, as did Eddie and DeBlieu.

"Disease-kateers. One for all and all for one," Eddie said, always the joker, the kind of guy who could lighten the mood in a morgue.

The canister lay on the blotter like an anesthetized patient. I hesitated. Maybe the director had been right. Maybe opening the thing would damage it. Maybe I'd been wrong in thinking people were hiding things from us. Maybe the film curled in there—if it was even still intact—had absolutely nothing to do with the cause of the hideous suffering going on only yards away from where we stood.

In the fluorescent light, the dents in the metal stood out. I had a vision of this thing encased in ice, waiting, years going by, snow falling, storms battering the wreck, bears wandering by the two mummified, ice-glazed corpses. The cellulose images in darkness until, one day, the *Montana* surfaced nearby.

Eddie said, "Change your mind?"

"No, Eddie."

"What are you waiting for?" said DeBlieu.

Slowly, holding my breath, I began working free the wedged-on canister lid.

NINETEEN

The film crumbled when I touched it.

The first three feet disintegrated; one second whole, the next—in despair—I looked down on an array of glossy shreds on the blotter.

I heard the men behind me breathing, and the crackling of aged cellulose. I tried another strip, gently, heard a noise like wax paper crackling, and another three-inch section broke off. Two inches remained intact. There was no picture on it. It was ghostly white, the image either long gone or, I hoped, this was an unused start to the roll.

Was I destroying evidence? I tried to unroll a third piece and the tweezers managed to pull out another intact two-inch strip.

"Attaboy," said Eddie.

I smelled DeBlieu behind me, a mix of Old Spice and Irish Spring soap, a whiff of a last meal, barbequed chicken. I held the strip firmly on the blotter. With my free hand, I gingerly slid a hand magnifier over it. The tensor light shone brightly, reflected off the magnifier and into my eyes. The shadows of the men behind me fell on the blotter. I felt the lab rock gently from ship movement as I leaned down again, put my eye to the piece.

I said, "Got something!"

Leaping into view was a single frame, showing four soldiers in uniforms standing proudly before the front door of a Quonset hut, the middle man, clearly clown of the group, sticking his hand in his shirt, like Napoleon, and saluting. Long-dead buddies. The hats held at their sides were floppy brimmed, early-twentieth-century U.S. Army. The men wore suspenders and loose breeches stuffed into high boots. They had neat mustaches, long for my taste, and the two men not wearing hats had their short hair parted in the middle.

"This is turn of the twentieth century. It's a silent movie," I breathed. "Older than we figured."

What possible relevance could it have to the submarine *Montana*? I noticed a sign beside the Quonset hut door. I heard myself read the words with horrified reverence. They froze my blood.

"FORT RILEY, KANSAS, 1918."

Eddie whispered, awed, too, "Oh, shit."

DeBlieu asked impatiently, "That's important? What happened at Fort Riley in 1918?"

Neither of us responded, hoping we were wrong. After several more strips disintegrated, a long one rolled out. Perhaps the more deeply I unrolled the spool, the more protection the film had received, the better shape it was in.

DeBlieu said, "Hey, feel free to answer."

With unreal slowness, I pulled out film. I needed many frames just to see an elbow shifting, a leg lifting. I said, "They're packing now. They're filling knapsacks. They're going on a journey."

Maybe I should have stopped as the director had ordered, but by now I was too excited and frightened at what I suspected would come next.

I narrated to my transfixed audience. "They're inside a building now. A warehouse. I see stacked Springfield rifles. Machine guns. Other soldiers help them load it onto trucks. Wait! Someone's inserted captions now. Handwritten. Eddie, you ever hear of U.S. Army Project White?"

"No."

"It says 'part two.' Do you think that first section, the busted-up one, was part one?"

"I'll take part two if we can get it."

The pressure of the eyepiece against my face seemed to penetrate my sockets. Eddie groaned. "They're only loading rifles, right? Arms, right?"

DeBlieu repeated, as if we'd not heard his previous plea, "What about Fort Riley? This is a hundred years old. What does this have to do with us?"

I held up a hand to let him know I'd heard. It was too early to answer. The film must have been developed on the old boat. As I kept rolling, and the strip started dangling off the table, Eddie scrounged around behind me and created a way to roll up the film as it uncoiled . . . He cut a knife groove into a wooden dowel. He inserted the film edge into the slit. He rolled film up as it unspooled. I figured—when we were done, we'd spool the film back up, if we could.

There were bare frames and that was so frustrating. It was like watching an old movie but only seeing every fourth or fifth frame . . . sometimes nine or ten in a row before a strip broke off.

Then the film seemed to stabilize enough so that I could pull it, frame by frame, beneath the hand magnifier.

I read out loud, peering down from a century ahead, to the century behind, "OFF LIMITS. AUTHORIZED PERSONNEL ONLY."

Little figures moved jerkily. The soldiers were on a dock now, in civilian clothing, loading the crates of grenades and Springfield rifles onto a boat. Time leaped in jerks. The gangplank seemed to bow with weight as men went back and forth onto a small, private, forty-foot-long boat, and there was a long shot of the name, *Anna*. The clown guy, the one who had acted like Napoleon before, did a sailor jig on the dock, hands on his belt.

"Now we're at sea," I said, seeing gray rolling waves, which were still out there, unlike the men who had shot this. A whale spouted. Then there were three whales. I said, "Shit," as a whole section of film tore off, and when I resumed, the men were in a rocky forest. "Whole bunch of new guys now with them, and mules, and the crates are on the animals. They're moving through a trail cut through high fir trees."

DeBlieu said, "Project White. Delivering arms."

It was like some old Charlie Chaplin movie. Real humans didn't move like this. Now the clown guy was standing on a stump, watching the mules go by, pretending to be an ape, hunched over, swinging his arms, scratching his armpits, beating his chest.

"He just broke out coughing," I said.

"You want to tell DeBlieu? Or should I?" said Eddie.

I felt a wave of devastation sweep over me. Now the clown guy must have had the camera, because the other guys—long overcoats on, rifles over their backs, military caps on—had paused for a group photo. The coughing wasn't the point of the shot. Clown guy had just happened to cough when they were rolling. The camera panned away, and there was a gap in the forest, and through that I saw a fuzzy moving blob in the distance.

"Guys coming on horseback. About thirty of them. A village there, too. Thatched roofs. Timber walls. The riders wear fur-flapped caps and baggy trousers and have rifles on their shoulders. Small horses, skinny. Bandoliers . . . these guys look like Cossacks. Man, handlebar mustaches!"

The Americans waved. It was an arranged meeting. Close up, the riders seemed to stare at the camera, angry that it was there. Their clothing was a ragtag collection of peasant patchwork, some foreign military uniforms, and one man even wore a stylish bowler, low brimmed, above a coat more appropriate for the theater, long and hemmed with fur.

"Colonel, where are they?" asked DeBlieu.

"They've got a flag. It's the two-headed eagle, the Russian imperial eagle, above a coat of arms. Russia." I sat back. I looked at DeBlieu. Now I understood. "They're bringing guns to the White Russians fighting the Reds."

DeBlieu looked puzzled. "Wait. America fought against Russia in 1918?" he said.

"Yeah, Woodrow Wilson sent in troops to help fight the Communists," said Eddie, a student of military history.

"He did?"

I felt DeBlieu's hand on my shoulder as he leaned closer. "What happened to those soldiers?"

I snapped, "You want me to explain, or keep going?"

His hand fell away. I glanced up. He looked angry, but he'd shut up.

I continued rolling, feeling guilty because I was getting to see the story, not them.

"They must have transferred the arms because now they're back on the boat. Mission accomplished! They're slapping each other's backs. They're toasting the mission. Clown guy is really coughing in this one. All done! Except, whoa! Now they're being chased by a gunship . . . Bolshevik ship . . . I can see the deck gun firing at them . . . a splash . . . the shell just missed them."

The Bolshevik ship was getting closer. I prayed for our guys to get away. Now the view shifted abruptly, the camera in front of the boat. The clown guy on the prow, not smiling, pointing forward, as if urging more speed. There was a cloud bank in the distance . . . I imagined the guy shouting, *Faster!*

"They're still not hit."

The film tilted. Brown spots, age spots ate up the picture. It was gone. I kept rolling. Eddie kept spooling up the film.

"They're back," I said, relieved. "It's cloudy all around . . . no . . . they're in mist. I guess they got away, escaped into it. They're in front of the boat, looking ahead. There's a caption: TWO DAYS LATER. Oh, oh, shit, man, they must be really north because *they're in the ice!*"

Only it wasn't the kind of ice the *Wilmington* was in, or the kind I'd seen near the *Montana*. Unrolling before my eye was the monster ice I'd read about in history books, seen in old lithographs. These were ice mountains. This was the Andes, the Alps, of ice. The walls surrounding the little *Anna* seemed to grow higher, frame by frame. I noticed one of the other men coughing, too, now.

I sat back. "They sailed too far north," I said. "Got away, but they're getting sick."

DeBlieu said, "These are the bodies the sub found?"

"Has to be."

The film jumped again and my heart did, too, because I saw it. I'd known we would end up here, but I'd hoped I'd be wrong.

"Take a look," I told DeBlieu.

I held the magnifier in place. He bent down. I resumed drawing the film toward me. I heard DeBlieu groan.

"They're all sick now," he said. "With the same thing."

Eddie sighed. "They kept filming, One. Till the end."

It was a death film now. At first I didn't realize that the man I watched in a bunk was clown guy. There was no smile now. No jumping around. A close-up showed him bleeding through his nose, like patients from the *Montana*. The camera pulled back. Another sick guy lay in an upper bunk, eyes closed, lethargic. The eyes opened. The mouth moved. History consumed his words. There was no technology to capture them. The hand of an unseen man laid a compress on clown guy's forehead. The camera shook violently. Maybe the man taking the photo was coughing, too, doing his job, distracting himself from what they probably all knew was to come.

Eddie took over at the eyepiece, described what came next, which was a foregone conclusion. Three of the men on the boat struggling with the corpse of clown guy, rolling it over the side, in a shroud. A shot of an ice mountain. Then the vessel locked in place, caught by ice coating the gunwales and ice on the ceilings. The deck was slick with ice, the men coughing, throwing up as they tried to chip it away, get free. Cut to the mast, which was now an ice pole. Another body went over the side, and flopped, in its sheet, onto a floe. A bear bent over it.

DeBlieu commanded, "Enough! You know what it is! Explain. Now!"

Explain? It's funny the way you can know something horrible, even be sure of it, but not want to say it because that will be the final step of transforming it into something real.

I said tiredly, "They called it the Spanish flu."

"Even though it didn't start in Spain," Eddie said.

"It broke out in 1918, near the end of World War One."

DeBlieu looked pensive, riveted.

"Nineteen eighteen," I said. "Imagine it. The world at war. Millions of men in trenches. Chemical bombs. Fighter planes for the first time. Tanks for the first time. And then, out of the blue, on top of everything else, a new disease appears."

"At Fort Riley," said Eddie. "Kansas."

"Wait, I heard of the Spanish flu," DeBlieu said. "It started in *Kansas?*"

"Just like the Wizard of Oz," said Eddie.

"I thought it killed millions in Europe."

"Oh, it did. But that's not where it started. We learned this on our first week in the unit," I said. "That flu was the worst disease outbreak in history."

"I thought the black plague was that."

"No. The story—the *theory*—is that soldiers enlisting at Riley, guys from pig farms nearby, came in already infected. Then it spread. Doctors had never seen anything like it. It hit the younger people the worst, the healthier ones, ramped up the resistance system like crazy, so a more vigorous person, those guys were more likely to die. Victims fell ill in the morning and died that night."

"Like on the *Montana*," DeBlieu breathed.

"Yeah. And like on the *Anna*. Those guys probably didn't know they were infected when they sailed off. Other Riley troops got sent to Europe. The disease amplified there, in the trenches," Eddie said. "But it didn't stay in the trenches. In the end, five hundred million infected. Twenty to fifty million dead, some estimates go as high as eighty million. It changed the war, altered battle plans, killed more people in one year than the black plague did in four. Fifteen thousand dead in Philadelphia. Theaters closed across the U.S. Schools closed. If the war hadn't been on, taken up the headlines, every schoolkid in the U.S. would know this story. But it was downplayed at the time. Oh, you knew that people in *your* city were sick, in *your* family, but no one outside of governments knew the whole picture."

I said, remembering photos we'd seen, "Crowds, people were too afraid to congregate. Cops and firemen stopped going to work in places.

In some countries the dead were bulldozed into pits. The flu burned across earth. Hell, go to a New York Yankees game in September 1918, half the people in the stands wore masks. Neighbors avoided each other. In parts of Alaska, Eskimo villages suffered a ninety-five percent death rate. Alaska—the Eskimos—got it the worst."

DeBlieu said, aghast, "How did they stop it?"

I shook my head. "They never did. It just ran out. It morphed into something less lethal. But the fear has always been that it will come back, in the original form. The question . . . we got this at the unit, in seminars, we read papers about it, it comes up at conferences. If it didn't have a name like flu, if it had a name like plague, believe me, you'd have heard of it. The question is, the fear has been, for a hundred years, *if that flu comes back, can we stop it this time?*"

DeBlieu said, "But it died out, you said?"

And Eddie said, "So did the black plague. First it appeared in 600 A.D. in Turkey. Then it came back in 1347, in Europe. Then it died out again. Then it returned in 1890, in China and India. Each time, millions died."

"And now the Spanish flu is back," I said.

Eddie said, "The White Plague."

■ ■ ■

DeBlieu fell into a chair. For a moment nobody spoke. Then DeBlieu said, struggling with hope, "Well, we've got better medicines now, right? I mean, in 1918, doctors didn't know a lot compared to now."

"Right," I said.

"Like those sprays and pills you're treating patients with in the hangar. All new. Wasn't even penicillin in 1918. So you can't compare now and then."

"Definitely," Eddie said. "You're right."

"So this time," DeBlieu said, fantasizing, "tell me that even if it's the flu, this will be like other diseases that once were dangerous, but aren't anymore. Polio. Cholera. Terrifying in the past, but now pretty much gone. You can beat it. That's why you took the sick aboard. You have a whole arsenal of medicines. We're just looking at something scary in the past."

Eddie was expressionless. I sighed. What we faced downstairs from the lab represented precisely the prediction we'd made to the Defense Department that had brought me to the director's attention five years ago. That a disease would erupt in the High North, not the Tropics.

I said, "I wish I could tell you that, Captain. But if we're seeing bodies from Fort Riley, we're dealing with the original strain. And we have no idea if people in the last hundred years have built up resistance to it, or whether, you know . . ."

Eddie added morosely, "Or whether we're looking at an even more lethal mutation."

DeBlieu argued doggedly, as if trying to change fact, "But if you've all been expecting it, why hasn't anyone worked on it all these years?"

"How can you work on it when you don't have samples of the original strain? Look, Captain, just in the last two years researchers have unearthed old corpses, flu victims, in Alaska, Russian Eskimo villages, trying to reconstruct the virus. It's been controversial. Some scientists fear that could start an outbreak in itself. But the benefits were supposed to outweigh the risk, and truth is, some virus has been reconstructed, but not the original strain. Not what we have here."

Eddie said, glancing down, as if he could see through the deck to the makeshift hospital ward in the hangar. "Now we'll find out, I guess."

DeBlieu, horrified, was reeling from the impact. He said, in a low, enraged voice, "You brought it onto *my ship?*"

"We didn't know that's what it was until five minutes ago. And we weren't going to abandon U.S. sailors on the ice. Look, we keep watching the film," I soothed. "Maybe there's something here that tells us what to do. An antidote. Something *they* didn't even know but *we'll know* when we see it."

"If they had an antidote, don't you think they would have used it?" DeBlieu demanded, backing away.

"Maybe they didn't know they had it. Maybe they only got seventy percent of the work done, but we can do the rest. Meanwhile, like you said, we've got new medicines. And we'll try them. We're using them right now."

"Maybe," DeBlieu repeated, as if the word, the doubt in the word "maybe," represented an affront to his sense of right.

"Maybe is the best we can do," I told him.

The enormity of the revelation seemed to suck air from the lab. DeBlieu absorbed the blow physically. He stood absolutely still, a vein throbbing on his forehead. He was an engineer by training, the commander entrusted with keeping the nation's lone icebreaker safe. The competing pressures inside him had to be enormous—the responsibility to his crew, the training stressing rescue. DeBlieu stared down at the bits of film, as if the celluloid itself crawled with a mass of microbes.

I'd expected to see fear on his face. Or hardness. But not sadness. That was what entered the brown, intelligent eyes. "No, the best we can do, Colonel, is that I'm pulling my people from the hangar. I'm sorry about the patients. I'm sorry they're sick. I have a different responsibility. You will remove every one of those patients and put them back on the ice," he said.

Eddie said, "What ice? We're past the tough ice. We're closing on Barrow. What do you want us to do, put them in a life raft?"

DeBlieu stood straighter, moved back a step. "Do what you have to do," he said with disconcerting decisiveness. "But get them off. Meanwhile, Colonel, I'm afraid I'm going to have to relieve you of command."

I jerked up sharply.

He said, "My orders—as you know—were to relinquish control to you unless I felt there was a danger to the ship."

"Captain, we don't have time to argue over—"

"I agree completely. So we'll find a stable area of ice, or even if we can't, we will—no, sorry—*your Marines*—will remove the sick from the ship, unload them onto the ice, or rafts, along with whatever provisions will make them more comfortable. Medicines, tents, heating, whatever you need, if we have it, you'll have it."

"It's a bit late for that," I told him.

As if to punctuate the point, Del Grazo appeared suddenly in the doorway, looking disheveled, looking as if he was trying not to seem afraid. It wasn't working.

"Colonel Rush, you better come. Clinton is really sick," he said.

TWENTY

FIVE VOICES IN WASHINGTON

"Do you think Colonel Rush will watch the film?"

"Unfortunately, yes." The director nodded. "He's too dedicated not to do it, orders or not."

It was dusk in Washington, and the lights remained off in the third-floor corner office of the four-story townhouse, diagonally across from the White House, on the north side of Lafayette Park. Outside, temperatures topped ninety-two degrees, and a gray, smoggy urban light—part sun, part rush-hour effluence—filtered in through mesh curtains covering the floor-to-ceiling windows.

During prior administrations, lesser White House officials had occupied this building, Council for the Environment, Council on Safety in the Workplace.

But the current National Security Advisor, Dr. A. R. Klinghoff of Michigan State University, the "Kissinger of the twenty-first century," as pundits called him, preferred the weathered but homey building to the more impersonal gray, massive, Eisenhower-era, ornate, too-hot-in-winter, *too-air-conditioned-in-summer Executive Office Building across Pennsylvania Avenue.*

Klinghoff was the youngest son of World War Two–era Viennese refugees, a professor and a civil lawyer, who fled the Nazis when Germany took over that country in 1938. He had grown up hearing dinner table stories of the bad things that happen when overt threats are ignored, and had made a career of predicting how to cope with them.

All five people present—they'd been at this discussion for more than eight hours—were old enough to remember a time when the view outside included cars moving on Pennsylvania Avenue past the White House, along an area now turned into a pedestrian mall shielded from truck bombers by concrete barriers. All here were acutely aware of the way the lockdown of official Washington had grown over the last two decades. Each person present had a responsibility relating to national security. Each had, in their own way, inherited the nation's nightmares.

Admiral Bud "Red" Burgoyne was chief of Naval Operations of the United States Navy. At fifty-six, he was florid-faced, bowlegged, with a pugilist's nose on an oddly thin, fluid body. He had, at age seventeen, considered a career in dance. Instead, he'd enlisted, become a champion Navy middleweight boxer, used the footwork to dodge punches, and never looked back.

Judge Eileen Marcus—Homeland Security Secretary—had risen to national prominence after presiding over two New York–based terrorist trials. She was a widely respected jurist whose purview included the operation of the nation's lone icebreaker. She was, at sixty-one, a grandmother of four, a painter of vintage rural railroad stations in her spare time, and a lover of saxophone jazz and crossword puzzles.

Also present was Nate Grady, who had served under two presidents of opposite parties as a media advisor. Grady, thirty-nine, had no use for extremists on the left or the right. Time *magazine had called him "one of the last professional Washingtonians who speak from the center." Having no so-cial life, he lived in a two-room apartment on Connecticut Avenue, went home each night and ate takeout soup or Mexican food, and drove a fourteen-year-old Honda. Physically, he resembled consumer advocate Ralph Nader, tall, ascetic, boxy brown suits, rubber-soled shoes. He slept well each night, when sometimes, smiling, he dreamed of playing left field for the Boston Red Sox.*

Klinghoff's assistant National Security head, Dr. Joe Rush's fifty-one-year-old boss, sat in a corner. Elias Pelfrey wore a box-cut pinstriped suit in dark blue, a white shirt, and a maroon tie. His brown curly hair was mat thick, cut short to control the wild part, and his quiet demeanor was enhanced by the limp from an old college football injury. He'd come close twice to being named National Security Advisor. He could hold his own with everyone in the group.

"The President wants a recommendation on protocol five," said Klinghoff. "Hopefully unanimous, that we'll stand behind if things go public."

"Which they usually do," said Grady.

The windows were quadruple strength, bullet- and soundproof. Adobe-colored coffee mugs cooled on tables. The art was Ansel Adams photos: Yosemite, Grand Canyon, Grand Tetons. Klinghoff and his wife were avid hikers during his rare vacations.

Protocol five, drawn up in 2007, was a top secret plan to be put into effect if ever a limited area inside the United States—an office building, a small town, a prison—any place smaller than two square miles—had been infected with deadly, contagious microorganisms.

"Only fast, surgical action may prevent global catastrophe," the protocol read.

Activated by a button beneath Klinghoff's desk was a voice-recording system. This is what it picked up.

BURGOYNE: I advised you to order the film destroyed on the sub. But you preferred to save it.

KLINGHOFF: We'll continue our talk under the premise that Dr. Rush has seen it.

BURGOYNE: Which is unfortunately more than I can say for us. Still, the idea of destroying our own people . . . There must be another way.

GRADY: Would you rather they reach land? That the disease gets out? You saw the spread projections.

PELFREY: How can it reach land if we stop the ship? You keep her offshore, see if the disease burns itself out, or we figure a way to kill it.

KLINGHOFF: You know that's misleading, Elias. You heard the CDC. They can probably *decontaminate, but no one hundred percent certainty. They say if we put medical personnel aboard, they'd be at risk. They're unsure whether healthy crew members—even months later—might be carriers. We all heard Dr. Graves say that noroviruses—that knocked out half of Washington last December—can live on surfaces; books, toilets. And you'll recall the lab in Virginia where monkey Ebola broke out in 1990. A year later—after release from quarantine—two lab workers tested positive. Sheer luck made that strain harmless to humans. The entire building was destroyed.*

PELFREY: Oh, scientists never have one hundred percent certainty.

KLINGHOFF: Because they know they can be surprised.

MARCUS: If you would have listened to me two years ago, we could have avoided this. One icebreaker! I asked for more! Destroy that ship and it will end our ability to move around up there. The damn Russians have twenty icebreakers! If I had more icebreakers, one would have been close, would have reached the Montana *early on.*

BURGOYNE: If the Navy had icebreakers, they'd be armed.

KLINGHOFF: We'll talk about that later. For now, I already explained, we can opt to try to decontaminate. Hydrogen chlorine gas in the vents. Foot-by-foot cleansing. Then testing. Lots of it, before sending her out again.

GRADY: *And what happens if the thing breaks out anyway? Listen to yourself. "Try" to decontaminate.*

MARCUS: *Save the ship. Kill the crew.*

GRADY: *Save millions of Americans onshore. That thing gets out, even a one percent lethality rate would kill four million people. We've got a twenty-five percent rate right now and it could go up.*

MARCUS: *Disgusting!*

GRADY: *Maybe you have a better idea. There's simply no safe way to move so many infected and potentially sick to quarantine. Look, our group has commissioned two studies, two over the last six years, on decontaminating populated areas if worst comes to worst. All acknowledge the possibility of having to put the sick to sleep. And all recommend getting triaged people to isolation wards! But in this case that means transporting them hundreds of miles in planes or trucks that would have to be decontaminated or destroyed, putting new crews at risk, sending carriers into populated areas, to hospitals unequipped to handle so many isolation cases at the same time, so we're talking multiple destinations. One sick person gets out, one truck breaks down, one fuckup, one fucking germ out, in a whole chain of events and it's loose and we did it.*

PELFREY: *I'd like to point out that—*

GRADY: *I'm not finished. What is your suggestion, sir? Put the sick on a barge? In four weeks that ocean will freeze over. The locals can walk out to it. Or ice crushes the barge. You can't guard it, we've got no ships that withstand ice. So what to do? Tow the barge off? Where? No deepwater harbors! Tow it six hundred miles to Nome? You still get ice, in a bigger city. And let's not forget the fall storms. A barge might not even make it. And the whole thing on TV! Look, when it comes*

*to the Arctic, you knew there would be an emergency one day. You're
unprepared.*

MARCUS: *Then bring them into Barrow. There's an old Air Force base
there, an Arctic research center.*

GRADY: *Ha! Barrow's got a population of five thousand Eskimos, voters
and veterans, and I'll remind you that indigenous people were the
most susceptible to flu in 1918. Whole villages perished. The base is not
equipped for quarantine. Crews moving the sick would be at risk. The
Quonset huts are eighty years old and would need to be fixed up. Costs
in the Arctic are quadruple, so you're saying we do a rush job and then
cross our fingers that precautions are adequate? That the most deadly
disease ever to hit mankind—stewing only one mile from a populated
area—doesn't get out? You think those people in town are going to stay
quiet? You think Alaska's senators are going to shut up?*

[The tape records Grady making a sound of disgust.]

KLINGHOFF: *Eileen, we'd have a disaster on our hands.*

MARCUS: *And murdering two hundred American sailors and Marines,
you don't call that a disaster?*

PELFREY: *You don't have the corner on compassion, Eileen. Those are my
guys up there, too.*

GRADY: *A calamity, awful, terrible, but let's discuss how to limit damage. Scenario A: The White House learned there was a fatal, highly
contagious disease on board. After quarantining the ship, the President decided—in consultation with the nation's foremost infectious
disease experts—that in the interest of American families, the val-
iant crew—on death's door—was put to sleep. We bring her into
U.S. waters. We transfer the crew to a barge, tell 'em they're going
ashore. We put 'em to sleep peacefully, spray them. Figure out about
the ship after.*

MARCUS: *Gas 'em like Auschwitz.*

GRADY: I resent that. Every person in this room has known for years that we might one day face an outbreak. Now it's real. You didn't have a problem endorsing conclusions when they were theoretical, Eileen. Auschwitz? Those people suffered. I'm saying we put our people to sleep. We might even consider announcing that the disease may have been introduced by an enemy. We'll hunt down the people who did this. We will not rest until our dead are avenged. The President takes control, out of the gate. And we triple decontaminate the icebreaker. Of course, once there's a potential enemy out there, terrorists, Congress goes nuts. Every governor. Every mayor. Every senator. Every damn candidate for any office in fifty states. What do you mean, terrorists have a disease weapon? How did they get it?

KLINGHOFF: I don't think I like that can of worms.

BURGOYNE: Well, this scenario of yours assumes the crew will just go along. You tell them to hand over weapons. May I remind you there are twenty-five Marines aboard, who can easily blow a copter out of the sky. If they have any idea what you're up to, you'll have one hell of a fight.

GRADY: Okay, then, scenario B: We send her to the bottom. An accident. Like the submarine Thresher. One spread of torpedoes or missiles could do it. No one aboard would know what hit them. They're cut off. A tragedy. But if we're going to do it, we do it now!

PELFREY: Why can't we just leave the ship alone, see if Dr. Rush makes progress? The Montana *is quarantined at the moment so the illness can't spread, for God's sake.*

MARCUS: I agree. Drop supplies. Or ask for medical volunteers, I'm sure many doctors would help, even knowing the risk. We show compassion. We save as many as we can. After the disease burns through, we keep the survivors in isolation, make sure they're clean. That's America! That's the difference between us and . . . those other people.

KLINGHOFF: That doesn't sound so bad to me.

GRADY: Sure, it sounds fine at first, benevolent, except . . . first, we just said the survivors may not be clean, and second, let's put it in perspective. Remember President Jimmy Carter and Iran? You've got fifty-two American hostages taken. Instead of going in, attacking, endangering lives, Carter holds off, he's the humanitarian President. He wants to avoid needless death. But what happens? The second the press knows, it becomes the lead story every night. You think this won't be the same? DEATH SHIP, DAY ONE! DEATH SHIP, DAY EIGHTY! *Roll call of the dead, on every screen in the world. Photos. Interviews with families. Congress demands an investigation, and someone digs up the other part. Washington at a standstill. The Russia treaty? The health initiative? Good luck! And when you finally decide to take action, we're in court, blocked. Too late.*

KLINGHOFF: Hmmmmm.

MARCUS: May I remind you that all the Iranian hostages got out without a single death in the end?

GRADY: There was one death, and it was that Presidency. Tell me, what happens if Colonel Rush, who already disobeyed orders if he watched the film, has the Marines fight back? Or maybe someone on board gets on the Internet, blogs, or the film gets out. Oh, that would be us taking control, all right. The whole thing on YouTube.

BURGOYNE: We're fucked.

GRADY: What we need now is a kind of triage.

BURGOYNE: I'm afraid he's right.

GRADY: I say either try to decontaminate the ship after putting to sleep— humanely—people who are frankly getting sick anyway. Or blow the ship straight out.

PELFREY: They're not all sick. Some got over it! Some of them won't even get sick at all!

GRADY: *You don't know that for sure. The death rate could go up. And anyway, the bigger problem isn't even the ship. It's the other thing.*

MARCUS: *Sounds like you're talking about dogs. Put to sleep! Say what you mean. Murder!*

PELFREY: *Joe Rush and Edward Nakamura, I've worked with those two for years . . . I've been to their homes.*

[The tape records silence at this point.]

KLINGHOFF: *Eileen, you're certainly making it hard.*

MARCUS: *Ha! I'm making it hard, he says.*

KLINGHOFF: *Remember when the President interviewed you for your job? When you said you could make the tough choices? When you said you wanted to be the one to make them? That if he picked you, you'd never shirk.*

MARCUS: *That's not fair. I'm not shirking. I'm wondering which choice here is the best.*

[The tape records everyone talking at the same time. Snippets of voices . . . "Yes, but . . ." "I wish he'd destroyed the tape . . ." "How did the Chinese get that news . . ."]

KLINGHOFF: *It's time for a vote. I'd rather have this unanimous, if possible. All in favor? Scenario A: Try to move the living onto barges, if we can disarm the Marines, let the thing burn through, try to move the barges south. All for it? Only one? Okay, then! Scenario B: Give it thirty-six hours, maybe Dr. Rush pulls off a miracle, and then destroy the ship and announce the real reason. Nobody for honesty, eh? C: Missiles or torpedoes. An accident. Hmmm, three out of five. Eileen? Vote!*

MARCUS: *There has to be another way.*

KLINGHOFF: *The President expects me in twelve minutes across the street, with a recommendation.*

MARCUS: *I vote to quarantine.*

PELFREY: Sir, it's the thirty-six hours that bothers me. It doesn't seem like enough time. Colonel Rush will be giving medicines. He'll need time to see if they work. To see if it spreads, or just dies off. Can't we go longer?

KLINGHOFF: Mr. Grady?

GRADY: The longer you give them, the more chance the story will get out. Once it does, it's out of control.

KLINGHOFF: Oh, a few more hours won't make such a big difference. Shall we say, forty-eight hours, Director Pelfrey?

PELFREY: Can we say more?

KLINGHOFF (irritated): How much more?

PELFREY: Five days. We're not even sure what the latency period is for this thing. For God's sake, give my guys time!

GRADY: That's pushing it.

KLINGHOFF: Fifty hours then! Okay! Hands, please. Eileen, still no? Elias? Okay, to sum up, I will tell the President that after being responsible for the destruction of a U.S. submarine, the outbreak is spreading on a second vessel. We recommend a fifty-hour window to see if Colonel Rush can show progress. After that, the National Emergency Powers Act enables him to use protocol five. The President might ignore us anyway. It wouldn't be the first time.

PELFREY: Two days. My God!

KLINGHOFF: It's a bit more than two. Certainly enough time to see if any treatments are working. Dr. Graves said that antivirals kick in fast. We're compassionate people. We'll give them a chance. We're all here because we can make tough choices, and this one might be the toughest we will ever make. I thank you. Now, all, perhaps a brief moment of prayer is in order, for the sick, and for Colonel Rush's efforts, before I cross the street.

■ ■ ■

At the White House, the President thanked Klinghoff, and sat alone for a long time in the dark of the Oval Office. He was a midsized, plain-looking, tough-minded man, a former governor, and he'd come a long way from his boyhood as a lower-middle-class son of a Montana cattle rancher. He remembered his boyhood on that beautiful ranch, and the worst day of it, when he was eight. He recalled his father taking him out to the east range, where they looked over a herd of eight thousand prime beef cows. He remembered sobbing when his father told him that all those animals would have to be shot, burned, and buried, because one had been found to be infected with something called "mad cow disease," which ate away brains.

In order to protect people in the nearby town, and those who would one day eat Montana beef across America, the entire herd would be put down, even though this would cause his father to lose the ranch.

"That's not fair," the boy had blurted out.

"It is the right thing to do," his father had said.

"You said we'll lose everything."

"When you have a tough decision to make, the longer you wait, the harder it gets."

At 3 A.M., the President picked up the phone and called his old college roommate, now an Air Force general in Seattle. He told the general what he needed, but asked the general to do it as a personal favor. He said he'd understand if the general refused.

The Air Force general said, "Christ, Mike," but then he said he would do it. He added, "We've got thick cloud cover moving in up there again, so the satellites will be blind."

The President hung up. He had decided that two days was too long to wait.

In twenty hours, if there was no definite progress, the ship would be destroyed. Then the surface of the ocean would be sprayed with oil and ignited to cleanse any bodies or debris. Then the President would go on national television, and tell the truth about everything except the old film.

The President figured this would quite possibly end his career. His enemies would call for his resignation, possibly even prosecution, but he'd weather the second part, and anyway, neither was the point. He had campaigned for office by telling voters he was the man they wanted in office when the eventual 3 A.M. emergency—every President faced one—occurred. Now the moment had come.

He wondered how he'd live with it.

He said out loud, "You said it, Daddy."

The President looked out at the Rose Garden, beyond the glass, without seeing it. After a while the First Lady came in, having woken, seen his side of the bed empty, and known that his habit, when disturbed, was to sit in his "home office." She got a wool comforter from a closet and lay down on one of the two couches. It was her custom, when he was troubled, to sleep near him. He liked the company, even if he didn't talk.

She was still sleeping when the sun came up. He did not notice the light brightening, though normally the sight of the Rose Garden at dawn was—to the old rancher's boy, a kid who'd grown up under drought conditions, a kid who'd worked his way up after his family went broke—a dew-drenched delight.

TWENTY-ONE

Clinton was in bad shape. He lay wheezing on a cot, in row two, the last cot that had been open. Now there were no more cots left if new people fell ill. Body temperature, 103 plus. He was shivering. Sweat poured from his forehead, drenched his bedding. Janice Cullen had laid a knapsack as a pillow at the head of the cot, as there was no wall or other way to prop him up; and sitting up was better for patients whose lungs filled with fluid.

"We're out of IVs," Cullen told me. Her eyes were clear, her voice steady. She might be afraid of storms, I saw, but not disease outbreaks. She had guts.

Bending by his bed, mask on, she helped Clinton to drink water from a glass. *Keep them hydrated.* And thanks to the Chinese, we had plenty of antivirals, at least something good had come from that confrontation, and she stuffed a squeeze-bottle nozzle into each nostril, sprayed, and left the medicine on a makeshift night table, a wooden crate, within Clinton's reach. Each patient had one. They displayed eyeglasses, pill vials, even, as in a real hospital, donated books or magazines from the crew.

On Clinton's crate lay a copy of *Outside* magazine. The cover showed a happy couple cross-country skiing over a snow field. ADVENTURES IN THE OPENING ARCTIC! the headline read.

His cough sprayed mucus. His blanket was stained with vomit. Our masks had been coated with disinfectant, so I smelled that mostly, not the effluence of the ill.

This man had saved our lives and I remembered—ministering to him—what Eddie had told me. In 1918, the death rate from Spanish flu in Eskimo villages had reached 98 percent. Alaska's indigenous people had been among the worst hit. It made sense. Their numbers, since contact with Westerners, had been decimated by flu and other illnesses that might cause a single week of discomfort in Ohio, but kill in the High North.

"Swollen," I said, probing lymph nodes in Clinton's neck. "Get an extra blanket, he's practically convulsing."

"None left," said Cullen.

"Then a parka. Get extra jackets sent in here. Sweaters. Jackets. Anything the crew can donate, to help keep 'em warm. And leave all clothing outside, in the halls. Nobody new comes in here."

Cullen looked at DeBlieu for confirmation, and the captain nodded stiffly.

I told him, standing up, "It's too late to put anyone off. We don't know who's infected, including us. So unless you're prepared to empty this whole hangar, all hundred-plus people here—you, too—we stay."

DeBlieu looked like he was going to hit me. His breath vaporized with each exhalation. The sounds around us seemed magnified: wheezing, coughing. Someone moaned for "Linda." Someone was throwing up.

DeBlieu said, in a low voice so people around us would not hear dissension, "Goddamn you."

I bent down to the patient. "Clinton?"

His oval eyes were bloodshot, only vaguely attentive.

"Clinton, where do you hurt?"

He focused weakly. "Name a place."

"Where's it the worst?"

"Take my wife's phone number, for when you can call out. Give her a message."

"No need for that. We'll get that fever lowered and you'll call her yourself soon."

His tongue was coated with blue. His cough was steady, wet, and hideous.

Clinton closed his eyes. "Don't go to Barrow," he said.

"Excuse me?"

"Don't bring us ashore. I have two kids. I have a wife. I know what's happening, Colonel. The elders told us what happened when their grandparents were kids, and got sick after being around whalers. You're all whalers."

Meaning outsiders. Like me. "Don't count yourself out, my friend," I said, the word "friend" bitter in my mouth. "I'm going to take your blood, okay? Check it in the lab."

Clinton stared at me blankly. I thought the fever was taking him. Then he said, "We don't have funeral homes in Barrow, you know. We bury our own dead, Colonel Rush."

■ ■ ■

Major Pettit stepped into my path as we reached the stairway to the labs. Like the other Marines, he wore a medical apron and gloves. I tried to brush past. Pettit kept his voice low. "A moment, sir?"

Ten feet off, I saw Andrew Sachs mopping the brow of one of the sick. Karen Vleska was applying ice—no shortage of that here—to a feverish head. I kept hearing Clinton's words in my mind and they seared me. Had I made a mistake, jeopardized everyone here because I felt guilty over what I did in Afghanistan? Had I let personal problems get in the way of professional judgment? That's what *they* were thinking. The director. DeBlieu. Clinton. Everyone.

"I'm in a hurry, Major. If it's not urgent . . ."

"Sir, I just wanted to say—"

"Get it out."

He stood straighter, and his words vaporized as they emerged. "Colonel, I was wrong about you. I apologize for what I said before. I'm proud to serve with you and so are the men. They asked me to tell you. Marines don't leave wounded behind. You don't leave your people behind."

Stunned, I stared at my ex-wife's lover, and saw, in his eyes, a tough Marine's respect. He was the last person I would have thought would back me up, on anything.

I said gruffly, "That's not urgent, Major."

I pushed past, keeping my eyes averted, so no one could see tears I blinked back, stupid tears, I thought, enraged. Stupid, idiot tears.

■ ■ ■

The only good thing about the United States having only one ice-breaker was that whoever stocked it made sure its labs came with the best equipment—including an electron microscope, used normally, De-Blieu had said, to analyze walrus blood, or southern fish species moving north, or bottom sediment that the ship dredged up, as scientists tried to gather information to support a U.S. claim for undersea territory at the UN.

Now it would help me look at Clinton's blood.

The apparatus had its own room, and looked nothing like the old handheld microscope my parents had given me as a birthday present when I was eleven years old. It was built into a six-foot desk, and consisted of a periscope-shaped tower, dial controls, twin eyepiece, as in a periscope, and two monitor screens on which the produced image would show up.

I would not see Clinton's blood directly, as in a normal microscope. I would be looking at a 3-D picture.

Well, the director was right about one thing, and that's the quality of my thumb drive encyclopedia. I found no shortage of electron mike photos of Spanish flu cells. They've been widely published since 2005, when doctors at the CDC reconstituted some from a corpse dug up in Alaska. Let's see if Clinton's blood looks the same. That would confirm we're dealing with the 1918 strain.

I injected some of Clinton's sample onto a petri dish. I inserted the sample into the vacuum compartment and closed the tiny door, six inches up in the microscope tower. I flipped a switch, heard a hum as power came on. Hitting a second switch, I envisioned a stream of high-voltage electrons—shot by a gun—spraying down from the top, through a condenser lens onto the dish. The electrons would pass through and then widen out in a cone shape, like moving shotgun pellets, to be reconstituted—as in a copy machine—onto a fluorescent screen that I watched, riveted, through the eyepiece.

The electron beams created a 3-D image of Clinton's blood, magnified twenty thousand times.

I heard myself breathing. On monitor one was the original Spanish flu; enlarged into a small armada of brown ovoid submarine shapes floating toward a wildly exotic-looking sprouting of long green undersea leaves. I was in a nano-world, and the rounded surfaces of the attackers were covered with sharp spikes, like mines.

The magnified leaves were actually cilia, microscopic hairs lining the lungs of a pig infected with reconstituted virus. The brown floaters were flu microbes, incoming to infect.

Enlarged to 100,000 magnification, the undersea landscape disappeared to be replaced by clusters of cells, rod or ovoid shaped, red with dye, looking like massed versions of what you see in a lava lamp, stretching and contracting and dividing into new cells, as they attacked the healthy cells of the pig. Each invading cell contained a jellylike center, its nucleic acid, surrounded by a protective layer, a thin capsid.

I compared the two images, one on each screen.

I heard Eddie's sharp intake of breath behind me as a 3-D image hummed, complete with grooves and spikes and striations, good as a microbe identity card.

Eddie said, unsurprised but still horrified, "They're the same."

■ ■ ■

Air in the hangar downstairs would be saturated with the exact same particles, with more being sprayed out each time anyone coughed. My thumb drive had told me that the Spanish flu manifested itself in patients after an incubation period of between one and three days. We'd been in contact with the *Montana* for over twenty-four hours.

"Prime infection time, Uno," Eddie said.

"Do we have enough antiviral spray for everyone, even the healthy ones?"

"Thanks to our good buddy, Zhou, yeah."

"Then everyone's to start taking it, as a preventative. If there's enough left after that, we supply the rest of the ship."

"That stuff slows regular flus from replicating. But every flu is different."

"I'd really like to talk to the CDC."

"Hey, we're in better shape than in 1918, One."

He was Mr. Positive. I thought, *Yeah, better. Instead of eighty million dead, only ten million this time.*

I said, "Let's see what else we can come up with."

■ ■ ■

The only medicine that definitely worked so far was coffee. We'd plugged in a huge Coast Guard percolator—it made gallons of dark, strong brew—and the smell of Maxwell House permeated the wet lab. Thick sandwiches—slabs of pot roast on rye—lay on the desk and table counters, sent over by the mess, and left by cooks in a passageway outside. No contact was allowed between crew outside the hangar, and inside.

One thing the ship was overstocked with was food.

"Can I help?" asked the voice of Karen Vleska.

Advancing into the lab, she seemed more vulnerable, more tentative. The small, agile persona that had marked her originally was gone. I saw a blue vein fluttering in the side of her neck, a tiny freckle on the jaw as she pulled up a chair beside me. She wore corduroy trousers and a thick wool ski sweater with a moose logo on it, in brown. She wore black Merrell boots and she smelled, like we all did, of unlaundered clothes and shipboard chemical showers. In epidemic country, we wore masks all the time.

"Down there all I'm doing is running cool towels over foreheads, along with Del Grazo and Marietta."

"Believe me, the people you're doing it for do not consider it a small thing," I said.

Eddie was on his laptop, both of our computers having been brought down by the crew. We'd been poring over articles, reports, and speculations on the disease, exploring the reams of information on my thumb drive sticks, replicated onto his.

She said, "Tell me what we're looking for."

"Treatments. Old diaries. Any ideas to help," I said, my eyes burning from staring at the screen.

She rolled her chair beside mine. Knee to knee. "Four eyes beat two," she said.

■ ■ ■

More than ten million pages have been written about the Spanish flu since 1918: symptoms, history, speculations, treatments. There were hundreds of photos in here of turn-of-the-century schoolchildren with surgical masks on, terrified kids, patients occupying rows of beds in quarantined Army wards in France, frightened doctors refusing to enter wards, public health notices in newspapers, mayors in radio studios, urging people to stay home. And most recently, results on the reconstituted virus in Atlanta, by the CDC.

The problem wasn't that we had too little information. The problem was that we had too much.

"Everything but a cure," Eddie said.

I found a diary written by a doctor working on a South Dakota Sioux Indian reservation in 1918. *Patients sitting up in bed survived at a higher rate.*

Eddie read aloud from a memo written in Philadelphia General Hospital, mid-outbreak. "'*We've had some success inoculating healthy people with blood from survivors. Rate of infection went down.*'"

Karen breathed audibly. "You mean, just shoot blood from one person into another?"

"Yeah," said Eddie. "That's what they did a hundred years ago."

"And that worked?" she said, shocked.

I rubbed my eyes, exhausted, groped for coffee. I stirred in three packs of sugar. Anything to get my attention span up. "Survivors have antibodies in their blood."

"But what about all those warnings about sharing fluids? Like in AIDS?"

I nodded. "The first blood transfusions happened in the 1700s in France, Karen. Doctors joined hoses to patients, ran a foot pump, circulated blood, one person to another. Crude as it gets, and no disinfectants, and it killed some people, but it also worked sometimes. But we didn't know about different blood types then."

Karen made a noise deep in her throat. "You're suggesting that we collect blood from survivors, and inject it into the sick? It sounds so . . . desperate."

"It is desperate. And not just the sick. The antibodies would act as a preventative in the healthy, in theory. And we'd also be transferring in lymphocytes, active virus-killing cells. I wonder, Eddie, can we collect blood from survivors, enough to vaccinate a lot of people, if they're the same blood type? Enough—if the medicines don't work?"

"Can we pool blood from different donors?"

"Too dangerous. More chance of rejection. One to one. And blood type to blood type."

It wasn't exactly the ideal treatment. But we called down to Lieutenant Cullen via ship phone and asked how many hypodermics were on board, just in case. She told us there was a shortage. If we wanted to inoculate, we'd need to reuse hypodermics.

"Great," I said. "On top of everything else, dirty needles."

"We could disinfect after each shot," suggested Eddie. "If it comes to that. Lab sterilizers."

"We get Chief Apparecio up here, and other survivors. Draw blood. It will have antibodies. We heparinize syringes. Put a couple milliliters of heparin in there so the blood doesn't clot. Then we'll give fifty cc's per patient, make the stuff last. Worst comes to worst . . ."

Eddie finished it. "Worst comes to worst, we try Dr. One's patented homemade miracle vaccine. Stops hair loss. Stops gout. Builds muscles. Kills flus."

Morose, I said, "It would help if we had Elisa kits."

Karen asked, "What's an Elisa kit?"

"A way to test for the presence of disease-related proteins," Eddie explained.

"Speak English."

"You take a microtiter plate and—"

"A what? A what? I said speak English!"

I sighed. "It's a plastic plate with little wells in it. You put blood samples in each well. You add a reagent. It enables you to isolate proteins. We want to ID viral proteins, or enzymes to try to disable. If we can ID them, if we had computer-aided designing . . ." I cursed. A wave of futility swept over me. "Goddamnit! The goddamn CDC can do this. *They* have equipment. We're just three people bumbling around on a ship. Why did they fucking cut us off?"

Karen gripped my forearm, clearly to get my mind on business again, "What do these microplates look like, Joe?"

Joe. We rummaged the wet lab. We found no Elisa kits aboard. Nothing in the dry lab either. That would have been too easy.

Back at the screens I drank more coffee, but even the caffeine was failing to stimulate me now. I said, sighing, "Let's give the medicines a chance to work before we start injecting people."

"How long before we know that?"

"Could be fast. A day. Two."

Karen Vleska got up, stretched, picked at the foods on the table that the cooks had sent over: Chips Ahoy! chocolate chip cookies; red shiny Washington State apples; PowerBars; packs of Nestlé's cocoa.

She chose an apple, lowered her mask, exposed her mouth, and bit into it. The crackle was like a signal for all of us to take a break.

I tore open the wrapping of a PowerBar. Apple cinnamon flavor. Eddie went for the cookies.

Karen said, after a few moments of eating in silence, "You know, my boyfriend, when he was a kid, went to an ethical culture school . . ."

I thought, *Right! The boyfriend. Good. I can stop thinking about her.*

Then I thought, *I can't believe I'm thinking about this now anyway.*

"Ethical culture school?" asked Eddie.

"It was a private school for atheists," she said, leaning back, exposing the long neck vein, the dark small freckles there, a constellation of three, swell of breasts tight on the moose logo sweater. The shiny silver hair was up, pinned. "His parents didn't believe in religion but still wanted their kids to learn values. My boyfriend—Carl—said they were given a problem in fifth grade. A museum is on fire. You can save one thing. Do you choose an old woman or the hundred-and-fifty-year-old Renoir masterpiece painting?"

Eddie snorted. "I'll be sure to send my kids to this school when we get back. See what happens when you eliminate God? You kill the people and save the BMWs."

"Well, we're at a table at a seafood restaurant. He's telling me about being in class, arguing. *I'd save the old lady! She's someone's grandmother! No! I'd save the painting! The old lady is probably sick anyway!*"

DeBlieu's voice suddenly crackled onto the ship intercom. He was addressing the healthy crew, the people outside the hangar, in the mess, on the bridge, in the cabins, people probably staring up at intercom boxes, hearts beating loud in their chests. "This is the captain. You need to know that the survivors of the *Montana* may be infected with a highly contagious illness. Anyone feeling ill is to report immediately to sick bay. We're on alert, just like drills. More hand washing. More disinfecting. Double shifts at meals. I want fewer people at each table. Regular disinfection of bathrooms. No more than three people in any cabin at one time. All lounges are closed. This is serious. Please know that our medical personnel are working very hard to . . ."

Eddie watched the intercom. "That'll go over big."

Karen's eyes had gone large, were fixed on mine. Perhaps I imagined it, but it seemed that a new note had entered her voice since the boyfriend came up. It wasn't affection, or missing the guy. It seemed to be more like distance. She said, "You know, you always hear that saying, there are two kinds of people in the world! People who shut off televisions when they enter a room and people who turn them on! People who follow rules and who don't! Well, I have one. People who want to save the contagious, and those who want to destroy them. That's what's going on, isn't it, in Washington? That's why they cut us off? They're getting ready to do something bad here."

"Not necessarily," I said.

"That's why they don't want us calling out."

I said, not really believing it, "They just want to manage the news. Damage control."

"Uh-huh. You don't believe that any more than I do. Did they give you any time frame? A deadline to get results? Any idea what they plan exactly, or is that classified, Joe? You're not supposed to tell us?"

She kept using my name, "Joe," like a weapon. I flashed back to a hot plain in Afghanistan. I saw the truck coming. I felt the grips of the machine gun on my hands. I heard myself counting down seconds, praying that the oncoming truck would stop. "Nine. Eight." I remembered thinking that if I fired, if I killed everyone in that truck, I'd save the people on the base. It was math. It was triage. I couldn't believe it was a choice I'd ever put myself in a position to have to make.

"No deadline that I know of," I said.

How will they do it? Sink us? Gas? If they use gas, they could keep the ship for later.

"But it's a whole ship," she said, as if monitoring my thinking. "It's over two hundred people. It's *me*," she said, and laughed suddenly, loudly, completely self-aware.

"Maybe it won't come to that," Eddie said.

Hours passed.

Karen dozed after a while. Then Eddie.

I jolted awake.

I'd been asleep too long.

■ ■ ■

"Triage," Karen said, back at work. "Notice how, whenever people want to do something horrible, they invent a sanitized word for it? Like 'surgical strikes' for drone attacks?"

Eddie finished up more cookies, which kept coming. He started on a ham and cheddar sandwich. He reached for a can of Dr Pepper. "Ah, we'd probably do the same thing."

"No!" A fierce look, anger and challenge, animated her features. Her eyes bored into mine. She snapped out, "We *were* them! We *had* the choice back there, and we're *not* doing the same thing. *We took everyone aboard!*"

I thought, stunned, in wonder, *She said "we." She wants to be part of that decision.*

Eddie burped and sighed. "Hey, forget the cosmic questions, Karen.

Let's get down to the real stuff. What did old boyfriend Carl save in the museum? The old lady? Or the painting?"

Perhaps it was the fluorescent light, or exhaustion, but it seemed for a moment that her expression flickered through her time on Earth: Karen the kid, face unlined; Karen the tough engineer; Karen with the weight of choice on her, like gravity tugging down the corners of her mouth.

"He chose the painting," she said softly.

"You would have chosen the old lady?" said Eddie.

Instead of answering, quite violently she sneezed.

■ ■ ■

There was a moment of silence, then she held out her hand, and in her small palm, lay a quivering mass of yellowish bile. Her hand began slightly trembling.

"Anyone could sneeze," I said.

Eddie said, "Hey, I sneeze all the time."

It was not the best moment for Major Pettit to show up again, a stocky presence in the doorway, blunt, V-shaped, blocking light. "Colonel, a moment?"

"Bad time, Major."

He stepped inside anyway, damn him, looking like some Arctic bag man bundled into his parka, beneath the apron, gauze mask, and plastic gloves. "I think you ought to see this, sir," he said as Karen Vleska used a napkin to wipe away the bile on her hand, but I knew those tiny particles were drifting in the air around us, expanding and contracting as in a lava lamp, like on the slide.

"Colonel, you *really* want to see this," Pettit said.

■ ■ ■

Eddie would check her throat, ears, nasal passages. *How many more will I kill?* I thought as Pettit led me down the narrow passageway between labs, and into one filled with electronics, and banks of at least twenty monitor screens.

"Major, just say it," I snapped.

"Sir," he said, taking a swivel chair at a console and activating a monitor, "they use this room normally for checking sea bottom images. These screens on the right? They show sonar pictures of sediments. I guess State will use this to apply for undersea territory, Mr. Sachs said."

"I'm running out of patience, Major."

"But the right-hand screens are cameras. You can call up images from anywhere on the ship."

Instantly I grew more interested.

Pettit plumped down into a swivel chair and adjusted a dial. I was seeing the hangar below, from an elevated angle. The cots. The sick. Lieutenant Cullen inserting one of those aerosol containers into the nose of a woman. I saw Marietta Cristobel wiping a man's forehead. Sachs spoke with Del Grazo and they broke apart. Pettit said, "Watch the difference between Sachs and Del Grazo."

There was only one reason Pettit would have called me in here, and it was that he thought he'd ID'd the spy. I felt my heart speed up. The black-and-white picture came in clear as the cable TV back home in Anchorage. Sachs went cot to cot, down a row, stopping by each cot, clearly asking each patient, *Need anything? Are you okay?*

If a guy shook his head, said no, Sachs moved to the next person. If a guy responded, Sachs stayed.

Pettit said, "Like all the volunteers. *Bed to bed.* Now," he said, adjusting the picture. "Watch Del Grazo."

I saw the lieutenant sit for a while with one patient, talking, nodding, taking his time, listening to what the man said. He turned his back to the camera. I saw his arms moving. What was he doing? Then he put something in his pocket and rose. But instead of going to the next cot over, where a man looked up at him, clearly expecting him to stop, Del Grazo scanned the rows, then went off in a different direction.

"Huh!" I said.

He passed by two dozen patients, including one waving for him to stop. He seemed to ask another patient—a sub crewman—for directions, then the patient pointed left and Del Grazo went that way.

Del Grazo arrived at a cot on the far end of the hangar. He bent over *that* man, and began talking, wiping the guy's head, looking attentive again.

Pettit said, "He never goes cot to cot."

I wished I could see what Del Grazo was doing when he again turned his back to the camera. There was something familiar about those arm movements. "Maybe he carried a message from one guy to a friend."

"I asked DeBlieu if they have tapes of the hangar. Del Grazo never talks to two people side by side. And he always turns his back, like he knows the camera is there. I wondered, why? Why those specific guys? So I called Apparecio up here and we watched together. And the last *four* guys he attended to?"

"Yes?" I was watching Del Grazo's back, the way his right hand seemed to extend straight out, toward the patient, and stay there. The left hand went out where I couldn't see it, but I could tell it was moving in small circles. Both hands went into his parka pockets.

Pettit turned his face to me fully. "Those guys he talks to all work with the prototype torpedo, Colonel. He passed up everyone else. He just talks to torpedo crew."

Softly I said, "Does he?"

"And before that, on the tapes, it was guys who work the reactor.

Never a cook. Never the guy who runs the ship store. Never a third mate . . ."

"Pretty risky of him," I said.

"It's mayhem down there. Everyone running around. No one pays attention. And if it's risky, whatever the hell he's doing, sir, with his hands, *maybe that's his mission.*"

Pettit and I stood up at the same time. I felt a dull throb of rage begin in my temples.

"The communications officer," I said.

"Yeah. Fixes everyone's computers. Maintains the sat equipment, radios, access to the ship," he said.

"Seems a talk is in order," I said.

And Pettit suddenly said, "Oh shit!"

■ ■ ■

On screen, Del Grazo had stopped walking, and was gazing up, directly into a camera. Del Grazo frowning, thinking, then looking around quickly. Del Grazo's gaze moving again, up and left, toward another camera.

"He's checking the cameras."

Del Grazo looking left now, then right, scanning the hangar. Looking for . . . what? Pettit? The guards? Del Grazo lowering his head, moving now, slow but steady, looking neither left nor right, but heading past patients toward the hangar door, hands in his pockets, taking an Arctic stroll. A plodding walk. A walk outside.

"This is happening right now?" I said, turning to go.

"This was ten minutes ago."

"Fuck," I said.

We ran for the hangar.

But Del Grazo was gone.

TWENTY-TWO

DeBlieu swore softly. "So the only way to go look for him is to infect the whole ship," he said. "Send Marines forward, expose just about everyone aboard."

"Do you know a better way?"

"I know that you never should have brought them all on," he said bitterly as we watched Pettit and his men head forward, a search party every bit as serious as if they approached a potentially hostile village in Afghanistan.

We were outside the bridge, above the prow and looking down, but views below were compartmentalized, blocked by superstructure, awnings, decks, antennas. DeBlieu had ordered nonessential personnel—anyone not searching for Del Grazo—to the mess, the only room big enough to hold them, while two-man Coast Guard teams—armed from the weapons locker—had been dispatched as guards to the engine room, central power plant, auxiliary control areas, and at strategically located hatches.

DeBlieu had also ordered Del Grazo to report to the bridge, over the intercom. A command unanswered. Big surprise.

Light was fading. To port, I saw that we'd pushed our way out of even the thinner ice, and had arrived at a generally open area of ocean, which probably would have been frozen solid fifty years ago this time of year. But other than a few pathetic ice rafts bobbing, we were free of the white prison, and idling in place, in case Del Grazo had gotten off.

A voice on the radio said, "Weapons locker secure, Captain. He didn't get in here."

Below, on deck, crew went from evacuation station to station, checking the life rafts to see if they were still there. To lower the motorized Zodiacs, brake releases could be operated by hand. The boat would then lower by gravity to the sea. There, anyone inside could disconnect the hook, start the motor with a button, and drive off.

I don't see any Zodiacs moving away on the water, so where is he?

"*My* officer," said DeBlieu savagely. His face was twisted in pain, the combined surges of guilt, rage, and humiliation that come with betrayal. "*My* communications man," he said as we flashed over the enormous damage such a man—having access to every computer on the ship—could do.

DeBlieu muttered, "He could have piggybacked Chinese listeners onto every sat talk, hacked into every laptop, inserted software to monitor every study we've done for the State Department over the last two years."

Is the damage over? Is Del Grazo putting some new plan into effect? Or is he just terrified, running like a kid, seeking a hiding place before the inevitable apprehension?

"If he's smart, he had an escape plan," I said. "Or he's stashed a weapon. You say you've had him here for two years?"

DeBlieu's jaw seemed to be grinding, his breath puffed out in bullet bursts. "Two goddamn years. But why not just take a Zodiac? He had a lead on us."

I shook my head. "And go where? He knew we were onto him. He figured he didn't have time to push off and get out of range. The Marines could plug him at three hundred yards."

Eddie had taken over in the monitor lab, and was going camera to camera, like the exec on the bridge, searching for a glimpse of the running man, a flash of movement, a face staring back; in a passageway, in the laundry, the gym, the cargo hold.

A couple of big, burly, armed chiefs sent to search Del Grazo's cabin had found, of course, nothing.

The sun was starting to sink in the heavens. We were far enough south so that, at exactly the worst time possible, natural light would disappear. The last rays sparkled and formed gray areas of shadow on the tiny passing ice floes. Reports flowed in from frustrated search parties. He was not in the aft cargo area. Not in the quarantined area. Not hiding in the copter control shack.

DeBlieu grunted as we heard that all Zodiac boats remained securely on board. "*Lieutenant Peter Del Grazo to the bridge, please,*" came a normal-sounding announcement, as if the guy was simply late for a shift.

DeBlieu said, "He was always helpful. Always volunteered to do extra."

He'd ordered his searchers over his radio, "If you find him, we want to talk to him. But if you have to defend yourself, shoot."

I kept thinking, *What was Del Grazo doing with those patients when his back was turned from the camera? What the hell was he up to?*

In all, at least forty people were scattered through the ship, looking for the fugitive. The Coasties were armed with M16s, but they were not warriors. They had not joined up to fight.

"At least he didn't get a weapon." DeBlieu sighed.

"That doesn't mean he's not armed. Do you search your crew each time they come on board when you're in port?"

"No."

"Do you sweep lockers, looking for drugs, weapons, contraband?"

"There's no need . . ." he started to say, and stopped.

"Then he could have brought on a weapon at any time, or could have taken one from the *Montana*."

DeBlieu headed into the bridge to join his officers, and I pulled out my Beretta sidearm and stepped inside and clomped down a stairwell. Now I was searching, too, for our human infection. Our saboteur. Our Chinese spy.

But the ship was a miniature city, and Del Grazo had a thousand places to hide, or to have stashed weapons. The *Wilmington* had multiple levels. It was stuffed with gear lockers and fan rooms, workshops, machine shops, store and supply rooms, prop shaft area, bow thruster room, twenty thousand cubic feet of cargo storage space alone. The ship's planners had maximized the use of space. There were no spare inches.

I went cabin to cabin. I opened a door slowly; no one was supposed to be in the junior officer stateroom. I scanned empty bunks, a desk, a poster of the singer Adele, as a soundtrack left on played Kelly Clarkson doing "Stronger." In the next cabin were books, *Farewell to Arms*, *Old Man and the Sea*, someone here taking the college lit class on board, taught by a professor from a university in Indiana.

A wallet lay on a deck. People here trusted each other.

No one under the bunk. Or in the shared bathroom separating two single-officer cabins.

In a male crew bunk room, twelve well-made steel berths were stacked in two-man tiers. It was quiet, except for the hissing of air whooshing from vents above the corners, and a muted scrape of an odd ice bit hitting the hull. For some reason, I smelled bananas.

I climbed through a hatch leading down—through a narrow hole, to a cargo hold. I stood amid a tumble of wooden crates and a thousand shadows.

Nobody!

"Level 04 clear, Captain, looks like!" my radio said.

You could search for a week and not find someone who knew the layout. You could search for two weeks if that someone kept moving, staying one cabin ahead, I thought.

If we find him, afterward we'll try to disinfect. They must have bleach on board. We can wash down every wall, every cabin. But odds are we won't get everything. Odds are the thing is out among the crew now.

Then my thoughts were interrupted. The ship's alarms began ringing, as in the drills we'd practiced, except this time I had a feeling that Del Grazo was behind the alarm.

"Fire in the chief's mess," the overhead voice said. And then, sharply, no surprise, "This is not a drill."

The chief's lounge, most comfortable cabin aboard. The break room for lifers, petty officers. They'd had me in there once for a poker game. Best coffee. Best music. Plushest Barcalounger furniture. Either a football or a baseball game seemed to be playing at all times.

He's not just hiding. But what is he doing?

Distraction? Sabotage? Escape?

■ ■ ■

Passages and stairwells filled with rushing, shouting figures in fire retardant suits, masks on, axes out, any panic on board previously now magnified. The danger was real now, and all anyone had to do to appreciate the extent of it was to see Marines, formerly quarantined, moving among the healthy crew.

Another announcement burst forth, five minutes later. "Fire in the radio room!"

Site of the long-range communication equipment and the cables running to the bridge.

The ship was a maze of machinery, electrical works, condensers. Fuel. Wiring. All vulnerable to fire. What had he done, I thought as I searched. Planted incendiary devices beforehand? Because the radio room was on a different deck entirely from the first fire.

It was always locked, but Del Grazo would have had a key and the combo to get in.

Four figures in fire-fighting gear unrolled a hose at the entrance of the science lounge. I glimpsed a sofa in flames, billowing black smoke. There was water on deck. The passageway smelled of burned foam. Maybe hell smelled that way also.

But I already knew that we'd sailed into white hell.

■ ■ ■

We'd done drills for accidental fires on the *Wilmington*. Drills for collisions and oil spill control, drills practicing fast boats down to evacuate a tour ship. Drills for ice hits, drills for heart attacks.

There were no drills for sabotage on the *Wilmington*.

I ran, Beretta out, down the main deck passageway, which connected—if you passed through a series of hatches—both ends of the ship, fore to aft. It passed the commissary and deck machinery equipment room and main generator room and auxiliary boiler room. There was a fire now in the engineering control center, up on level one.

SNAFU, situation normal all fucked up, as Eddie would say. At Quan-

*tico when we do searches we're always in three-man teams. Watch your part-
ners. Never go into a room alone. Always wait for the corner men to go in first.*

Heart in my throat, I went into each room alone.

I was the corner man and also the main man. I opened the door of
the commissary. I shoved it into the wall to make sure nobody was
behind. I flicked on the light and advanced forward, pulse slamming.
Inside were stacked shelves of logo T-shirts and sweatshirts, *Wilmington* hats, and red wool caps for designated "polar bears," who had gone
through the Arctic hazing. There were shaving kits for sale, and feminine hygiene products. There was no Peter Del Grazo crouching behind
a stack of long-sleeved shirts showing a grinning walrus.

I continued aft, along the passageway. It was quiet at first down
here, no footsteps, no shouting, but then I heard people coming and
two burly white-suited figures with fire axes approached. I stared at the
faceplates. It was impossible to see inside due to the sharp reflected
overhead light.

I tightened my grip on the pistol. The figures came abreast, passed,
disappeared. They were probably also checking compartments.

I kept going.

Ahead, on the right, three minutes later, I came upon a small bathroom, a head, in an isolated turn of corridor just before the hatch leading to the science area. I reached for the knob. The door creaked open.
It was dark inside.

The light flooded on and I jumped. Five feet ahead I saw a figure
but it was me, scared as shit, pointing a Beretta at a mirror.

But suddenly there was a white-suited figure behind me in the mirror, too, maybe one of the two guys who had passed earlier, except now
his ax was raised, swinging down, toward me.

It was too late to turn around. Reflexively I dropped as the ax
swished past my ears. I heard the metallic smack of steel on steel, saw

the blade bounce off the door frame as my body slammed into the deck and pain exploded inside.

Falling onto a steel deck is like being hit with hammers. An electric current jolted into my left kneecap. A fiery torch had been thrust into my right shin. My elbow was numb. I saw the Beretta drop to the deck, heard it clatter away, beyond the looming figure storming in from the corridor. I rolled left, slammed into a wall, just as the ax hit the spot where I'd lain a moment earlier. The room was too cramped. Each leg motion sent streaks of agony up my spine. He jabbed the ax at me. I rolled as it glanced off the sink and sliced through a toilet paper roll, easy as skin.

He went for my head, staying far enough away so I could not reach him. My ankle made a popping noise when I pushed back. I tried to scramble up but a giant seemed to tear in two the tendons on my ankle. I kicked out with the other leg, kept him back, but a fifty-ton truck must have rolled over my leg.

Why did he come back for me? Maybe he thought I recognized him through the faceplate.

His face inside the shield was bulging and white and streaming sweat. The formerly pleasant features were twisted with rage. Perspiration flooded my eyes. There was no room to back up. I gathered all my strength and, when he jabbed again, swung the bad leg in a roundabout kick, making contact with the side of the ax head with my boot, pushing it left as I screamed from the pain.

The momentum swung him off balance. I tried to lunge past him and reach the Beretta, and actually touched it, actually felt fingers brush steel, but then he was on me. His hood fell off. His breath smelled of garlic. His eyes were huge and furious. I saw veins in his nostrils, and dandruff caught in an eyebrow. His fingers were vises, pressing into my throat.

"You . . . should have . . . killed them," he said.

I could not breathe but I pulled the trigger, heard the M9 go off. Nothing. I fired again, heard ricochets in the corridor. I felt a sting at the edge of my ear. The ricocheting bullet had winged the marksman.

He straddled me. I was losing consciousness. His right knee pinned my left hand on deck, his hip blocked movement of my right. I needed all my remaining strength to push the gun three inches toward his belly. I pulled the trigger, and with my oxygen cut off, sound seemed louder.

He was still there.

Maybe the noise had attracted attention, because I heard running, and someone shouting, "Hey! Hey!"

I could breathe. He was running off. A woman's face was bending over me. I recognized the small blonde, an Alabaman, an officer who worked night shifts on the bridge.

"Colonel? Are you all right? Colonel?"

I gasped for air. I forced out, "Where'd he go?"

"Into the stairwell. Look, he left something in the sink. It's another one! Carla! Call the incendiary crew!"

Two minutes later, limping, I found the other white-suited figure who had been with Del Grazo, crumbled, around the corner, blood spurting from a wound opening his left side. Ribs caved in. Just a kid. An eighteen-year-old who'd not known the figure he was running with was the man for whom he'd been searching.

"Colonel, we're fighting four fires now! He left devices all over the place!"

As for Del Grazo, he was, once again, gone.

His words a drumbeat in my head.

You should have killed them.

■ ■ ■

By the time the ship exec spotted him, the radio room was wrecked, the fires were under control, but the Zodiac was overboard, and he was inside, pulling away in the dark, hoping to be absorbed into the inky blackness, natural color of the Arctic sea in summers these days, not white, as it had been for centuries until now.

With satellites blocked off and the radio room burned, the only two means of communication remaining with the outside world were the line-of-sight handhelds, good at a measly six miles . . . and the long-range radio from the bridge, that is, if atmospheric conditions cooperated, and if, the huge *if,* the cable running from the radio room had not melted.

But if the cable was out, we had no way of reaching the mainland, or any ships, or anyone at all more than six miles away.

Del Grazo was waiting for darkness to get away. He was using the fires to give him time, and distract the crew.

He'd needed only a few minutes to manually release the Zodiac, climb in, ride it down to the sea, and disconnect the hooks.

Del Grazo turning black also, man blending in with sea.

"Night vision," I snapped, watching Del Grazo disappear.

Crew lined the railings. Some held binoculars. Others, like me, wore cyclops night vision monoculars, which used ambient star or moonlight to—under normal circumstances on the *Wilmington*—track whales surfacing in dark, or walrus, seals, polar bears.

"What is this guy, invisible?" said Eddie, scanning.

"Where the hell could he be going?"

"He's using that berg piece as cover. There!"

I'd spotted a human figure two hundred yards off, a silhouette actually, at the Zodiac steering console, staying low, knees down, as he emerged from behind a three-foot-high protruding bit of ice, just high enough to shield a man. I heard M4 fire beside me in a three-round burst. The figure kept moving, well within range, but now that we were out of the ice, the open water was choppy. The ship rocked back and forth, the Zodiac up and down. It was hard to hit anything at this distance when both parties were moving in three directions at the same time.

Del Grazo slipped behind another small ice bit, and must have slowed down, because he didn't come out.

DeBlieu ordered another Zodiac lowered.

Pettit came up and joined the Marine marksman, pointed to where the figure had disappeared. Both men resting elbows on the railing, staring fixedly into the gloom ahead.

Pettit muttering, "I think he moved behind another piece. See the ice shaped like an hourglass?"

"The two humps? The camel shape?"

"Yeah."

"Wait, sir, there's two pieces camel shaped," the other Marine said. "The two o'clock? Or the four o'clock?"

"You think two o'clock looks like a camel?"

"Well, what do you think it looks like?"

"I don't know. Breasts," suggested Pettit.

The kid looked up, astonished. "You think a camel looks like breasts?"

DeBlieu interrupted. "Stop the fucking Rorschach test. The Zodiac is down."

Eddie came up beside us, stamping to keep warm. "Do you mind telling me where the hell he's going, middle of nowhere? Guy'll freeze to death in a few hours. *What is he doing?*"

Del Grazo's ice shield was a ghost bit beneath a speck of moon, but even that faded as clouds thickened, massed low, cut down on even ambient light. The damn Arctic weather seemed to change every ten minutes here.

Inside the ship, I knew that crew searched for more incendiaries, moving from cabin to cabin. But the fires were out.

"I just don't understand . . . oh shit," moaned Pettit. "Look!"

I did and my heart sank as it all came together. I saw—in green—five hundred yards off, a frothing, surging milkshake of activity, foaming water erupting, and then the big sub thrust upward, bigger than a bowhead. Biggest thing under the sea. Welcome to the new Arctic.

"He's *baaaackkk*," said Eddie morosely. "Let's hear a big round of applause from the studio audience for Captain Zhou!"

The sub came out clean, smacked back down, and sent up spray. The black eel-shape positioned itself to block any more shots at Peter Del Grazo. We couldn't see him anymore. He must have called them. He'd set up a rendezvous with his masters, then delayed until he could get off the ship.

Eddie said, "Hey, look at the bright side. Maybe he'll infect *them*, send them to the bottom, One."

"Yeah," muttered Pettit. "Like the *Montana*. Goddamn spy. Goddamn turncoat. Hail the conquering goddamn traitor."

But that's not what happened.

Because ten minutes later, as we watched, stunned at one more turn of events, they shot Del Grazo as he argued with them on their deck.

TWENTY-THREE

They shot him.

It happened like this.

First we watched the Chinese sub surface, an immense dark moray eel shape with greenish current flowing past, and occasional bergy bits. Then the hatch opened and fur-hatted soldiers climbed out onto the deck, followed by two crew members wearing bulky-looking hazmat suits.

Eddie saying bitterly, "Looks like Zhou believed you about the sickness on the *Montana*."

Eyeing the suits, I recalled the circular motions of Del Grazo's arm earlier on the monitors, when his back was turned. I understood what he'd been doing suddenly. I'd seen it enough in hospitals. His left arm—from behind—straight out. His right arm making little circles.

"He was taking samples," I whispered.

Eddie spun toward me. I nodded. "Mucus. Sweat. Blood."

Eddie looked thoughtful. "Zhou did ask us to send blood samples over for analysis. Trying to sound helpful . . . but . . . do you really think they believe it's a bioweapon? That we have a bioweapon that got loose?"

"I don't know what to think," I said. My whole body hurt from the fight with Del Grazo. I limped when I walked. My head pounded.

Now through the monocular I saw a head—Del Grazo—appear above Zhou's deck on the far side, body shielded from us. The Chinese must have thrown him a rope ladder, and he'd climbed up, and now stood.

I made sure the Marines had all weapons lowered. The sub was Chinese territory, not to mention that it carried torpedoes, and a pissed-off Captain Zhou.

"Nobody shoots," I said.

"Why did he do it?" said DeBlieu, as if unsure to be enraged, baffled, or both.

"Who knows? Money? Sex? Who the hell knows? But I'm sure there will be one heck of an investigation to figure it out when we get back."

Del Grazo, on deck, seemed half bent from his exertions, getting his breath back, I imagined, as he glanced our way, and I also imagined him feeling a surge of triumph, relief, maybe superiority. I remembered the rage in his face as he tried to choke me. I wondered if he felt trapped, his options over, his traitorous dreams in shambles. Del Grazo left with a life, but one he'd live far from home, in a foreign land.

I watched him pull something from his parka pocket. I adjusted focus, trying to see better. Larger images like his body grew blurry. But the object in his hand crystallized into what looked like a ziplock bag.

Meanwhile, the Chinese stayed back from him except for the hazmat guys, but even they approached gingerly, stopped ten feet away, and extended a metallic retractable arm, mechanical pincers to grab the bag, and bring it back.

"They're disinfecting it," said Eddie as the hazmat figures started spraying the outside of the bag, then wiping it off, with great rigor. Then spraying again.

Del Grazo took a step toward them, clearly wanting to reach the protection of the inside of the submarine. But the soldiers jerked up their bullpup assault rifles, as if to pantomime, *Stay back*.

The Del Grazo silhouette halted in the shadow of the tower, looking like one of those Indonesian shadow puppets, a figure half hidden by translucent curtain, arms out, frozen, mid-step.

Eddie narrating, as if we couldn't see it anyway. "He looks like he's arguing, *Let me aboard! I did what you wanted! You promised!*"

Two figures appeared on the bridge of the sub, the high point, looking down at Del Grazo, like priests atop an Aztec ziggurat. I adjusted focus again. I saw fur hats with red stars pinned in front, faces beneath them. I'd never seen Zhou, at this particular angle, but I was pretty sure I was looking at him and his British-accented translator. Yes, it was the translator, because I saw the guy's thick-framed glasses. Fat face. Fat frames. Zhou was smaller, features tight.

Del Grazo's movements growing more agitated.

Zhou—looking down, listening, then shaking his head.

Del Grazo took two quick steps toward the hatch and the guns came up. And now he was shouting in pantomime, waving his arms, body bent into his screaming as the hazmat guys disappeared into the sub, with the ziplock, then all the Chinese soldiers but one filing down into that hole, to safety, then there were only four figures out there. Zhou and his translator up high. Del Grazo and a single soldier below.

Eddie gasped. "They're going to leave him."

I shook my head. "No. If they leave him, we pick him up. They won't leave him."

"Then what are—"

Del Grazo must have panicked. He lunged forward. Later I'd try to figure out what had happened. All the pressure he'd been under—the spy normally assigned low-key missions, a computer hacker, not a saboteur. A sneak, not a warrior, suddenly pressured to do more as the stakes shot up.

We saw the gunfire before we heard it, blossoms of light in the dark before the snapping sound, a faint pressure on the eardrums over the humming idling of the icebreaker.

He crumbled. He was on hands and knees. I felt sorry for him for a moment. He crawled a few feet toward the edge of the deck, and then he toppled, disappeared, dropping into the sea.

Back to Zhou now, through glass. Zhou, on the bridge, riveted, eyeing the spot where Del Grazo had disappeared. Zhou, motionless for what seemed a long time. Then Zhou's right hand came up, and he saluted the spot where Del Grazo had been last with that stiff, palm-up motion favored in the People's Republic.

Eddie said, "One, you want to tell me what the hell just happened over there?"

"He's honoring him," I said.

"Oh, honoring. Some honor. Shoot a guy and salute him."

I turned to Eddie, who, close up, was as green as the Hulk. "Zhou had the same choice we did. Zhou decided—or was ordered to—keep the potentially infected guy off. He knows what happened in the *Montana*. He got the samples for analysis. They've probably got that bag in a locked freezer that no one will go into until Zhou gets home."

"Honoring," said Eddie.

"I think so. Yes."

"Yeah, so how will they honor us? A torpedo?"

Zhou turned to us, as if he felt our eyes on him, and knew we tried to figure out what he was doing. I felt him staring back. Maybe he even had a photo of me.

But oddly, probably because we were both motionless, it was not a tense moment. I had no sensation of antagonism across the black water. Just a sort of connection through the green world of night vision, as if we both understood that we'd faced the same choices, that the consequences of missteps in the microbial world we'd been thrust into had spiraled far from human control.

It was, I knew, just a feeling. And feelings can be dangerous. That *feelings* in a confrontation can—if you deceive yourself, if you fall victim to wishful thinking, if you get tired, as I was, and were scared, as I was, and confused, as I knew myself to be—lead to disaster.

And yet the moment lengthened, and I could not help but believe that a fellow consciousness linked our two vessels.

He would protect his crew *better than I did mine*, I couldn't help thinking. He would take the samples and disappear below and turn west, staying in international waters, heading toward the U.S.-Russian border, then veering south into the narrow Bering Strait, and the northern Pacific, the main sea lanes, and ultimately to whatever secure lab awaited that ziplock and its contents somewhere in the People's Republic of China.

That's what I figured would happen.

But it did not happen.

The submarine remained on the surface. The real truth, I saw, was that whatever was going on lay far beneath any surface that I knew. Zhou stood there, looking back, as the sub began turning in our direction.

I didn't have any torpedoes with which to protect us this time. There wasn't even a single deck gun on board.

"Shit," said DeBlieu, and told the bridge to start us up again, head

south again, full speed ahead in relatively clear seas, no point in hanging around waiting to see what Zhou intended. In fact, if he was going
to fire, why leave the ship sitting broadside to him, fat and open?

I felt the icebreaker's engines rev, felt us turning.

"Sweet Jesus," said Marine Lance Corporal Frederick Fastbinder
beside me at the handrail.

Waiting . . .

Waiting . . .

Then minutes later we got a message on our handheld radios, channel 13, required to be monitored on all vessels. Our ship radios were out.

"Captain Zhou wishes to escort you as far as the U.S. twelve-mile
limit."

"That will not be necessary," I replied.

"Captain wishes me to say that you are in no danger. He would appreciate it if you might be so kind as to allow us to trail behind you, like
one of your research vessels. We do not wish to encounter ice. Even
small amounts might damage our hull. Please to not be alarmed. If you
like, we can coordinate speeds. Again, we have no hostile intent."

He wasn't asking permission, I knew. He *sounded* like he was, but
he was informing us, not making requests. There was no way for us to
stop him.

"Hostile intent?" said Eddie. "This is a guy who threatened to kill
us all yesterday."

"My captain heard that and assures you that the situation is quite
different now."

"Different how?"

"The *Montana* has gone to the bottom. We are on a humanitarian
mission."

All fires on board were extinguished, and a vague smell of burned
rubber drifted from the ship's vents, and across deck, a dirty, infected

odor, a whiff of destruction, enhancing the sense of near escape that worsened moment by moment, along with the growing sense of danger. The *Wilmington* steamed south, 300 more miles to Barrow, 288 miles to U.S. waters, seventeen hours minimum, if we could hold top speed, and the British-accented voice of the Chinese translator clear and bright, all of us aware that, thanks to Peter Del Grazo, there could be listening software anywhere on the ship. Zhou's people might be riveted right now hearing any private talk between us.

Eddie said, "Fucking Del Grazo."

Zhou repeated patiently that his intents were honorable, that he understood that we might not trust him.

I asked him what his intentions were exactly. Or rather, why he felt it necessary to escort us at all.

When he answered, when the stuffy British-sounding translator spoke next, Eddie turned bone white.

TWENTY-FOUR

I've come to believe that all human actions are explicable. Understand motivation and you can reconstruct an act. You may be horrified by it, you may be disgusted or appalled, but at least you see how it happened. The madman's murders make twisted sense if you understand his delusion. The future acts of an Adolf Hitler might be predicted if you observe his unique twisted growth, his particular step-by-step path in life.

Now the *Wilmington* hit full speed in the iceless summer waters. Only now we had an escort, mile for mile. But even if Zhou submerged, his top speed would exceed ours. From the bridge, or on monitors, or from the fantail, anyone could follow the dark fin shape, frothing at the bow.

Zhou's words to me were ice in my veins, as I recalled his answer to why he was staying close.

He had said, through his translator, that low voice clear over the handheld radio, "To help, if you need it."

"Considering what happened earlier, that is hard to believe."

After a hesitation, he said stiffly, "I've been instructed to tell you, in order to alleviate any concerns you may have, that in light of new developments there's been an . . . adjustment of our policy."

"What is that supposed to mean, Captain?"

"I've been instructed to tell you that there's been a reappraisal on my end. I am ordered to make myself available to you should emergency assistance be required."

"Oh, we're friends now," I said skeptically.

There was no answer, and then the voice said, devoid of emotion, "If it makes you feel better. Good luck."

He clicked off. The radio buzzed with static. But that *click* didn't mean Zhou couldn't hear us.

"Hey, One," Eddie said, "remember those vultures in Afghanistan. The way they'd appear magically, in the air, following guys, troops, Taliban, watching, circling. Those fucking carrion birds, just waiting for people to die."

"I remember."

"What's he really been ordered to do, swoop in if we're dying?"

On the monitor, from the aft camera, I could see the sub back there as a sort of luminescence, a frothy V-shape marking the forward-most progress of the black hull.

"Captain Zhou Dongfeng, everybody's buddy," said Eddie.

"There's nothing we can do about him. There's no one we can even tell about him. Let's get back to work," I said.

■ ■ ■

"Good luck," Eddie repeated as we went cot to cot, taking temperatures, peering into eyes and throats, hoping the medicines had had an effect, seeing that they had not. "Good luck. Like he's wishing *us* good luck?"

"Ever get the feeling he knows more than we do?"

"I get the feeling everyone knows more than we do."

"It's goddamn creepy, having him back there. Maybe he doesn't know the long-range is out. Maybe he's waiting for us to send a general SOS. Then he swoops in and boards the *Wilmington*. He's got the ship. He's got," I said, "the film." I stopped. My left eye was hurting. "It can't be the film, can it?"

"Give me a break, man. It's a hundred years old. Forget the film. We can't even see the first part of it. What I can't figure is, why does Zhou stay on the surface? Why advertise that he's here? He'd be safer submerged, from the ice, from Washington seeing him on satellite, from someone at the Pentagon deciding he's aggressive."

The throb in my left eye spread to my temple. "Plus," I said, "if Del Grazo planted listening devices aboard, he could monitor us remotely. Like those hackers who broke into the Defense Department, or the banks. Hell, those guys were on other continents."

Eddie blew out air, turning possibilities over in his mind as we moved between patients. "I read this article in *Time* magazine. About bad guys driving around suburban neighborhoods, and they can *see* what's going on inside homes 'cause they hijacked the owner's webcam. It's called drive-by programs. They hack in, or you click on an infected website—and then they access you remotely whenever they want, use your own mike to listen to you argue with your wife about money, activate your webcams to watch your daughter get undressed as they jerk off. Anyone can buy this shit at spy stores, and God knows what the really sophisticated stuff that governments have can do."

"You mean, like, the sub is a drive-by?"

Eddie looked at the ship camera, which would be picking up our images, broadcasting them to the bridge. "Hey, Zhou! You listening? You watching right now? You studying us, Zhou? You waiting to see on your monitors how we die? Little research for your guys? What we look like when we get sick? How fast it jumps from person to person? That's it, isn't it? Help us? Give me a break! Break out the popcorn over there! Help us! You're just watching the guinea pigs get sick!"

"Maybe he needs to stay surfaced to watch. Maybe the programs Del Grazo planted won't work if he's submerged."

"Fucking maybes. Fucking goddamn maybes. Maybe he's from Venus," Eddie snapped.

■ ■ ■

We continued our rounds, checked for the twentieth time—in despair—to see if we'd made progress.

We reached Clinton's cot. The big Iñupiat was worse now, his breathing jagged, bile dripping from the corners of his mouth, a tearing, ripping noise coming from him with each exhalation. Clinton lay beneath the piled parkas and extra sweaters and on sweat-soaked sheets, breaking into shivers so violent that they approached convulsions. Clinton's fever at 104, hitting possible brain damage level. Clinton hooked to the IV that had been freed up when one of the *Montana* crew died. Clinton muttering Iñupiat words. I had no idea what they meant.

"How many people in the United States, Eddie."

"Three . . . four hundred million?"

"Triage," I said.

"Don't go there, amigo. We have no control over what Washington does. Let's concentrate on us."

I gave Clinton his prescribed three-hour dose of aerosols. We covered him up and moved down the row. I felt my heart tearing inside me.

I was responsible for this scene. I kept hearing Zhou, even though I tried to block it out. *Good luck.*

Had I misread the tone? It would be easy over distance. Had I misread intent? It would be simple with a translator involved. Was Eddie right? They were just watching and recording us, trying to deal with the disease? *Triage.* What if *Zhou* was here to blow us up? What if he was waiting while some high-level negotiations were going on between Washington and Beijing? *We can't blow up our own ship, so you guys do it.* My imagination was getting the better of me. I saw a room in Washington. I saw the director meeting with men and women whose faces I knew from the nightly news. I knew the decision that faced them, because wasn't it the same one I'd faced in Afghanistan, on a smaller scale? Blowing up a truck instead of a ship? Killing eight men to save thousands, instead of hundreds to save millions?

Good luck, Zhou's translator had told me.

I told Eddie, "Well, we can use luck either way."

■ ■ ■

But there was no luck, because what we were seeing was worse than the 1918 strain; that much was evident. The death toll aboard hit twenty-one. Eddie and I went back to the microscope, and saw differences that we'd missed before—minuscule alterations—between the oblong microbes in the photos that the CDC had sent out, and the view of inside Clinton. Reconstituted version versus real-life disease.

"Extra spikes on Clinton's strain," said Eddie an hour later, staring at the two pictures. "It's narrower in the middle, and that tiny hook on top, see the way the two strands entwine? The curl is more pronounced, and the tail."

Three Marines were down with fevers of over 103, coughing up bile, skin patchy, blotched blue.

"Not getting oxygen," Eddie said.

Six *Wilmington* crewmen, who had been stationed elsewhere in the ship when Del Grazo escaped, new patients, had been carried to the hangar, in similar shape.

The cook had gone in one shocking two-hour period from merrily serving breakfast to breaking out coughing, to collapsing in his bunk after throwing up on the man below.

He had then died.

The hangar was a nightmare filled with sick and dying. DeBlieu stayed permanently forward, now that he'd left the quarantined area anyway. He ran the ship from the bridge. I heard his announcements regularly, and my respect for the man grew. He kept the crew busy with a steady stream of jobs: clean decks, check equipment or lifeboats, or do one more drill, or work harder trying to fix the radio room, get the long-range working since the fire. He was trying to snuff out panic before it began. DeBlieu on the intercom saying, "If you want to help the doctors, do your jobs."

XO Gordon Longstreet lay in row two, close to the sliding door of the hangar. Karen Vleska was one cot over, she and Clinton the patients I had the most trouble viewing. But I sat by her side, put my hand on her forehead. She was ashen, shivering, asleep.

I must have fallen asleep myself, sitting there, and this is what I dreamed. I was in the back of a troop truck with eight Marines, in Afghanistan. There were oil drum bombs lashed to the sides, and I smelled alkaline desert, diesel fuel, unwashed guys, and roast lamb. I felt the hard hum of tires on dirt road, felt the jolt each time we hit a rut. Guys smoking. Guys shutting their eyes to doze. Me filled with dread, knowing that something awful was coming, and opening my mouth to warn them, but I couldn't talk, and then I could not move, not even a toe.

And then there were two of me, because I was also watching the truck approach from the guard post bomb barrier, and I was yelling into a radio for the truck to pull over and stop. I gripped the handles of the .50-caliber. I felt the weapon buck. Suddenly I was inside the truck again, with the doomed troops, instead of firing at it.

The chassis rocked. The blast seemed to pierce my eardrums. I was pinned. The truck had turned over. I smelled fire. I was on fire myself. I tried to move but still could not.

"Wake up, One. You were having a nightmare."

I jerked out of it, gasping for breath, and still feeling hot flames licking at my trousers. I was surprised to see the hangar around me. I looked right. There was Karen Vleska, still asleep and looking very white, very small.

"I screwed up, Eddie."

"No."

"Zhou was right to shoot Del Grazo."

"One, keep your mind on the job. You got some shut-eye. You're a new man, One. You'll figure it out."

"We'll prepare the inoculations, Eddie. Put out a call for anyone who got over the flu to come to the lab. We'll reuse syringes if we have to. Time to take blood. No more time to wait."

I looked down and Karen's eyes were open. They were watery and red but still focused, like her pupils were the only healthy part left. I felt something cold touch my hand. It was Karen's hand. I took it. I felt the bones of her knuckles, and her tremors, and I heard the creaky whisper of double pneumonia attacking her lungs as she forced air in or out. Perspiration flowed down skin turned gray as death.

"You didn't make a mistake," she croaked. "You hear me? You didn't. You saved the old woman, not the painting."

"At the moment I prefer the painting. How do you feel?"

"Like I look. Like shit," she said, smiled weakly, a skull smile, and let go, and then she closed her eyes.

But she kept talking. "My father used to say, when I was little . . ."

"What did he say, Karen?"

A flicker, at the corner of the mouth, of a smile. "He'd say, things are hard because they aren't easy. Dumb, huh? He was full of stupid sayings. He was . . . a great guy. And I think . . . Colonel, that so . . . are . . . you."

We left Andrew Sachs with her, mopping her brow, mask off; the guy seemed unconcerned for his own safety. I placed my hand on his bony shoulder, saw the watery iron-colored eyes turn up toward me in a question. I guess everyone was thinking of mortality, getting out the good comments while we could.

"Mr. Sachs, you're a jerk under normal conditions, but pretty damn good in an emergency," I said.

He grinned with an almost pathetic look of gratefulness, a broad sunny smile, and I saw his past in that moment; I saw other, bigger kids making fun of him when he was young, on a Boston street corner. I saw skinny Andrew being chased down a street outside of a school. I saw nerdy Andrew in college, winning A grades but looking yearningly at the baseball field. And later taking refuge in officialdom, as many in Washington do. What's the old saying? Politics is show business for ugly people? All those power brokers on the surface walking around, chests thrust forward, thinking, inside where you can't see, *I'm big now. I'm smart. So how come I still feel like that jerk of a kid?*

An hour later, Eddie and I had twenty men lined up in the lab, sleeves rolled up past their elbows; all *Montana* crew who had survived the outbreak. We dabbed forearms with alcohol-soaked cotton balls. We inserted needles into blue veins. We measured out blood into test tubes and stoppered the stuff; each container holding antibodies to whatever strain of flu was rampant on this ship.

But I felt like a medieval doctor, a barber with a knife and slimy leeches, about to do things to patients that would never be permitted in a modern hospital. I knew that if one of the men we'd taken blood from was infected with HIV, I'd be dooming anyone to whom I gave that preventive shot.

We diluted the collected blood with plasma from sick bay, to help supply other immunity proteins. Then we took the vials downstairs to the hangar, and the needles, about forty of them still in wrappers, and we also carried bottles of rubbing alcohol. We'd flush the needles with saline and autoclave the parts after each shot.

As we started going cot to cot, administering the shots, Eddie looked up at one of the hangar cameras, but he wasn't really thinking about watchers on the bridge. "Hey! Hey, Zhou! You! Two orders of kung pao chicken, with an extra container of rice! And no MSG like last time!"

Elsewhere on the ship, I knew, DeBlieu had ordered sheets laid over computers, in case the cameras were being operated remotely. He'd ordered quadruple duct tape layers and foam padding over computer microphone openings, and all mikes turned off, or at least set that way.

Still, I had the disembodied feeling, at all times, that foreign eyes watched me, that we were on a TV screen somewhere, maybe with a Shanghai street outside the viewer's window, maybe a military base near the Vietnamese border, or outside Beijing. *Now Lieutenant Colonel Rush is examining another patient. Now Lieutenant Colonel Rush is shaking his head; he looks frustrated, exhausted. Now a man in row number two has died, and two Marines are carrying him out, covered with a blanket.*

Another hour passed.

And another.

No change in the patients, I thought. *But it's still too soon. Wait until tomorrow. Give it time.*

Eddie and I took a break, went outside, mugs of strong Maxwell House in hand. The ice was gone now. We were 140 miles, maybe eight more hours, from shore, if we maintained speed. The water had a light chop, a low, early moon sneered at us above, and suddenly I saw in the sky aurora borealis, as luminous streaks of emerald lights began pulsating above. I'd never seen one this clear. I was in another universe. The clarity was beyond comprehension, and all around it, day as night and night as day, earth's processes all mixed in an Arctic blender, a million stars, each one a hint of more that you could not see, far stars, burned stars, dangerous stars, as many stars as microbes. Each one a private world.

A shooting star streaked into aurora borealis, seemed to be consumed and burned by it, then reappeared as a smear that dropped below the curve of earth and was gone. And then, to starboard, only a mile off, I saw solid whiteout. The planet was gone.

Maybe the inoculations will need a little more time.

The ship's medical officer Janice Cullen suddenly appeared on deck with us, not even having put on a parka. Her face looked flushed. I thought she was ill at first, but then, for the first time, saw animation instead of fear or exhaustion. She was gripping the hand railing. But the eyes were bright, and I thought I saw—at least for an instant—what to me seemed like hope.

"Something is happening in the hangar," she said in a breathy voice. "You better come look."

"The serum?" I said. "So *fast?*"

"No, not the serum. It's . . . it's actually . . . Colonel, I'm not sure just what it is," she said. "But you have to come see for yourself. *See for yourself!*"

She turned without waiting for an answer, and hurried into the hangar.

Heart slamming against my ribs, I followed, hearing Eddie's bootfalls behind.

TWENTY-FIVE

Watching the soldiers refuel the fighter plane was so cool!

In Barrow, Seth Itta, age nine, and Leo Nuna, also age nine, best friends, peered out the window in the North Slope Rescue Squad office on the second floor of the squad's hangar at the airport, at the recently lengthened runway and tarmac and the fascinating, gleaming predator-shaped plane that had landed thirty minutes before, and was now parked below.

The lone runway was empty, the brown tundra grass waving behind it, a big white owl there, staring back. Yesterday's Alaska Air flight to Anchorage had left an hour ago—delayed by mechanical problems—and no private planes were due in, and the wind outside scuffed the tops of high grasses, and blew the red wind sock to the southwest.

"It's an F22," announced Seth.

"How do you know?" challenged Leo.

"Because Uncle Elmore showed me pictures. He fixes those things in Anchorage. He says they can go over a thousand miles an hour. He says they're the fastest thing in the sky."

Outside, in early September, it was light again, twenty-seven degrees, but it was one of those rare days when aurora borealis, the northern lights, was so strong that the sky rippled green lines that undulated above the ocean, and tundra to the south, shimmering and snaking and luminescent even during daylight.

Their third-grade teacher had said that aurora borealis was caused by "sunspots," huge gas explosions on the sun, and that this year there were "extra strong" sunspots, and that was why the lights could be seen even during the day. He'd said this year's display was the best the North Slope had seen in twenty years.

Normally the light show would have captivated the boys, but it paled beside the fighter jet. Flown-in Air Force crew had driven the fuel truck out to it, attached the hose, and were pumping in gas.

"Where are the bombs?" Leo asked Seth.

"Inside the plane, dummy!" announced Seth.

"Why do you think the plane is here?"

"Why do you think? To blow up bad guys! My grandfather was talking about walrus ivory smugglers last night, over by Wainright. Men from Nome. Maybe the bombs will blow their boats out of the water, like, boom! No more smugglers killing walrus!"

Seth made an explosion noise and swept some papers into the air, as if the explosion had dislodged them.

"Dead smugglers!" shouted Leo.

"Bust 'em to pieces!" cried Seth.

And then another voice, a male voice, and an unfamiliar one said quietly, "What are you two doing up here?"

The black man who advanced into the room in an Air Force flight suit had short gray hair and very straight posture and a stern voice, although his face looked friendly, as did his copper-colored eyes, catching overhead light. The rescue squad office was empty. It was large and lit well and broken into *partitioned-off cubicles for the pilots, and a side office for the head of the department.*

Just now the pilots were out, one on a rescue mission to pick up a hunter who had broken his leg two hundred miles inland, at a fishing camp; one to ferry a couple of electrical maintenance men three hundred miles west to Point Hope, on the coast, so they could fix that village's electrical generator.

The boys had been told by Seth's uncle, Drew, who ran the rescue squad, that they could hang out here and listen to the emergency radio. If they heard someone calling for aid—maybe the pregnant lady with "complications" in Atqasuk, maybe a fisherman whose engine had died at sea, maybe someone with appendicitis at a hunting camp—they were to call Drew on his cell phone, at the AC Value Center, the big supermarket, where he'd gone to the pickup counter for fried chicken and cheeseburgers and fries and fried onions and a liter of Mountain Dew soda for dinner for them all.

Drew had a radio in his Outback, but while shopping, even for a few minutes, he preferred to have someone at the office, listening in case something went wrong.

Uncle Drew had taught Seth to use the radio. Seth was to tell whoever was calling to wait, hold on, while he contacted Uncle Drew.

The boys told the man in the flight suit this, and he just smiled, and shrugged, believing them, and he looked out the window over their shoulders at the jet, and said, "Nice bird, isn't she?"

"Terrific," breathed Seth.

"She came in so fast," Leo said. "Whooooooosh!"

The boys were dressed in mid-weight jackets and T-shirts—New York Giants logo for Seth, Carlsbad Caverns on Leo, and new blue jeans from the AV, and their banana seat bikes were leaning against the hangar outside, not far from where the taxicabs idled during breaks, their Pakistani or Korean drivers chattering away in foreign tongues, waiting for tourists to take to the hotels, or scientists to take up to the research campus.

*The boys had had a great summer riding around in broad daylight at all
hours of the night, going out to fishing camps, and hunting camps, and now,
with autumn coming, they were looking forward to high school football games
on the blue Astroturf field by the beach, to ice coming back, and not particularly to schoolwork, especially math lessons.*

*The man in the flight suit asked if there was coffee anywhere here, and
Seth directed him to the big Krups fourteen-cupper by the Zenith TV, where
the pilots relaxed on Sundays and watched cable TV football games. The man
poured brew into a ceramic mug, stirred in coffee creamer and sugar, and
plopped onto the couch. He seemed friendly, but also worried, Leo thought.*

Leo said, "Are you the whole crew?"

"Yep."

"Like, the only one in there?"

"That's me, son."

"Where did you come from?"

"Anchorage. Elmendorf."

"What kind of bombs are inside?"

*The man's head swung up, and for a moment the boys were frightened by
the intense look on his face. At first Seth thought he was angry. But then he
saw that the question seemed to have aged the man by ten years. There were
furrows by the mouth that had not been there earlier. There were wavy lines
on the forehead, and the posture, which had been straight and proud, looked
more like an elder's posture, bent.*

"Who told you I'm carrying bombs?"

*"My uncle said they go inside. He also said the Navy planes have missiles
that can sink ships."*

"Yes, harpoons," the man said in a low voice.

*Which got the boys giggling, because "harpoons" were what their fathers,
uncles, and elders worked on, in garages and toolsheds and in the Heritage
Center, all winter, to use on the bowheads during the spring hunt in May,*

and the upcoming fall hunt in October. The boys were now old enough to go out to the hunting camps with their uncles, at the edge of the ice, where they'd run errands, be quiet, or be sent home, study the way the men waited for the big whales to appear, the way they'd positioned their sealskin-covered umiaqs—open boats—to be ready when the bowheads showed up, coming from their summer feeding grounds in Canada, heading toward their winter grounds to the west.

The man seemed to understand why the boys were laughing. He smiled. "Oh, right," he said. "Harpoons."

Whale hunts were more exciting than fighter planes, but Seth asked the man in the flight suit, "Are you going to blow up bad guys with your bombs?"

And the man in the flight suit looked up at them and sighed. Then he looked at his watch. He seemed to be waiting for something, "orders," Seth would later insist when he told his friends the story.

The man in the flight suit shook his head and looked sad, just about the saddest man they'd ever seen. He didn't answer. He stared into space. For a moment he reminded Seth of the scary way his cousin Elliot had looked on the night before he shot himself.

"No, boys, I'm not going to blow up bad guys," he said in a dead voice. "Not the bad guys at all."

TWENTY-SIX

Clinton's fever was dropping.

I stood beside his cot, staring down with hope at the thermometer. There was no doubt about the two-degree change, down from a raging 104 two hours ago, to a dangerous but better 102. Eyes more focused. Chest sounding a trifle clearer. Mucus still clotted and yellow, but the sweat running at a sheen on his broad forehead was not a flood anymore.

"Clinton?"

The eyes were red, exhausted, but did I see a spark of interest there that had previously been absent?

"Don't land," he said weakly.

"How do you feel? Any better?"

"I'd be better if you stayed away from Barrow."

Fevers, of course, wax and wane. The new development could be a temporary abatement. It did not mean he was getting better, and if he was, it did not mean the medicine was responsible. He could be manifesting natural resistance. After all, a majority of the stricken, so far, had recovered. But Janice Cullen took my arm and excitedly pulled me to the next cot in line, this one occupied by a *Montana* fire control technician, a lean Italian-American from Rhode Island, one of the original sick, who had been gray as death last time I'd come by. The hand-scrawled chart at the foot of the cot read age thirty. Last time I'd checked, he'd looked more like seventy.

Now I saw a spot of color on his cheeks. I watched the chest moving in and out more regularly—still fitful, but an improvement. I hoped it wasn't just a coincidence.

Cullen whispered, "Everyone in this row is getting better. But, um, *only people in this row.* No one else."

I blinked, uncomprehending. "Repeat that, please."

She nodded. "Nineteen of them, all improving. I don't understand it either. Why just this row?"

I gazed in puzzlement around our makeshift hospital, the rows of cots, three for the sick, and the other, separated section for quarantined people—the rest of us—who showed no signs of illness yet.

Clinton lay in the second row over from the hull. His row contained a mix of patients: a twenty-two-year-old female yeoman from the *Montana*, a twenty-nine-year-old male electronics technician from the *Wilmington*, a nineteen-year-old machinist from the *Montana*, a forty-two-year-old chief from the *Wilmington*.

"Coincidence?" said Eddie, frowning, leaning close.

I didn't answer in words, just a disbelieving look.

"Then why?"

Something clear and sweet moved into my throat and caught there. It was the taste of hope, replacing the sour flavor of despair. Oh, I knew the old saying: *When hope is hungry, everything feeds it.* So I tried to think dispassionately, to lock away pure hope, to be the scientist fathoming intellectually what this medical officer was telling me, because it made no sense yet, none at all. Row two was getting better but everyone else remained as sick as before.

"Go ahead, check it out," challenged Cullen.

I took a walk between rows two and three, trying to contain the excitement. On my right, in row three, patient after patient continued showing the debilitating effects of disease. But on the left, only feet away, all down row two, violent heartbeats had slowed, fevers were less, eyes seemed more focused, and patients more animated, as if collectively they sensed the change not only in themselves, but in others, too.

Eddie said, "What the hell?"

Okay, what is happening? What's the reason?

My eyes ran over the walls, vents, carts of medicines, rolling steel door. Overconfidence is a killer, and there was no proof that what we saw meant anything more than a temporary and coincidental upswing.

"Eddie, what is different about people in this row? They got the same medicine. They got the same food. They're adjacent to two other rows, so it's not environmental. They're cared for by the same people."

"The venting system?"

We looked up. A huge vent lay directly overhead, but air spewing from it would spread over the entire hangar.

"No."

"The time when they got here!"

"Eddie, most of these people arrived at approximately the same time."

I double-checked with Janice Cullen to make sure that Clinton's row had received the same medicines as other patients, and she affirmed that was the case. Same dosages of zanamivir and xapaxin. Two snorts into each nostril, every few hours.

"Well, *something's* not the same."

I tried to clear my mind of preconceptions, although, when it comes to preconceptions, you never know that you have one until it's too late. I walked to the front of the row and started back again slowly, glancing back and forth at the deathly gray faces on one side, the slightly more alert ones on the other. I let my eyes rove over blankets, parkas, makeshift night tables. Eddie walked beside me, doing the same thing, hoping some difference would jump out.

"Huh!" Eddie exclaimed.

We turned back, guards on patrol, started up the row in the opposite direction. My guts were grinding. A spike drove into my right eye. My fists clenched, as if I felt the presence of an unknown vulnerability in our enemy. My ankle, where I'd been hurt, was swollen, bandaged, on fire. I could feel the steady hum of the powerful engines of the icebreaker, driving us south, and wished we would leave international waters and reach the border of the United States.

I halted midway down the line, concentrating on the array of items on top of the crate night tables: pill vials and plastic aerosol containers, trinkets, books.

"You're *sure* they got the same medicines, Lieutenant Cullen?"

"I administered them myself."

"You're *sure* nobody came along and did something special, different to people in row two?"

"Not to my knowledge. And I've pretty much been here the whole time, except for bathroom breaks."

I bent down at a crate, stenciled U.S. COAST GUARD PROPERTY, let my gloved fingers hover above a Timex watch, a plastic mug of water, a dog-eared copy of *The Sun Also Rises*, the white plastic aerosol container that . . .

I froze.

Eddie asked me, "What?"

I called over to Janice, the vague suspicion coming as my heartbeat sped up, "Who got the medicines that we brought in? And who got the Chinese stuff?"

"But it's the same!" she protested.

"Is it?"

I started down the row again. The first patient in line was Alice Richler, age nineteen, her chart read, a food service specialist on the *Wilmington*. Temperature at 103 two hours ago, at 101 now. Black curly hair tied back. She was breathing easier. The baby blue eyes showed a flicker of hope. She sensed, as the more alert patients did, that something good might be happening. She'd been at death's door last time I'd checked.

On Alice's crate lay a pair of pink plastic reading glasses, a ring of keys, a pen flashlight, a lucky bracelet with tiny charms, and a small white aerosol container.

Picking it up with my gloved hand, I read the label out loud. "Xapaxin." And, "Manufactured in Shanghai."

I reached across the aisle, to the adjacent night table, and picked up the aerosol container that sat there. It was shaped slightly differently, more bullet shaped, less bulgy at the center. I read the label.

"Xapaxin. Manufactured by Pacific-North Pharma."

I moved on to the next pair of cots, and stopped. I read the next label on the right side. "Shanghai." But the shape of the container told me that beforehand.

"And on the left side, Pacific-North Pharma."

"But what . . ." said Cullen, and shut up.

Now we split up and the three of us went from cot to cot, reading labels.

Cullen moving down row two, saying, "China . . . China . . . China . . ."

Eddie in row one: "P-N Pharma . . . Pharma. But, One, I don't get it. It's manufactured in two places but it's both xapaxin, the same stuff."

And I said, holding two containers up, a bullet-shaped one from Pacific-North, a more rounded version from Zhou's donated supply, "All we really know, Eddie, is that the labels *say* it's the same."

■ ■ ■

"It's not the same," I said thirty minutes later.

"Not even close," breathed Eddie.

We were in the lab upstairs at the electron microscope again, comparing medicines, magnified 20,000 times on screens. Night and day. Yin and yang. *Xapaxin,* or at least the version manufactured in the United States, was an aquamarine crystalline bouquet, a shimmering jewel collection of bright surfaces, molecular clusters absorbing and sending forth the microscope's internal bright probing light.

Xapaxin molecules, the sort that Zhou had donated, showed up as rust-colored clusters of grape-shaped ovals, thicker in the middle, small and bulging on top.

Eddie and I sat back. My pulse beat in my throat—strong and steady, a mix of hope, excitement, and bafflement.

"Is it possible?"

"Do you think?"

"But if it *is* an antidote," I told Eddie, "how did they get it? How did they goddamn even *have* an antidote for the 1918 flu? You want to tell me that?"

"And also," Eddie added, thinking out loud, "how did they know to bring it here? How did they know before we did, that we're even *dealing* with the 1918 flu?"

"Unless *they're* the ones using the bioweapon," I said, "and this is it. They somehow introduced it into the sub."

"Then why give us the antidote?"

"Maybe they made a mistake using it. Maybe whoever used it did so without orders. So now they need to stop it, but not admit they did it. It's a screwup. They sent Zhou here to make the problem go away, before the truth got out," Eddie suggested. "If the truth gets out that they attacked us, Christ, One, that's an act of war."

I recalled our first confrontation with Zhou, the way the Chinese officer had threatened to blow up the *Montana*, had sent soldiers to seize it. Was it possible that the whole episode—the attempt at seizure at first, the supplying of drugs when military action failed—had all been some kind of attempted cover-up, an effort to correct a terrible error made by someone on the Chinese side?

"No," I decided. "That wouldn't explain the disease breaking out because the *Montana* took hundred-year-old bodies aboard, and it sure wouldn't explain the connection to an old silent movie."

"Do you have a better explanation?" Eddie challenged.

"No."

"How about a worse explanation?"

"No," I said helplessly.

"Well, while we try to figure out *any* explanation," Eddie said, "we better get word to the director that we might have an antidote. I mean, if people keep getting better on it then . . . My God! An actual antidote!"

"And I'm going to ask Zhou what the hell this is."

■ ■ ■

I called ahead to the bridge to warn DeBlieu that I would be coming. It was the only way to try to use the long-range radio, that is, if it had been fixed. When I reached the bridge, the group of officers clustered at the control panel and chart table—a smaller group than usual, diminished by disease—moved back collectively, even though I was in my hazmat suit, with a surgical mask on instead of the faceplate, so I could talk.

The view through the windows stopped me dead. I'd not seen the sky for many hours, and it had changed. It seemed a schizophrenic rendering of two entirely different weather systems. To the northeast, a colossal northern light show—aurora borealis—turned the heavens astoundingly beautiful. The whole sky was luminous and deep cobalt, and against that background I saw enormous pulsating serpents in electric emerald, forming fantastic waxing and waning shapes—intertwined pythons, massive twirling ghost gyroscopes—while a solid arc of light stretched away, parallel to and fixed above the steep curvature of the earth.

But look left and I saw the ominous incoming mass of one more weather system, a thick solid gray. In minutes the cloud wall would slide between the lights and the ship, obscuring the glorious show, low and dark.

I turned to glance back. Behind the ship, a half mile away, was our follower, the sub, matching our speed.

DeBlieu's crew stood ready with bottles of powerful disinfectant. They would pounce when I left and scrub anything I touched, anything nearby. The captain showed me how to operate the HF radio, and explained that the crew had been working in the radio room, and they were ready for a test.

"But even if we got the thing working, you might have trouble due to that light show overhead," DeBlieu said.

When I switched it on, a gaggle of electronic scratches and screeches poured out. Nothing . . . nothing . . .

The whole thing went dead.

I could not call out.

I got on the handheld and called the submarine. While DeBlieu and the bridge crew listened, transfixed, I told the truth, that their medicines were working. I said that we knew now they'd sent aboard different stuff than ours. I told them that we'd compared medicines under the microscope, and the differences, chemically, were huge, no small modification. I thanked Zhou but also asked him, "Can you tell me what is in those containers? We're going to need more. We need to know what it is."

The static grew so bad that for an instant I thought that I'd lost him. The gray clouds were ominously closer in the sky now, racing toward us, closing the gap. The static climbed so high that I saw two of De-Blieu's crew cover their ears with their hands.

But then the voice came through.

"Colonel, this is excellent news. I've been instructed to tell you that we are pleased that medicines made in China have been able to assist you in a time of need."

He had not answered the question.

I asked, "But what *is* the medicine that you gave us?"

"I've been instructed to inform you that representatives from the People's Republic would be pleased to work out a way, with your government, of supplying more help. These discussions will be held at high levels so action can come fast!"

I felt as if he read from a script that had nothing to do with my questions. That he understood my questions perfectly and that no real answers would come. It was maddening. The man had studied English but just used it to talk in riddles. So I asked directly about Zhou's change in behavior, the switch from aggressor to helper, as the static poured forth, and the British accent—if I didn't know it came from a Chinese man, I would have envisioned someone in a bowler hat—came through again.

"I have been instructed, should you make this particular inquiry, to inform you that we work for a different superior now. The officer formerly in charge of our command is temporarily assigned to a different job."

Above, I watched the dark clouds consume the light show. Soon half the sky was gray, then 30 percent, then 10. The electric green undulations vanished, as if they'd never been there at all.

I said, "You're not going to tell me anything, are you? You're not going to give me any answers at all."

Nothing.

"Can you help us call Washington?" I asked, grasping at a new thought. "Patch me through?"

But they were gone. I cursed.

■ ■ ■

They were back.

"I've been instructed, Colonel," the voice continued in that maddeningly formal tone, "to inform you that we now intend to break off contact, submerge, sir, and leave you with our good wishes before your warplane arrives."

"Warplane?" A barb sliced into my belly. "What warplane?" I thought, *Was that a warning? From Zhou?*

"Colonel, considering the recent misunderstandings between our countries in the South China Sea, we do not wish our presence to be misconstrued as aggressive. We wish you continued success in thwarting the outbreak. I am instructed to say good-bye and wish you the best of luck, especially now that satellites cannot see what happens to you, with cloud cover so thick. We hope you suffer no accident."

He clicked off. He did not answer when I attempted to reestablish contact. I went out on deck and saw, beyond the aft deck and copter landing square and winches at the rear of the ship, the submarine fall back, slide low, and then there was a phosphorescent frothing at the bow, from microorganisms. Zhou's submarine began to disappear.

Captain DeBlieu—back on the bridge—had heard the whole conversation.

"What was that about a warplane?" he asked. "And an accident? And why the effing x do they know more than we do half the time? We need choppers, dropped supplies. *A warplane? An accident?*"

"How far are we from land, Captain?"

"Eighty miles, more or less. But I don't get it. How come they haven't sent us a copter by now?"

"Can I reach Barrow on the handheld?"

I tried. Of course no one answered. We needed a miracle. The goddamn radio had a range of a few miles.

DeBlieu said, not really believing it, "Maybe we'll get lucky, patch up the radio room. Yeah, maybe."

And I asked, "How fast can your Zodiacs go?"

"At top speed, twenty-six, twenty-eight knots."

"So almost twice as fast as the ship. What kind of radio do they carry?"

"Standard line-of-sight transmission. You've got to see the place you're trying to reach. On a good day, six miles."

"I'd need to be near shore, then, to reach it."

"If you even get there. There could be ice further south. It moves in packs. And you don't know weather conditions. Things change fast. Look, Colonel, it's an open boat, for work near the ship, but it's not for distance, not up here. If you encounter a chop, or waves, you could flip in a second. And you'll be in the dark. Hit ice at almost thirty miles an hour, and—"

"Lower a Zodiac, Captain. I need to get to Barrow."

DeBlieu had turned white now, and not from disease, and he came close. He did not want the others nearby to hear.

"You're saying that our own side is sending a plane to destroy us?"

"I'm saying give me a coxswain to drive the boat, the best person you have. I'm saying get someone on the radio, and stay on it, whether or not you think anyone can hear, and start screaming as loud as you can over the static: *We may have an antidote.* Keep sending, keep it up until you can't scream anymore, keep it up while your guys try to fix the cables, in case you get a temporary connection, and then have someone else take over, scream it louder still."

I started to leave, to get my gear, and turned back.

"Also," I said, "I advise you to change direction *now*, head off toward the last place anyone would ever think that you'd go. Turn off every light! Now! Run dark. No radar. No sonar. Find that whiteout we passed and stay inside it. Give yourself every extra second. Maybe, with that electronic disturbance up there, it won't be so easy to find you. Now, please, lower a Zodiac over the side!"

TWENTY-SEVEN

The coxswain was a master chief named John Kukulka. He was a big, strapping man from Ridgefield, Connecticut, built like a rugby player—ruddy face, fullback shoulders, curly hair and boyish cheeks, and a cheerful disposition as we sat in the Zodiac and were lowered down the starboard side of the *Wilmington*, to the Chukchi Sea.

"Ever go to Coney Island, Colonel?"

"Once, when I was a kid."

"Like the rides?"

"Why?"

I saw his even teeth through the dark, white as snow. We wore crash helmets over our balaclavas. We wore thermal underwear and water-proof zip-up mustang suits against cold that would increase at almost thirty knots. Waterproof shells. Waterproof boots. The sky had clouded over. Aurora borealis was reduced to sporadic massive explosions inside the massed clouds. The ship was hidden from satellites. With Zhou gone, there would be no witnesses to whatever was planned to occur.

Now I was one of those Marines on the truck in Afghanistan, trying to reach the U.S. encampment, and whoever had ordered a warplane to hit us was also me, some officer onshore, in the continental United States.

"Coney Island," John Kukulka said as I felt the buoyant Zodiac rock in the light swell, and as he button-started the motor. "At Coney Island, I liked the Cyclone roller coaster, the Tilt-A-Whirl, the Python, now *that* was a good one."

"And why are you telling me this, Kukulka?"

He grinned beneath his helmet. "Because *here we go!*"

The shock of the water on my face was immediate. The boat seemed to dig in and spurt forward and the bow lifted slightly but not enough so that John Kukulka—at the steering console toward the stern—could not see, with his night vision glasses, what was coming up ahead. The engine sounded monstrous. The ship fell back behind us, went from being a gigantic tanker shape, to a vague block of darkness with a few lights on, to those lights suddenly going off in the distance.

Something hard and angular flashed by at eye level on the port side.

"Ice bit," shouted Kukulka. "Didn't even know it was here."

Now I knew why he'd asked about Coney Island. The little boat corkscrewed and leaped, turned sideways and righted itself. Frigid spray came from three directions. Our floodlight stabbed ahead, bouncing, yet somehow reflecting back into our faces. The sky seemed to press down and try to smother us. I thought, *Warplane? What kind?* A Hercules that could drop a fire bomb to float down by parachute? An Apache equipped with ship-killing missiles? A Navy jet launching harpoon missiles from twenty miles away, to guide them electronically into the ship?

Radar, I thought. *Even with thick cloud cover, a warplane could light up that ship with radar.*

"Hey, Kukulka!"

"What, sir?"

"You married?"

"To Lizzie."

"Kids?"

"Ian. He's eight."

"Tell me about Ian."

The jolly voice called back, "He's got a birthday coming up."

"Get a present for him yet, Chief?"

"Yeah, Colonel," shouted the big man, only the jaunty tone was gone now, and something harder and diligent was there. "I'm going to give him an intact family. I'm going to give him a mom who's not a widow. And a dad who helps him blow out the candles on Lizzie's banana cake. I'm going to get you where you need to be, so you can reach someone over our fucking radio, excuse the word, sir."

At that moment, we hit something, wave, ice, log, who knows what, and we launched into the air again, corkscrewing and starting to flip. Kukulka slammed into the steering wheel, and bounced back. His hands flew off the wheel. His helmet hit the casing again. Blood blossomed from his right eye. I was no longer on the seat. I saw water below at a sixty-degree angle. Colonel Joseph Rush, no longer human, was flying. Colonel Joe Rush and coxswain John Kukulka, like Arctic birds, aloft, in the night.

■ ■ ■

In Barrow, the clouds blanketed the sky and the light show disappeared and the word finally came from Washington. The general stood up in the rescue squad office, at the airport, said good-bye to the two Eskimo boys. They'd been talking football, which had been pleasantly distracting. They were good kids, curious and smart, and joking with them had made the otherwise torturous wait go faster.

The general made his way downstairs, in his Arctic-issue shearling-lined hat and fleece pants. The F22 awaited him outside the hangar. The wind smelled wet. Inside the plane, huge kayak shapes, bombs, were finned and ready to be guided into the ship.

Their weight made takeoff longer than usual. Once in the air, he turned the Raptor to the north. He trimmed the wings. Dark sea raced by. He stayed below the clouds for better vision. He knew the last satellite coordinates for the Wilmington, *but his radar seemed slightly off, possibly due to the light show high above in the ionosphere.*

The Raptor had a top range of more than 1,800 miles and could reach air speeds of 1,500 mph, although today he was flying slower. The plane was capable, under combat conditions, of flying 500 miles, maneuvering, attacking an enemy, delivering payloads, and returning home. It was a miracle. He loved the Raptor. Today the route would be shorter, and finding the target should be simple with radar, despite the massive atmospheric disturbances wreaking havoc with satellites and sensors. Once he had visual confirmation of the target—as Washington wanted no mistakes, no bombing of some errant research or German tourist ship—he'd let loose with the 2,000-pound bombs.

The general knew the course that the Wilmington *was committed to, and the speed it had been going before the satellites lost view. So he should be able to locate the ship whether or not it lay dead ahead.*

He thought, We've got a tanker up here somewhere if I need a bit more time, need to refuel in the air. But if there are no problems, thirty minutes maximum. Thirty more minutes and I'll circle while she burns, to make sure the ship goes down, and then I'll go home, and resign and get drunk.

■ ■ ■

The Zodiac flew left and righted itself and smacked down into the ocean again as the prop bit into the water. The craft spun left. I fell back in. Kukulka lay on the bottom, facedown, in water, as another wave towered overhead.

I crawled to the wheel and managed to right us. We were climbing a wave, me at the wheel, fighting the pull. We topped it and sledded downward. In the trough, I cut speed, knelt, and turned Kukulka over, got the helmet and balaclava off. His head was bloody but he was breathing. His eyes looked glazed. I heard a rattling sound in his chest. Broken ribs.

"John? You with me here?"

No answer.

There was nothing I could do but make sure he was free to breathe. I took the wheel and continued south. *Was it south or had we turned around?* The engine fought me like an animal. The waves came sideways, and remembering what Clinton had said about snow, and wind lines, I aimed at the same angle into each wave, hoping this meant we were continuing in our prior direction. There were no stars. The compass needle swung left, then right. The bursts of explosions—more disturbances in the low clouds—pockmarked the heavens. The clouds seemed about to drop on our heads.

The turbulence let up and the engine sputtered but kept going. Kukulka was sitting up the next time I looked, then lying down again, but faceup, at least. The things you recall. The things you remember. I was a kid in Massachusetts. I used to stay up late on Sunday nights and watch black-and-white horror movies on our rabbit-ear TV with Dad. One creepy one, which I loved, was *The Incredible Shrinking Man*, and this old movie, ridiculous as it sounds, came back to me now. I recalled how in the film, a man in a motorboat—out for a weekend pleasure cruise—drives through mist on the ocean. A few days later the guy starts shrinking, losing weight. At first he likes it. He's trim! Healthy! Then, as he keeps getting smaller, he worries that he's sick.

By the end of a month the guy is the size of a midget, then a six-year-old, a two-year-old, and finally he's so small he lives in a doll-house, but he keeps getting smaller, and in the end he can't even be seen with the naked eye. He's so small that he slips out of the house through a mesh screen, to stare in wonder at the multitude of stars above, and decide that however small you are, you are still part of something great, something larger.

Bullshit. I never felt as small as I did on that Zodiac, bumping through blackness. Time seemed suspended. There was only horror in feeling helpless and disconnected and mute.

The ocean changed. Without ice to blanket down waves, swells grew larger. We jetted up the side of a wall, and coasted down, cork-screwing. Sideways, we hit a wall of water coming out of nowhere, but somehow I kept us afloat. We passed through soaking icy spray. In the bottom of the Zodiac I saw a flopping, gasping fish. I reached down with one hand, holding the wheel with the other. I picked up the wrig-gling, suffocating creature. I dropped it into the sea. Let something here stay alive.

Without stars, I had no bearing. I could have been driving in any direction, through hell, the world a weightless, directionless intensity, our speed immeasurable, the velocity of despair. The speedometer had jammed. I looked at my watch. Were we moving at almost thirty miles an hour? If we were, and we'd been eighty miles from shore when Ku-kulka hit the throttle, surely we'd be getting close to the north coast of Alaska by now.

I tried the radio. Nothing.

I tried again. It was soaking wet, like everything here, but DeBlieu had said the thing was waterproof.

Then I heard a rumble in the sky. I thought, *Shit, thunder, another storm.* The roar came from directly ahead. It seemed to sweep toward us. The sound grew enormously and then there was a mighty *whoosh* above and I knew I'd been wrong about the source as the fighter plane swept past, leaving a vague ghost of contrail from its massive nozzle.

I tried to reach the pilot on the radio. Maybe on flight band it might work. I shouted into the set that he should leave the ship alone, that we'd found an antidote, that the sick were getting better, that he should check with Washington, tell them the news.

I heard scratchy static in my ears.

Had DeBlieu changed course?

I hoped so. But there was no way, even if he had, that the *Wilmington* could evade that monster for long.

The engine sputtered . . . and caught, slowed, and surged ahead.

I thought in prayer. *Please God, let him miss the ship.*

Kukulka groaned and rolled onto his side, but his face remained above the water that sloshed in the Zodiac.

■ ■ ■

"This is Lieutenant Colonel Joe Rush of the Coast Guard icebreaker *Wilmington*. Is anybody there?

"Mayday! This is Lieutenant Colonel Joe Rush of the icebreaker *Wilmington*! If anyone is listening, please respond!

"This is an emergency. If you can hear me, I cannot hear you. Please call the following phone number in Washington and tell whoever answers that you've heard from me and *to call back the plane!*"

No answer.

I said out loud, "Hey, Clinton, are you sure this business about direction is right?"

Up was down. North was south. Maybe I'd turned us completely around, beneath the skyless heavens, and headed back toward the North Pole.

■ ■ ■

Kukulka was groaning, sitting up a little, and trying to get my attention. His face was a sheet of blood, but he was able to shout. I heard him over the engine.

"What, Chief?"

"How far away would a ship have to be, Colonel, for us to hear an explosion?"

"I don't know."

"We'd hear it, right? Or even see something, a light, a spark, something?"

I kept going.

I drove up and into the side of a massive, heaving wave.

■ ■ ■

"This is Joe Rush of the icebreaker *Wilmington*. Is anyone listening?

"This is Joe Rush from the *Wilmington*. If you can hear me, please call the following number . . ."

What's the point? I thought.

I heard a different kind of static, a burst that sounded like someone talking.

"*Buzzzz . . . static . . . buzzzzzz . . .* Seth!"

It sounded like a woman. Or a kid. I said, "Please try again. I cannot hear you. Hello?"

"*Buzz . . . buzzz . . .* my uncle Elmore . . . he said . . . *buzz.*"

"This is Lieutenant Colonel Joe Rush. Who am I speaking to?"

"Seth Itta! At the rescue squad office. My uncle said to . . . *crackle.*"

Three minutes later I was talking to an adult, telling him who I was, telling him where to call, telling him, as I saw lights ahead, low, flickering, yellow *streetlights*, a curve of shore . . . *Barrow*, who we were.

He understood right away, and clicked off, and minutes dragged by as we closed on the shore. I had no idea if he had any luck reaching Washington. It seemed like hours ago when the Raptor fighter had flown past.

Maybe they've got the landline to Washington. Maybe they can reach the F22.

He was back. He was nervous. He told us to stay offshore and not land, "Because you might be contagious."

I said, "I have a man here who needs a doctor."

"Aren't you a doctor, Colonel Rush?"

■ ■ ■

It started raining.

Rain in the Arctic. It was over. It had not worked. The fighter had destroyed the ship, the sick, the healthy, the crew, the Marines.

We drifted offshore, cold, wet, locked in our own failure, watching headlights move along a coast road a half mile off. I saw telephone poles, a garbage truck, lights on top of an office building. All of it might as well have been a thousand miles away.

Failed.

Kukulka was propped against the side of the Zodiac. *Concussion,* I thought. He drank lots of water. He weakly pointed and I saw the pinprick black dot approaching in the sky again, only this time it was coming from the ocean side, not the land side. It was the Raptor coming straight at us, low, over the water, as if it had a homing beam fixed on us.

Kukulka's lips forming words, "Oh, shit."

The thing grew enormous and the sound was a blast, an explosion, as it swept over our heads, circled, and came back, low, as if to make a run at us. It had blown up the ship. It had killed Eddie and Karen,

DeBlieu and Pettit. It had done what I'd done in Afghanistan, sent more than two hundred people to the bottom. Washington had waited until the cloud cover blocked view, kept the sinking secret, and now, as we sat there, the F22 would open up on us with machine guns or cannon.

The predator-like form seemed to slow, its wings to open, belly up, as it drifted above like a bird of prey. Then I saw what the pilot was doing. His doors were open. There were bulky kayak-sized shapes inside. I saw Kukulka's big face upturned in wonder, his lips moving soundlessly, as he counted the bombs that the pilot was showing us, as if we watched an innocent air show.

"One . . . two . . . Sir, *sir, he didn't bomb them!*"

Kukulka's shoulders started moving.

The big man was crying.

"You stopped it," he said.

TWENTY-EIGHT

It was hot in New Mexico during the day, cold at night, but still toasty compared to the Arctic. The Army guards stayed outside the fence, and we could take long hikes on the mesa and still remain in the forty-square-mile ex–Air Force base where we were quarantined. Two electrified barbed wire fences surrounded the place. Cameras looked down along the periphery. The twenty-foot-wide strip between the fences, we were informed in stern but kindly tones, contained mines.

Please remain in the camp.

First came the doctors, looking more—in their bulky suits—like radiation cleanup crews after an accident.

As soon as we settled in, they coptered in and we got more blood tests than astronauts. We were CAT-scanned and X-rayed, and fMRI-machined. We underwent stress tests and eye exams. We spent hours with psychologists who wanted to know—in fifty ways—about tension levels on the ship, or post-traumatic stress.

When the doctors left, the FBI arrived for debriefings, the agents using specially set up interrogation booths—protected compartments—for interviews. We sat behind thick glass but still the agents wore surgical masks.

When they weren't grilling us about Peter Del Grazo, they started in on us: bank accounts, drug use, family history, clubs we belonged to, e-mails we sent, former jobs, and political affiliations.

They asked me exactly when I decided to scuttle the submarine *Montana*. Before the Chinese arrived? Or after? They asked if I'd ever visited China, or had friends there, or had gone to college with people from China. They asked if I blamed my job for my divorce. They wanted to know if I was angry at Major Pettit for living with my ex-wife, and if that situation had affected my judgment.

"I see you wear a wedding ring," I told the agent, a man named Mulcahy. "Who's *your* wife sleeping with these days?"

"There's nothing personal in these questions, sir."

"Or in my responses either, asshole."

More investigators arrived—from Homeland Security, CIA, the National Security Council, the House Committee on Terrorism—to ask all the questions that probably should have been asked long before anyone ever boarded that ship.

When each session was done, I usually asked a few questions back, the same ones that we prisoners went over each night, in the dorm rooms we shared, making lists, calling contacts in D.C., gaming scenarios in our heads.

"How long did Del Grazo work for the Chinese?" I'd ask.

"We don't know that," was always the answer.

"How did they recruit him?"

"Ask your superiors."

"What exactly did he do for them?"

"I'm not part of that investigation."

"How did the Chinese get the antidote?"

"Your guess is as good as mine."

■ ■ ■

The director was more forthcoming during our daily encrypted tele-conferences.

"Del Grazo infected that whole ship with malware, Joe," he said wryly. "Laptops. E-mails. Cabins. The whole damn place was a gigantic open mike to Beijing. They were monitoring our research. They wanted advance notice of any plans in the Arctic. He was their man in place when the *Montana* had the fire. By the way, the icebreaker's been de-contaminated and the Coast Guard is tearing out the whole communi-cation system. It's a real mess."

"Why did he do it, sir?"

"Oh, money, looks like."

"How did they recruit him?"

"We're guessing, Joe. He ran up big gambling bills at Seattle casi-nos. Turns out the Chinese were silent partners in one, probably trolling for useful losers there, you can bet. Horses. Football games. Baseball. Anything you can bet on. He paid cash for a condo, great view of the bay. Cash for an Escalade. Cash in the lockbox we turned up. Joe, it infuriates me. Any half-assed check of the guy would have found this stuff, but the Arctic's such a low priority, no one did it. Believe me. Red faces all around."

I asked, "Director, were the experts at the archives able to get any-thing from the blank parts of the film?"

"No. But it's a good thing you opened it up and didn't listen to me. Still, next time, pay attention."

I asked the biggest question. "How did the Chinese get the antidote?"

On screen, he looked tired. "China's where most swine flus originate, so yeah, Jade Pharma is a subsidiary of Pacific-North, but they do their own research, too. A drug they were experimenting with worked. You were their guinea pigs, Joe. And the mislabeling? A mistake, they say, it happens there, but," he said, shrugging, "it's China, man. Nothing is what it seems. We're just happy things worked."

While I thought it over, he added, "Can you do me a favor? Can you muzzle your friend Andrew Sachs? His people are being bothersome. A tone-down at State would go a long way here."

"Bothersome?"

"They're poking into things. Look, the WH wants to talk up this incident as an example of friendship. And pissing in the mouth of the guy who helped you ain't that. For a change, we've got something positive to work with, so let's encourage it. No sour grapes, Joe. Know what I mean?"

"Of course."

I asked Sachs that night to increase his efforts. I wanted to know everything that his contacts could learn about Jade Pharmaceuticals, the Chinese subsidiary of Pacific-North, of New York City, New York.

I added, "Tell your guys I asked you to stop asking questions."

"Help you cover your ass, you mean? Well, you saved mine."

"I want the director to think I'm on his side."

■ ■ ■

I slept in officers' housing, and shared a suite with Eddie and Andrew Sachs and DeBlieu. At night there was Scrabble and a hundred channels of TV, but mostly we kept trying to figure out what had happened. There were air-dropped books. We took turns giving lectures. We considered a hundred theories as to how the Chinese had obtained the proper drug.

Clinton bunked down the hall with Pettit, complaining that the base was too hot. The Marines bunked with *Montana* and *Wilmington* survivors. Karen Vleska shared a room with Marietta Cristobel, in female officer housing.

■ ■ ■

Journalists came next, in an orchestrated parade, to interview—from a distance—the quarantined puppets; that is, after we suffered through a two-hour warning on the penalties of violating secrecy oaths, and a "suggestion session" on acceptable answers to questions.

The warnings contained words like "Leavenworth" and "the rest of your life."

I sat in a booth and eyed a reporter from the *New York Times* and told the agreed-upon story. That the *Montana* had taken aboard unidentified frozen bodies recovered from the ice pack, probably foreign, lost since 1918. That the illness that had broken out was from the thawed bodies, and not from any new kind of virus, and was therefore contained. That the public was safe because no other vectors existed. That the *Montana* had been scuttled to prevent further spread of the disease, and that all aboard both vessels—the *Montana* and the *Wilmington*—had acted heroically in the face of danger and death.

Peter Del Grazo was included in the list of dead from disease. There was no mention of spies. Or silent films.

The reporter was an attractive, thirtyish blonde who flirted during the interview, and doted on the part about my Zodiac trip in the storm. She asked, legs crossed, skirt tight, voice breathy, pen poised, "Any love interest in your life at the moment, Colonel?"

"I'm free of foreign entanglements."

"And divorced, I understand."

"My ex and I stayed friends."

"An attractive man like you, no girlfriend?"

"No, ma'am."

"I'm not a ma'am. I'm a Beth. And here's my card. Perhaps I'll be in Anchorage on a story and we can have dinner sometime," she said.

You're not the one I want to have that dinner with.

■ ■ ■

The medicine worked both as cure and preventative. The protocol called for a six-day treatment, and after four weeks on base, when no new cases presented themselves, a few braver VIPs began touching down—the Secretary of Health and Human Services; the Vice President; a couple of senators from terrorism committees—making sure they were shown on TV addressing "our Arctic heroes."

On Thanksgiving we got a terrific meal, turkey and cranberry sauce and pumpkin pies, donated by the State of New Mexico. The Discovery Channel featured stories about "the possible breakout of new viruses in the Arctic."

There also came gifts from around the country, so many that an entire Quonset hut was needed to contain the loot, including several hundred pairs of socks, four giant flat-screen TVs, a planeload of North Carolina barbeque from Wilmington, two hundred subscriptions to the beer-of-the-month club, dinners at restaurants in thirty-one states, and a smuggled-in package from Paramount Pictures offering a million-dollar contract for movie rights, just sign here and e-mail a copy back.

■ ■ ■

Families arrived next, and "personal contacts." There was a viewing area outside the fence, or in bad weather, relatives used the interview booths and spoke by microphone. Eddie's wife and kids visited me. And my ex-wife, Nina, showed up when her hours with Pettit were over. I was surprised by it. It was a bittersweet session, lots of memories, but she seemed a figure from a long time ago, and I actually wished her and Pettit well.

Among the visitors to the base was Karen Vleska's boyfriend, who took up residence in a motel thirty-five miles away and commuted daily. Since he was a lawyer for Electric Boat, he was here to prepare a corporate response should any angry civil suits be filed by relatives of the dead. This was unlikely, we'd been assured, but he stayed on anyway. He seemed a caring, loving man. I watched Karen go off often, eagerly, to sit and talk with him, or take walks along the fence, he on one side, she on the other.

I told myself she was lucky to have him. That she probably had all kinds of personal problems I'd discover if I got to know her better. That my feelings for her had been ratcheted up by danger, and that in normal day-to-day life, I'd probably lose interest in her fast.

I hated the boyfriend being there.

Meanwhile, the Spanish flu made headlines. The *Washington Post* ran a series reliving the horrible outbreak in 1918. The *New York Times* parked a science reporter at the CDC, and FOX-TV sent a crew to the North Slope of Alaska, after a scare in Wainright, a possible flu case which turned out to be a different, milder form.

Reuters headline: ANXIETY GROWS AROUND THE WORLD AS FLU SEASON ARRIVES.

We were growing more irritable by the day, and even the most conservative CDC doctors were signing their reports with the word "clean." Finally, we were told we'd be free in two more weeks, after a few last medical tests.

■ ■ ■

"What will you do when you get home, Karen?"

My favorite part of being on base were the hikes we took, and today we were on a mesa, humping through an old firing range, under a bright, cold sun, in forty-eight-degree weather. Around us grew buffalo grass and snakeweed, and prickly pear cactus. There was cholla cactus with porcupine-style barbed quills, and strands of cottonwood. A hawk watched us pass.

"Carl wants us to take a vacation," she said.

"Sounds great. Where?"

"Mexico. I think he's going to propose."

"Congratulations."

She turned and stared at me. She seemed annoyed with me lately, but then again, tempers were growing short all around. She was healthy, fully recovered, burned brown from the hikes, trim, small, and agile, hopping from rock to rock when we reached an arroyo, scrambling up onto high ground with a gymnast's joy. Her silvery hair, worn long again, was magnificent.

She said, "What about you? Back to Anchorage?"

"The old grind."

"You don't seem to mind it here like the rest of us."

I said, "I just hide it better." I thought, *That's because you're here.*

"Eddie told me about your ex-wife and Major Pettit."

"Eddie's as discreet as the *National Enquirer*."

"He's got some idea about you and me," she said, plopping down on a sunny flat rock.

"You *think*? Being around Eddie is like being on *Millionaire Matchmaker*, except for the money."

She reached into her rucksack and unwrapped today's sandwich, avocado and smoked turkey on a sesame seed roll, thanks to Uncle Sam's airdrop last night. There was apple juice in the water bottles. The sun on my face felt good. In the distance I saw a trail of rising dust approaching, which meant a jeep was out. Chief Apparecio spent his spare time repairing the old stock lying around. Trucks. Jeeps. Generators left to rust. About two million dollars of taxpayer money being intentionally left to rot.

"Eddie e-mailed me some interesting pictures," she said, and handed over her iPhone. I cursed inwardly and felt myself grow warm. There was a shot of me sitting beside her cot on the icebreaker, while she slept. There was a shot of me wiping sweat from her forehead with a cool rag. There was a close-up of my face, and only an idiot wouldn't see that the expression held more than professional concern. The fourth shot was of me asleep beside her, in the chair.

"That's what doctors do. Hey," I said, following the jeep's progress, grateful it was there. "That's Eddie and Sachs. They're waving."

Sachs had his binocs out, too, and he was pointing so Eddie could change course. The two men had become fast friends. The jeep raised dust behind it. Minutes later it stopped at the foot of the trail and the men scrambled out and headed up the steep trail. Sachs had acquired a tan, and definition in his muscles. Eddie always looked the same. He was built like a horse and, I thought irritably, sometimes about as smart.

Sachs opened his knapsack and, as they closed, pulled out papers. He thrust the sheaf toward me, even before they reached us. That's how eager he was.

"You were right, Joe," he said. "More right than anyone thought. My guys didn't want to make waves but I insisted. You won't believe how it started, but you'll sure believe," he said, flourishing a printout of the front page of today's *Wall Street Journal*, "where it's ending. Get this."

I felt my breath catch as I looked over the information; page after page, building it all up; the years, the names, the connections, the transactions.

A dizzy rage rose up inside me. All I could think of was, *You did it for this?*

TWENTY-NINE

The uniformed guards were polite and efficient, patting me down in the lobby. Another guard ran a scanner over me when I reached the second bank of elevators to the tower, the one that started on the forty-first floor. A third man handled the wand and hand search outside the executive suite. Normal precaution, he said. He had the look of ex-military; had the politeness, the firmness, the obvious strength.

"We're checking all visitors. There's been a threat," he apologized. I knew he was lying, and he knew I knew. He was looking for recording devices, not explosives. I didn't mind.

It was early December, three weeks after we finally got out of quarantine. Today's headline in the *New York Times*, sitting on the guard's desk, read:

PRESIDENT AUTHORIZES
SPANISH FLU VACCINATION PROGRAM.

THREE HUNDRED MILLION DOSES TO BE PREPARED.
BRITAIN, FRANCE & GERMANY CONSIDER
SIMILAR PROGRAMS.

The front page of the business section, partially visible below the A section, read, PACIFIC-NORTH STOCK SURGES! GREATEST ONE-DAY GAIN IN MARKET HISTORY!

Inside, the director's new office was three times the size of his old rabbit hole in Northwest Washington, glass instead of tired gray marble, eightieth-story view instead of basement, soundproofing, art consultant–picked canvases, Italian leather chairs, all the perks of upper floor life in New York. I remembered reading once that in jungles, some animals spend their entire lives in high tree canopies. They don't come down. They never experience the dirt of the forest floor. How like the tropical jungle this city was, I thought.

He rose from behind his old walnut Washington desk—an out-of-place and doggedly sentimental attachment—clad in a three-button pinstriped suit in dark blue, with light gray stripes. The shirt was crisp white, the tie Armani, the gold cuff links sparkled from sunlight slanting through floor-to-ceiling windows. The sky was urban blue, a washed-out vestige of what I recalled from the Arctic. Below rose the lesser towers of Gotham, their spires mere supplicants, straining, like the city, for more.

"Nice office, sir," I said, looking down at Fifty-seventh Street.

"Every time I come back, it takes getting used to, Joe."

The triple-strength windows blocked out any hint of unwanted sound. New Yorkers moved below as in a twenty-first-century silent movie. Or if you preferred the inside view, there was a big-screen TV, tuned to FOX Business, a built-in wet bar, and several colorful canvases. The photos of his wife and two girls in Bermuda were the same ones he'd exhibited in D.C. The wall of VIP photos showed the director in the old days, more hair, bigger stomach, nerdier glasses, with the President, the National Security Advisor, at a London conference on bioterror.

I said, "I bet you see pilots' faces when they go by."

He chuckled. "Oh, it's just more space I have to figure out how to fill. They hire people to help you do it."

I accepted a Tito's vodka on ice. The glass was crystal, the tongs silver. We made small talk, and at length, when it was time, I said, "You know the thing that keeps bothering me? It's who told the Chinese to send that submarine."

He shrugged, sipped single malt on ice. He'd told his secretary to hold all his calls. "Del Grazo, I imagine."

"No, he only knew we were going north. Zhou was dispatched before anyone on the *Wilmington* knew about the illness, yet the sub carried the antidote. Funny, huh?"

"Hmm. Now that you mention it, I do find it odd."

I felt his smooth, icy vodka spread through me. I reached into my breast pocket and pulled out a folded paper, and his pleasant expression turned curious.

"Records, sir, on some old Kansas pharmaceutical company. Maybe you heard of it. E.E. Worth & Sons."

He'd heard of it, all right, that much was evident in the slight straightening of shoulders, and briefest hesitation in the way his glass lifted toward his mouth. It's funny how loud silence can be. I heard an ice cube crackle in his glass.

"What's that name again, Joe?"

"Well, sir. E.E. Worth, a little company established 1887. They provided drugs to Fort Riley. Had a contract with the Army—headache powders, gargles, medical needs. Apparently had a research arm, too."

"Is that so," the director said in an interested voice.

"Yes, sir! Turn of the twentieth century. World War One, the bioweapons race! Total war! The French came up with tear gas in 1914, then, in '15, chlorine from the Germans, and phosgene from France. In 1917, mustard gas. A whole biowarfare effort, and E.E. Worth did their part."

"And how was that?"

"Andy Sachs's guys found this. Worth had a research farm near Fort Riley, Kansas. Experimenting on sheep. Pigs. Horses. Gasses and diseases, sir! Conditions must have been primitive as hell, poking around. No idea that viruses even existed yet. No containment. Just doctors and amateur chemists stumbling around dirty labs. Then, in 1918, the Spanish flu suddenly breaks out at Fort Riley, *in the middle of this race for new weapons!*"

The director's brows rose. "You're suggesting a connection?"

"So far, just facts. In 1931, Worth merges with Ashcroft Drugs of Chicago. In 1952, with Chicago-Midland; '64, Boyd & Sons; and *they're* absorbed into Pacific-North in '87. And P-N acquires Jade Pharma for their generics arm, an Asian arm in 2008, brings us up to today."

"Joe, I don't understand where you're going."

"Don't you?"

His eyes were in shadow. His shoulders did not move.

I pulled out another folded paper and felt his gaze slide to it, cool, gray, distant.

"What I couldn't figure out first . . . well . . . actually, what none of us could figure out, was why all records relating to that old farm—bills for services, invoices, details of work projects, you name it—nothing was in the archives."

"*Tsk!* No one keeps work orders a hundred years old."

"Oh, archives did for the other forts, sir."

"An oversight, then, with a war on."

"Maybe."

"Lost then, certainly."

"Oh, definitely. Lost." I nodded. "But why?"

"I think you're about to tell me."

This time when more papers came out, he slid forward in his chair a few inches. I heard the creak. It seemed actually to come from inside his body, not from the chair.

"It's a family history excerpt, sir. One of those privately printed works; family wants Granddad commemorated. A CEO wants a book to give his kids. This one was commissioned by the head of a Sacramento software company, great-great-grandson of E.E. Worth. The guy hired a writer to do his autobiography. You pay the writer fifty thousand dollars and get your own book, but these things still get cataloged by the Library of Congress. That's where I found this."

The director said nothing.

I unfolded the pages, read out loud:

My inspiration has always been my great-great-grandfather, E.E. Worth, who looms in our family history. After the Spanish flu first appeared at Fort Riley, great-great-grandfather tirelessly threw himself into research to try to cure it. It was almost as if, my dad told me, E.E. blamed himself for the disease breaking out, for the death of his infant son Kyle from the illness. E.E. poured all his profits into the search for an antidote. Long after the outbreak subsided, he spent nights in his lab, insisting that one day the disease would come back, that mankind would need a cure.

Toward the end of his life, feeble minded, he would break into tears and tell doctors that he'd caused the Spanish flu; he had done experiments with pigs that went bad, and caused soldiers to get sick . . . but that he had prayed to God and that God had finally forgiven him and let him discover an antidote, and it sat in the company freezers.

He never lost his preoccupation with the flu.

And while it is true that he had dementia, my dad drilled into me that even in the grip of insanity, E.E. remained dedicated to helping humanity. He was our example. His quest to find a cure for that long-dead plague made me equally committed to humanitarian causes, which is why . . .

I looked up. "And so forth," I said.

The director relaxed, slid his chair back, crossed his legs. "A family history?" he said. "Uncorroborated? An old man babbling that he created the flu? Please. You ought to hear the stories at *my* dinner table. By the time they're told for the fifth time, they have no resemblance to the truth."

I said nothing. I just waited.

At length, the director broke the silence. But he seemed easier, as if danger had approached and slid past. "Joe, think, if someone had an antidote for this disease back in the 1930s, don't you think they would have patented it, *advertised* it?"

"Why? Patents are only good for twenty years. He had a cure for a disease that no longer existed! If they patented the drug in 1930, there was a good chance that by the time the disease returned, they wouldn't own the patent anymore. So they kept it quiet. It didn't hurt to put the thing in a freezer, and wait until it was needed. You yourself said many times, *All diseases eventually come back.*"

"Ah, ties in with *your* theory, that the melting Arctic will rerelease old diseases."

"It's not a theory after what just happened."

"So you're actually saying," he said, grinning now, "that this alleged *cure* sat in company freezers, passed from corporation to corporation for eighty years, and finally lands up with *this* company's subsidiary in China."

"You needed to keep it a secret," I said, flourishing the newspaper headline about the announced vaccination program, "until you knew it worked. So *you* told the Chinese—your own guys—to send the antidote. Maybe you already knew you were going back to work in the company. Maybe you negotiated the job when you realized what was happening. Either way you had access to old records. *You* knew about the outbreak before I did. *You* had time to make the call. *You* had the Chinese mislabel the stuff in case it didn't work, to protect the formula. If it didn't work, no one would know. You'd go back to waiting. If it did work, you'd capitalize on the drug."

He broke out laughing. He stood up.

"If there weren't so many holes in this," he said, "I'd be offended. But tell me, Joe, if there was such superb coordination between New York and China, why did the Chinese almost blow you to smithereens, instead of just handing over the drug? Not exactly self-interest!"

"That bothered me, too, at first. But then I realized the answer. It's because someone made a mistake. You treated Chinese executives the way you'd treat American ones. You forgot that in China, the military *owns* companies, *especially* ones that deal with drugs for the military. By alerting them, you were also unwittingly letting the Chinese Navy know that a U.S. sub was out of commission."

"Oh, I find this incredible!"

"And their military people," I continued, "wanted it all. The *Montana*'s torpedoes for the Navy. The drug profits for the company, for themselves. Here's a photo Andrew's boys found of a board of directors' meeting of Jade. See these guys here? An admiral. A general. Heavy on the military side, sir. I'm guessing that the Chinese double-crossed you. They tried to get both, the sub and the profits. Maybe they fought over it. After all, the original admiral who gave Zhou instructions was replaced after the fighting, right?"

"And that's your theory," said the director.

"Yes."

"Well, I have an old college roommate who is now a film producer in Los Angeles, and he would probably like this idea for a cute science fiction piece."

"Good, because then I could give him the real film we found, did I mention that? Especially the first part, which wasn't really blank, sir. We lied to you. It showed the program at Fort Riley, *the creation of the Spanish flu, which we tried to introduce into Russia.* That film's on about two hundred cell phones now, ready to go out."

This was the bluff I'd been building up to since the session started. It had to come at exactly the right moment, and I watched the bomb hit home. There was no mistaking the reaction. He was an accomplished dissembler, but he'd been sure I'd used all my ammunition, he'd allowed himself to relax, think he'd beaten me, I was done, and now just for an instant the blood drained from his face and his fingers clawed at the sides of his chair.

He saw me see it. He knew that words were useless. He knew that he'd just admitted it, and that lies would not convince me otherwise anymore. He canted his head, seemed more like a professor regarding an especially smart student, and then his smile broadened approvingly.

"Was that the truth, Joe? Copies?"

"Yes."

"Uh-huh. Then by the way, where *is* the original first part? Throw it out? Hide it? Oh well, either way, that was very well done. I always admired the way you could put things together. Kudos, man."

I felt the rage engulf me then. That he could have sent in the antidote from the first moment. That he could have avoided the suffering and death. That he'd played me and Eddie for fools and almost killed us and two hundred other people, almost started a war.

But the director seemed more proud than embarrassed. He opened his top desk drawer, extracted a report, tossed the thing on his blotter, backward, so I could see the title of the White House executive order:

300 MILLION DOSES TO BE DISTRIBUTED.

"All Americans will be protected, Joe, for the rest of their lives. Like polio vaccinations. Or typhoid. Thanks to you, to this, we're saving lives."

"And what is your personal profit, sir?"

He snorted. "The profit! What are you saying? That it's wrong to earn profit and help people at the same time? I didn't think you were that liberal, Joe. Why do you think that people like me go back and forth between private industry and government? It's a system that keeps both sides honest. Good policy *is* good profit. Good profit encourages good policy. This system is old, practical and moral both."

"A class of rulers, you mean. A *class*."

"I saved your life. Why do you think that Chinese captain warned you? Eh? Or would you rather we played amateur hour with the fate of our country? Yes. A class. Tell me a single great benefit that humanity has enjoyed, that's made lives easier, and that didn't make someone a profit. Polio vaccine? Building codes? Flight? Heart transplants? I challenge you. One!"

"And that was your goal, the good of all."

"Soon three hundred million people will be protected against the very danger that you've warned against, which would *not* have happened if we'd rushed the drug up, given it to the crew, and hushed the whole thing up. Yes, we'd have saved a few dozen people, but then what? The drug goes back into hibernation. The company gets nothing for hard work. There's no supply when the disease *does* reassert itself. And meanwhile, people like you take it for granted that you're owed anything you need at any given moment. *I'm sick. You owe me.* Well, Joe? We don't owe you. People owe us something and it is called thanks."

I turned to leave and heard him call me back.

"Oh, stop it! You're angry."

I reached the door.

"Cool down, man. Sit a bit. I said sit! For Christ's sake, *sit down!*"

I opened the door.

"Joe! There's more!"

I stopped.

"Thank you. Now sit. Sit if you want to hear. Good. Very good. Take a breath, Joe. Joe? Focus! Look, I couldn't tell you earlier, but with my position vacant, the White House is looking for a replacement, and your name is in the mix. I know that at the moment you're steaming. I'd be mad, too, if I were you. No one likes to find things out this way. I understand. I do. I sympathize. Another drink? I'm not an ogre. No? No drink?"

I said nothing.

"Joe, when you can think clearly, you'll see that you can continue your good work by taking the job."

I said, stunned, "You're trying to buy me?"

He shook his head, sitting on the arm of my chair now. "No, I'm offering you what you always wanted, a chance to be one of the people who decide things. And, Joe, I don't have to buy you. I just threaten you. Ten minutes ago when your theory was conjecture, and you had no evidence, you might have made a weak case for sharing your theories with a reporter, a blog. But now that you know facts, your oath binds you to secrecy. Any violation will be met with an immediate response. Joe, listen to me carefully. I have your best interests at heart. *Immediate response* means something legal to most people, arrest, trial, Leavenworth, but to others, to more radical elements, *immediate response* can be . . . well . . . think of it as triage. Sacrificing a few to save the many. You do know what I mean, right?"

There are many powerful drugs but sometimes I think that words are the strongest. They bind you, paralyze you, spread through your bloodstream faster than an antibiotic. A man sits in a chair, stunned, unmoving, just from words.

"I . . . we . . . we'd be killed?"

"Do you really think that you'd be allowed to reveal that the worst outbreak of disease in history, the deadliest plague to ever hit mankind, fifty to eighty million killed . . . in allied nations, our friends, our great-grandparents, that a starting point for modern flus that have killed thousands was *an accident that came from a U.S. Army laboratory?* Do you have any idea of the damage? The lawsuits? People are *still* dying every year. International Court. UN. Justification for any terrorist revenge attack . . . The utter destruction of our credibility when it comes to situations involving chemical or biological weapons overseas. Joe? Are you seeing it? The damage you would do? And the people who did it in 1918 aren't even around anymore, so *what is the point?*"

"Once you know you can make secrets, you make more," I said.

"So what? Look, maybe it's for the best that you figured things out. In fact, that is exactly the case. I'm glad! Now you can stop poking around. And I'd advise you to stop your friends also. Me? I'm safe, whatever you do. You're the one—*they're* the ones—who are not."

On the way out, I heard him say, "The truth is overrated, Joe. You should know that by now. Come back and let's have dinner when you calm down. And take the job when they call!"

■ ■ ■

The elevator doors opened and the guards let me pass. I was in the lobby. And then I was outside, on the plaza, beneath the bronze statues of Salk and Pasteur and Jennings, surrounded by thousands of New Yorkers going about their daily business, perhaps already making appointments with their doctors to arrange vaccinations—when the drug became available—against the Spanish flu.

My friends had been waiting and they crowded around me: Sachs and Karen, Eddie and Clinton, Marietta, Pettit, DeBlieu. Their voices were a far-off chorus. The cacophony seemed to merge into one word, the director's word: triage.

They asked, *Did you tell him? Did he admit it?*

I told them that we had been wrong and he had shown me conclusive proof that the drug had been made in China. I said that our guess about the Spanish flu being a hundred-year-old bioweapon was wrong, too. The first cases had not been at Fort Riley, but somewhere else, it turned out. I said that the director's move to Pacific-North had been planned for a long time, predating the emergency, and was not a result of anything that had happened in the Arctic. I said it had been a privilege to serve with them.

I turned and walked away.

There really was nothing to be gained by telling the story, I thought sometime later, sitting on the last stool in the ground floor bar of the Three Mark Hotel on Fifty-ninth Street, downing a third glass of Svedka. And there was plenty to gain by accepting a job as new director, and continuing the work I had been doing at a higher level, having *input*, as the director would say, *at the top.*

Maybe I'd find myself at meetings in the future, with the director as an equal. Maybe I'd be the one planning triage next time, to a town, a city, a ship. It's what I'd wanted. It's what I'd lost my first wife over. It's what I'd cut myself off from people for. It's what I'd chosen, and so, I told the bartender morosely, "He was right. I'll go along. He was right."

"Who was right?" the bartender asked.

"No," I said loudly as he stared. "He *wasn't* right."

I didn't want to use my cell phone and there didn't seem to be any land phones anymore in New York City. I walked for blocks before I found one of those antique phones which now took credit cards instead of coins, and cost more for one call than a monthly charge for my iPhone.

But no one, I knew, was listening when I punched in the number on the card I extracted from my wallet. And no one stopped me after I made the phone call, as I walked over to the Forty-first Street, headquarters of the *New York Times*.

The truth is overrated, the director had said, and I wondered how you could assign it a numerical value. Maybe it was a line in the dirt. Maybe it was the ultimate gift that God gave to Adam and Eve. Maybe it was simply a case-by-case choice.

I stood looking up at the *Times* building, from across the street. The curb was like a line in the dirt, cross it and the world would change. The reporter was waiting for me. But I didn't move. And then I felt something brush my hand and I whirled, and was surprised to look into the open, scared face of Karen Vleska.

"You, too?" she said.

"This isn't the way to do it either," I said after a moment, aware of the hundreds of people on the block flowing past, going to work, shopping, oblivious to the nation's old secrets and new ones, needing to know more about some things, I knew, but, I realized suddenly, not needing to know all.

Was I already becoming like the director?

"We need to go to Washington," I said.

Our fingers had become entwined, and I knew that to anyone on the street we looked like lovers, holding hands, walking away from the *Times* building, toward the happy bustle of Broadway. A couple in deep loving conversation. A couple so involved with each other that we seemed cut off from the world. A couple strolling out of Times Square and later, through green, lovely Central Park, and after that, into a Central Park West hotel.

Lovers? Well, we spent the night together, all right, but not that way . . . Karen dozing fitfully, waking from nightmares occasionally, me awake, too alert to sleep, with my sidearm within reach; me aware of every creak in the hallway, every ring of a phone through the wall, every honk of a cab far below.

He tried to bribe me with a job, and then he threatened my life. Were we followed here? Maybe we should not have waited, should have just gone to the *Times*.

The early Metroliner brought us into the capital at rush hour, when the highways around Washington were as clogged as arteries, tubes carrying life blood from the body's extremities in or out of the pumping heart. Andrew Sachs had called ahead, had made arrangements, had reached his counterpart at the Pentagon, and so we were expected when we arrived, ushered through security, and along the bustling hallways, and into the muted, wood paneled room from which emanated directions guiding millions of U.S. servicemen and women around the world.

Up close, the Secretary of Defense looked smaller than he did on television, but more robust, with a thoughtful bluntness. He served us coffee himself, added two sugars to Karen's, milk to mine. He told us to relax, although he didn't seem that way himself. He leaned forward in his leather chair and kept his hands flat on his desk blotter, beside the Remington sculpture of an Indian hunting buffalo. Behind his head was a photo of the President looking down, and four oil paintings of World War Two battle scenes, one honoring each branch of service. Naval aircraft carriers under fire in the Pacific. Army troops in their foxholes among the wintery French woods. Marines storming ashore at Normandy. Coast Guard rescuers taking survivors aboard after a U-boat sank a merchant marine ship off Maine.

"Sir, we have a story we think you should hear," I heard myself say.

He told me to tell it slowly, to take my time. He never took his eyes off my face.

(reprinted from the *Wall Street Journal*)

BIG PHARMA SUICIDE ROCKS WALL STREET

Top executives at Pacific-North Pharma, one of the Dow's biggest gainers this month, were rocked Sunday night at the news of the suicide of the head of their generics division.

Elias Pelfrey shot himself to death at his suburban home in Westchester. Bedford Hills police said that Pelfrey left a note saying that he was depressed over personal matters. His wife told them that she heard the shot around 2 A.M., rushed into his study, and found him dead of a wound to the head. He had shot himself through the mouth.

Pelfrey had recently taken over the generics division of Pacific-

North, the group responsible for designing the vaccine effective against the Spanish flu. The drug has been responsible for saving millions of lives, said spokespeople at the Surgeon General's office. It also made Pacific-North Pharma Wall Street's biggest gainer recently.

Pacific-North Pharma stock price seems unaffected by Pelfrey's death.